John Boyne was born in Ireland in 1971. He is the author of eleven novels for adults, five for young readers and a collection of short stories. Perhaps best known for his 2006 multi-award-winning book *The Boy in the Striped Pyjamas*, John's other novels, notably *The Absolutist* and *A History of Loneliness*, have been widely praised and are international bestsellers. In 2015, John chaired the panel for the Giller Prize, Canada's most prestigious literary award. His latest novel is *A Ladder to the Sky*.

www.johnboyne.com
@john_boyne

By John Boyne

NOVELS
The Thief of Time
The Congress of Rough Riders
Crippen
Next of Kin
Mutiny on the Bounty
The House of Special Purpose
The Absolutist
This House Is Haunted
A History of Loneliness
The Heart's Invisible Furies
A Ladder to the Sky

NOVELS FOR YOUNGER READERS
The Boy in the Striped Pyjamas
Noah Barleywater Runs Away
The Terrible Thing That Happened to Barnaby Brocket
Stay Where You Are and then Leave
The Boy at the Top of the Mountain

SHORT STORIES
Beneath the Earth

Crippen

A Novel of Murder

JOHN BOYNE

BLACK SWAN

TRANSWORLD PUBLISHERS
61–63 Uxbridge Road, London W5 5SA
A Random House Group Company
www.transworldbooks.co.uk

CRIPPEN
A BLACK SWAN BOOK: 9780552777438

First published in Great Britain
in 2004 by Penguin Books
Black Swan edition published 2011

A CIP catalogue record for this book
is available from the British Library.

Addresses for Random House Group Ltd companies outside the UK
can be found at: www.randomhouse.co.uk
The Random House Group Ltd Reg. No. 954009

Typeset in 11/12½pt Giovanni Book by
Kestrel Data, Exeter, Devon.

10

Penguin Random House is committed to a sustainable future for
our business, our readers and our planet. This book is made from
Forest Stewardship Council® certified paper.

Printed and bound in Great Britain by Clays Ltd, Elcograf S.p.A.

For Lily and Tessie Canavan

Contents

Acknowledgements

Special thanks to my friends in the Wexford Bookshop
for a wonderful year in their company while writing
this book; especially Angie Murphy, Conor Dunne,
Joanne O'Leary, John Harper, Linda Cullen, Lindsay
Tierney, Luke Kelly, Maggie Niotis and Paula Dempsey.

Thanks also to Ann Geraghty, Anne Griffin, Bob
Johnston, James Lowry, Shane Duggan and Tim Hendy
for all the visits and their loyal friendship, and Paul
O'Rourke for getting me there and back again.

1

The *Montrose*

She was over 575 feet in length, with a beam almost an eighth of that size. She weighed approximately 16,500 tons and had a capacity of over eighteen hundred passengers, although today she was only three-quarters full. Stately and impressive, her hull and paintwork gleaming in the July sun, she seemed almost impatient to depart, her chimneys piping steam cautiously as the Scheldt river crashed noisily against her side. She was the SS *Montrose*, part of the Canadian Pacific fleet of passenger ships, and she was preparing to set sail from the port of Antwerp in Belgium for the city of Quebec in Canada, some three thousand miles away.

For over two weeks, the *Montrose* had been settled in the Berendrecht lock as her crew of sailors and engineers prepared her for her next voyage, and the *Sinjoreens* of the small Belgian city took pride in the fact that a fatal voyage had never set forth from their shores. There were almost two hundred employees of the Canadian Pacific Company who would sail with the ship when she left the harbour, from the navigator at the helm, through the coal-skinned, muscle-ripened recluses who stoked the engines, to the younger,

13

orphan boys who swept out the main dining hall after the evening's entertainments had come to an end. Few of them, however, had spent much time at the harbour since they had docked there in early July, preferring to enjoy their vacation and shore leave in the busy town of Antwerp, where there was enough food, drink and whores to satisfy all.

A taxi pulled in near a series of large steel containers, and Mrs Antoinette Drake opened the door and placed a felt slipper gingerly on the sea-slimed pavement outside, curling her lip in distaste at the filth which clung to the cobblestones. The slipper was of a dark-purple hue, the same colour as her hat and extravagant travelling gown which covered her enormous body like a sheet of tarpaulin covers a lifeboat. 'Driver,' she said impatiently, reaching forward and tapping him on the shoulder with a gloved finger; she rolled the 'r' in 'driver' regally. 'Driver, surely you can park a little closer to the ship? I can't be expected to walk through this. I'll ruin my shoes. They're new, don't you know. They won't take to all this water.'

'No further,' he replied, making no effort to turn around. His English was poor; rather than trying to improve it, he had discovered over the years that he needed to employ only a few stock phrases with foreigners, and so he stuck rigidly to them. That had been one of them. And here was another: 'Three schillings, please.'

'No further? What nonsense! What's he talking about, Victoria?' Mrs Drake asked, turning to look at her daughter, who was rooting through her purse for the fare. 'The man's a fool. Why can't he drive us any closer? The ship is all the way over there. Is he simple-minded, do you think? Does he not understand me?'

'This is as far as he's allowed to drive, Mother,' said Victoria, fishing out the money and handing it to the driver before opening her own door and stepping outside. 'Wait there,' she added. 'I'll help you out. It's perfectly safe.'

'Oh really, this is too much,' Mrs Drake muttered irritably as she waited for the seventeen-year-old to come around to her side of the taxi. Victoria had chosen a far more suitable travelling costume and didn't seem concerned about the dangers of footwear on the damp stones. 'I say it's really not good enough,' she added in a louder voice. 'Do you hear me, driver? It's not good enough, all this taking money for a job half done. It's a disgrace, if you want to know the truth. If this was England, you'd be taken out and flogged for such a thing. Leaving a lady of my years and station stranded like this.'

'Out please,' the driver replied in a pleasant, sing-song voice, another of his handful of useful phrases.

'What's that?'

'Out please,' he repeated. He drove tourists to the harbour every day and had little time for their complaints, especially the English ones, especially the *upper-class* English ones who seemed to believe that they should not only be driven to the ship but should be carried aboard on a sedan chair.

'Well I never did!' said Mrs Drake, astonished at the man's impertinence. 'Now look here, you—' She intended to drag her body weight forward and remonstrate further, perhaps employ a little light violence if necessary, but by now Victoria had opened the side door fully and was reaching inside, gripping her mother's arm, placing a foot against the wheel to act as a makeshift fulcrum and wrenching the older woman out. The vast bulk of the elder Drake found itself pouring on to the stones of the Antwerp harbour before any more complaints could issue from her mouth; a sound like a vacuum filling was heard distinctly from inside the car. 'Victoria, I—' she gasped, head held low, bosom crashing forward, the words seized from her mouth and mercifully whisked away, unspoken, into the heavens. 'Victoria, take a care! Can't you just—'

'Thank you, driver,' said Victoria when her mother was safely out of the car and attempting to recover her dignity by flattening the creases in her dress with a suede glove.

'Look at me,' she muttered. 'What a condition to be seen in.'

'You look perfectly fine,' her daughter said in a distracted voice as she looked around at the other passengers making their way to the ship. She quickly closed the door, and the driver immediately sped away.

'Victoria, I wish you wouldn't treat these people with such deference,' Mrs Drake remonstrated as she shook her head in frustration. 'Thanking him, after the way he spoke to me. You must understand that so many of these foreigners will take advantage of people like you and I if we show them any sign of weakness. Don't spare the rod, that's my adage, my dear, and it has served me well.'

'Don't I know it,' Victoria replied.

'Their class don't understand any better. In truth, many of them will respect you for it.'

'*We* are the foreigners here, Mother,' Victoria pointed out, looking around to inspect her surroundings. 'Not them. This is Belgium, remember? The man didn't mean to be rude. It's not worth our concerning ourselves with such trivial matters.'

'Not worth it? That's three schillings we've spent on a taxi ride to the ship, and look at us! Another mile to walk on wet cobblestones, and who's to clean the hem of my dress when we're on board? I fancied I would wear this on a dinner evening after we had set sail. That's out of the question now. And my legs are not what they were when I was a girl. You know I hate walking.'

Victoria smiled and linked her mother's arm with her own, leading her in the direction of the ship. 'It's hardly a mile away,' she said patiently. 'Two hundred yards, no more.' She considered pointing out that it had actually been four schillings she had spent and not three, for she had given the man a tip, but she decided against it. 'Once we're on board you won't have to walk again for eleven days if you don't feel like it. And I'm sure there will be a maid to help with the clothing. All our luggage should have already been unpacked in our cabin, you know. Who do you think did that? Mice?'

Mrs Drake sniffed but refused to concede the point. She remained silent, however, as they approached the gangway. 'Don't be insolent,' she said finally. 'I only mean that there is a correct way and an incorrect way to conduct one's business, and if one is dealing with an underling one should bear that in mind at all times.'

'Yes, Mother,' said Victoria in a sad voice, employing the tone of one who has grown accustomed to dealing with the complaints of a small child. 'But we're here now anyway, so let's not worry about it.'

'And you have to remember that we are Englishwomen. And Englishwomen of a particular class at that. We cannot let ourselves be bullied or taken advantage of by some . . . *European.*' She spat out the word as if it was a fly she had inhaled. 'We must remember ourselves at all times when we're sailing. Now, here's a boy to take our tickets. Oh, take a look at his face. He looks as though he hasn't washed in a week. Filthy child.' She lifted her cane and waved it in his direction, as if she was flagging down a passing motorist. 'Have them ready for him there, Victoria. Let's not waste time on ceremony. And for heaven's sake don't get too close to him. He may be diseased. Oh, what's that noise? For heaven's sake, get me out of this place!'

'That noise' was the sound of Bernard Leejik, the Drakes' recent cab driver, pressing firmly on the horn of his car as he narrowly avoided mowing down several other innocent travellers making their way towards the

Montrose. Mr John Robinson had to jump back when the vehicle sped past him, his legs moving a lot more nimbly than those of the average forty-seven-year-old gentleman. A man of quiet sensibilities who disliked any sort of commotion or trouble, he stared around at the disappearing vehicle with distaste. 'These new motor cars will be the death of everyone,' he said, recovering his balance and directing his attention towards his youthful companion. 'I think someone should do something about them before we all get knocked over and killed. Don't you agree?'

'I've never driven in one . . . Father,' came the boy's cautious reply, as if he was trying out the word for the first time.

Mr Robinson both smiled and felt awkward at the same time. 'That's it,' he said quietly, resting a hand on the lad's shoulder for a moment as they walked along. 'Well done. You have the tickets, haven't you?' he added, his hand drawn to his face as he felt the bare space above his upper lip which was now devoid of the moustache he had worn for almost thirty years. In its place, he had started to grow a beard along his cheeks and chin, and after four days it was coming along quite nicely. Still, this face, this new sensation along his cheeks and lips was unfamiliar to him and he could not stop himself from constantly touching it. 'Edmund,' he said, with as much strange formality as the boy had uttered 'father' a few moments before.

'They're in my pocket,' he answered.

'Excellent. Well, as soon as we're on board, I think we should go straight to our cabin. Settle in and take a little rest. Not create any sort of fuss. When the ship is safely at sea we can take the air perhaps.'

'Oh no,' said Edmund, frustrated. 'Can't we stand by the railings and wave at the people as we set sail? When we left England you wouldn't allow me to do it. Can't we do it now? Please?'

Mr Robinson frowned. In recent days he had grown almost pathologically careful about drawing any unnecessary attention to himself or to Edmund. 'They're only people,' he pointed out, hoping to dampen the boy's enthusiasm. 'Growing smaller in the distance. It's nothing to get excited about.'

'Well, if you'd prefer we didn't . . .' Edmund muttered, looking down at the ground disconsolately as they approached the ship. 'But it would mean a lot to me. I promise I won't speak to anyone. I just want to feel some of the excitement, that's all.'

'Very well,' Mr Robinson conceded with a sigh. 'If it means that much to you, I don't see how I can possibly refuse.'

Edmund smiled at his father and hugged his arm tightly. 'Thank you,' he said. 'Look,' he added, pointing ahead to where two women were remonstrating at the platform with a uniformed member of staff. 'Some sort of commotion already.'

'Just ignore them,' said Mr Robinson. 'We'll show our tickets and climb aboard. No need to get involved with any little local difficulties.'

'There's a second queue,' said Edmund, reaching into his pocket and displaying the tickets to another member of the crew, who examined them carefully before staring into the faces of the father and son and ticking their names off on a master sheet.

'Your cabin is number A4 on the first-class deck,' he said in an affected voice, one which had studied the vowel sounds of the upper classes and was mimicking them unsuccessfully. Mr Robinson could tell that he was probably originally an East End Londoner who had worked his way up through the ranks of the Canadian Pacific Company to the position he now held and wanted to pretend that he was of more impressive stock than was actually the case. This is what came of mingling with the rich for a career, he knew: one

19

wanted to feel part of their society. 'Nice set of rooms, sir,' the man added with a friendly smile. 'Think you'll be very comfortable there. Plenty of stewards around if there's any problems.'

'Thank you,' said Mr Robinson, ushering Edmund along, a hand on his back, not wishing to become engaged in too long a conversation.

'Like one of the lads to show you the way, sir?' the attendant asked, but Mr Robinson shook his head without turning around.

'We'll be fine,' he called out. 'I'm sure we can find it.'

'I *specifically* ordered a room on the starboard side,' said Mrs Drake, her arms flapping like a seagull in flight as she craned her neck to look at the sheets which the first crew member was holding before him on a clipboard. She turned around irritably as Mr Robinson and Edmund brushed past her, as if she couldn't understand why others were being allowed to board while she was stuck here making conversation with an impoverished person. 'I find this simply too outrageous. Victoria, tell the boy that we ordered a starboard room.'

'Cabin, ma'am.'

'What?'

'Madam, the cabin which was booked was a first-class cabin. We don't specifically note which side of the ship it's on. That's not a service we offer.'

'It's fine, really,' said Victoria, reaching out for the key which the crew member was holding.

'It's far from fine,' said Mrs Drake firmly. 'Where's the captain? Surely there must be some *adult* in charge of this boy? They can hardly allow him to take charge of things on his own with a filthy face like that. Living on the sea, too. Haven't you ever heard of water?'

'The captain is busy right now,' he replied between gritted teeth, ignoring her comments. The truth was that he had been working since early morning and the Drakes were among the last passengers to board. Standing on the dock of the Antwerp harbour over the course of several hours involved a lot of dust in the air travelling one's way, and he was damned if he was going to apologize for not carrying a cloth in his pocket to wipe his face clean before every single passenger climbed on board. 'Believe me, Mrs Drake, when we're at sea, there's no real difference in the view, whether you're port or starboard. It's water, water everywhere and not a drop to drink,' he added in a false tone of jollity, as if this would end the situation and make these people board sooner. He wasn't travelling with the ship himself and the sooner she sailed, the sooner his working day would end and he could return home. A queue of about a half-dozen people was lining up behind them now and Mrs Drake was growing more aware of their presence, although embarrassment was a sensation unfamiliar to her. She turned to look at the first couple, a well-dressed husband and wife in their sixties who were staring directly ahead, silently pretending that this contretemps was not taking place at all, and she frowned. Pursing her lips, she gave them a discreet nod, as if they, her social equals, could understand the frustration of having to converse with the little people.

'So sorry to detain you,' she said obsequiously, beaming from ear to ear. 'Some mix-up over our room. Mrs Antoinette Drake, so pleased to meet you,' she added, enunciating each word perfectly.

Before her new companions could have an opportunity to answer her or add their own names, Victoria had reached across and taken the key quickly. 'A7,' she said, reading the inscription. 'Is it a nice cabin?' she asked, reaching down to lift the hem of her skirt to prevent it dragging behind her as she made her way up the gangway.

'One of the nicest, miss,' came the reply. 'I guarantee you'll find it comfortable and relaxing. All the cabins in A and B section are reserved for our finest gentlemen and ladies.'

'You'll be hearing more of this, I assure you,' said Mrs Drake, giving in now as she prepared to follow her daughter on board. She tapped the young man on the shoulder twice with her cane, sharply, as if about to ennoble him. 'So sorry to detain you,' she repeated to the people behind her, shifting tone once again in an attempt to create a solidarity with them. 'I dare say we shall meet again on board ship.'

'Charmed,' said the old man in a dry voice which suggested he wanted her to get out of his way . . . and quickly.

'Really, Mother,' said Victoria.

'Really, Victoria,' said Mrs Drake at the same moment. 'I just believe a person should receive what a person pays for. Nothing more and nothing less. Is that so wrong? If a person pays for a starboard cabin, then a person should be given a starboard cabin. And there's an end to it.' They climbed aboard and saw a sign pointing towards a staircase bearing the legend *First Class Cabins: A1–A8*.

'This way, Mother,' said Victoria, and they made their way along a narrow corridor, looking at each door as they passed, Mrs Drake sighing in frustration with every step, torn between complaining about the condition of her knees and the cleanliness of the carpet.

Outside one of the rooms, a middle-aged man and his teenage son seemed to be having some difficulty with the lock of their cabin door.

'Let me try,' said Edmund, taking the key from Mr Robinson's hands and sliding it into the lock carefully. He twisted it several times and shook the door sharply before it opened, almost falling inside as it gave way before him. The cabin itself was a decent size and contained two bunk beds, a sofa, a dressing table and a small en-suite bathroom. A porthole offered a pleasant view of the sea beyond.

'Bunks,' said Mr Robinson, his face falling a little.

'Never mind,' said Edmund.

'I do beg your pardon,' said Mrs Drake, leaning into the room, her massive body taking them both by surprise. Mr Robinson pushed his pince-nez a little higher up his nose in order to take in this large, purple creature. 'I just wondered whether the cabins on the starboard side were as nice as those on the port. I ordered starboard but was given port. What do you think of that, eh? Have you ever heard the like?'

'I was unaware you could state a preference,' said Mr Robinson. 'Or that anyone could even have one.'

'Apparently you can't,' she said, replying to the first sentiment and ignoring the second. 'Mrs Antoinette Drake,' she added. 'So pleased to meet you.'

'John Robinson,' he said quietly, not having wished to make any acquaintances this early on and regretting not having immediately closed their cabin door after entering. He gave a polite bow. 'My son Edmund.'

'Lovely to meet you both,' she said, looking them up and down with narrowed eyes as if to define whether or not they were her type of people. In the end she let the initial letter on their cabin door decide for her. 'Edmund, what a charming suit you're wearing,' she added, reaching forward and touching his lapels casually, causing him to take a step backwards in surprise. 'Oh, I'm not going to bite you,' she said with a laugh. 'Don't worry. But that's a new suit if ever I saw one.'

'We just bought it yesterday,' Edmund acknowledged, blushing slightly and looking at his shoes.

'Well, it's a charming one, and I applaud your taste. How old are you anyway, seventeen or eighteen? How lovely for you. And such delicate features. You must meet my daughter Victoria. We will be looking for suitable companions on the voyage.'

'We were just about to get ready for departure,' said Mr Robinson after a moment, stepping forward to usher her back through the door and out into the corridor.

'Now I must get on,' she said immediately. 'My daughter and I are in Cabin A7. Port side, to my shame. I'm sure we will become fast friends as the voyage progresses.'

'No doubt,' said Mr Robinson.

She took herself out of the room and Mr Robinson and Edmund looked at each other nervously. 'Don't look so worried,' said Edmund. 'There are a lot of passengers on board. We have to be prepared to speak to them. No one knows us here.'

'Perhaps,' said Mr Robinson dubiously.

While Mrs Drake was settling into Cabin A7 and finding fault with as many of its features as possible, forty feet below her, in Cabin B7, Miss Martha Hayes was sitting on the edge of her small bed, willing herself not to burst into tears. At twenty-nine years of age, Martha looked as if she was about to turn forty. Her hair was beginning to spring with jagged wires of grey and her skin was taking on a rough appearance. Still, for all that, she was what could be referred to as a handsome woman. She had been on board for almost an hour now and had spent that time quite happily arranging her clothes and belongings around her small cabin. Now that this was done, she had little left to occupy her time. She was travelling alone and had as yet formed no alliances. In Antwerp, she had considered buying a dozen new novels and secluding herself in her room for the entire voyage, but had eventually decided against that anti-social idea and instead limited herself to three books and a new hat to shield her from the sun, in order to encourage lounging on the deck. From her pocket she took a gold watch and, opening it up, stared at the face of Léon Brillt, the Belgian teacher with whom she had been embroiled for almost eighteen months. She stared at his dark face and caramel eyes and bit her lip, forcing herself not to cry. Snapping the case shut again, she stood up and shook her body violently.

'A new beginning, Martha,' she said aloud. 'No more of this nonsense.'

And at that very moment Martha Hayes, Mrs Antoinette Drake, her daughter Victoria, Mr John Robinson, Master Edmund Robinson and the 1,323 other passengers of the *Montrose* all jumped in unison as the stately ship's horn above them blew one long, deep snort, and the voices of the crew cried out in unison as a heavenly choir: '*All aboard! All aboard!*'

The *Montrose* was ready to sail.

Henry Kendall's love of the sea stretched back to his childhood, when his father, Arthur, would read him stories of life on board ship from the small collection of books he stored on a shelf above the fireplace. Father and son shared a favourite story, the one concerning William Bligh and his adventures on board HMS *Bounty*, but for very different reasons. Arthur sided with Fletcher Christian and the mutineers, for he hated sadism and pompous authority. For Henry, however, it was the moment when Bligh first set foot on the small boat to navigate the seas by means of a compass and the stars that the narrative truly came to life; all else was prologue. He despised the mutineers and their blatant disregard for naval authority, and his ideal conclusion to the story would have been to see Fletcher Christian hanging by his neck for his crime, rather than living out his days as a free man on the South Sea islands.

Henry joined the navy as a sailor at the age of fifteen. A lifelong bachelor, he devoted himself to the sea from the start and made slow but steady progress through the ranks of naval officer, but to his great disappointment failed to gain his own command. At the age of forty-two, he learned that an independent company, the Canadian Pacific, was looking for experienced first officers to captain a new fleet of six transatlantic ships and he applied immediately, surprising himself at his willingness to abandon Her Majesty's Navy. His experience and reliability stood him in good stead at the interviews and he took command of the *Perseverance*, making regular voyages from Calais to New York, three months later. Now, at fifty years of age, he was captain of the passenger ship the SS *Montrose*, sailing from Antwerp to Quebec, and on the morning of Wednesday, 20 July 1910, he stared at his reflection in the mirror of his cabin and wondered sadly what the sailing world was coming to.

He had come on board some two hours earlier, as was his custom, to study the charts in private, plotting the voyage and route by the winds, and had been greeted by a young man in his late twenties who introduced himself cheerfully as Billy Carter, the new first officer.

'The new what?' Captain Kendall asked in surprise, irritated at even having to open his mouth, fill his lungs with air and find the energy to address this impertinent fellow. Carter was a cheeky-looking individual with a mop of sandy-brown curly hair, deep-blue eyes, an impressive set of dimples and a row of freckles across his nose, all of which made him look not so much like a man as a comic-book creation, animation brought to life; and Kendall was a captain who detested having to converse with anyone other than the most senior officers. There was a chain of authority on board ship, a chain which should never be broken, and he believed that this should extend not just to duty but to conversation as well.

'First officer, sir,' Carter replied. 'Billy Carter. At your service. Pleased to meet you,' he added with a wink and a toss of his curls.

Kendall frowned, appalled by the fellow's familiarity. 'And where is Mr Sorenson?' he asked in an imperious tone, refusing even to meet the fellow's eyes.

'Mr Sorenson?'

'First Officer Sorenson,' Kendall explained irritably. 'He has been with me for seven years, and it was my understanding that he would be undertaking this voyage too. The crew listings state this to be the case. So I ask again, where is he?'

'Lord, haven't you heard, sir?' asked Carter, scratching his head furiously, as if a civilization of lice might lurk beneath and he needed to scrape them away. 'He was taken into hospital only last night, screaming like a baby who's had his rattle stolen. Appendix burst is what I heard. Not a pretty thing. I got a note from HQ early this morning asking me to take over his duties on this trip. They said they'd informed you too. Didn't you get their note?'

'No one has informed me of anything,' the captain replied, his heart sinking at the loss of his most trusted colleague, worry for his friend filling him entirely. Kendall and Sorenson had built up mutual trust and professional respect over seven years of sailing together; they were also fast poker friends and had enjoyed many late-night games in the captain's cabin over a bottle of whiskey. Sorenson was, Kendall had often realized, his only intimate. 'Damn these people. Who are you anyway? What's your experience?'

'Like I said, the name's Billy Carter,' he began, before being interrupted by his superior.

'Billy Carter?' he asked, spitting out the words like undercooked meat. '*Billy*? What kind of name is that for an officer, might I ask?'

'Short for William, sir. My father's name before me.

And his. Not *his*, though. *His* name was James. Before him there was another—'

'I'm not interested in your family history,' Kendall snapped.

'They always called me Billy as a boy,' the young man added helpfully.

'Well, you're a man now, aren't you?'

'My wife says I am anyway.' Another wink.

'You're married?' asked Kendall, appalled. He disapproved of officers who had taken wives: nasty, smelly creatures. Kendall had never met a woman who interested him and he could scarcely imagine the horrors that married life would impose upon him; he found it incredible that anyone would be interested in pursuing such a path voluntarily. The truth was, he disapproved of women as a gender, considering them entirely surplus to his requirements.

'Two years now,' replied Carter. 'And we've got a kiddy on the way. Due around the end of August. Not sure if I'm supposed to be excited or terrified,' he added, shaking his head and laughing, as if casual chit-chat was all that shipboard life was about. 'Got any kids yourself, sir?' he asked politely.

'Mr Carter, I'm sure you'd make an excellent first officer for the *Montrose* but I really fail to see how—'

'Half a mo', Captain.' He reached into his pocket and produced the note which the Canadian Pacific Company had sent him earlier that morning. 'Here's my orders, sent to me like I said. I've been a first officer on the *Zealous* and the *Ontario* for two years and eighteen months respectively. We only sail around Europe most of the time and I get to go home more often. Don't think I want to spend too much time going back and forth across the pond – not with the kiddy coming soon, anyway – but they asked and I didn't have much choice but to jump. They promised I'd be back in time for Junior's birth. But I am experienced, Captain, and I know what I'm doing. Truth be told, I'd rather be back on my regular ship now too, just like I'm sure you'd rather have Mr Sorenson with you now than me. But there we are. Life's funny that way.'

Kendall read the note silently, hearing only scattered portions of Carter's speech, selecting the information he needed and discarding the rest without a moment's thought. He sighed and stroked his heavy white beard reflectively, realizing that he would have little choice but to accept this new state of affairs. 'And Mr Sorenson?' he added after a moment. 'He'll be out of commission for how long?'

'A good six weeks is what I've been told. Seems like there was a fairly messy operation involved. A burst appendix isn't a lot of fun, you know. But don't worry, sir, you won't have to put up with me for long. He should be up and around in a few weeks.'

'Very well, Mr Carter,' said Kendall, accepting the situation but determined to set his guidelines from the start. 'However, I think it would be appropriate if you visited the ship's barber before we set sail today. Your hair is unkempt and I cannot abide untidiness aboard ship, especially not in my senior officers, who should be setting an example to the men.'

Carter hesitated but, after a moment, he nodded. He ran a hand through his curly mop defensively, as if a cut would deprive him, like Samson, of his powers. 'Very good, sir,' he muttered quietly.

'And when walking the decks, I'll thank you to have your cap with you at all times, either worn on your head or tucked discreetly under your arm if conversing with a lady passenger. These are small matters, you understand, but I believe they are crucial to professional conduct. Discipline. Unity. Obedience. All important watch-words aboard the *Montrose*.'

The first officer nodded again but said nothing. Kendall licked his lips and was surprised to find them dry and slightly chapped; if he was to break into a sudden smile, he thought, they would crack and bleed.

'Perhaps you would also be good enough to bring me complete crew and passenger lists, in case there are any other small surprises about which our employers have failed to inform me. We set sail at two o'clock, yes?'

'That's right, sir.'

'Then we need to make sure that all visitors are ashore by one-thirty at the latest and that all passengers are on board by that time. You'll find I'm a punctual man, Mr Carter, and I can't abide unnecessary tardiness. The business of transatlantic crossings is guided by punctuality and speed. We compete against faster and better ships every day and I have a duty to our passengers and to the Canadian Pacific fleet to ensure no delays. That's why I expect so much from my officers and sailors, Mr Carter. That's why I'll expect a lot from you.'

'I'll bring the lists to your cabin immediately, sir,' said Carter in a quieter voice; he was unaccustomed to the kind of stern authority that Captain Kendall was displaying towards him.

An hour later, the captain sat alone in his cabin and listened as the ship's horn sounded, alerting those not destined for Canada to return to the shore immediately. He glanced at his watch. One o'clock. It usually took about half an hour to clear the decks and board the final passengers, which would bring the time to one-thirty precisely, exactly as he had instructed Mr Carter. For reasons unknown to him, he felt irritated by this, even though he had issued the order and it was being followed exactly. He realized that he expected to find many faults with Mr First Officer Billy Carter and wanted to iron them out immediately. However, if the man continued to mask his shortcomings, it would prove difficult to discipline him.

'A man like that,' he declared out loud, even though there was no one else present in his cabin to hear him, 'would never have survived in the navy.' And then, standing up and inspecting himself in the mirror, he placed his cap on his head, pulled his jacket straight and stepped outside to issue his navigational instructions to the crew.

Having packed their clothes away into the small dresser and wardrobe opposite the bunk beds, Mr John Robinson allowed Edmund to persuade him that they should watch the disappearance of Antwerp from the deck of the *Montrose*, although he would have been quite happy to remain in his cabin reading *The Hound of the Baskervilles*. He stepped inside the small bathroom and splashed some water on his face to refresh himself. A grey towel, rough and smelling of detergent, hung on a rail by the sink, and he stared at his reflection in the mirror as he dried his face. Like Captain Kendall, he found himself disturbed by his own appearance, which seemed like that of a stranger; his new features – no moustache, but a flourishing beard – were taking some getting used to, but, added to that, his face seemed a little more drawn now than it had in London, his skin a little more pasty, the dark bags under his eyes more pronounced.

'That's just lack of sleep,' said Edmund when this was pointed out anxiously. 'We've had a busy time in Antwerp and very little rest. But we have eleven days to relax on board. You'll be a new man by the time we reach Quebec.'

'I quite enjoyed our time in Belgium,' said Mr Robinson in a quiet voice, tapping his cheeks gently to see whether any further colour would emerge, any memory of youth. 'You aren't missing home yet?'

'Of course not. I have to get used to it now anyway. Canada will be quite different from London, I expect.'

Mr Robinson nodded in agreement. 'Do you suppose we'll ever return?' Edmund asked.

'To England?'

'Yes.'

'Perhaps. Some day. We have new lives to start now though, and it's best that we focus on them. A few weeks from today, you'll have forgotten all about it and won't want to go back. England will be nothing more than a bad memory. A few months from now, we'll have forgotten the names of all our old friends. *My* old friends, I mean,' he corrected himself after a moment.

Edmund wasn't so sure but he allowed the observation to go unchallenged. He slid the last of the suitcases under the lower bunk, and the tightly sealed hat box which had been contained inside one of them went on top of the wardrobe. Edmund had secured it earlier with tape and rope to prevent it from spilling open.

'Why do you insist on bringing that thing with you?' Mr Robinson asked, looking up at it and shaking his head. 'It's such an encumbrance.'

'I've told you. It contains my most private belongings. It's just the right size and shape.'

'Well, it's just as well you kept it in the suitcase,' he said. 'Imagine a boy carrying a lady's hat box with him. We would have had some strange looks at the harbour with that.' He tapped his fingers lightly against the side of the dresser as he glanced towards the door anxiously. The deep boom of the ship's horn continued to sound every few minutes and the noise was giving him a headache.

'We're getting close to departure,' said Edmund.

'You can always go up there on your own,' Mr Robinson pointed out. 'If you want to watch as she sails, that is. You don't need me with you, surely?'

'I don't *need* you with me. I *want* you with me. I want us to see Europe disappearing into the distance behind us together. I think it would be bad luck for me to be up there alone. Besides, I get nervous on my own. You know that. I'm not used to . . .' He held out his palms as if to indicate that he couldn't even find the words to explain this situation. '. . . all of this,' he said finally.

Mr Robinson nodded. 'Very well then,' he said with a smile. 'If it means that much to you, we'll go together. Let me fetch my coat.'

Edmund grinned. His powers of persuasion were second to none; even on trivial matters like this, victory gave him a tremendous sense of power.

The wind was blowing quite strongly on the deck of the ship and, as many of the passengers had decided to remain below decks, they did not have to struggle to secure a place along the railings; the first-class deck was separated from steerage anyway, leaving them a lot more room to walk around or to relax on deckchairs. From where they stood, the harbour of Antwerp was spread out before them, and it seemed as if there were thousands of people walking around busily, working, travelling, collecting or despatching their loved ones, looking lost.

'It wasn't as nice as Paris, was it?' Edmund commented, buttoning his coat against the breeze.

'What's that?'

'Antwerp. I didn't like the city as much as Paris. We had more fun there.'

'That's because Paris is the true city of romance, or so they say,' said Mr Robinson with a smile. 'I'm not sure there are many cities in the world that can compete with it. I read somewhere once that when good Americans die, they go to Paris.'

Edmund laughed. 'And are you one of those?' he asked. 'Are you a good American?'

'Of those two things,' he replied, 'I am certainly one.'

A gust of wind blew quickly from behind them and, without even thinking, Mr Robinson's reflexes reacted and his hand shot out to grab a lady's hat before it was blown over the side of the ship and into the water below. He stared at his catch, amazed to see the dark-blue bonnet he was holding, and turned around to see a woman standing a few steps behind them, her own hands clasped on either side of her head where they had remained for a moment after the hat blew away.

'Your hat, madam?' he asked, surprised.

'Thank you,' she said, laughing gently as she retrieved it and tying the bow securely under her chin in a double knot. 'The wind took it right off my head before I could stop it. I was sure it was lost. It was very quick of you to catch it.'

He gave a polite half-bow and tipped his own hat slightly to acknowledge this courtesy. Lost for words, he was unsure whether it might be considered rude of him to turn around again to face the port, for then he would be offering his back to her. However, she saved him the trouble for she immediately walked to the railings herself and, folding her arms in front of her, stared into the distance as the ship began to move.

'I imagined there would be more people,' she said, looking ahead.

'Really?' Mr Robinson replied. 'I don't believe I've ever seen so many. They say the ship can hold eighteen hundred souls.'

'I meant, to see us off. I expected crowds of men and women waving their handkerchiefs in the air, crying at the loss of their loved ones.'

'I think that happens only in books,' he said. 'Not in the real world. I don't think people care about others that much outside of fiction.'

'Thank heaven for that,' she replied. 'I don't care for crowds myself. I was going to stay in my cabin until we were out at sea, but then I thought I might never see Europe again and would regret missing my last sight of it.'

'That's what I said,' Edmund chipped in, leaning forward to look at the lady, a little suspiciously. If there was to be conversation, he was determined to be part of it. 'I had to persuade him to come up here using that very argument.'

She smiled and looked at her two companions. 'I'm sorry,' she said. 'I should have introduced myself. Martha Hayes.' She extended her hand to each of them in turn. 'Pleased to meet you both.'

'John Robinson,' came the reply. 'My son Edmund.' As he named him, he gave the boy a sideways glance that suggested this was the very reason he would have preferred not to have come up on deck. Although the trip would take about eleven days, he was convinced that the fewer people they encountered the better, even if it meant a period of enforced isolation in each other's company.

For her part, Martha had been immediately drawn to Mr Robinson as he had an air of quiet respectability which she liked in a man. She had heard stories that transatlantic crossings were notorious for the numbers of lotharios on board, but she could sense that he was not such a character. His downcast eyes and despondent air stood in contrast to the excited glow of the other passengers.

'Are you going specifically to Canada or travelling on from there?'

'Travelling on, most likely,' he replied, even though this was not the case.

'Where to?'

He thought about it and licked his lips. He pictured the map of North America in his mind and wondered what destination he could name that would make sense. He was tempted to say New York – but then the question would be raised, why he had not taken a ship directly to that city instead. And of course there was nowhere to travel to north of Canada. He closed his eyes and felt a dull rush of panic begin in his chest and work its way up towards his throat, where the words flickered away and were lost.

Fortunately, Edmund saved the day by changing the subject. 'What deck is your cabin on?' he asked, and Miss Hayes hesitated for only a moment before answering, turning her head to look at the boy.

'B deck,' she said. 'Quite a nice room, all in all.'

'We're on A,' said Edmund. 'Bunk beds,' he added with a frown.

'Mr Robinson! It is Mr Robinson, isn't it?' A loud voice from behind them forced all three to turn around. Standing there, grinning like the cat that had got the cream, was Mrs Drake from Cabin A7, with her daughter Victoria standing gloomily by her side. Mrs Drake was wearing a different hat from the one she had worn earlier, a much more elaborate affair this time, and she carried an unnecessary parasol. Her perfectly round face was glowing with happiness to see them there, although she looked Miss Hayes up and down distastefully, as if she suspected the woman of being a member of the working classes and therefore unsuitable for polite company.

Victoria stared at Edmund and narrowed her eyes suspiciously.

'It's Mrs Drake,' the older woman added after a moment in order to save the embarrassment of a lack of recognition. 'We met while my daughter and I were looking for our rooms.'

'Ah yes,' said Mr Robinson. 'Mrs Drake. How nice to see you again.'

'What a coincidence that we should meet downstairs and then, when we come up to take the air, you're the first people we see. I said to Victoria, I said, "Look there's that nice Mr Robinson and his son, let's go and say hello to them. They'll be delighted to see us again." I said that, didn't I, Victoria?'

'Yes, Mother,' said Victoria dutifully. 'Doesn't the city look far away now?' she added to no one in particular. 'We've only been out five minutes and the mist is already taking it from sight.'

'And a good thing too,' said Mrs Drake. 'I didn't care for Antwerp, not one little bit. The place smelt foul and the people were thieves, every last one of them. Don't you agree, Mr Robinson? I dare say you felt the same way. You look like a man of breeding to me.'

'We didn't like it as much as Paris,' Edmund admitted.

'Oh. Were you in Paris recently then?' asked Mrs Drake, turning her head to look at the boy. 'Only, Victoria and I were there for the winter. Where did you stay? We have an apartment there. It's convenient, because we spend at least three or four months there every year. Mr Drake generally stays in London, where his business interests are. I love the theatre particularly. Couldn't you just die for the theatre, Mr Robinson?'

'This is Miss Hayes,' he answered, directing her attention towards the fifth member of their group and ignoring her question. While they were speaking, Martha had felt slightly awkward, wondering whether they were all old friends, and she had even considered slipping away without a word, unsure whether anyone would notice if she did so, or if they would even care. 'A fellow traveller,' he added.

'Charmed, Miss Hayes,' said Mrs Drake, extending a gloved hand in such a regal manner towards the younger woman that she wondered whether she should curtsey and kiss it. Resisting the urge, however, she shook it forcefully instead. Mrs Drake curled her lip a little. 'What a firm grip you have,' she said critically. 'Very manly. Are you travelling alone?'

'There must be a thousand people on board,' Martha replied, aiming for a little humour but seeing it backfire immediately as Mrs Drake considered her remark to be rude.

'I meant, do you have a chaperone? Your mother, perhaps, or a favoured aunt? A paid companion perhaps? Some of the ladies go in for such things, I know. Not I, of course, but one hears about such things.'

'I am entirely alone,' said Miss Hayes after a moment in a voice of such dignity that Mr Robinson was forced to stare closely at her, wondering whether her reply had referred not so much to her status aboard ship as to her life as a whole.

'How unfortunate for you, you poor, miserable, god-forsaken creature,' said Mrs Drake. 'I never travel alone myself. Nor would I allow Victoria to go abroad without me. She's too young still, you see. Only seventeen. How old are you, Edmund?' she asked.

'The same age,' said Mr Robinson, answering for him. 'I too prefer to keep him with me.'

'Ah, but he's a boy at least,' said Mrs Drake, as if this changed everything. 'Practically a man. Men aren't in such danger. Even ones with such delicate features as your son.' She stared at him more closely, narrowing her eyes. 'Have you been in a fight though, Edmund?'

'No,' he replied suspiciously.

'But the scar above your lip,' she said, noticing the thin pink gash that ran from beneath his right nostril down to his lip. 'Surely that's the result of an altercation of some sort. Boys can be so mischievous,' she added, smiling. 'The little scamps.' Edmund felt himself begin to blush and touched the place she had mentioned self-consciously. He was aware that the eyes of the others were on him and he despised Mrs Drake for it. 'Young ladies are always in peril, I feel, if they travel alone,' she continued finally, oblivious to his discomfort. 'I think perhaps we understand each other, Mr Robinson.'

'I believe I can look after myself,' said Martha, already feeling a general dislike for this large bulk of a woman, this supercilious sow looking down her nose at her. 'I have become accustomed to it recently.'

'Have you indeed,' said Mrs Drake dismissively, intrigued by what the younger lady's circumstances were now but not willing to flatter her by showing her any further attention. 'How nice for you. Now, Mr Robinson, as we are practically neighbours, I do hope that we will be able to dine together some evening? It makes a voyage pass so much quicker, I feel, when one makes friends and acquaintances along the way. I favour fan tan, but am equally adept at whist and baccarat. The first-class dining hall takes reservations, and I have it on the best authority that tables are booked up early. Perhaps I should reserve a table for four for tomorrow evening?' She didn't look in the direction of Martha, who allowed herself a brief smile at the snub. Mr Robinson, on the other hand, looked increasingly flustered and his hand went to his moustache, as it always did in moments of crisis, only to find that it was no longer there. His eyes opened wide in surprise.

'Where's your mother?' Victoria asked Edmund in an inquisitive tone. She had removed herself from her mother's side and had worked her way to the end of the railing so that she and Edmund stood a little apart from the adults and out of earshot. 'Is she dead?'

He looked at her, surprised by the forthrightness of her question. 'Yes,' he said finally. 'She died some years ago.'

'What did she die of?'

'She caught the plague,' said Edmund in a level tone. 'And it did for her.'

'The plague?' Victoria asked, shocked and stepping back a little, as if it might be contagious. 'Are you serious?'

'No, of course not, I'm teasing. Heavens, this is the twentieth century after all. Medical science has travelled on a little. No, she died of tuberculosis.'

'Ah,' said Victoria, relieved. 'I'm sorry to hear that. My aunt Georgiana had that, and she had to spend the last ten years of her life in Switzerland for the air. She died when a bird fell on her.'

'When a *what*?'

'A bird fell on her head one day. While she was out walking. It must have died in the air and just fell to earth. Killed her outright. It was a very *big* bird, you see. Not a pleasant way to go. Especially after only moving out there in order to stay alive. Why, she could have come home and lived her days out in England without the fear of random objects falling out of the sky and killing her. But that's the Swiss, I expect. They're a strange people, don't you agree?'

Edmund nodded and raised his eyebrows a little, wondering whether bird and animal life could actually assume a national identity. 'Where's your father?' he asked, returning the question. 'Is he dead too?'

'He's in . . . London,' she replied, shaking her head as if it took a little time to remember his exact location. 'He's in banking. He travels from time to time but is based there. We're going to Canada on a holiday to visit my uncle and aunt who emigrated there twenty years ago. Mother hasn't seen them in all that time. They're very wealthy.'

'How nice for them,' said Edmund sarcastically.

'Mother *says* that she wouldn't allow me to travel alone,' she continued, ignoring his tone. 'But next year I will be eighteen, and then I come into my money. When that happens she won't see me for dust. I'm going to do a little private travelling of my own. Kick up my heels.'

Edmund smiled and looked across at Mrs Drake, who was standing in a troika with Mr Robinson and Miss Hayes but directing all her questions at the former, who looked as if he might conceivably jump overboard at any moment. 'Don't let her hear you say that,' he said.

'Oh, she can't hear me from over there. Not over the sound of her own voice anyway. She could drown out the engines if she really put her mind to it.'

'And where will you go?' he asked. 'With your money, I mean.'

Victoria turned and looked out to sea with a casual air and a wide smile. Her long dark hair blew behind her gracefully and Edmund could not help but admire her perfect skin and the pale prettiness of her features. 'Wherever the wind takes me,' she said dramatically. 'And wherever there are eligible young men to fall in love with me.'

Edmund gasped and gave a little laugh.

'Do I shock you?' she asked flirtatiously, narrowing her eyes.

'No,' he replied firmly, unwilling to allow her this small thrill.

She looked immediately disappointed. 'Oh,' she said, deflated. 'Why not?'

'It takes a lot to shock me.'

'Perhaps you don't have my sense of adventure,' she said.

'Perhaps you don't have my experience of life.'

'After all, you're still travelling with your father.'

'As you are with your mother.'

'But you're a boy,' she said. 'Like my mother said, practically a man. Don't you want to go off somewhere without him? Do a little seduction of your own?'

Edmund allowed a thin smile to cross his face but he didn't look at Victoria. Already he knew that this was the kind of girl he disliked, but standing there at that moment he felt he had the power to tease her, a sensation which made him feel an extra three feet tall.

'Victoria, dear, don't slouch over the railing like that,' called Mrs Drake, and they turned to face her. Edmund strolled back towards their company and Victoria was forced to follow. She was irritated by the boy's apparent indifference to her, a new response. In London, where the Drakes lived, and in Paris, where they spent much of their time, she was considered quite the catch and

41

enjoyed the game of stringing innocent boys along, making them fall in love with her and then dismissing them as soon as a new possibility appeared. This took place in the private life that her mother knew little of. One boy in particular, a nineteen-year-old stockbroker's son named Kenneth Cage, had become obsessed with her the previous summer and announced that he would slit his throat if she did not agree to marry him; but then he had pretensions towards being an artist and believed in wild statements such as this. Unmoved, she had informed him that if she was to reach the age of twenty *without* some fellow killing himself for the love of her, she would consider herself a great failure. In the end he had swallowed two pots of emulsified paint in an attempt at self-poisoning, but it had gone horribly wrong and, rather than dying or impressing Victoria sufficiently for her to succumb to his charms, he had merely suffered a severe case of diarrhoea for two weeks and pissed several shades of primary colours for months afterwards. And now here was Edmund, a boy her own age – a strikingly good-looking boy at that, with sharp cheekbones, tender red lips, smooth cheeks and the most beautiful eyes she had ever seen. A slim body, the kind she found devilishly attractive. And not only was he making no effort whatsoever to make love to her, he seemed entirely indifferent to her and had even walked away from her without being dismissed. She would win him over, she decided. Before the voyage was over she would make him fall in love with her. Then she would use him and discard him and teach him what it was to lose a person such as her.

'I think I may return to my cabin,' said Martha Hayes when they were all reunited. She had barely got a word in edgeways while Mrs Drake had been talking to Mr Robinson, and she had no desire to stay any longer in order to be ignored. Decorum insisted that she take her leave politely, however.

'Lovely to have met you, Miss Hayes,' said Mr Robinson, doffing his hat.

'And you,' she acknowledged. 'And thank you again for saving my hat. Mrs Drake,' she added with a curt nod. 'Miss Drake.'

'Goodbye, Miss Hayes,' said Mrs Drake in a loud voice, watching her walk away and shaking her head in amazement. 'The things some people wear when they travel,' she said with a gentle laugh, before turning back to Mr Robinson. 'The poor girl probably can't afford anything better, I expect. But a delightful manner, wouldn't you agree, Mr Robinson? Very homely.'

'I think perhaps Edmund and I should also return to our cabin,' he said.

'Already? But the sun is just beginning to come out. I thought perhaps you might take a turn around the deck with me. Stake out our territory, so to speak. I'd love to learn a little more about you.'

'And you will, no doubt,' he said, taking Edmund by the arm. 'We have many days ahead of us, I fear.'

'You fear?' she asked, surprised.

'I'm not the world's best sailor,' he explained. 'I think I may rest for a little while.'

'Ah. Find your sea legs, you mean. Well, certainly, Mr Robinson. I'll look forward to seeing you later then. In the meantime Victoria and I will discover what entertainments are laid on for the first-class passengers.'

'Excellent. Until later then,' he said, walking away. 'What a woman,' he whispered to Edmund when they were out of earshot. 'She could talk for England. Don't leave me alone with her again. I might end up throwing her overboard.'

'I'll look out for you if you'll keep the daughter away from me,' Edmund replied. 'Stuck up – well, I can't say the word. Are you really a bad traveller?' he asked after a moment.

'Not at all. I just wanted to go back to the cabin, that's all. With you.'

Edmund smiled. 'You only had to say as much,' he said, reaching into his pocket for the key.

Billy Carter had spent the previous hour in the barber's saloon, a small cabin on one of the lower decks of the ship which was not as elaborate as its official title made it sound. Usually, Jean Dupuis, the French-Canadian barber who had spent the last ten years travelling back and forth across the Atlantic Ocean without ever setting foot on either of its book-ended continents, was to be found there alone, comfortably close to a bottle of vodka. There were those sailors on board who worried about letting a man, half blood, half alcohol, get close to their ears with a sharp pair of scissors, but none had yet reported any accidents and so M. Dupuis had maintained his position and his free accommodation for a decade unchallenged. Carter was forced to wait for the barber's reappearance, however, as the older man was up on deck, sober as a judge, nervously awaiting the arrival of his supplies for the voyage ahead.

'A haircut already?' he asked, stepping into the cabin and stopping in surprise to see the young first officer standing there, hands in pockets, looking around at his belongings. 'We're not even out of port yet. Can't it wait a few hours?'

'Captain Kendall insisted,' replied Carter. 'He said my hair was too long and ordered me down here sharpish.'

Dupuis narrowed his eyes and cocked his head slightly, as if judging for himself whether the younger man's hairstyle was in fact an affront to taste. 'It's not so long that it can't wait a day or two,' he suggested. 'Only I wanted to arrange my things before we set sail.' By 'things', he meant the crate of vodka which had arrived for him and which he liked to secrete in various parts of his cabin, working his way around the room methodically as the voyage continued, making sure that the draining of the last bottle would coincide with their arrival on the other side of the Atlantic. He knew better than to binge, as it would only lead to days of sobriety.

'The captain insisted,' Carter repeated in a tone which suggested that he was not leaving without submitting himself to the clippers. 'Sorry,' he added.

'All right, all right,' Dupuis sighed, directing him towards the chair in front of the mirror. 'Take a seat then if it means that much to you.'

Carter sat down and looked at his face in the mirror while the barber wrapped a towel round his neck and rifled through a cigar box filled with scissors and combs for a particular one. 'I think the old man's already taken a dislike to me,' he said to fill the empty air. 'So I thought it best to do exactly as he says. Otherwise I wouldn't insist on doing this right now.'

'It's fine,' said Dupuis, who merely wanted to cut his hair as requested and then get him out of there. 'I don't know you though, do I? Are you new?'

'Billy Carter. I'm acting first officer.'

'First officer?' He stopped in surprise and looked at Carter's reflection in the mirror. 'What happened to Mr Sorenson?'

'Sick. Appendix. Hospital,' he said in quick, staccato tones. Dupuis made a tut-tutting sound and reached forward, grasping a clump of the younger man's curls between his thick, cigarette-stained fingers.

'The captain won't like that,' he said.

'He seemed . . . irritated by it,' Carter admitted.

'Well, they're thick as thieves, those two,' said Dupuis. 'Always together.' He clipped away quickly without appearing to be watching what he was doing as curls fell to the floor.

'Just a trim,' said Carter nervously, realizing that he

45

had not yet been asked what style he wanted, but his hair was already being snipped away.

'A trim, yes,' the barber said. 'A *Kendall* trim. I think I know what the old man likes.'

Carter tried to relax in the chair and allow the barber to get on with his work. He thought of his wife back home and began calculating the dates in his head for the thousandth time that day. All going well, they would reach Quebec by about the last day of July, 1st August at the latest. The *Montrose* herself was not scheduled to make the return trip for another week after that, but the Canadian Pacific fleet company had promised him that morning that he could return to Europe on board one of their sister ships, scheduled to leave Quebec on the 3rd of August, meaning there was a good chance he would be home again within a month, by the middle of August. The baby was due a few weeks after that, so there was no chance he would miss the birth. Had that seemed even remotely likely, he would have refused this commission, regardless of the consequences.

'What's he like then?' he asked after a few silent minutes had passed, frowning as great clumps of his brown curly hair fell to the floor around his feet, revealing more of his boyish face than he was accustomed to seeing. 'The captain, I mean. You've sailed with him before, right?'

'I don't know him very well,' replied Dupuis, who had learned a long time ago to listen to any gossip which the sailors brought to him but, like a priest confessor, to reveal nothing that could come back to haunt him. 'I know he runs a tight ship, believes in order and discipline, and is a martyr to punctuality. They say he doesn't believe in God but keeps a copy of William Bligh's memoirs in his cabin and reads it every night as his Bible. When he sits in this chair, he barely says five words to me.'

'Captain Bligh?' said Carter, raising an eyebrow in surprise. 'Crikey, that's all I need. Thank God this is the twentieth century, that's all I can say. I'm not in favour of the rum and keel-hauling school of sailing myself. Do the job and get paid for it, that's my motto. Nothing more, nothing less. Captain Bligh!' he repeated in a quiet voice. 'Well, I never did.'

'There,' said the barber, finishing off and stepping back to admire his handiwork. 'How's that? Quick and easy.'

Carter nodded and stood up, slipping a few coins into the man's hand as he stepped outside again, stroking the back of his head curiously now, intrigued to feel the slightly bumpy scalp which had been revealed. A breeze blowing through the deck felt chilly against the back of his head and he muttered, 'God save us!' under his breath impatiently. Looking around, he realized that he would have to make a serious effort over the next twenty-four hours to understand the structure of this ship; the last thing he needed was to get lost while walking around. She was designed in a similar way to the *Zealous* and the *Ontario*, the sister ships on which he had served, but she was a little more modern than either of them, and many of the architectural oddities employed in their construction had been ironed out by the time the *Montrose* came to be built. Technologically, she was more advanced as well, having been the first ship in the fleet to install a Marconi telegraph machine, which enabled them to communicate with, and receive messages from, land.

Usually he could instinctively tell the way to the deck with his eyes shut, simply by the swaying of the boat and the smell of the sea; he had honed his senses over the years to such a sharpened point that his brain acted as his own navigator. Something about this ship, however, gave him pause for thought. The gleaming woodwork contrasted with the darkened hallways, and the creaking of the vessel seemed to numb his wits to the point where he found himself distrustful of his own abilities. Finally, stepping through the first-class deck, he could see the stairwell in the distance and the shaft of light pouring down which would lead him back to the main deck. Coming towards him was a man in his late forties with what appeared to be a teenage boy following directly behind. Immediately he remembered that he was not wearing his cap, or keeping it tucked discreetly under his arm as Kendall had instructed, and he bit his lip. He decided to return to his own cabin and retrieve it without delay.

'Afternoon, gents,' he said, pausing in the hallway to greet the two passengers, the older of whom looked a little irritated at being addressed. 'Ready for the trip, then?'

'Yes, thank you,' Mr Robinson replied, seeing the door of Cabin A4 only a few feet away, a holy grail which it seemed almost impossible to attain without conversing with half the Christian world first.

'Billy Carter, first officer of the *Montrose*,' he said with a nod of his head. 'Any problems or queries on board, feel free to ask me or any of my men. Looks like a nice day's sailing,' he added in a pleasant tone. 'Water's quite steady, isn't it?'

'I'm just going for a lie down,' said Mr Robinson, pressing past him. 'You'll forgive me if—'

'No problem, sir,' said Carter, stepping out of his way. 'Feeling it a bit, are you? Not to worry. You'll soon find your sea-legs. Everyone does. How about you, young man? Been to sea before, have you?'

'Only once,' said Edmund. 'A shorter voyage. Never for as long a trip as this.'

'By the time I was your age I'd already spent two or three years at sea. Couldn't get enough of it myself. But I was sick as a dog at the start too, so don't mind if you are. It'll pass.'

'I think I'll be fine,' said Edmund, feeling somewhat patronized.

'Right you are.'

Mr Robinson turned the key in the lock of his cabin and stepped inside, closing his eyes briefly, relieved at the peace and quiet which seemed to lie within. He turned around, prepared to call Edmund inside in a sharp tone if necessary, but the young sailor was passing out of sight now and his companion was stepping into the cabin.

'Finally . . .' said Mr Robinson in an exhausted voice. 'Do you suppose everyone on board is determined to speak to us? Those people on deck. That sailor.'

'He's the first officer,' said Edmund in a distant voice, looking back towards the corridor as he shut the door behind him. 'We should feel honoured.'

Mr Robinson snorted. 'Nonsense,' he said irritably. He took his hat off and hung it on a hook on the wall. Staring through the small porthole at the sea, he felt his headache growing stronger. He massaged his temples lightly and closed his eyes, feeling tense inside and nervous of discovery. To his relief, however, Edmund stepped up behind him and wrapped his arms around his chest from behind, pressing their bodies together. Mr Robinson turned around gratefully.

'Is this too difficult for you?' he asked, pulling apart slightly and looking down at the boy's elaborate outfit which they had purchased in Antwerp the day before. 'Do you think I've made a farce of you?'

'On the contrary,' said Edmund, reaching down and opening his tunic slightly, loosening the tight binding beneath. 'I've quite enjoyed it, really. It's rather daring, pretending to be something one is not.'

'Not for me, it isn't. Do you think we got away with it?'

'You have to relax,' said Edmund, unbuttoning Mr Robinson's jacket and dropping it on the floor.

'Everything is going to be fine. I'm sure of it.' He leaned forward and their lips met, tenderly at first, then with more force, their bodies pressing tightly against each other as they slipped awkwardly down on to the lower bunk.

'My only one,' said Mr Robinson, between kisses, his breath and consciousness almost taken away by the force of his passion. 'My only one.'

2

Youth

When Mr Josiah Crippen and his wife Dolores arrived
at the Holy Cross Church in Ann Arbor, Michigan, to
witness the wedding of their son, Samuel, to his second
cousin, Jezebel Quirk, they were in two, very different,
frames of mind. Josiah smiled all the way through the
ceremony because he was completely drunk, while
Dolores pursed her lips together so hard they became
numb, for in her mind the idea of her precious boy
becoming devoted to any woman other than herself
was an outrage. She had brought him up to revere and
idolize her and (although she was quite unaware of it)
she had only succeeded in making him despise her for
her coldness. However, in his new wife he had found a
loving and beautiful girl, and within a year Jezebel had
given birth to a son, whom they named Hawley Harvey
Crippen.

The year between their wedding and their parent-
hood was the only happy year of the Crippens'
life together for, once she was with child, Jezebel's
character changed entirely, as she set aside her earlier,
fun-loving ways and adopted a more puritan lifestyle.
Where she had once enjoyed accompanying Samuel to

a dance, she now considered such evenings improper and encouraging of licentiousness. Where she had once been known to invite their neighbours, the Tennetts, around for an evening of cards, she now thought such entertainments immoral and broke off her relationship with the otherwise harmless couple. Having never previously shown any sign of moral fervour in her life, Jezebel Crippen found that pregnancy delivered her not only of a new child but also of a new best friend: Jesus. And He didn't like her having any fun.

Hawley was, from the start, a quiet child. He had no brothers or sisters, owing to the fact that his mother's labour was so arduous and lengthy that she became a traitor to her own name after the birth and refused thereafter to allow her husband even to sleep in the same bed as her, let alone engage in acts of love.

'You've defiled me often enough, Samuel Crippen,' she said during those early months when he believed that deft persuasion on his part would enable him to make her change her mind, just as his father before him believed he had done when breaking down the defences of Dolores Hartford. 'I will never allow a man to touch me in that filthy way again.'

'But my dear,' he protested. 'Our marriage vows!'

'I have only one true husband now, Samuel. And His name is Jesus. I cannot betray Him.'

Samuel was eventually forced to realize that she was not going to relent and that, thanks to her Messiah, for him a life of celibacy beckoned. He would have railed against the cruelty of her decision but was fortunate enough to learn of the existence of a brothel, some ten miles outside Ann Arbor, where he could pursue his romantic interests with less emotional involvement, a prospect which suited him just fine.

As a boy, Hawley was encouraged by his mother to enjoy his solitude; they would spend long hours sitting on their porch, staring at the sky together while she directed his thoughts in the direction of the Lord. She believed that where there was just the two of them there was less occasion for sin. Her one purpose in life became ensuring that he arrived successfully into the kingdom of heaven, even if she had to put him there herself ahead of schedule.

'God's glorious sky,' she would say, smiling the smile of the mentally disturbed as her eyes fixed on each rolling group of clouds and the quick bursts of sunlight blinking through from behind. 'Give thanks, Hawley, to the good Lord for such a wonderful day as this.'

'Thank you, Lord,' he replied dutifully, blinking through the brightness.

'God's glorious work,' she would state while she cheerfully swept the house clean of dust and cobwebs or cleared the grime from the windows with a greasy rag. 'Give thanks, Hawley, to the good Lord for creating dirt all around us, that we may have the honour of cleaning up in His name.'

'Thank you, Lord,' he replied suspiciously, coughing at the dust in the air.

Dinnertimes were a quiet affair in the Crippen household. Samuel would return from his job at the grocery store by six o'clock, when his wife would lay out a spartan meal for the three of them. Typically, this consisted of a dry cooked vegetable and perhaps a little chicken or pork, undercooked slightly, the resulting diarrhoea or digestive problems being offered up for the poor souls in purgatory.

'God's glorious bounty,' Jezebel would say, smiling at her menfolk beatifically and extending her palms, as if she was the reincarnation of Jesus at the Last Supper. 'Give thanks, Hawley, to the good Lord for blessing us with such a sumptuous feast.'

'Thank you, Lord,' he replied, his stomach churning, his legs weakening as his bowels began to give way to God's glorious digestive problems.

As Jezebel entered her thirties and began to see God's glory in every blessed moment of the day, Samuel began to spend less and less time at home, preferring either to work late at the grocery store or to spend the evening at a local saloon, where he would drown his frustrations in alcohol. While this behaviour was frowned upon by his wife, he maintained enough distance to ignore her complaints. They mainly came when he was drunk anyway, so they hardly mattered. On one particular occasion he returned home towards midnight, unsteady on his feet, his cheeks puffy, his nose red and leading his way like the Christmas reindeer. He entered the house, singing a bawdy song which related to the adventures of a well-endowed sailor and his visit to a certain house of ill-repute in the city of Venice.

'You are *not* the man I married,' Jezebel cried in disgust, fetching a kitchen pail as her husband's bloodshot eyes and unsteady expression made it clear that he might soon be emptying the contents of his stomach on to the living-room floor. 'Coming home at this time of night in such a condition. And in front of our Hawley. What have you been drinking anyway? Whiskey? Beer? Tell me, Samuel.'

'God's glorious alcohol,' he replied in a sing-song voice, before belching loudly, adopting an amazed expression and falling unconscious to the floor.

'Thank you, Lord,' Hawley intoned piously, as he had been taught.

It was Jezebel's idea that her son be taken out of the village school and instead be educated at home by herself. Hawley didn't mind; at school he was used to being bullied because of his dark, formal clothing, which made him look like Oliver Twist when he was acting as a funeral walker for the Sowerberrys, and because of his delicate features, which forced some of the boys to suggest that he was not one of them at

54

all, but a lousy girl. Investigations proved otherwise, leaving the child feeling even more humiliated and despised than before.

'We will begin with Bible studies,' Jezebel told him on their first morning of home study. 'And then, before our second period of Bible studies, you will start to learn to read properly, using the Book of Psalms as your text. After a period of reflection on the Mysteries of the Cross, we will end classes for the day with some soul-enhancing Bible studies.' By the age of nine, Hawley was able to recite all one hundred and fifty Psalms in order, and he knew the exact line of ancestry from Adam to Jesus Christ. No one begat anyone without Hawley being in on the action. Jezebel made a party trick of it for Christmas, when the Crippens and the Quirks would gather together in her front room for a sumptuous feast of barley water and dry cake.

'Who begat Enos, Hawley?' she would ask, plucking a name from her memory as the boy screwed up his face and worked his way through Genesis in his mind.

'Seth,' he said.

'Correct! And who begat Methuselah?'

Hawley thought again. 'Enoch,' he pronounced.

'He most certainly did, the filthy beast. And Nimrod?' she continued, pushing the game to breaking point. 'Who begat Nimrod?'

'Cush,' said Hawley triumphantly.

'Cush it was! And Nimrod became a mighty hunter before the Lord. And the beginning of his kingdom was Babel, and Erech, and Accad, and Calneh, in the land of Shinar,' she continued gleefully, clapping her hands together in orgasmic delight, the crazed sparkle of religious fervour skipping like electricity from her sunken eyes.

For a woman who couldn't bear to be touched by her husband's hands, Samuel could not help but feel that she seemed a little obsessed with the process of

55

begetting. He wished for his son to lead a more active life outside the home, and he was sure that the boy was missing out on some of the joys of childhood.

'Missing out?' Jezebel asked, laughing at her husband's imbecility. 'You think this boy is missing out on something? How ridiculous. Watch this, you stupid man. Hawley – "For I was envious at the foolish, when I saw the prosperity of the wicked"?'

'"For there are no bands in their death,"' Hawley replied immediately from his position in the living-room window where he was sitting and staring at the sky in silent contemplation. He moved his eyes slowly from left to right as he spoke, as if reading the words directly from the page. '"But their strength is firm,"' he added, almost as an afterthought.

'Psalm number?'

'Seventy-three, Mother.'

'Verses?'

'Two and three.'

Jezebel looked at her husband triumphantly, her yellowing teeth pushing through her lips as she tried to control her rising emotions. 'Samuel Crippen,' she announced, 'your son's a prodigy.'

The early teenage years brought yet more strife for the boy Hawley. A sudden inflammation of acne around the time of his thirteenth birthday coincided with an almost pathological amount of bed-wetting, an act which caused great consternation in the Crippen household. Waking every morning at 5 a.m., his bed sheets soaked as a result of his exotic dreams, he would lie awake in dread of daybreak and the moment when his mother would enter the room, turn up her nose at the foul stench in the air and brand him a wicked boy and worse than a baby, beating him soundly about the head. When she overheard Samuel informing his son of a convenient way to cut down on these nightly emissions, she collapsed on the wooden floor of the kitchen in a swoon, bruising the back of her head badly, and had to be revived with smelling salts.

And yet, as time went by, Hawley did in fact manage to find in his tumultuous adolescence the opportunity to develop his own interests. His education began to extend beyond the Book of Revelations as he took it upon himself to read literature, poetry and works of non-fiction in the secrecy of the small library in Ann Arbor. As a fifteen-year-old he discovered a book entitled *The Human Body & Its Many Strange & Unusual Functions*, by Dr A. K. Larousse; and this became his new Bible as he digested every word pertaining to the study of the bodily organs and the respiratory functions. The Larousse work led him to many others on the same subject, and his later teenage years became fuelled by his study of science and biology, his theories about the creation of the universe, the workings of human and animal bodies, and the very nature of life. Most of these books he kept secret from his mother, who believed the study of science to be sinful, since it was attempting to understand the mind of God.

'If God wanted us to live for ever,' she pointed out, 'he never would have visited the seven plagues upon us. Now there was a God who knew how to deal with evil. He needs to get back a little of that old *chutzpah*, if you ask me.'

Without Jezebel's knowledge, Hawley began to purchase and store under his mattress copies of *Scientific American*, a brand new and radical publication from the state of New York, pulling them out only late at night when his parents were asleep in their separate rooms and he could light his candle and flick through their contents, furtively licking his lips with every new morsel of information which came his way. Each page seemed to offer a new theory or the possibility of a scientific revolution. Every contributor was working on new medicines, intricate equations or new definitions of words such as 'life', 'man' and 'existence'. Hawley could only hold his breath in excitement each month in anticipation of what would come next.

By his seventeenth birthday, however, the stack of *Scientific American* magazines beneath Hawley's mattress began to grow more noticeable, despite the fact that they were spread out evenly from pillow to base, forming an extra layer of inquisitive softness. Returning home from the library one afternoon in June, he sat on his bed to remove his boots and was surprised to feel a little more give under him than usual. Lifting the bed slightly to see what changes had taken place, he was horrified to discover that his collection of magazines had been stolen. His face grew pale and then scarlet with embarrassment; he felt his stomach contract inside him and was forced to sit down again, his heart pounding within his chest as he tried to think up an explanation. He waited in despair for his mother to come through the door in anger but there was no sign of her as yet, and it was only when he heard his father return home in the evening that he was summoned downstairs, where the pile of magazines he had invested in over the past two and a half years had been placed one on top of another on the kitchen table. He stared at the collection as if he had never laid eyes on any of them before and he swallowed nervously; although ready to deny them, they were still precious to him and he wanted them back unharmed. His mother stood by the fireplace, her arms folded, her face betraying her fury, while Samuel stood somewhere between them, unsure what position he was supposed to be taking.

'All this time I thought I knew you,' Jezebel said. 'I thought you were a decent boy. I thought I had brought you up right.'

'You do! I am! You did!' he protested, answering each charge deliberately, but before he could say anything further her shouts were drowning his voice out.

'A decent boy doesn't keep filth like this under his mattress. It's disgusting! Have you seen these magazines?' she asked her husband, who shook his head sheepishly before picking one up and flicking through it carefully, his excited face becoming more and more disappointed as each page was turned and he came closer to the end.

'They're interesting to me,' Hawley pleaded. 'It's science. It's educational.'

'It's *filth*,' she insisted. 'Why on earth would anyone waste their money on diseased rubbish like this?'

'I read them for the articles,' he said defensively, his voice rising ever so slightly. 'I'm interested in the human body—'

'Hawley! Not in this house!'

'In how the world was created. In what we are.'

Jezebel shook her head furiously and plucked the magazine from her husband's hands, throwing it into the fire then pushing it further into the coals with an iron poker.

'Mother, no!' Hawley cried as she reached for the next magazine, and the next one, and the one after that.

'It's for your own good,' she said, watching as his years of study charred and flickered in the fireplace. 'Better that these pages should be burning here right now than you should spend an eternity roasting in Hades' flames. I couldn't live with myself if I knew you were spending eternity in Hell.'

'This is ridiculous,' shouted Hawley in disgust, the first time he had ever raised his voice in this house. Both his parents looked at him in amazement as his face grew red and eyes became wild with anger. 'Just ridiculous!' he repeated. 'And these magazines fascinate me. Don't you understand, I want to be a man of science.'

'Science?' Jezebel shouted in amazement. 'This science is the devil's work, nothing more. Is that what I educated you for?'

'I don't care, that's what I want,' he cried, disgusted by her ignorance. And watching as the magazines disappeared in flames up the chimney, he found the words to express what it was he was put on earth to do. 'I intend to study medicine,' he told his parents. 'I will be a great scientist.' He leaned in towards his mother so that she had to hold herself steady to prevent herself from taking a step back in fear. 'Maybe that's God's plan for me,' he added quietly.

Jezebel threw a hand to her mouth, as if he had just uttered the words which would bring damnation around all their ears.

'God's glorious plan, Hawley,' said Samuel, confused, perhaps a little drunk.

With Hawley's twenty-first birthday came a series of changes. Much to his mother's disgust and his father's surprise, he started to assert himself, refusing to allow Jezebel to dictate the terms of his existence any longer. Risking her censure, but refusing to ask her permission, he continued to purchase copies of *Scientific American*, and now he offered them pride of place on the top of his dresser, where any casual visitor could take note of his perversion. To these he added quarterly issues of the *American Journal of Human Medicine* as well as *The Medical Practitioner's Bi-Monthly Review*, scholarly works whose in-depth analysis of the state of the sciences in the United States would have been beyond the reach of most laymen, but whose complex writings and diagrams fascinated the young Crippen and convinced him that here was the life he craved. Their gratuitous display, removed from under the mattress, justified them and made Jezebel think twice before consigning this latest bunch to the fireplace.

He applied to the University of Michigan to study medicine, but it was only when he received their prospectus that he realized that a desire on one's part to study was secondary in the mind of such an establishment to the ability of a potential student to pay for it. In order to become a doctor, he would have to undertake four years of courses at a rate of over $500 per year. Since leaving school he had worked as a grocery clerk at his father's store, but he still earned no more than $33 week, a third of which he was forced to return to his mother in order to pay for his food and board. There was no possibility whatsoever that he could afford the tuition fees.

'You have to understand,' he said to his parents one evening when he explained his dilemma to them, 'that being a doctor is the most important thing in the world to me. I feel it's my destiny, my vocation in life.'

'Now, Hawley, don't use words like that in such a context,' Jezebel said, delighted that he was coming begging to her again. Although her attitude towards his interests had relaxed a little over the previous couple of years, she could not help but still protest at what she considered her son's anti-Christian sentiments. 'A vocation only exists when the good Lord calls you to His service.'

'Perhaps that's what He's doing,' he replied. 'Calling me to serve the sick, to make them better. Perhaps He wants me to be a doctor. It's a noble profession, after all.'

'The Lord sees the art of medicine as a heathen one, you know that. Why else would He visit sickness upon the little children if there were others who could simply take that sickness away? It is best to leave well alone. His will be done.'

Hawley sighed. He had recently grown a moustache and had taken to stroking it gently in times of stress. He tried not to lose his temper, since that would only lessen his chances of success. 'Mother, please,' he said quietly. 'Can't you see how important this is to me?'

'How much do you need?' Samuel asked, not daring

to look at his wife although he could feel her venomous stare darting through his body like a thousand spears and he knew he would pay for it later.

'The course costs five hundred dollars per year—'

'Five hundred dollars?' Jezebel cried in surprise. 'It's out of the question.'

'It's expensive, but it's worth it,' Hawley protested. 'I can manage perhaps one hundred dollars a year if I get a night job. It would be difficult to study during the day and work at night, certainly, but these are the sacrifices I would make.' He added this last part to appeal to his mother's sense of martyrdom.

'So you need four hundred dollars a year over four years,' said Samuel.

'Yes.'

'Sixteen hundred dollars.'

'Effectively.'

'It's absolutely impossible,' Jezebel stated firmly.

'I suppose we could re-mortgage the store,' his father said, thinking about it and stroking his face now with a gesture that imitated his son's. 'The bank *might* allow it, but there's no guarantee that they'll—'

'We are *not* re-mortgaging the store,' Jezebel said. 'Samuel, it's taken us all these years to finally own it outright and I am not going back into debt just so that Hawley can carve out a place in the devil's quarters for himself.'

'Oh, Mother!' he cried in frustration. 'If you could just look beyond your own self for a moment.'

'I'm sorry, Hawley,' she said. 'I know it's a disappointment to you, but you know how I feel and you cannot ask me to change. I simply will not see a son of mine move into a profession like that. If you feel you have a vocation to help people, then why not become a teacher? The state is crying out for young teachers and you would be perfectly suited to such a life. Or a cleric?'

'But I don't *want* to teach,' he shouted. 'And I *certainly* don't want to preach. I want to be a doctor! I want to practise medicine! Why do you find that so hard to understand?'

Jezebel closed her eyes and rocked back and forth in her chair, humming 'Amazing Grace' quietly to herself. This was her usual method of suggesting that the conversation had come to an end.

Hawley looked across at his father, his last line of defence, but Samuel merely shrugged and glanced towards his wife as if to imply that hers was the final decision and there was nothing more he could do about it. Frustrated beyond reason, Hawley had little choice now but to contact the university and tell them that, despite his desire to become a student there, he could not afford the tuition fees. He hoped briefly that a scholarship might be offered to him; but instead the admissions board accepted his decision immediately and thanked him for his interest in a letter which showed no hint of sympathy for his situation.

The formal practice of medicine therefore became an aspiration which Hawley was forced to put out of his mind for ever. However there were other courses, less expensive ones, through which he could indulge his fascination with science, and he began to investigate these, numbing his disappointment by convincing himself that this was the next best thing. In an issue of *The Medical Practitioner's Bi-Monthly Review*, he read that the Medical College of Philadelphia offered a correspondence course in general health studies which, over the course of a twelve-month period, could lead to a diploma. It cost $60, an expense which would eat into his income over the year, but he decided it was worth it, applied and was quickly accepted as a student.

In order to fund the diploma, he went in search of a night job and was offered a position in the McKinley-Ross Abattoir where, from 9 p.m. until 6 a.m., three nights a week, he received the carcasses of sheep or cattle, and skinned them, gutted them, cleaned out their entrails and sliced them up.

Although Jezebel and Samuel were horrified, it seemed a natural job for Hawley to do while beginning his studies. He had spent enough long nights tracing his finger around the various parts of the human body depicted in his *Gray's Anatomy*, learning their names and functions, understanding how easily each could be broken or worn down. He knew where the weak points of ligaments and tendons lay and, although he had never sliced a knife through a cadaver as yet, he had dreamed about it and had decided already where each incision would be most appropriate for the cleanest possible dissection. Although it wasn't ideal, he rather relished the idea of being presented with a recently dead animal and having full responsibility for separating its bones from its muscles, its skin from its organs, collecting the blood separately and delivering the corpse into chops for the dinner table. While some might have found the process disgusting, Hawley Harvey Crippen found himself licking his lips at the thought of what lay ahead.

On his first evening at McKinley-Ross, he was partnered by a sixty-two-year-old veteran of the abattoir named Stanley Price who, he was informed, would train him at the craft. A skinny devil with a slightly humped back and grizzly white hair, the first thing Hawley noticed about his teacher was the fact that his hands were lined in red from thirty-seven years of chopping up dead animals, the pores so deeply dyed that the innards of millions of animals could be identified all over his exposed skin. 'All the washing in the world won't take that away,' Price told him proudly. 'I've got more blood on my hands than any of them murderers in Chokey. And I'm better with a knife. You ever cut up a dead animal before?'

'Never,' Hawley admitted, laughing as if the idea was preposterous. As if he had spent the long, lazy summer days of his Michigan youth randomly slicing dogs and cats open on his front porch.

'Got the stomach for it?'

'I believe so. I'm studying to be a doctor with the Medical College of Philadelphia.' This was only a white lie; the recipients of diplomas in general health studies from the MCP were not entitled to call themselves doctors, although they did clearly have some medical training. Hawley thought there would be little to lose by boosting his credentials a little and that it might even earn him some respect.

'And if you're studying in Philly, what the hell are you doing still in Michigan?'

'It's a correspondence course,' he explained.

'A correspondence course to be a doctor?' the older man asked sceptically.

Hawley nodded and stood firm.

They stared at each other for what seemed like several minutes before Price breathed in heavily through his nose and, shaking his head, looked away. 'Don't come to my rescue if you see me falling over, sick. A doctor by correspondence course,' he muttered under his breath. 'What's the world coming to?'

'How many animals do we cut up a night?' Hawley asked, wanting to change the subject and return to the business at hand. He tried to phrase his question in as serious a tone as possible, not wishing to sound blood-thirsty.

'Me, I can go through five cows on a good night and maybe two or three sheep for variety. All the way, from just dead to sliced up for mincemeat. You?' He looked the boy up and down as if he had never seen a less likely candidate before. 'Your first few months, you'll be lucky to manage one a night without assistance. It's not a question of numbers, Crippen. Remember that. You have to have the same level of skill for each animal, and if that means you only do one-fifth the work of someone else, well, so be it. But don't rush a job just to move on to the next one. You'll ruin the meat.'

'Right,' said Hawley, bouncing from foot to foot and feeling the blood rise within him in his excitement. 'So when do we get started, then?'

'Anxious, ain't you?' said Price. 'Well, don't worry, we'll be starting soon enough. Soon as that bell over there sounds.' He nodded towards the clock on the wall which was edging towards nine o'clock. The day shift of abattoir workers finished at 7 p.m., when the cleaners came in and scrubbed the floors, disinfecting the workbenches in time for the night shift to begin. McKinley-Ross never shut. There were always slaughtered animals to be cut up.

Finally the bell sounded and the doors opened; the forty night-shift workers entered a long corridor along which hung rows of pristine white jackets, such as scientists might wear in a laboratory.

'It's one size fits all around here,' Price said. 'So just take the first one that comes to hand and let's get to work. Don't know why they bother with them myself. They're all covered in blood by the time we're finished.'

Hawley took a jacket and put it on, enjoying the fact that its appearance made him feel like a real doctor. He grinned at Stanley Price, who stared back at him suspiciously, shaking his head as if he was watching an idiot child being led to his execution, completely unaware that what lay ahead would not be pleasant.

Price walked towards a corner of the massive auditorium within and looked around, pointing out the various features to his new protégé. 'Over here's all our tools,' he said. 'Saws, carvers, slicers, all sharpened twice a day. Don't bother testing the blades with your fingers unless you want to lose one of them. A hose over here where we can wash blood away into the drain. Gets collected down below.' He nodded towards the corner of the floor where a sudden steep slope indicated where it would disappear. 'When we get started, we press this button.' He reached out and pressed a green button by a conveyor belt, and it immediately chugged into action. All around the massive room, Hawley could hear similar buttons being pressed and in a moment a series of dead animals entered the room on an overhead conveyor belt, hooked through the neck by massive steel claws. 'You struck gold,' Price said in a dry voice. 'We got a cow.'

Sure enough, the body of a cow turned slowly around on the conveyor until it was situated directly over the drain, at which point Price pressed a red button and the animal clunked to a stop, rocking back and forth on its hook precariously. Hawley reached forward and touched the skin; it was cold and the hairs were slightly extended forward along the neck, much like the hairs on his own forearms which bristled attentively. The cow's eyes were open and stared back at him, massive dark pools of blackness in which, when he leaned forward, he could see his own reflection.

'All we need's the torso,' said Price, 'so first things first. Press that green button again till the cow's over the bench.'

Hawley did as he was asked, and then Price reached to one side and pulled a yellow lever downwards, a movement which took some force. Hawley jumped back in shock as the cow appeared to come to life before his eyes. In fact, the lever had extended the hook backwards so that the animal's head was slowly turned around. When it was released, the carcass fell the remaining distance directly on to the workbench with a massive thud. Years of experience had ensured that, when the older man pressed any button or pulled any lever in this room, he knew exactly when to stop it and, sure enough, the cow had landed directly on its side, in a perfect position for the amputations to follow.

'We need to cut off the head,' said Price in a calm

voice. 'Then the tail and each of the legs. Then we'll drain the body of blood, skin it, take out the organs, hose down the cadaver that remains and chop it up for the dinner table. How's that sound to you, sonny?'

This was not the first time that Price had trained a new recruit in the art of reducing a recently killed animal to its basic components and he took a perverted pleasure from the way each one of them, even the most hardy, waited until this very moment, after that very speech, to step backwards awkwardly and reach a hand to their mouth before running, charging out of the room into the cold air beyond, where they would throw up whatever dinner they had been foolish enough to swallow earlier. But now, for the first time in years, he looked across at his trainee and saw, not the disgusted face of a novice, squeamish and terrified, but instead a serious-looking young man whose cheeks, if anything, had *gained* some colour. And was he seeing things, or was that the beginnings of a smile stretching across the youngster's face?

'My oh my,' he said, surprised at what he saw, even a little disturbed. 'You are a cold one, ain't you?'

3

Mrs Louise Smythson's First
Visit to Scotland Yard

London: Thursday, 31 March 1910

Not even her closest friends could have suggested that
Mrs Louise Smythson was a friend to the working classes.
A product of a poverty-stricken upbringing herself, she
had dragged herself out of the gutter and felt nothing
but contempt for those still wallowing there. When she
had met her future husband Nicholas, she had been
working as a barmaid at the Horse and Three Bells
public house in Bethnal Green. He had been smitten
by her beauty immediately, while she had been won
over by his silver cigarette case, the oak carved cane he
carried and his gentleman's manners. When she served
him at the bar and he opened his wallet to reveal a
brace of £20 notes, it only added to the attraction. After
serving him a frothy beer followed by a small brandy,
she had whispered to her friend Nellie Pippin that she
would marry the young man seated at the corner table
poring over *The Times* or die in the attempt. Six months
later, still alive, she married him in a small ceremony
in a church off Russell Square, in Bloomsbury, attended
only by his closest family members, many of whom were

heard to say that the pretty girl with the affected vowels had landed on her feet and no mistake. Still, married they were, and from that moment Louise decided that being the wife of a gentleman automatically made her a lady. In this she was incorrect. She refused to speak to any of her family any more – 'Common as muck, most of 'em, ain't got no manners, can't even speak proper, none of 'em, not even ol' Uncle 'Enry and 'im as 'ad three years of schoolin' when 'e were a lad' – and didn't even acknowledge her old friends. She developed an eye for fashion by sitting in her upstairs bay windows, watching the well-dressed ladies walk by, writing down what they were wearing in a notebook and presenting its contents to her tailor, demanding that he reproduce them exactly. She bought the latest and most stylish shoes and hats and she insisted on eating out almost every night of the week in popular society restaurants, where she ate little because she was conscious of her figure and dined mainly off the luxurious atmosphere. Nicholas, a man with few brains but a lot of money, continued to dote on her, always giving in to even her most outlandish demands, and his own friends finally grew to accept that love can be not only blind but also lacking in taste.

Although she was quite fond of her brother-in-law – he had, after all, played an important part in convincing the Smythson family that Nicholas should be allowed to marry whomever he wanted, even if she was a cheap tart with no class or upbringing to speak of – Louise's dearest wish was that the Honourable Martin Smythson would die. It was well known that he suffered from all manner of ailments, including a dislocated vertebra, one non-functioning kidney, an arthritic knee and a heart flutter, and that he had been in and out of hospital all his life. His own father was also at death's door, which meant that Martin would soon inherit the title of Lord Smythson. Recently married himself, Louise prayed nightly that he would succumb to one of his illnesses before his wife found herself with child, otherwise the possibility of the title passing to Nicholas would fade. She was determined to become Lady Smythson, and if that meant leaving a few extra windows open when Martin came to visit, or undercooking his meat a little, well what of it? It was all in a good cause.

On the morning of Thursday, 31 March 1910, however, thoughts of the dress she would wear to any of her in-laws' funerals at some future date were at the back of her mind as she marched determinedly along Victoria Embankment towards the offices of New Scotland Yard to report a murder.

It was at breakfast that morning when she had come to her decision. She had been thinking about it all night, ever since the meeting of the Music Hall Ladies' Guild the previous evening at the home of her friend Mrs Margaret Nash. In fact she had hardly slept when she had returned home, and for once it had not been the snoring of her husband in the bed beside her that had kept her awake. Sitting at their breakfast table by the bay windows in the living room shortly before nine, the window above them open to let in a little fresh morning air, he had been surprised by her air of distraction, watching her, half amused, as she spread the jam on her toast before the butter and, realizing her mistake, sought to eat it quickly rather than draw comment.

'Are you all right, my dear?' Nicholas asked, taking his pince-nez off his nose and peering at her, as if his spectacles hindered his sight.

'Perfectly fine, Nicholas. Thank you for asking,' she replied formally.

'It's just you seem a little *distrait*,' he said. 'Didn't you sleep well?'

She sighed and decided to confide in him. 'I didn't, if you want to know the truth,' she said in a sad voice. 'I

71

had a conversation last night that's left me not knowing what to think.'

Nicholas frowned. His wife was not normally as mysterious as this. He rang the small bell on the table and when the maid came he asked her to clear away the breakfast things, informing her that they would take coffee by the fireplace. Sitting on the sofa, Louise thought the whole thing through then turned to her husband. 'I was at my meeting last night,' she began. 'You know, the Music Hall Ladies' Guild?'

'Of course, my dear.'

'And I was talking to Margaret Nash. We talked of many things, but eventually the conversation turned to Cora Crippen.'

'To whom?'

'Cora Crippen, Nicholas. You know Cora. You've met her several times. A lovely woman. A fine singer. She was married to Dr Hawley Crippen.'

'Oh yes, of course,' he said, remembering. 'Bit of a milksop, that Crippen man, if you ask me. Bit hen-pecked. Let his wife bully him something dreadful. Decent enough sort, other than that, I expect.'

'Nicholas, really! The poor woman has only been dead a short time. You can hardly speak ill of her at a time like this.'

'But hadn't you decided not to talk to her again?' he asked, recalling an unpleasant event at the Crippens' home a few months earlier. 'That's right, she insulted you and you determined to have her expelled from the Music Hall Ladies' Guild.'

'She was upset, Nicholas.'

'She was drunk.'

'Really, you shouldn't speak in that way about some-one who isn't alive to defend themselves. And I didn't plan on having her expelled. I merely thought she should reconsider her actions in polite society.'

'I apologize, my dear. That was insensitive of me.'

She shook her head, dismissing it. 'The thing is,' she continued, 'that Margaret mentioned seeing Dr Crippen a few weeks before at the theatre. Andrew was entertaining some business associate in London – apparently he's a bit of a drama buff – and they all went to see a performance of *A Midsummer Night's Dream* in the West End. And during the interval they were having a drink in the crush bar when Margaret saw Dr Crippen standing near by. Now, she hadn't seen him since we all heard about Cora going off to America and then dying there, so naturally she went over to say hello to him and offer her condolences.'

'Naturally,' said Nicholas.

'Of course she was surprised to see him there at all. The poor woman had only been dead a couple of weeks. It did seem a little heartless to come out of mourning so soon.'

Nicholas shrugged. 'We each of us deal with grief in different ways, my dear,' he suggested quietly.

'Of course, and it's neither here nor there, but still one can't help but feel a little ashamed of his behaviour. Anyway, when Margaret approached him, Dr Crippen was actually quite rude to her, speaking for only a few moments before walking away.'

'Well, perhaps he was upset. Perhaps he didn't want to talk about it.'

'But he had a young lady with him, Nicholas. A pretty young thing, apparently, but rather common. That young woman we met at the Crippens' house one evening, the one with the scar running from her nose to her lip. You remember her?'

'Vaguely,' said Nicholas, not recalling her at all.

'The first time we went there. Over a year ago now. When that nice young man who was lodging with them was so entertaining,' she added, remembering the young man, whose name was Alec Heath, fondly.

'I'm sure I was there, Louise,' he replied. 'But really, I

can't be expected to remember every social function I attend, can I?'

'Whether or not you remember the woman is immaterial,' she said irritably. 'The point is, she was wearing a blue sapphire necklace that Mrs Nash had seen Cora wear on several occasions in the past, along with a set of ear-rings that she knew to be her favourites. Don't you think that's astonishing?'

Nicholas scratched his chin and thought about it. He couldn't quite see her point.

'A lady doesn't go to America without her best jewellery,' Louise said finally, egging him on, listening for the sound of his brain clicking into gear. 'She just doesn't do it. And she *certainly* doesn't allow any jumped-up tart to wear her favourite things in her absence.'

'My dear, you're too excitable. Her absence is permanent. The poor lady has died.'

'She didn't know she was going to die when she went abroad, though, did she?'

He shrugged.

'I'm worried, Nicholas, that's all. I know it sounds ridiculous, but I have an idea that some mishap might have come to Cora Crippen and I'm determined to get to the bottom of it. Margaret feels the same way.'

'Oh really, Louise,' he said with a laugh, actually quite amused by this sudden spurt of curiosity in his wife. 'Now you're not going to go around to the poor man's house and bother him, are you?'

'I most certainly am not,' she replied. 'And have that hussy open the door to me? Maybe even refuse me entrance? Not on your life! I intend to do the only thing a respectable woman can do when faced with such a dilemma.'

'Which is?'

'I intend to go to Scotland Yard and report that Cora Crippen's death came about as the result of mischief.'

Nicholas's mouth fell open and he could not help but laugh. 'My dear, you're too much,' he said after a moment, shaking his head in amazement. 'Is that *really* what respectable women would do at such a time? Go to Scotland Yard? What an astonishing idea!' He was shaking now with laughter and love. His father could call Louise all the names he liked; she made her husband's life a sheer joy with her unpredictability. 'I believe you've been reading one too many detective novels again.'

'I have not,' she said, offended. 'Cora Crippen is simply a friend of mine and—'

'Oh come on. You haven't spoken to her in ages. Not since that dreadful night when she seemed to lose her reason with us.'

'We were members of the same guild,' she insisted, conveniently ignoring the events of that evening. 'And as such there is a sisterhood between us. No, I've made up my mind, Nicholas. I intend to visit Scotland Yard this morning and see to it that the police investigate this case further. I won't be dissuaded.' She spoke with such determination that Nicholas knew better than to argue with her.

'Very well, my dear,' he agreed. 'If you insist. But try not to make unwise accusations. After all, Dr Crippen is a member of our society, a little removed from us perhaps in station, but we must have many mutual friends. There's no point stirring up a hornet's nest of trouble if we can avoid it.'

'Don't worry, Nicholas,' she replied, standing up to leave the room and change into a dress appropriate for a police interview. 'I know what I'm doing. I believe I have an understanding of how society works. I am, after all, a lady.'

'Of course you are, my dear. Of course you are.'

*   *   *

Louise strode towards the desk. The young police-man seated behind it, sensing a storm on the horizon, looked up warily. Tall and thin, with jet-black hair combed dramatically away from his face, she found herself momentarily distracted by his cheekbones and lips as she approached him, for she had rarely seen such a striking youth as this. She had seen people before like this: men and women with such features that they were almost beyond gender. Only the clothing defined who was male and who was female. How easily any of us could be fooled, she thought.

'I'm Mrs Louise Smythson,' she proclaimed to the room as a whole and to the officer in particular, as if she was announcing her candidacy for the highest office. 'Good morning to you, constable.'

'Good morning,' he said hesitantly, staring at her, waiting for her to continue.

'Are you aware,' she asked after a moment, 'that in polite society when one introduces oneself and offers one's name, it is considered good manners to offer one's own name in return?'

He thought about this and blinked several times. It was a few seconds before he understood what she meant. 'Police Constable Milburn,' he said then in a shy voice, like a little boy who has just been scolded by his mother.

'Well, Police Constable *Milburn*,' she said, stressing the surname, 'I am here to make an official complaint. Well, perhaps not a complaint as such, more of a state-ment. Yes, I'd like to make a statement, please.'

PC Milburn reached for a file containing a list of names and their alleged offences. 'You've been told to come down here to make a statement, is that it?' he asked.

'Well, no. No one's actually asked me—'

'Regarding which case, ma'am?'

'There isn't any case at the moment,' she said irritably.

'I'm here to *make* the case. To express concern about a missing woman.'

'You want to report a missing woman?' he asked. This is like pulling teeth, he thought, before regretting the analogy; he had been forced to have a tooth extracted when he was fifteen years old, and the memory of it haunted him still. The dentist had been more of a sadist than a man of medicine; in his entire life he had never experienced such pain.

'In a manner of speaking. She was reported to be dead, but I don't believe it, owing to a little matter of a blue sapphire pendant necklace and a lovely set of ear-rings – the missing lady's favourites, I might add. I think she's come to mischief. As does my friend, Mrs Margaret Nash. Now just wait a moment, please,' she said, reaching into her bag and extracting a small pad of paper, which she leafed through quickly trying to find a particular entry. 'It's here somewhere,' she muttered, then pointed dramatically at it. 'Here it is,' she said. 'I'm told there are five chief inspectors at Scotland Yard who handle the most serious cases. Inspectors Arrow, Fox, Frost, Dew and Cane. Can this be right? Are those really their names or are they pseudonyms, invented to excite the public?'

PC Milburn looked at her as if she was mad. 'Of course they're their names,' he replied. 'Why wouldn't they be?'

'Well, Arrow and Cane – similar sorts of things. Frost and Dew. I need hardly tell you. And then Fox. Well, I'm not sure what the link is there,' she admitted, a puzzled expression crossing her face. 'It just seems slightly odd to me, that's all. They're not invented for the newspapers then?'

'Not at all.'

'Not made up to put criminals off the scent in any way? You can tell me, you know. I'm quite discreet.'

'I assure you that all five of those gentlemen are

inspectors,' he said determinedly. 'Now if there's anything further that you—'

'Not that it really matters,' she concluded with a laugh, interrupting him and dismissing the case of the monosyllabic inspectors without a further thought. 'I'd like to speak to one of them immediately. Could you fetch one, please?'

PC Milburn laughed and then, forced to disguise it upon seeing her frown, turned the chuckle into a cough.

'What's the matter, young man?' she asked. 'Am I amusing you in some way? I've come to report a crime. Surely this . . . Scotland Yard, as you call it, is interested in pursuing the matter? Or is this a vaudeville of some sort?'

'Miss Smythson—'

'Mrs Smythson,' she corrected him. 'Potentially Lady Smythson one day, if God is good, so have a care.'

'Mrs Smythson, the inspectors are very busy men. I'm afraid they can't just see any caller who comes in with a complaint. That's what our detectives are for. That's what I'm for.'

'Police Constable Milburn,' she said in a firm tone, as if she was dealing with a child of limited understanding, 'perhaps you are unaware of whom you are speaking to. My father-in-law is Lord Smythson. My brother-in-law is the Honourable Martin Smythson. We are a titled family. We are the quality. We are not common people, asking for the police to investigate the case of a pair of missing knickers, ripped off our washing line in the middle of the night by some cheap trollop next door who can't afford her own pair.' She seemed to get all that out without pausing for breath, her volume increasing steadily as the sentence progressed; the young constable's eyes opened wide in surprise at the change in her tone and vocabulary. 'We are respectable personages,' she added, quieter now. 'I am here to make a statement and I demand to see an inspector.'

PC Milburn nodded and did what he always did when he had a difficult customer: he played for time. 'If you could just take a seat,' he suggested, nodding towards a row of chairs by the wall, 'I'll see what I can do.'

'Very well,' she said, nodding briskly as if she had got her way already. 'But see that you're not long about it. I have a busy day ahead of me and no time to waste. I'll expect to see an inspector within ten minutes.'

'It may be a little longer than that,' said PC Milburn. 'I know for a fact that three of the inspectors are not in the building at the moment. And a fourth is questioning a witness. I'm not sure where Inspector Dew is, but—'

'Well, track him down, Police Constable Milburn!' she roared, slapping her hand on the desk in front of her. 'Track him down! Use that well-trained brain of yours to discover his whereabouts. Do a little detective work of your own. Get a magnifying glass. Question witnesses. Trace his last known movements. But bring him to me within ten minutes or I shall return to this desk and I shall want to know the reason why, and you, young man, will come off the worse for it. I can assure you of that.'

He nodded and swallowed, his Adam's apple rising nervously as she finished her sentence. 'Right you are,' he agreed, scurrying away. She watched him disappear into one of the back rooms, his uniform clinging tightly to his trim body. She licked her lips and smiled. What I wouldn't give for a piece of that, she thought to herself, her natural upbringing springing to the fore.

'What you in for, then, love?' a young woman sitting a few seats away from her asked. Louise, sitting erect and poised, rolled her eyes to the left but didn't move her head, ignoring her in the hope that she would simply stop talking. 'I said, what you in for?' she repeated. 'Didn't you 'ear me?'

'I heard you perfectly well, thank you,' said Louise, affecting her poshest possible voice, as if this alone might frighten the girl into silence. 'And I do beg your pardon, but I am not in a position to converse at the moment.'

'Oh lardy-dar!' said the woman, one Mary Dobson, in a sing-song voice. 'Get you.'

'Thank you,' said Louise, nodding slightly as if she had been complimented. No further words were exchanged for a few minutes and she thought the worst was over, but then, without asking permission, Mary Dobson stood up and moved to the seat next to Louise, sitting down heavily and folding her arms as she sat back in the chair.

She examined the other woman up and down, noting the fine stitching of her dress and the neatness of the lace gloves. 'They 'ave me come in every week, you see,' she said, as if they were continuing a conversation already begun. 'Got to tell 'em what I been up to, where I been workin' and that. They say they 'ave to keep an eye on me although I says to them I don't see why no more 'cos I don't do nothing that no one else don't do and I know what's mine and what ain't mine and I don't ever confuse the two. Not like the old days when—'

'I'm sorry, do you mind?' Louise said, pulling at her dress a little, for Mary Dobson had sat down on the edge of it. She tugged it out from under the young woman and stared at the corner of the garment distastefully. It would have to be steamed later. Perhaps discarded altogether.

'I don't mind at all,' said Mary. 'I bet they've got you from down behind the King's Road, am I right?'

'From behind the – ?'

'You don't fool me,' she said with an admiring laugh. 'I can spot a high-class whore when I sees one. That's why you makes the money, I expect, and good luck to you, that's what I says. 'Cos you know what a gentleman's after. Not like me. I just give 'em a little slap and tickle, 'ow's your father, pull 'em, kiss 'em, bang 'em, I don't care, and that'll be sixpence please, thank you very much.'

'I don't know *what* you're implying, miss,' said Louise in an outraged voice, although she did know perfectly well. 'But I can *assure* you that I—'

''Ere, what you reckon to them two over there, then?' she asked, moving on to another subject immediately and staring across at a middle-aged couple who were sitting in the corner. The woman had a black eye and the man had a miserable look on his face. 'That'll be what they call a domestic dispute, I expect,' said Mary.

'I make it a point not to interfere in other people's business,' said Louise. 'I find it a very good policy. Perhaps you could do the same.'

'Oh, is that right?' Mary asked, not willing to be condescended to. 'Well, go on then if you're so 'igh and mighty. What you really 'ere for then, eh?'

'I am *here*,' said Louise, happy to be able to set the record straight, 'because a dear friend of mine has gone missing and I want to report the matter.'

'And where's 'er 'usband then? Why don't he report the matter?' She uttered the last three words in a snooty tone, mimicking Louise's.

'It's precisely because he hasn't that I'm worried,' Louise explained. 'That's why I'm here, you see. To inform the police of her disappearance.'

'And there was me thinking that you made a point of not interfering in other people's business. Must have misheard you, did I?'

Louise looked at the woman with a snarl and leaned forward so that only she could hear her. 'Why don't you piss off to another seat, you smelly little whore,' she whispered. 'Piss off before I clock you one.'

Mary Dobson shot up in her chair and her mouth fell open in surprise while Louise sat back in her chair and gave her a kindly smile, as if she had said all that she had to say on the subject and could quite possibly drag her out by the hair if she attempted to speak again.

'Mrs Smythson?' She turned and saw a middle-aged man in a tweed suit addressing her. He had a kindly look in his eye and so she smiled, nodding. 'I'm Inspector Walter Dew,' he said. 'Sorry for keeping you. Won't you please come this way?'

He held up the wooden partition separating the lobby area from the rooms beyond, and allowed her to enter. She stepped through and followed him as he led the way. She paused only momentarily to turn and look at PC Milburn for a final time, on this occasion surprising even herself by sticking out her tongue at him and giving him a quick wink. He blushed scarlet and turned away, busying himself with the papers on his desk to prevent anyone seeing his embarrassed face.

Inspector Dew had a small office with a window overlooking the Embankment on the third floor of the Scotland Yard building. He opened the window immediately after they stepped inside, for there was a distinct scent of cigar smoke in the air that he hadn't noticed before leaving the room; and he invited Mrs Louise Smythson to sit down on a threadbare armchair opposite his desk. Looking at it with distaste, she finally lowered herself on it with a victimized sigh and smiled across at him. Although she had never met a chief inspector before, she was reassured by his age and his distinguished manner. Her eye was taken by a picture on his desk, and she looked at the pale young man in the etching with curiosity. 'Your son?' she asked.

'Oh my, no,' said Dew, shaking his head quickly. 'No, that's a picture of Police Constable Joseph Grantham. Have you heard of him?' Louise racked her brains for any reason why she might have, but failed. She shook her head. 'Well, no reason why you should have, I suppose,' he said, sounding a little disappointed. 'Considering he's been dead for about eighty years.'

'Dead?'

'PC Grantham was the first member of the Metropolitan Police to die in the course of his duty. I keep his picture as a reminder of what we're here for. It helps to keep me focused.'

'How thoughtful,' said Louise, unimpressed.

'So, what can I do for you, Mrs Smythson?' he asked, disappointed by her reaction. 'PC Milburn said you have a missing person to report.'

'Well, in a manner of speaking,' she said, leaning forward as Dew began to take notes. 'A friend of mine, Mrs Cora Crippen, she died recently.'

'I'm sorry to hear it.'

'Thank you, but I have reason to think she came to harm.'

'Really,' said Inspector Dew, raising an eyebrow. 'And why would you think that?'

'Her husband is Dr Hawley Crippen,' she said. 'He lives in Hilldrop Crescent. In Camden. Do you know it?'

'A little,' he said, urging her to continue.

'Well, I've known the Crippens for a few years now. They're not entirely our sort, you understand, but I took her under my wing in a charitable sense. Recently, however, Cora went to America to tend a sick relative – she wrote a letter to me as secretary of the Music Hall Ladies' Guild to announce that she would be away for some time – and then, the next thing we knew, Dr Crippen informed us that she had died while she was out there.'

'And you have reason to doubt him?'

'Well, not specifically, no. Although I wasn't aware of any illness she had. She was always a very . . . robust woman. It's just that last night I discovered that some weeks ago a friend of mine went to the theatre where she met Dr Crippen, and he was with a young lady.'

'Ah.'

'And the young lady was wearing some of Cora's jewellery. A blue sapphire necklace, to be precise. And some very fine ear-rings.'

'And you believe it's too soon after the death of his wife for this Crippen fellow to be escorting another lady around town, is that it?' Inspector Dew's eyes seemed to glaze over, as if he had to deal with this kind of thing all the time and it was high time the desk constables received better training at weeding out people like this.

'Well, there's that, certainly,' Louise admitted. 'But that's a matter for his conscience and for polite society to deal with. Naturally, my husband and I would not be able to associate with such a man any more.'

'Naturally.'

'The fact is that I just don't believe that Cora Crippen would go to America and leave her jewellery behind her. It doesn't make sense, Inspector.'

Dew thought about this for a few moments, then nodded his head. 'This Crippen character,' he asked, 'what sort of fellow is he?'

'Oh, I suppose he's quite a respectable man,' she admitted grudgingly.

'Not the violent sort? No trouble in his past?'

'None that I know of. Although I did hear that he was a widower when he married Cora. Might there be something in that? My husband – Nicholas Smythson? He might be Lord Smythson one day, you know – my husband calls him a milksop of a man. He doesn't care for him. He's not my type either, of course, but still. Not your typically suspicious sort. But still . . . two wives. Both dead. You can't help but wonder, can you? He's always seemed very quiet, almost *too* quiet, if you know what I mean. There was something about him I never quite trusted. It's in the eyes, Inspector. There's a tip for you. You can always tell a killer by the look in his eyes!'

Without giving any warning, Inspector Dew closed his notebook firmly and, standing up, practically picked Mrs Smythson out of her chair and steered her towards the door. 'It was very good of you to come in and express your concerns,' he said. 'But it doesn't sound to me as if there's anything for you to be worried about. If the woman has died in America, then she has died in America. That's not our jurisdiction. And what she chose to do with her jewellery when she left England, well, that's a matter for—'

'But, Inspector, don't you think it even a little strange?' she asked irritably, disliking the way he was manhandling her out through the door and back along the corridor as if she was an hysteric or a common criminal.

'Not particularly,' he said. 'There's no case to answer here, Mrs Smythson. I suggest you return home and not give it another thought. Let the poor woman rest in peace and if Dr Crippen wishes to take company with another woman, then that's his own concern. I realize that you were a friend of his late wife but—'

'That's *not* why I'm here,' she protested. 'I'm not angry about that.'

'Thank you, Mrs Smythson. Glad to have been of service.'

Without further ceremony she found herself back in the main lobby of Scotland Yard, shocked by his casual treatment of her, her face growing a little red as people stared in her direction.

A voice piped up from the back of the room, and she recognized it as that of Mary Dobson. The whole room listened as the woman shouted. 'Don't worry, darlin',' she yelled. 'The Peelers only take in prossies to give them a lecture, first time out anyways. They won't bother you if you stick to your own area. Try round Leicester Square or Covent Garden next time. Always a market for upper-class whores like you there.'

Mrs Louise Smythson, who had aspirations towards the nobility, felt her mouth drop open in shock as a room full of people stared at her, looking her up and down, sizing her up, pricing her in their minds.

'Well I never did,' she said out loud, before storming through the door and turning round to look back at Scotland Yard as if the building itself had ruined her day. 'Some mischief has come to her,' she shouted up at the windows of the top floor, forgetting her upper-class accent once again. 'You'll find out, Inspector, and then you'll want me to come back and tell you all the details. And I bloody well won't bother!'

4

The First Mistake

Detroit; Utah: 1884–1890

Hawley didn't last long as Price's apprentice; within a week he was allowed to begin his own dissections. A month after that, he was getting through up to seven or eight a night, a new record, and earning extra money as a bonus for his speed and precision as a surgeon. The floor manager stated that he had never seen such meticulousness in a cutter before, and he took particular pleasure in the way Hawley managed to separate the organs and the bones carefully from the remaining carcass, distributing them at various parts of his work area so that when the moment came to dispose of them separately into the different tanks, he could do so in the quickest possible time, leaving barely any sign of a disturbance behind.

Such was his success that, one night before beginning work, he was summoned to the office where he met Leo McKinley, one of the owners of the abattoir. 'They say you're the best prospect we've had in a long time,' he was told. 'A good arm, resilience, and you're quick.' It made him sound as if he was being accepted as a professional baseball player.

'I enjoy my work,' Hawley replied modestly.

'Enjoy it, eh? Three nights a week, you do. What would you say to a full-time position? Five day shifts, leave your nights free for the ladies, eh? What do you think of that?'

Hawley shook his head. 'It's out of the question,' he explained. 'I'm studying to be a doctor.'

'There's better prospects here, son,' he was told. 'I'm talking about a twenty per cent raise. You won't get a better offer than that. What if you want to settle down one day and take a wife? You'll need money then. Trust me, sonny. The women today expect a man who'll look after them.'

Hawley laughed, flattered that he had been considered for the position, but he continued to decline it, preferring to keep his unsocial hours and his ambitions alive.

Jezebel complained when he returned home, stained with blood, in the mornings. 'Take a look at yourself,' she said, shaking her head in disgust. 'What must the neighbours think? They'll say you're some kind of vicious murderer, going out all clean and decent in the evening time, coming home in the early hours covered in blood and reeking of death. What kind of a living is that to make? It's hardly the Lord's work.'

'It's not a living at all,' he stated coldly. 'It's a way of *making* a living.'

Sure enough, that first year at McKinley-Ross saw him earn his diploma from Philadelphia and then another, this time as an eye and ear specialist from the Ophthalmic Hospital in New York City, all thanks to his three nights a week as the best cutter in the Michigan abattoirs. He dreamed of the moment when strangers would ask his name for the first time, and he would finally be able to give a polite bow and lean forward, extending a hand and offering the version which he had dreamed of for such a long time. 'My name,' he would say proudly, 'is Doctor Crippen.'

While it takes no more than an hour to travel from the town of Ann Arbor in Michigan to the city of Detroit, Dr Hawley Harvey Crippen's decision to move there in the spring of 1884 was seen by his mother as a deliberate attempt to escape her influence. In this she was correct.

On the basis of his two diplomas, from Philadelphia and New York, Hawley was offered a position as a physician's assistant at a busy general surgery in downtown Detroit. His job, which would more usually have been done by a nurse, involved long hours and low pay, but he had the opportunity now to work with actual human beings rather than with dead animals, and that alone made it worthwhile to him. The surgery was owned by four doctors, ranging in age from thirty-three to sixty-seven, the youngest, Dr Anthony Lake, being the son of the eldest, Dr Stephen Lake; they allowed their colleagues to address them as Dr Anthony and Dr Stephen respectively in order to save confusion. Hawley worked for Dr Stephen, and he got along with him quite well, for the older man could identify in his new employee the makings of a good doctor. He had rarely seen such enthusiasm, not even in his own son, who had more or less drifted into the profession when his father had purchased him a place at university.

'Why didn't you go to medical school, Hawley?' Dr Stephen asked him one evening when the surgery had closed for the night and they were enjoying a light supper together in the kitchen. 'You know as much about the workings of the body as an average student approaching his finals. I've seen less efficient qualified doctors. And you have excellent hands. Some of your suturing is quite brilliant.'

'I couldn't afford it,' Hawley explained. 'The tuition fees were too expensive. I worked as a clerk in my father's grocery store, and it just wasn't possible. I only managed to afford the diploma courses because I worked in an abattoir three nights a week.'

Dr Stephen pulled a face, although squeamishness was the thing furthest from his mind. 'One of life's cruel ironies,' he said. 'The good Lord gives you the talent but the great god of commerce doesn't allow you to pursue it.'

Hawley smiled; mention of the Lord's name brought back memories of his mother. He had left the two of them behind in Ann Arbor and rarely thought of either any more.

'By the way, while you're here, in front of the patients I mean, you will always be addressed as Dr Crippen. Of course you are not really a doctor, but most medical students adopt the title because it sets the patients at ease. It's simpler that way.'

'I think it has a certain ring to it,' said Hawley.

He lived in a small room on the top floor of a house a few doors down from the surgery. It belonged to Dr Anthony Lake, who had offered their new employee the room shortly after his arrival in Detroit, deducting a third of his weekly wages as rent. While the house itself was large and well furnished, Hawley's room was small and poky and contained little more than a bed, a broken wardrobe, a desk and a washbasin. He had the impression that it had been used as a storeroom in the past and on more than one night he woke at five o'clock in the morning, feeling as if he was about to be choked by the dampness and dust in the air. A small skylight gave the room its only ventilation but, because it was quite dirty on the outside and impossible to clean without climbing on to the roof itself, it offered little in the way of natural light.

'If you want to climb out there,' his landlord told him, 'you can clean it. But there's more chance you'll fall off and break your neck, and there won't be a doctor in the world who can save you then.'

Dr Anthony was ten years his senior and yet Hawley did not have as pleasant a relationship with him as he enjoyed with his father, and he was grateful that he was not the younger man's assistant. It was well known that medical students survived with Dr Anthony for no more than a month or two at a time, just as it was common knowledge that only the prettiest were ever employed by him. A married man with a small child, he lived in this house during the week but left the city at the weekends to join Mrs Lake at their more expensive retreat on the outskirts of the city. Hawley only met her once during his residency at Eaton Lane, and he was immediately taken by her beauty, blushing furiously when she spoke to him and stuttering his responses nervously. The ladies were still a mystery to him.

Upon arriving at the surgery in the morning, the first face he saw was that of Charlotte Bell, the young receptionist who had begun working there only three days after him. Originally from California, she had lived in Michigan for over a year and had left her previous place of employment, as a receptionist in an ophthalmologist's surgery, only when the doctor there had died. It was this connection that encouraged her to strike up a friendship with the nervous young man.

'I believe you studied ophthalmology in New York?' she asked him as they ate their lunch together one day. Hawley considered the question, wondering whether he should be honest and point out that it had been by a correspondence course or tell a lie and make himself seem better travelled than was really the case.

'That's right,' he replied, deciding quickly.

'I've always wanted to visit New York,' she said, look-ing out of the window dreamily, as if it was possible, if she tried hard enough, to see the Statue of Liberty in the distance. 'But I think it would scare me a little. Is it as noisy and crowded as they say?'

'Certainly,' said Hawley, who had never set foot

outside the state of Michigan in his twenty-three years. 'There must be a million people living there.'

'A million!' she repeated breathlessly. 'Impossible to imagine!'

'Everywhere there are crowds rushing along the sidewalks, streetcars blowing their horns. Noise and music emerging from every corner. It's a lively place, that's for sure. Not a city for a single young lady, I feel.'

'I only asked because I worked for an ophthalmologist myself before I came here,' said Charlotte. 'Dr Abraham Rubens. Did you know him?'

Should I? he wondered. 'I don't believe so,' he said slowly, watching her face carefully for her reaction.

'Really? He was one of the top men in his field. I can't believe you haven't heard his name. Our waiting room was always filled with important people. Alice Darson, the actress? You've heard of her, of course?'

'Of course,' he said, despite the fact that he had never heard her name in his life, his interest in the arts section of the newspapers being minimal.

'She came every week. I shouldn't tell you this, but she's going blind. Can't see a thing out of her left eye any more, and her right one's on the downward slope. Didn't want anyone to know in case the theatre managers heard about it and wouldn't give her a job any more. Now that the doctor's dead I don't know what she's going to do. He was the only one she trusted, you see. She'd been seeing him for years.'

'Indeed,' said Hawley, unsure whether he should be impressed by her connections or offended by her loose tongue.

'And then there was the governor,' she added, looking around nervously, as if he might have political enemies everywhere, even here in the small kitchen area of a local surgery. 'He sees double. Can barely focus on anyone standing in front of him. He has to decide which is the real person – the one on the left or the one on the right – and focus directly on that choice, hoping he's picked correctly. And he doesn't always, I can tell you. He had a five-minute conversation with me once and addressed all his remarks to a ficus plant. Anyway, the doctor went to see him in the governor's mansion, of course. Only right and proper. You couldn't expect someone important like that to come to the surgery. This place isn't the same. We don't seem to get any famous people in here,' she added with a sigh.

Her breathless enthusiasm made Hawley smile despite himself. When she looked out of the window – which she did frequently, dreaming of bigger and better things – he stole the opportunity to stare at her breasts, the tops of which were visibly straining against her low-cut bodice. A stranger to women, he found himself drawn to Charlotte Bell.

Their friendship continued over their many lunches, and within a month he had agreed to accompany her to the theatre for an evening out to see a production of *King Lear* at the Detroit Playhouse. The actress Alice Darson was playing Cordelia, even though she was clearly twenty years too old for the role; her slim figure and some carefully applied make-up ensured that she did not look too much out of place. Her eyesight must have been getting worse, for she refused Goneril's kingdom rather than her father's, and she balanced precariously over the orchestra pit, almost falling in on several occasions.

It was Charlotte who had bought the tickets to the play and who invited him to join her, a forward step which both shocked and excited him. She found it difficult to decipher Hawley's frame of mind when they met outside the Playhouse. Expecting him to be nervous and gentlemanly, she found instead that his hands were bunched into fists and, although he was being polite and courteous towards her, she could tell that he was preoccupied. She hoped he hadn't thought her forward by inviting him to the play, but she had done so because she had enjoyed their conversations so much and she sensed in him a quiet, lost soul, the type she found fascinating. Throughout the performance, whenever she looked across at her companion he seemed to be distracted and staring off into the wings, much as the Governor of Michigan might have done if he was speaking to someone directly in front of him.

'I don't think you enjoyed tonight,' she told him quietly as they strolled along the river when he walked her home.

'You're quite wrong, Miss Bell,' he said. 'On the contrary, I enjoyed the play a lot, although I confess I know little of the arts. And . . .' He hesitated for a moment, wondering whether he was being too forward in saying such a thing but decided that he had little to lose '. . . also I enjoyed your company very much,' he added. 'Very much indeed.'

'You're very sweet,' said Charlotte, turning to look at him with great affection. In the half-light of the night-time streetlamps his face took on a more defined look as he walked along, tall and erect, his moustache neatly combed, his thin, sharp nose lending him an almost aristocratic appearance. If only he was a little bit taller, she thought to herself. For although he was pale, his hair a little mousy, his voice a little weak, and his manner a little more reserved than she would have liked, she thought him a much nicer sort than any of the other young men whom she had gone out with on evenings in the past – especially that Dr Anthony Lake, who had given her a cheap meal at a local restaurant before practically dragging her back to his house, which she had left without allowing him to have his way with her. 'Chateau Lake', he had called it and she had been forced to bite her lip to stop herself from giggling at his pomposity. She had nearly lost her job for refusing to sleep with him, but somehow, in a moment of boredom, he had decided to allow her to stay at the surgery and had simply ignored the event ever since.

They stopped outside Charlotte's front door, where a light was on in the porch. Hawley noticed the curtains twitching slightly, and he frowned. 'Mother and Father will still be awake,' she said after an embarrassing pause. 'Would you like to come in to meet them? Have a cup of tea perhaps? It's been such a lovely night.'

Hawley shook his head. 'Not tonight,' he said. 'I believe I should return home now. Thank you very much for agreeing to accompany me, however.'

'It was *you* who agreed to accompany *me*,' she said, laughing. 'I was the brazen hussy who invited you along, remember?'

He was surprised by her language, but it amused him too. He couldn't help but break into a smile, and this made Charlotte smile too. She almost never saw him grinning like this; it made him seem more boyish, not the serious-minded young doctor he aspired to be. She reached forward and placed a hand behind his head, enjoying the sensation of his hair against her fingers, then she pulled his face to hers, kissing him lightly on the lips, his first kiss. She lingered for only a moment before releasing him and opening the door to her home. 'Goodnight, Hawley,' she said, smiling at him one last time before disappearing inside.

'Miss Bell,' he whispered, thoroughly bewitched.

Reader, they married. And with their marriage came a change of circumstances. Dr Anthony Lake decided that Dr Crippen's upstairs room was too small for two people to share; although he did not hold a grudge against Charlotte following her rejection of him, he could not fathom how she could turn down his offer and yet marry a man like Hawley Crippen, so clearly his social and sexual inferior. Neither Hawley nor his new wife was particularly concerned about that, however; Charlotte had told her husband of the advances her earlier suitor had made towards her, and they had both agreed that they should find a new place to begin married life. However, to add insult to injury, Lake also decided that Charlotte could no longer work at the surgery.

'Doesn't look good, Crippen,' he explained, leaning against the wooden frame of the door in his room as Hawley packed. 'A married woman working like that. Sure, if you were both poor and she wanted to take in washing a few days a week, that would be one thing. But you're not poor. You're almost respectable.'

'We have barely two cents to rub together,' Hawley protested.

'Yes, but you're not in the gutter, are you?' he replied, frowning. 'And what would people think if they knew that you were sending your wife off to work every day, eh? They'd think you a poor excuse for a husband. Even Charlotte might. That's no way to start a marriage. Do you think *my* marriage would be such a success if I packed Mrs Lake off every morning with two sandwiches and an apple to some godforsaken office?'

Hawley raised an eyebrow; he wasn't sure the Lake marriage was the one he should be using as a standard. 'Very well,' he said finally. 'I'll tell her myself, though, if you don't mind.'

'Don't mind at all,' Dr Anthony said, already visualizing the interview procedure for the new receptionist. He thought it would be a nice idea to hold it at the house rather than the surgery. Perhaps in the evening. Over a glass of wine. 'I'm delighted you see it's for the best. A new start for both of you. Best thing in the world, if you ask me.'

Hawley nodded, but it took a few moments for those words to settle in. 'For both of us?' he queried. 'Why both of us?'

'Oh, come on, Crippen,' the other said with a false air of bonhomie, punching Hawley casually on the arm as if they were old friends. 'You don't want to stay around our stuffy old surgery, now do you? You need to find yourself a position with some prospects. What if you were to have a family? How would you survive then? Children cost, you can take my word on that. Believe me, I'm doing you a favour.'

'You're firing me?' Hawley asked, astonished.

'I'm opening up new opportunities for you.'

'You can't do that,' said Hawley, summoning up the courage within himself to debate the point. He could hear the nervousness in his own voice as he spoke more loudly and he cursed his own weakness. 'I work for your father, not for you. You don't have the right to let me go.'

Dr Anthony breathed heavily through his nose and stared at the floor for a moment, shaking his head as if he was being put in an impossible situation and couldn't understand why. 'I *have* spoken to Father,' he said. 'I've made him see that it's for the best. *I'm* not letting you go, *he* is. So don't shoot the messenger.'

Hawley felt a sudden urge towards violence. He didn't want to throw a punch – he knew that he would come off worse in any such confrontation – but if he could disable this man in some way, he could think of a far more suitable punishment for him. His mind swam with images from his abattoir days. He pictured Dr Anthony stretched out on his work table, unable to escape, while Hawley set about him with a saw and a No. 9 blade knife, his blood pooling on the tiled floor below before being washed down the drain.

In the end, however, cowardly and uncertain of himself, there was no outlet for these emotions and he had little choice but to carry on packing his bags and he arranged to meet his new wife at her parents' home as originally planned. There, he told her the bad news and, after a long night's discussion, they made what plans they could for the future.

He found his next job in much the same way as he had found his last: through the Appointments section of *Scientific American*. A new ophthalmology hospital in Utah was set to employ a dozen trainees to work in their research department, and Hawley applied eagerly for the position, although Charlotte was not so sure about moving to another state.

'Utah?' she asked. 'What's in Utah?'

'Well, what's in Michigan, my dear? Nothing much. Utah will be a fresh start for us.' He frowned when he heard himself repeating the words and sentiments of young Dr Lake but dismissed the memory quickly. 'It looks like the hospital will be one of the most advanced in its field. It will be tremendously exciting for me to work there.'

'But the baby, Hawley,' she said. 'Is it a safe place for us to bring the baby up?' By now, Charlotte was six months pregnant, something of a miracle in itself. 'I hear that crime is a real problem in Utah, that people get murdered there every day.'

'Crime is everywhere, my dear,' he replied. 'Murders take place every day. You'd be surprised how many average people wake up in the morning, and before the night is over they've taken a life. It doesn't just happen in Utah.'

Over the course of the next three years they lived quite comfortably on the top floor of a house that was owned by a retired couple who lived downstairs and who protested constantly about the noise that little Otto made, despite the fact that he was an uncommonly peaceful child. Hawley enjoyed his work at the hospital, although the hours were long and he was not given as many responsibilities for research as he had hoped for. Indeed, of the original dozen new employees who had been hired at the same time, only three had been promoted high enough to earn the right to plan their own research projects. The others, Hawley included, were little more than assistants to the more trusted members of the team. He could tell that his employers did not think highly of him and he resented the fact that yet again he was being held back from advancement.

Married life was also proving difficult for him at times. Charlotte Bell was the first female whom he had ever kissed. Needless to say, their wedding night was the first occasion when he made love to another human being – although it was more Charlotte who found herself making love to him, rather than the other way around. At first their intimacy was embarrassed and unfulfilling. As time went on, it also became infrequent. Otto's conception had come about on a rare evening when Hawley had drunk too much brandy and Charlotte had taken advantage of him, for she was desperate to have a baby.

'Your mother has written again,' she stated over the breakfast table one morning as Hawley was reading the newspaper. He looked over the top of it irritably; she knew that he did not enjoy conversation first thing in the morning and yet she insisted on it. If they used up family discussions now, what would they speak of tonight when he got home?

'Has she indeed,' he commented in a dry tone.

'Yes, she wants to come on a visit,' said Charlotte, turning the pages of the letter quickly and scanning through it for any unpleasant news, before returning to the start and reading it more carefully. 'Or she wants us to visit her. Says it's up to us which we'd prefer.'

'I would prefer neither,' said Hawley. 'Should we write and tell her that?'

'She wants to see little Otto again. She must miss him dreadfully.'

Hawley frowned. 'The last time she saw him, she walked straight into the living room and doused him immediately in holy water. It startled the poor child so much that he burst into tears and couldn't look at her for days.'

'I remember,' said Charlotte, trying to suppress a smile. 'She thought she was doing the right thing.'

'She was wrong.'

'She thinks we're not Christian enough.'

'We are perfectly Christian enough for our needs. I do not need Mother coming here and telling us how to bring up our own child. She has the most outdated ideas. I told you how she made me hide copies of my research magazines—'

'Under the bed, yes. You have mentioned it once or twice,' said Charlotte in an exasperated tone. 'Really, Hawley, that was years ago. I do think you might try to move past it.'

'I'm a scientist, my dear, not a priest.'

'Well, shall I tell her that she can come on a visit then?'

'Heavens, no. Tell her that we'll come to Ann Arbor after Christmas. Then, when it gets to late December, we'll write and say that Otto has the croup.'

'Hawley! Don't tempt fate!'

'There is no fate, my dear. We are masters of our own destiny. And believe me, my suggesting that Otto will get the croup will no more bring the illness on him than my saying that we will today inherit a hundred thousand dollars or that I will succeed to the throne of Sweden. Really, my dear, you are very sweet about such things, but quite an innocent.'

Hawley believed implicitly in what he was saying about fate and destiny, but nevertheless Charlotte did not think it very nice to joke about their child's health. She pretended that it was not the case, but she could tell very well that her husband found it difficult to demonstrate love for his son. She could accept his intimate rejection of her; after all, they managed to live together perfectly peacefully, with only the rarest of arguments. She had long since stopped hoping that he might become a slave to his passions overnight or that he would begin to show her any real affection other than the most formal kind. She had chosen her life and was content to live with it. But his awkwardness with Otto pained her. It wasn't that he was cruel to the boy, or resentful of his presence; nothing as stark as that. It was simply that he seemed at pains not to be left alone with him. When she watched them playing together she always got the impression that he wanted to be elsewhere, and his conversation with the child was stilted and formal. Sometimes she felt that she was conducting two separate relationships in their home, one with a man, one with a child, and that she was not part of a family at all.

These were the thoughts which ran through Charlotte's mind as she walked down McGraw Way towards the centre of town, wheeling Otto in his perambulator in front of her. It was a cold day and she had wrapped the child up warm in two jumpers and a blanket, but she had neglected to do the same for herself and regretted wearing neither hat nor gloves when leaving the house. She had spent the morning composing a letter to Jezebel Crippen, replying to all the questions which had been asked in the previous letter, thanking her for the many prayers she was offering up for all three of them and informing her, as Hawley had suggested, that they would be delighted to visit their relatives during the Christmas holidays. As she considered the letter she would have to write some months later cancelling the visit, her eye was taken by a young couple across the street.

They were not much older than Hawley and her – no more than twenty-five or twenty-six years of age – but they were laughing as they walked along, the young man's arm wrapped protectively around the woman.

Suddenly, without any warning, he whisked her up off the pavement and spun her around in his arms, while she gave a squeal of delight and begged to be returned to the ground, pounding on his shoulders while laughing. As he did so, their lips met and they kissed passionately. Charlotte watched as the woman's hand moved to the back of her lover's head, pulling it closer to hers in order to make their kiss even firmer and more urgent. Their bodies were pressed very close to each other – almost indecently so – and she was amazed by the wanton display of their embrace. And envious of it. A rush of colour came to her cheeks and she sighed as a stirring within her made her realize that right then, at that very moment, she would give up everything, her husband, her life, even her child, to be locked in such a passionate embrace with a man. To feel loved. To feel sexually alive. She grew almost weak with hunger as her eyes focused directly on them, while her mouth became dry and her body stirred within itself; she did not even notice the other people who walked past the couple, either ignoring them completely or staring at them distastefully. Charlotte was so removed from her own body at that moment that the strong wind saw its opportunity and whisked the letter she had written to Jezebel Crippen out of her hand, spinning it in the air, arcing it along for a moment or two then allowing it to fly back and forth over the road joyfully, before depositing it firmly in the middle of the road.

'Oh my,' said Charlotte, snapping out of her daydream and watching as the letter disappeared into the air, 'my letter.' Without giving it a single thought, her other hand let go of the pram and she jumped out into the road to retrieve the letter, looking neither to left nor to right as she did so. The streetcar which was coming towards her was only a few feet away at the time and had no opportunity either to stop or to alert her to her danger. Within a second her body was pushed forward by the speeding bus, her heels were dragged under, and its wheels crushed her beneath its carriage. It drove over her almost immediately before pulling to a screeching halt as people in the street screamed and looked away from the bloodied, mangled body which lay on the ground before them, legs stretched apart, one arm almost ripped from its socket. A couple of teeth rattled along the road towards the kerb, stopping just short of a drain.

Hawley took the news of his wife's death with little emotion. He remembered when they had met and how she had seduced him. He recalled their evenings at the theatre and the weight of responsibility he had felt to marry her. He thought about much of their three years of married life together, but the one thing he could not remember was having ever loved her very much. Oh, he knew she was a perfectly pleasant woman without a malicious side to her. He believed her to be an excellent mother and a sensible lifelong companion for him. But love? That had not been part of it. And so he did what he had to do in order to move on. He organized a funeral, he buried her, and he put Otto on a bus to his maternal grandparents, who had agreed, much to his relief, to take over responsibility for his upbringing.

At the age of twenty-eight, Dr Hawley Harvey Crippen was once again a man alone.

5

The Passengers of the *Montrose*

The Atlantic Ocean: Thursday, 21 July 1910

Mr John Robinson had never experienced much trouble in sleeping until the start of February, when events had seen to it that his nightly eight hours rarely went uninterrupted. But the first night on board the *Montrose* had been almost unbearable. Edmund and he had finally separated and climbed into their two separate bunks at around 11 p.m., Edmund taking the top one and falling asleep almost immediately. Mr Robinson, on the other hand, had lain awake in the lower bunk for over an hour, feeling so warm in the cabin that he was forced to take all the sheets off his bed and try to sleep uncovered. The first-class cabins were of a decent size, second only to the Presidential Suite, whose occupants he had not yet met, but the air was restrictive and he swore that he would leave the porthole open all day from now on. The rocking of the boat made it even more unpleasant and when he finally drifted off, some time after two in the morning, he dreamed that he was dancing around the edge of the tallest building in the world while wearing roller-skates and it was all he could do to keep his balance. When he finally slipped and fell in the direction of the traffic on the street below, he awoke with a start, drenched in perspiration, and immediately reached across to the bedside table for his pocket watch so as to check the time. Three thirty. He sighed in exhaustion and wiped his face, trying to eliminate the bad memories which floated before his eyes. From then on, he slept only in fits and starts and shortly after seven o'clock he rose quietly, attempting not to waken Edmund, and washed himself in their small bathroom. His eyelids were almost stuck together with exhaustion but he believed that a turn around the deck and the early morning air would bring him back to life. Dressing in yesterday's suit and tie, he closed the door to the cabin behind him and made his way towards the stairs.

It was a bright, warm morning that first day, and he immediately felt cheered by the blue sky and sparkling sea; the sun caught the waves as they pressed against the ship and they sparkled in the morning light. Sea birds squawked as they dived into the water in search of their breakfast. Walking towards the railing, he looked overboard, leaning slightly forward so that a little of the spume from the water caught him in the face from time to time. Squinting, he could make out the dark shadowy shoals of fish swimming alongside the boat, their speed surprising him, for they were keeping pace perfectly, while the *Montrose*, he reasoned, must have been travelling at about ten or eleven knots. With a good harpoon, he thought, I could kill some of them.

Despite the early hour, there were already several people on deck, passengers like him who had found their first night on board ship to be less than comfortable. Billy Carter, the first officer, was accustomed to these early-morning strollers, although there were a few more on this occasion than he expected as he surveyed the deck from the helm. He noticed two sailors standing together, talking and smoking cigarettes, and he called them over to him, issuing what were always his first instructions of the morning, a task neither one looked particularly happy about undertaking.

'Get some buckets of water, lads,' he told them, 'and go around the sides of the ship, pouring them down the stern. The boat will most likely be covered in sick from people who haven't been able to keep last night's dinner down, and any passenger looking out to sea today doesn't want to be confronted with that.'

There was an officers' mess on C Deck where traditionally Carter would have eaten, but on this first morning he made his way to the first-class passengers' dining hall instead, not because he wanted to be fed better than anyone else, but because he believed it would make a good impression to show his face to the quality and answer any questions they might have about the crossing. They'd only track him down later if he didn't.

A buffet had been set up along one of the walls of the room and he helped himself to large portions before looking around to see who else was present. There were not many people eating breakfast as yet, and he was about to walk towards a table where three fashionable and attractive young ladies in their mid-twenties were breakfasting together when he noticed a rather older and less striking woman attempting to catch his attention at another table. She was waving her napkin in the air, and he felt rather like a bull being tormented by a matador. He smiled at her and, unable to pretend that she had not caught his eye, walked reluctantly in her direction.

'Good morning, young man,' she said with a wide smile; a small scraping of butter from her toast clung to her chin and Billy Carter wondered whether he should draw her attention to it, but decided against. 'Won't you join me, I've been waiting for my daughter, but she is quite delayed. Heaven knows what she is doing.'

'I'd be delighted,' said Carter, sitting down and casting only a quick, longing glance towards the sirens at the other table, who were giggling with each other in delight. One of them gave him a brief, flirtatious glance before looking away. 'First Officer Carter,' he added, giving a polite nod of the head.

'Oh, how delightful,' came the reply. 'An officer. I'm Mrs Antoinette Drake. Cabin A7. Travelling with my daughter Victoria.'

'Good morning,' said Carter, tucking into his food hungrily. He could already sense that Mrs Drake was one of those passengers who might cling on to him for ever if he was not careful, and he did not want to give her the opportunity by staying too long in her company. 'Enjoying the journey so far, are you?'

'Oh delightful, delightful,' she said. 'Although I did find the motion a little rough last night. Perhaps you could have a word with one of your sailors about it?'

Carter smiled. He wondered whether she thought the boat was crossing the ocean courtesy of a galley of Roman slaves below decks, chained together and rowing away relentlessly. 'I'll see what I can do,' he said politely.

'Victoria and I are light sleepers, you understand and I . . .' Here she gave a small, girlish giggle and looked at him coquettishly while tapping his arm. 'Well, I do need my beauty sleep, Mr Carter.'

'Of course,' he said, not realizing that she expected him to contradict her. Her smile froze for a moment, before turning into a frown. How rude, she thought, before remembering her motivation for calling him over to her in the first place.

'Now you must tell me,' she said. 'The captain of the ship. What's his name?'

'Captain Kendall, ma'am.'

'Captain Kendall, yes. Such a strong name. Fills one with confidence. And he dines here every evening, is that right?'

'I expect so, ma'am,' he said, already knowing where this was heading. 'This is my first voyage on the *Montrose*. The regular first officer was taken ill.'

'It's just that my daughter Victoria, she would be so thrilled to take a meal with him one evening, and I do so want her to enjoy this voyage. I take it he invites some of the first-class passengers to join him at the captain's table for the evening meal?' She raised her painted eyebrows slightly and licked her lips, practically feeding him the lines she wanted to hear. Without warning, her tongue nicked out, like a lizard's, and drew in the dab of butter which she seemed to have been storing on her chin for later.

'I'm sure he does,' said Carter, surprised to find his own stomach churning for once. 'Would you like me to arrange for you both to be seated at his table one evening?'

'Oh, well I would never ask for such a thing myself,' she replied quickly, shaking her head. 'I just take my meals whenever they're served to me, of course. I'm not at all fussy. But if you wanted to, for Victoria's sake, that would be lovely. Very kind of you in fact.' Her opinion of him shifted back again. 'Very kind indeed.'

'No problem,' he said, gobbling his food down quickly so that he could make an early escape.

'Where is that girl, anyway?' Mrs Drake asked after a moment, looking towards the door in frustration. 'She knows that I don't like her being tardy. She'll miss her breakfast if she's not careful. If I go back to that cabin and she's still in bed, there'll be trouble, Mr Carter, I can assure you of that.'

Mrs Drake need not have worried, for Victoria was not still asleep in bed at all. In fact, she had risen a few moments after her mother had left their cabin, and she spent twenty minutes in the bathroom, washing herself, combing her hair, and applying some of the small make-up items she had acquired in Paris a few weeks earlier. Opening the porthole and feeling the warmth of the sun and the cool air pouring in upon her, she decided to dress less formally than on the previous day, and opted for a pale blouse which exposed the tops of her shoulders, along with a long navy skirt. Poking her head out of the door of the cabin, she looked up and down the corridor to ensure that she was not being watched, before skipping quickly along to the door of Cabin A4, where she put her ear to the door and squinted slightly, as if this would improve her hearing. It took a few moments, but eventually she could hear the sound of movement within and, her heart beating quickly in her chest, she ran back to her room and left the door slightly ajar while she hovered inside. She stood there, arms folded, listening intently, for a further ten minutes or so until she heard the door on the other side of the corridor open, at which she immediately opened her own and stepped outside, slamming the door loudly behind her.

'Oh, good morning,' said Edmund, turning around at the sound. 'It's Victoria, isn't it?'

'*Yes,*' she said irritably, as if he was trying to be awkward by pretending that he was unsure of her name. 'And you're Edward, yes?'

'That's right. How are you this morning?'

She stared at him quizzically. 'Is it Edward or Edmund?' she asked after a moment.

'Oh! Ed . . . *mund,*' he said after a pause, a little colour rising in his cheeks. 'Isn't that what you said?'

'Well, you don't sound so sure,' said Victoria. 'Don't you even know your own name? And no, I said "Edward" originally.'

'Well, why did you say that if you knew it was wrong?'

Victoria stared at him and ignored the question. 'Are you going to breakfast?' she asked. Edmund nodded. 'Where's your father, then? Still asleep?'

'He got up an hour or so ago. I think he had difficulty sleeping.'

'Mother too. The *old*,' she said dismissively. As they stepped out on to the main deck, the sun poured down on both of them and she took the opportunity to get a proper look at Edmund in the light of day. He was not as tall as some of the beaux she had seduced in the past – he was no more than five foot seven or so – but she had rarely seen a boy with such clear skin and beautiful eyes. His hair was a little longer than fashion dictated and he wore a hat which obscured it slightly, the hair itself being jet black, fine and thick. She felt an overwhelming urge to rip his hat off and run her fingers through that lustrous thatch. And his lips! Cherry red, full. Simply begging to be kissed. When his tongue appeared momentarily between them, she felt quite weak. Even the thin scar running from his nose to his lip was attractive. Her heart fluttered slightly and she forced herself to turn away so that he would not catch her staring.

'There's Miss Hayes,' said Edmund after a moment, pointing towards the railing where Martha Hayes was standing in much the same position as she had been in when they had chatted the night before. 'Shall we say hello?'

Victoria sighed irritably. Although there was no chance that Edmund could possibly be interested in a woman as old as Miss Hayes – who was almost thirty, after all – it annoyed her that he preferred to speak to her than remain alone with a beauty such as herself. Most likely a ruse to toy with me, she decided. He's playing hard to get.

'Miss Hayes,' Edmund called as they reached her, and the older lady looked across at them and smiled.

'Well, hello, children,' she said, quickly putting her locket back inside her bag and snapping it shut. 'How lovely to see you again.'

Children! Victoria thought irritably. How dare she! We are both almost eighteen years old!

'Surely you haven't been here all night?' Edmund asked, smiling. 'You didn't come back on deck after we all went below, did you?'

'Oh no,' she said with a laugh. 'No, I retired as soon as I reached my cabin, I assure you. I just came back on deck myself a moment ago. How are the breakfasts, Victoria?' she asked. 'Tasty or foul?'

'I haven't had mine yet, *Miss* Hayes,' Victoria replied, considering the other woman very forward by addressing her by her Christian name. 'I've only just come on deck myself.'

'Oh really? I could have sworn I saw you running up and down the corridors earlier.'

'Me?' Victoria asked in surprise.

'I thought perhaps you were calling on Mr Robinson and his son to invite them to accompany you. Did I not see you outside their room a little earlier?'

Victoria gasped and felt herself torn between laughing it off and punching her. She could tell that Edmund had turned to look at her with an intrigued expression on his face and she blushed quickly. 'I really don't think so,' she said firmly. 'What an odd thing to suggest.'

'Outside *our* room?' Edmund asked, ignoring her denial. 'Whatever for?'

'I was nowhere near your room,' Victoria replied, her voice deepening slightly, eager to change the subject. 'It must have been one of the steerage passengers, playing games in places where they have no business being. We should speak to the captain. They're thieves, most of them, anyway. Gypsies, too.'

'Yes, that must be it,' said Miss Hayes. 'It would be easy to mistake you for one of them. Some of you young girls have a very similar look. It's the fashion, I suppose.'

Victoria stared at her venomously. Who was this awful

woman, she wondered. Why were they continually being bothered by her?

'Will you join us for breakfast, Miss Hayes?' Edmund asked, and Victoria sighed again.

Captain Kendall himself opened the door to the dining room for them as they stepped inside. He had just finished his own breakfast, which he had taken in the kitchens, for he was not in the mood for early-morning conversation, and he stepped outside on to the deck, breathing the air deeply into his lungs. A fine morning. He noticed two of his best young sailors pouring water over the side of the boat, not into the sea but along the paintwork itself, and he strode across to them curiously.

'What goes on here, men?' he asked, confused. 'What on earth are you doing?'

'The new first officer,' one of them explained. 'He asked us to do it.'

'To throw pails of water over the side? Whatever for?'

'He said the passengers had been getting sick overboard and we should wash it away. Gives a bad impression, he said.'

Kendall glared at him and looked over the side of the boat; he couldn't see anything himself. 'Ridiculous,' he said. 'Stop it immediately. The sea will wash away whatever needs washing. Attend to your other duties at once.'

'Yes, sir,' they replied in unison, happy to be freed of this task and rushing away with their pails.

Kendall shook his head irritably. 'Washing away vomit,' he said under his breath, missing his old friend now more than ever. 'Captain Bligh would have washed *him* away. Oh, Mr Sorenson,' he added to the winds. 'Who *have* they saddled me with?'

*   *   *

Eighty deckchairs lined the perimeter of the first-class deck of the SS *Montrose*, which was sealed off from the rest of the passengers, and about a third of them were filled later that afternoon as the sun continued to beat down on the boat. Some of the travellers had chosen to relax in their cabins, some were snoozing in the sunshine or reading books, some played cards in the games room. On the steerage deck, children ran wild, chasing and fighting with one another, looking for mischief, while their parents smoked and chatted together amiably. Both men and women wore sun hats and several ladies carried parasols as they strolled along, attempting to find diversions on board. Those who were seated were in the main keeping themselves to themselves; some early friendships were being nervously struck up between couples looking for conversation, but all were wary of being stuck with bores for the next nine days. At the far end of the deck, sitting alone, a dark-haired boy of about fourteen was leaning forward in his chair, squinting in the sunlight. His features were already tanned and his skin was the sort that took the sun easily. However, he was perspiring as he sat there and he kept brushing his dark hair out of his eyes. He wished that he had gone for a haircut before leaving Antwerp as it was beginning to irritate him. As he considered the last few months of his life, he thought it remarkable that he was on this boat at all. It was as if his entire life had been suddenly taken away from him and he was being forced to embark upon a new one.

This was his first time at sea, and it was a trip being undertaken under unfortunate circumstances. He had never known his father, who had been killed in the Boer War when he was just six months old, and his mother, a French lady named Céline de Fredi, had died of tuberculosis a few months ago. They had lived in various cities around Europe, and Tom found himself able to communicate in a variety of languages. His only surviving relation was his late father's uncle, to whom Céline had written shortly before her death, begging him to take care of the boy if anything should happen to her. He had agreed and had arrived in Paris a week before she passed away. Céline had taken the opportunity to let him know how troublesome his task might be: Tom was proving to be a difficult teenager, out of control on the streets of the city, and had become a source of constant worry to his mother. Inexperienced with children, she wondered whether his new guardian would be capable of looking after him, although there was no one else she could entrust with his upbringing. It was either him or the orphanage, and if she chose the latter it would only be a matter of time before her son traded in one form of imprisonment for another. After she passed away they continued to live in Paris for a month, settling Céline's affairs, before travelling to Antwerp, where Tom's uncle lived. Business called him to Canada, however, and he had chosen the *Montrose* as the vessel to take him there, booking the most expensive cabin on board, the Presidential Suite.

There were not many boys of Tom's age on board the ship, and he was not looking forward to another nine days of boredom with only his uncle for company. Already he missed his Parisian friends – although in truth it had been they who had been leading the lad astray for over a year, breaking into houses in the dead of night, stealing food from shops and acting as pickpockets on the streets, even though none of them was particularly in need of money. These memories added to his distemper. But that was all behind him now, and in Canada lay the future. Not to mention his new relative, whom he was still learning to trust, but who appeared to be a decent, if somewhat distant, gentleman.

'There you are,' came a voice from beside him, and he looked up, shielding his eyes from the sun with his hand, squinting to see who was addressing him.

'Uncle Matthieu,' he said, acknowledging him. 'What's wrong?'

'Nothing's wrong, my boy,' the man said, sitting down and looking around the deck with a distracted air. 'I was simply looking for you, that's all. When I couldn't find you I was afraid you'd fallen overboard. Imagine my sense of loss.'

Tom frowned. He found his uncle's sense of humour difficult to decipher at times. 'I've been sitting here, trying to think of something to do,' he said after a moment. 'This has to be the most boring trip I have ever taken. Maybe I'll actually die of boredom. If I do, you can bury me at sea.'

'Rest assured that I will,' said Matthieu, nodding his head. 'I myself am finding it very relaxing, however. Eleven days crossing the ocean without a worry in the world. No one to bother me with any business problems. Excellent cabins. Good food. Pleasant company. I believe I could do with several more weeks of this. It's the only way to travel.'

'Yes, but you're old,' Tom explained. 'You probably need the rest. I'm young. And I'm bored senseless.'

'Indeed,' he replied, unimpressed. To a casual observer, Matthieu Zéla was a man approaching fifty years of age. A little over six feet in height, with thinning grey hair, he was, without realizing it, already cutting a dashing figure on board ship with several of the ladies. His trim shape and fine clothes, combined with the fact that he could afford the most expensive suite on board, made him an object of much interest to several of them, particularly the single ones. The fact that he was a widower and was travelling without a female companion made him even more attractive . . . excellent husband material. 'Perhaps you should try reading a book?' he suggested to his nephew. 'Broaden your mind a little. What have you read recently anyway?'

Tom thought about it. Although he had grown up in a home surrounded by literature, he had never much taken to it. He remembered his mother reading *The Man In The Iron Mask* to him when he was about eleven, and he chose this book as his reply.

'Ah,' said Matthieu happily. 'Dumas. An excellent choice. Perfect for the youthful mind. Adventure, history, suspense. Just what you need in a novel. I'm sure there's a library on board somewhere. Perhaps we could take a look later and see whether we can find something suitable for you along those lines. I'm sure it will make the voyage go even faster. I'm almost never without a book myself. Did I ever tell you that I once attended a reading by Mr Charles Dickens in Covent Garden?'

'Where's that?' asked Tom, who had never been to England.

'London, my boy! London!' replied Matthieu. 'Astonishing, the ignorance of the young,' he added, shaking his head sadly. 'You should read some of Mr Dickens's novels. Many of them tell of orphans, just like you.'

Tom frowned. That was especially tactless, he thought. But one thing he had learned about this Mr Zéla since they had met was that he spoke his mind with little consideration for tact.

'And what happens to these orphans?' he asked, considering it.

'Most of them find that, once their parents have died, their new guardians – often older men – become cruel and abusive. They don't feed them, they beat them mercilessly, and they make their lives so painful that they are forced to run away without so much as a pair of shoes on their feet. Ultimately, however, they triumph.

How was your bed last night, by the way? Did you sleep well?'

Without warning a ball appeared in front of them, appearing from the other side of the ship where a game of tennis was being played by some children, quite careful to avoid losing it to the sea. Matthieu turned around to see where the ball had come from, and in that moment Tom scooped it up in his hands and tossed it into the water, where it landed with a distant plop. Sniggering to himself, he leaned back in his deckchair and folded his arms, pretending to be asleep. Matthieu stared at him, amazed by what the boy had done.

Two small children appeared within moments and looked around the deck desperately for their ball.

'Excuse me, sir,' said the smaller one, a polite little girl with ringlets and green eyes. She was wearing a very formal dress for the middle of the afternoon. 'Our tennis ball, sir.'

Matthieu opened his mouth and closed it again, unsure what to say, regretting that he might have to lie to such an innocent. 'I'm sorry, I haven't seen it,' he said.

The girl narrowed her eyes, suspecting otherwise. 'Yes you have,' she said in a deeper voice, pointing her finger at him before bursting into a sudden rush of tears and being escorted back to the tennis court by her brother. 'You stole it!' she cried as her parting shot, displaying more fury than he knew a child could muster.

Matthieu turned to his nephew in frustration. 'Tom!' he exclaimed. 'What a charmless thing to do. Why did you throw that ball away?'

Tom shrugged, still smiling, delighted by his trick. 'Nothing better to do,' he said in a quiet voice.

'Well, it was extremely childish of you,' Matthieu scolded him. 'I believe you should go over to those children and apologize. Tell them it was a mistake by all means, that you were trying to retrieve it for them when it escaped you, but apologize.'

'Why?' he asked. 'Who cares?'

'I care,' Matthieu insisted. 'Now do it. This instant. I'm serious.'

Tom thought about it. The rules of their relationship were still being defined; the level of Matthieu's authority over him was still in some question. Although he was fourteen years old, he was still a child and hadn't quite reached the point where he believed himself strong enough to disobey his elders. Also, although he scarcely wanted to admit it to himself, he worried what would happen if this man, who had never laid eyes on him until a couple of months earlier, was to decide that he was a bad lot after all and leave him destitute. Matthieu Zéla was clearly wealthy; he could help him in his future life. There was no point antagonizing him unnecessarily. Deciding to play the scolded child on this occasion, he gave an exaggerated sigh and stood up, dragging his body around the deck as if it weighed two hundred pounds.

Matthieu shook his head. For his part, he had little experience of children and this one had been rather foisted on to him; he was far from sure that he could manage *in loco parentis*.

'You were right to send him to apologize,' a voice beside him said, and he turned to look at the young lady who had just sat down in the deckchair next to his.

'You saw it then?' he asked, a little embarrassed for his nephew. 'You saw what he did?'

She nodded. 'He's just a boy,' she said, excusing his actions. 'And he's bored. But you were right to send him over there. Manners are important.'

Matthieu nodded and looked into the sea, before remembering his own manners and turning back to his companion. 'I do beg your pardon,' he said, extending his hand, 'I should have introduced myself. My name is Matthieu Zéla.'

'Martha Hayes,' she replied, shaking his hand happily.

'Delighted to meet you, Miss Hayes. You are returning home to Canada or travelling there for the first time?'

'A little of both,' she said. 'It will be my first time there, but I hope to make my home in Quebec. I've lived in Europe all my life and have had quite enough of it.'

'I know what you mean,' he replied, smiling. 'I'm something of a traveller myself. I never seem able to stay in the same place for very long. Circumstances always come along and force me to move.'

'That must be exciting.'

'Sometimes. But I'd quite like to settle down for a while. I'm not getting any younger, after all.'

'You look very sprightly to me, Mr Zéla,' she said, warming to him already.

'Matthieu, please.'

'Well, you look very sprightly, Matthieu, then,' she repeated.

He shrugged. 'Appearances can be deceptive,' he muttered. 'How are you enjoying the journey so far?' he asked, changing the subject. 'Found your sea-legs yet?'

'Just about,' she said with a laugh. 'It's very relaxing.'

'That's just what I was saying to my nephew,' said Matthieu. 'He seemed to consider *that* to be the problem.'

'Your nephew?'

'Yes, I'm Tom's uncle. Acting as guardian for him for the moment. His parents are both dead. His mother quite recently, I'm afraid.'

'I'm so sorry,' said Martha. 'The poor boy. I suppose that, under those circumstances, throwing a tennis ball in the water is not such a major crime. He's only, what . . . fourteen?'

Matthieu nodded. The psychology of the youth was not one in which he was particularly interested. As far as he was concerned, the boy had suffered a loss, he should mourn his mother, come to terms with it and move on. He himself had been forced to do much the same thing and at a younger age than Tom, for Matthieu's own mother had been killed by her violent second husband, leaving him and his younger brother also orphaned, only without a guardian. They had survived though.

'I hope he will have a happier life in America,' he said after some thought. 'A fresh start can be a healthy thing. And he's young, of course. He can create a new world for himself there. I'm travelling to Canada on business, but will probably move down to the States afterwards for a time. If things work out, we may stay there. Tom has proved something of a handful in Paris; I hope to steer him back on to the straight and narrow. Assuming he doesn't go stir crazy over the next week or so and jump over the side of the ship.'

'Oh, he'll settle down,' Martha said reassuringly.

At that moment, Tom reappeared from the other side of the deck and stood before them, staring at Miss Hayes suspiciously. 'Ah, Tom,' said Matthieu. 'Let me introduce you. This is my nephew, Miss Hayes. Tom DuMarqué.'

'Pleased to meet you, Tom,' said Martha, shaking his hand.

He nodded at her but said nothing, standing quite close to the chairs and as far away from the railing as possible. Although he could not have admitted it to his uncle, he had a morbid fear of water, and every moment on board was a trial to him. He avoided thinking about the great expanse of sea surrounding him and had resolved not to look over the railing once during this journey.

'Well? Did you apologize?' Matthieu asked when it became clear that he was not going to offer anything to the conversation.

'*Yes*,' he cried in an exaggerated tone. 'They have about twenty tennis balls around there, so I don't see what all the fuss was about anyway.' He continued to stare at Martha, refusing to sit down, and she suddenly felt uncomfortable in his presence. He had a certain look in his eye which made him seem dangerous and unpredictable.

'Well, it was lovely to have met you, Mr Zéla,' she said, standing up and smoothing down her skirt.

'Matthieu, please.'

'Matthieu,' she acknowledged. 'And you, Tom. But I believe I will continue my stroll now. I'm sure we'll see each other again.'

'O God, thy sea so great, my boat so small,' Matthieu said with a smile, nodding as she walked away. 'What a charming lady,' he said quietly when she had disappeared from sight. 'You might have made her feel a little more welcome, Tom. Really, your manners are astonishingly crude.'

'Pfff,' came the reply, a dry snort through the boy's lips, a bubble of spittle sticking there for a moment before he wiped it away.

Tom might have added more to this eloquence had his eye not been taken by the form of Victoria Drake who was standing some twenty feet away from them both at the railing, staring out to sea. His eyes widened, his mouth dropped open and he experienced the first pangs of desire. Sensing that she was being stared at, she looked around slowly in his direction, caught his eye, and gave him a disdainful glance before looking away again. Tom felt himself blush and pressed his lips together tightly. Matthieu, who had been watching the whole pantomime, could not help but be amused.

'Why, Tom,' he exclaimed. 'You've gone bright red. Are you in love?'

'Pfff,' he said again, as if the very idea was ridiculous. (Yes, he thought.) Matthieu looked over at the object of his nephew's affection and nodded slowly. Despite himself, Tom felt his eyes wandering across to Victoria again, but now she had vanished out of sight.

'Ah,' said Matthieu, for he had been in this position himself many times. 'I believe I understand.'

Captain Kendall had learned through many years' experience that it was not a sensible thing to become too friendly with the crew. In his early days as a captain he had sought to ingratiate himself with the officers and sailors under his command, hoping that earning their comradeship would inculcate a better atmosphere on board. However, that had been taken advantage of on the *Perseverance* when he had begun to detect complacency among his crew, who hardly saw him as the disciplined leader which had so inspired him in the story of the *Bounty*. He altered his manner considerably when he took command of the *Montrose*. Now, while he was not exactly feared by the men, he was nevertheless treated with deference, and his moods were legendary. He could be perfectly obsequious to a first-class passenger one minute, and come close to striking a sailor the next. The rule of thumb was to follow his orders but not to get too close. The only person who had – the appendicitis-stricken first officer, Mr Sorenson – had made himself even more unpopular with his colleagues for his sycophancy, and the captain was aware that he was the only man on board who regretted his stay in the hospital. Sitting at the desk in his cabin later that afternoon, his compasses spanning across the blue charts, he made quick notes on a piece of paper by his side, calculating distance through longitude and latitude and using their knot speed to determine whether they would arrive in Canada when they were supposed to. He was pleased to note that they were making good time. Clear skies and a light breeze behind them this afternoon had given them a great advantage, and they had even picked up speed a little, despite the fact that he had only ordered four of the six boilers to be opened as yet. Captain Kendall was a great believer in not overtaxing a vessel and rarely employed the boilers to full capacity. Unlike his hero, Captain Bligh, he believed in sticking to the schedule and had no interest in beating the clock. They were supposed to land in Quebec on the morning of 31 July, and as far as he was concerned that was the only date that would do. To arrive on the thirtieth would be too showy, to arrive on 1 August would be considered tardy. As things stood, however, they would make it exactly on time, and he gave a smile of satisfaction as he sat back and picked up the newspaper he had purchased before leaving harbour. He glanced only briefly at the headlines – trouble brewing over strike action in the Belgian liquor industry, a manhunt going on for some fellow who'd killed his wife and chopped her body up into little pieces, a report of a wealthy grandmother who had recently married a boy of eighteen. He tossed it to one side, irritated by the stupidity of the world. This was why he preferred living at sea, he reasoned.

He thought of Mr Sorenson, languishing alone in an Antwerp hospital. The man had probably already had his appendix removed and would be recovering from the operation, possibly waking up from the anaesthetic around now and wondering whether the ship had sailed without him, knowing of course that it would have. As he set his cap on his head and tugged his jacket down sharply, the captain wondered whether he should use the new Marconi telegraph in the wireless room to send a get-well message to the hospital, but decided against it. It would be difficult to explain to the radio controllers why he wanted to be left alone there, and if they found out about the message his carefully honed image as a tough taskmaster might be undermined. Still, he hated to think that Mr Sorenson might feel he didn't care. Shaking his head roughly, he dismissed the idea from his mind and stepped outside the cabin, locking the door behind him.

From his vantage point on the deck he could make out the figure of Billy Carter in the wheelhouse, pointing out to sea and sharing a joke with one of the navigators. He was drinking a cup of tea himself, something that the captain expressly forbade in that room. He marched around the steerage deck, avoiding the children and their parents, making sharp lefts and rights whenever he saw some annoying individual ready to catch his eye and begin a conversation. They're all taken by the uniform, he thought to himself, which was true. He cut a dashing figure in his black naval attire, sporting what appeared to be a row of medal ribbons along the pocket but which were actually the various insignia of the Canadian Pacific fleet. Compared to the cheap travelling clothes of these passengers, he was quite the dandy. He gave a brief sigh of relief, but only a small one, as he made his way on to the first-class deck. These people, he knew, could be even worse, because they, unlike their steerage counterparts, did not look up to him. On the contrary, they looked *down* on him, believing that he was little more than one of their butlers or servants. And he was generally forced into politeness with them. Plus, every one of them would be angling for an invitation to dine at his table, a nightly ritual that he dreaded. Mr Sorenson was usually good at weeding out the bores from those who might at least entertain him, but there was always a hierarchy anyway. The residents of the Presidential Suite were always invited, along with several other first-class passengers. But without Mr Sorenson to sort the wheat from the chaff, what hope had he of enjoying his meal or digesting it properly? He singled out small pieces of conversation as he passed several passengers, and he even heard one complimentary – and unexpected – comment from a young boy whom he passed as he made his way towards the helm.

'It's a dashing uniform, isn't it?' said Edmund to

Victoria as they sat on deckchairs, playing a game of cards, his eye caught by Captain Kendall as he walked by them. 'The officers look very smart.'

'Very,' said Victoria, pleased to express an interest in the other men on board, hoping that this might finally spur him into showing her more attention. 'Have you seen the first officer? He's very handsome.'

Edmund smiled but said nothing, discarding a red Queen on a red eight. This was the fourth game of rummy they had played and he had lost each of the previous three, which surprised him as he considered himself quite good at cards. He was trying to concentrate now, not wishing for a complete whitewash.

'Last card,' said Victoria as she turned up the nine of spades and bit her lip in anticipation of another victory; she gave a whoop of delight when it came. 'Gin,' she cried, clapping her hands together happily.

'Four in a row,' said Edmund, shaking his head. 'You're on a roll.'

'Mother and I play cards all the time,' she confided in him. 'Don't tell anyone, but we play for money and she always loses to me. I consider it something of a private income at this stage.'

'A card shark,' he replied, smiling. 'Really, Victoria. I'm surprised at you, taking advantage of me this way.'

She raised an eyebrow, wondering whether this was the beginning of a flirtation with her at last, but he had already reached for the pack and was shuffling them, ready to deal another hand. She sighed. Looking around, she searched the deck for any other eligible young men but there didn't seem to be any. It was a most disappointing selection. Usually when they travelled, there was at least a dozen who would vie for her hand. And on those rare occasions when she herself found someone to whom she was desperately attracted the competition alone would make them jump into action. They continued their game and when it became clear that Edmund had meant nothing particularly teasing in his 'taking advantage of me' comment, she felt herself growing more irritated with him. And completely at his will.

'Do you know that boy over there?' Edmund asked after a moment, torn between concentrating on his cards, determined to win, and noticing the young, dark-haired lad watching them from a distance. Victoria turned around quickly to look at him and, as she did so, he turned away and looked out to the sea before stepping quickly back in fear of falling in, his hands pressed flat against the funnel behind him.

'No,' she said, turning back to Edmund. 'I did notice him earlier, staring at me though, but I have no idea who he is.'

'I believe you have an admirer,' he replied with a smile and, despite herself – not to mention to her utter amazement – she felt herself begin to blush.

'I hardly think so,' she said. 'He's just a child. He can't be more than fourteen or fifteen.'

'Well, you're only a couple of years older than that yourself,' said Edmund. 'Perhaps you could develop a shipboard romance.'

Victoria snorted. 'Not with a little boy,' she said. 'What do you think I am, some sort of cradle-snatcher? I do have some standards, you know. I hardly need to start trawling the kindergartens for excitement.'

Edmund laughed. 'I have no doubt of it,' he said.

'And what about you?' she asked, ready to delve a little deeper into his psyche. 'Have you found any young ladies on board who take your fancy?'

He shifted uncomfortably in his seat and she was delighted to notice his discomfort. 'No,' he said gruffly before playing another card. 'Why can't I win?' he asked the heavens.

'Don't change the subject, Edmund.'

'I wasn't aware we *had* a subject.'

'We did. It was romance.'

'And I thought we were just playing cards.'

She smiled at him coyly and within a few moves had the game won once again. Edmund sighed in frustration. 'I seem to have no luck,' he said, picking up the pack and shuffling it again. After a moment he stopped and began to count them. 'There's only forty-nine cards here,' he said, looking across at his companion in surprise.

'What's that?' she asked innocently.

'I said, there's only forty-nine cards in this pack. I thought there was something strange going on. There's no . . .' He counted again and searched through the cards before nodding forcefully. 'I thought as much,' he said. 'There are only two Kings instead of four and we're missing an Ace as well. No wonder I can't win. I was counting on some of those cards.'

'Oh,' said Victoria, feigning surprise. 'That must be an old pack. We've been playing with them for weeks. Maybe we left some of them behind in our rooms in Antwerp.'

'Indeed,' Edmund said suspiciously, pleased now that they had not been playing for money.

'Well, I hope you're not suggesting that I've been *cheating*,' said Victoria, her hand rushing to her throat as if the very idea took her breath away.

'Of course not,' he replied, although he wasn't so sure. 'It's just a game, after all. But I think we'll need a fresh pack if we're to continue.'

Victoria thought about it and she now wondered whether she actually had the nerve to go through with her plan. She had hidden the three cards earlier before bringing the remainder of the pack on deck with this eventuality in mind. Indeed, she had been a little surprised that it had taken Edmund so long to discover that some cards were missing and had begun to wonder whether they were destined to spend their entire afternoon playing gin rummy together outside, short of two Kings and an Ace. Finally she decided that if she did not act now, then he never would and, steeling herself for rejection, made her brazen suggestion. 'I have another pack in my cabin,' she said, not catching his eye. 'A new pack. Let's go and get it.'

Edmund narrowed his eyes. 'I'll wait here if you like,' he said. 'I'll mind the chairs.'

'There are plenty of chairs,' she said, laughing as she looked around. 'You don't mind walking with me, do you? I don't want that boy to follow me.'

Edmund nodded. 'Well if you like . . .' he said slowly. They stood up and she took his arm, her heart beating a little faster now that she had him where she wanted him. Walking quickly along the deck and passing Tom DuMarqué without so much as a glance, she led him towards the companionway and back to her cabin, thrilled by the prospect of what lay ahead.

Captain Kendall watched them from his vantage point in the wheelhouse and recognized them as first-class passengers. Something caught his eye about Edmund as he disappeared out of sight, but he couldn't quite put his finger on what it was. There was something unusual, however. Something—

'Captain,' said Billy Carter, interrupting his reverie.

'Oh, what is it man?' he asked in an irritated tone, causing the younger man to raise an eyebrow in surprise. Kendall closed his eyes for a brief moment in order to regain his equilibrium. 'What?' he repeated in a calmer voice.

'I was just going to say that I'm going off duty now, but I'll be in my cabin if you need me,' he said.

'Very well.'

'And on the desk over there I've left a list of the names of those passengers who'll be dining at your table to-night.'

'No bores, I hope, Mr Carter?'

'Only myself, sir.'

'You?'

'Well, it's tradition, isn't it, sir? For the first officer to dine at the captain's table on the second night of a voyage.'

Kendall thought about it. Was it a tradition? If it was, it was a new one to him. Mr Sorenson ate with him every night on board anyway, but that was just their habit. He was unaware that there were actual rules governing it. Still, not wishing to appear ignorant of the fact, he nodded gruffly. 'Of course,' he said. 'Who else then?'

'Well there's Mr Zéla and his nephew, a Master DuMarqué.'

'The Presidential Suite?'

'Of course.'

Kendall nodded. 'Zéla?' he asked. 'DuMarqué? What kind of names are those?'

'They're Frenchmen, sir.'

'Frenchmen,' the captain repeated, exasperated. 'God help us all.'

'And then there's Mrs Drake and her daughter Victoria,' continued Billy Carter. 'Mrs Drake was very keen to join the party.'

'Rich? Annoying? Obsequious?'

'A very pleasant woman, I'm sure, sir. And then I've invited Mr Robinson and his son Edmund and also a Miss Hayes, as they seem to have struck up a friendship together. Should be a lively group, sir.'

'I am moist with anticipation,' said Kendall in a dry tone.

'Yes, sir,' said Carter after a moment, surprised by the comment. 'Well, if there's nothing else then, Captain, I'll retire until dinnertime.'

'There's nothing else, Mr Carter. Off you go.' He watched as the first officer climbed down the steps and disappeared into the crowd on the steerage deck. He checked his watch. Five thirty. Two and a half hours until the meal ordeal, and then an hour or two of forced conversation and bonhomie before he could retire himself. For the first time in his career he began to wonder whether he was really cut out for this job.

Although dinner was served at any time between seven thirty and ten, invitations for tonight's captain's table had been set for eight o'clock, as this was the time when Captain Kendall preferred to eat. While he was adjusting his tie in the mirror of his cabin, all of those fortunate enough to be joining him were in varying degrees of excitement about the meal ahead, and each was preparing for it in a slightly different way.

In Cabin A7, Mrs Antoinette Drake was leaning closer to her mirror and adjusting the light; she could see a faint wisp of a moustache returning above her lip and she sighed in exasperation. She had gone for a beauty treatment in Antwerp but the silly girl who had taken charge of her had forgotten to wax her upper lip. She reached for her powder puff and dabbed at it gently. Mrs Drake had chosen an extravagant dark-green dress and a brassiere which practically pushed her breasts over the top of it. They rose upwards as she breathed in and one could almost hear them arguing with each other as to which would be released first. Staring at her reflection, she managed to convince herself that she still had the sexual allure of an eighteen-year-old debutante.

'Victoria, do try to cheer up a little,' she said, catching her daughter's eye in the mirror. 'You should be excited about tonight. How many girls of your age get to dine with a ship's captain?' Fully dressed in a splendid red evening gown, Victoria was sitting at the side of her bed staring into space, the humiliation of the afternoon still playing on her mind. 'What's wrong with you this evening anyway? You look as if your whole world has just come to an end.'

'Nothing's wrong with me,' she snapped. 'I'm just hungry, that's all. Aren't you ready yet?'

'I'm going as fast as I can. Don't rush me.'

'It's almost eight o'clock.'

'It's a lady's privilege to be late,' explained her mother. 'That's a thing you have to learn, my dear. Keep the gentlemen waiting. If we were to be the first to arrive at the table, it would be an embarrassment to all.'

Victoria was already feeling more than embarrassed at what lay ahead, for she knew that one of her dining companions would be Edmund Robinson and she prayed that the table would be large enough for her to keep as far away from him as possible. Their afternoon had come to an abrupt end when she brought him back to her cabin to find the new pack of cards. Closing the door firmly behind them, she had invited him to take a seat while she looked for them, but instead he had gone over to the dressing table and looked at the few photographs which Mrs Drake had arranged there in their frames.

'My father,' said Victoria, stealing up behind him and looking over his shoulder at the image of a thin, ageing man, his dark eyes staring angrily at the camera, his shoulders hunched. 'He doesn't like having his picture taken. Gets quite furious about it in fact.'

'I can tell,' said Edmund, looking at him with a frown.

Before moving away, Victoria's eyes swivelled slightly to the left and she was immediately transfixed by the pale, clear skin of Edmund's neck, so entirely unblemished, so perfectly white, like a garden of snow which has not yet been walked upon. She breathed in his scent as she forced herself to step away and Edmund turned quickly, feeling a tickle on his ear.

'It's clever of you to bring extra cards,' he said and she turned around and stared at him, momentarily forgetting the reason they were there.

'Oh yes,' she said. 'The cards. Now where did I put them?'

'Victoria, are you listening to me?' She snapped herself out of her daydream and turned to look at her mother, who was standing at the door now, ready to leave. 'Come on,' she said. 'It's five past eight. The others should have arrived by now. Time to go.'

She frowned and stood up, shaking the memory from her head. 'Coming,' she said.

Martha Hayes had chosen one of her favourite dresses for the evening as well, a white chiffon gown which Léon Brillt, the one true love of her life, had bought for her after their engagement. She had thrown away most of Léon's gifts, but this dress was so beautiful – and so expensive – that she could not bear to part with it. And even though it reminded her of the evening he had presented it to her, one of their most memorable evenings together (the evening, in fact, when she had given herself to him for the first time), she forced herself to dismiss the memory and enjoy the way she now felt in the dress instead. Leaving her cabin, she met Billy Carter, who was in his formal white uniform and who was also making his way to the dining hall.

'Why, Miss Hayes,' he said, impressed by her transformation. 'You look very fetching tonight.'

'Thank you, Mr Carter,' she said with a smile. 'And thank you again for the kind invitation. I will feel quite privileged to be dining with the captain.'

'You're very welcome. We have a nice group together tonight, I think. And Captain Kendall is always keen on getting to know the passengers. He's a very friendly man,' he lied. He just hates me, he thought to himself.

'You've sailed together often?'

'This is our first time actually,' he replied. 'The regular first officer, Mr Sorenson, has been laid low by appendicitis.'

'Not really?' she exclaimed, surprised. 'My fiancé

almost died three months ago from a burst appendix.'
The words, although quite true, were out before she
could stop them and she felt an immediate urge to take
them back; before she could say anything more on the
subject, however, they were entering the dining hall and
Billy Carter was leading her over to meet the captain.
The table itself was circular and five of the other guests
were already seated, the captain, Matthieu Zéla and his
nephew Tom, and John Robinson and Edmund.

'I believe you know the Robinsons,' said Billy Carter,
pulling out Martha's chair for her as she sat down. 'But
have you met Mr Zéla and his nephew?'

'We met earlier today,' said Martha, acknowledging
the man with a nod of the head. 'Lovely to see you again.
And Tom,' she said, looking at the boy, who was staring
at her with the same degree of suspicion he had shown
earlier. Within a moment, however, his eyes were elsewhere as Mrs Antoinette Drake strode into the hall with
her daughter two feet behind her and marched over to
the table as if she was about to announce that she was
taking command of the ship and they should all fall to
their knees and pay homage.

'Apologies to all for our tardiness,' she said, taking
the empty seat next to the captain and to the left of Mr
Robinson, who edged along the table a little. 'I hope we
didn't keep you waiting. I was applying my face.'

'I just arrived myself, Mrs Drake,' said Martha Hayes.
'A lady's privilege, as they say.'

'Oh! Miss Hayes,' Mrs Drake replied, her smile fading
a little as she noticed her sitting opposite. 'Why, you're
simply everywhere, aren't you?'

Martha smiled graciously, wondering what on earth
she had ever done to incur the lady's dislike.

There was only one empty seat left, between Billy
Carter and Tom DuMarqué, and Victoria was forced to
take it. Tom licked his lips like a lion about to pounce
on its prey, but preferring to sniff at it a little first.

Formal introductions were made and the captain gave the signal to the steward to serve the first course.

Edmund, sitting across the table from Victoria, tried to avoid her eye during the meal but he could not help but be drawn to look at her from time to time. He too was embarrassed about what had happened earlier, but they seemed to have made an unspoken pact not to mention it now. After Victoria had finally retrieved the fresh pack of cards, he had stepped towards the door of her cabin but she had blocked the way, smiling at him suggestively.

'Something tells me you don't want to be left alone with me,' she said.

He shook his head, surprised. 'Not at all, Victoria,' he said. 'Why would you think that?'

'I don't think you trust yourself with me.'

'Victoria—' he began, but before he could continue she stepped forward and immediately silenced him by placing a finger on his lips. The sensation was thrilling to her and she could have stood like that for hours, her fingertip pressed against his full, red lips. She knew immediately what she wanted to do and, removing her finger, closed her eyes and put a hand behind his head, pulling him forward to kiss her.

'Victoria!' said Edmund, breaking away from her embrace. 'This isn't a good idea. I think we should return to the deck.'

'In a moment,' she purred.

'Victoria, no,' he insisted, pulling away and shaking his head. 'Please stop.'

'What is wrong with you?' she asked, furious, her eyes sparkling with anger. 'Aren't you attracted to me? Don't you know that I was one of the most sought-after girls in Paris? Why are you treating me like this?'

'I'm not treating you in any way,' he said defensively, making for the door now. 'I just think you might be feeling the effects of the sea a little.'

'The *what*?'

'Really, Victoria, I don't think we should . . . Anyway, I promised my . . . my father that I would meet him in our cabin around now. I should be getting on my way.'

And with that he raced from the room, failing even to close the door behind him – which she did, loudly, before spending the next ten minutes pacing around, cursing Edmund under her breath, damning herself for being so forward, and yet falling for him even more. His innocence, his fear of intimacy, beguiled her. It must be his first time, she thought, dazzled by the idea.

'This is such a charming way to spend an evening,' said Mrs Drake, her voice carrying over the conversation of all the others. 'My husband, Mr Drake, and I have been on boats before but never have we dined at the captain's table.'

'A pleasure to have you, ma'am,' muttered the captain.

'Miss Hayes was telling me earlier that she's engaged to be married,' said Billy Carter, tucking into his steak with gusto. 'Does your fiancé live in Canada then?' he asked her.

'Oh!' she exclaimed, surprised and embarrassed that he would bring this up at the dinner table.

'Engaged!' said Mrs Drake, as if the very idea was preposterous. 'Well, how lovely. And tell me, my dear,' she added, staring at Martha's naked fingers. 'Where is your engagement ring then?'

'Congratulations, Miss Hayes,' said Matthieu Zéla simultaneously. 'We should have a toast.'

'No,' said Martha, shaking her head. 'I'm afraid that Mr Brillt turned out to . . . that is, Mr Brillt and I . . . well I'm sorry to say that we have been forced to end our engagement.'

'I see,' said Mrs Drake, her nostrils flaring at the whiff of a scandal.

'Did he get another woman then?' Tom asked, turning

135

to wink at Victoria, who stared at him as if he was the source of a bad smell.

'Tom,' said Matthieu quietly.

'It's a private matter,' said Martha, unable to look at any of them and instead staring down at her meal in embarrassment. 'I'd rather not go into it, if you don't mind.'

'Perhaps we should change the subject,' said Mr John Robinson, looking around hopefully and sorry for her discomfort.

'Quite right too,' said Matthieu. 'Tell me, Edmund,' he said quickly, turning to his left. 'What business are you hoping to go into in Canada?'

'I'm a doctor,' said Mr Robinson, answering instead. 'I hope to set up my own surgery. Edmund will continue with his studies.'

'Is that right?' said Matthieu, looking at him and nodding slowly. 'And how old are you, Edmund?'

The boy blinked and thought about it. 'Seventeen,' he said.

'And you, Captain Kendall,' Mrs Drake said, 'your wife must miss you terribly while you're at sea.'

'Seventeen. A fine age,' said Matthieu. 'You must be pleased to have found a companion on board in Miss Drake, then?' he asked, nodding across at Victoria, who glared at him furiously.

'I am a single man,' the captain said formally, a quick flicker of a frown crossing his face. Half hearing the other conversation, he remembered seeing Edmund and Victoria disappear back to their cabins together earlier and he suspected licentious behaviour.

'You've never been married? Not even a widower?'

'All the passengers I have met seem very friendly,' said Edmund, not wishing to single out Victoria especially.

'Indeed.'

'My wife's back in Antwerp. About to have a baby,' said Billy Carter.

'I've always found widowers to be very charming.'

'Some are not as friendly as others,' said Victoria.

'You're very quiet, Mr Robinson,' said Matthieu Zéla. 'Enjoying your meal?'

'How lovely for you,' said Martha Hayes. 'Is it your first?'

'I can be pretty friendly, you know,' said Tom, his hand lowering beneath the table to squeeze Victoria's knee.

'Delicious,' said Mr Robinson, carving his chicken expertly, separating the legs and breast with ease.

'Of course a widow is a different matter entirely. Some of them can be very crude. It's because they finally have control of the finances, you see. I expect some widows have tried to capture your attentions on board, Captain, haven't they?'

'First of many, I hope!'

'*Get your hands off me right now, you little shit, or I'll cut off your balls with my knife*,' Victoria whispered, and Tom removed his hand immediately, swallowing nervously but finding himself incredibly turned on.

'Where are you from, Mr Robinson, originally? Were you based in Antwerp?'

'I perform my duties on board, Mrs Drake. Nothing else,' said the captain with a dry laugh. This kind of questioning of his personal life was one of the reasons he hated these meals so much.

'I thought we might have a game of bowls in the morning, Victoria,' Edmund suggested, keen to mend fences with her and noticing the angry look on her face, unaware that it was actually caused by the unwanted attentions of Tom DuMarqué.

'And will you be home in time for the birth?'

'What a charming idea. Victoria would enjoy that, wouldn't you, dear?'

'No,' said Mr Robinson. 'I've been based in London for many years. I'm from America originally.' Edmund shot him a look, unsure just how honest he should be with this group.

'Oh yes. I wouldn't miss it for the world.'

'Perhaps,' said Victoria, unwilling to commit herself. Regretting it now, are you? she wondered.

'What part of America?'

'Is there any dancing later on, Captain? If so, I would so enjoy it if you would accompany me.'

The captain tapped his glass quickly with his knife, producing a clear ring that brought them all to silence.

'Ladies and gentlemen,' he said to the table as a whole. 'I give you the *Montrose*. And to a safe voyage.'

'A safe voyage,' they all intoned, before taking a drink.

'When I lived in Paris,' said Tom DuMarqué, breaking the sudden silence which followed the toast, 'people said I would come to nothing, on account of my getting in trouble all the time for stealing and breaking and entering. But when *I* go to America,' he added, glaring at Edmund whom he had already identified as his natural enemy, 'I'm going to end up in Hollywood and be a film star.'

'Gracious!' said Mrs Drake, unsure which element of that sentence scandalized her more, his criminal background or his intended career. Victoria merely snorted, as if the very idea was preposterous.

'A what?' asked Mr Robinson, looking across at the boy.

'A film star,' he repeated. 'It's all the rage now, you know. They're setting up studios in Los Angeles and anyone can go there and be in the pictures. You must have seen some of them.'

'Perhaps one or two,' he said, trying to remember. 'I've visited the nickelodeon once or twice. But surely there's not a *living* to be made in it, is there?'

'More than a living,' said Tom with certainty. 'They

say a fellow who gets in at the start of it could make a million dollars before he dies.'

'What nonsense,' said Victoria.

'They won't take off,' said Billy Carter. 'You'll never beat the music halls. They're the most fun there is. That's where I met my wife, you know,' he added. 'She was a chorus girl there.'

'A chorus girl?' asked Mrs Drake. 'How shocking!'

'Women like that,' said Mr Robinson in a quiet voice, 'are nothing but trouble. They parade themselves around like cheap whores, hoping to trap some fellow, and then, once they've got him, they bleed him dry. If I had my way, they'd close down every music hall in the land.'

The table descended into silence; his words had been spoken in an inappropriate tone and Mrs Drake could see how his knuckles whitened as he gripped his knife and fork.

'Well, not my Delilah,' said Billy Carter finally to break the tension. 'They broke the mould when they made her.'

Captain Kendall pushed his plate aside and signalled the steward to begin clearing the table, even though several of his companions were still eating. Pulling out his pocket watch, he flicked it open and exclaimed loudly, 'Oh my, the time!'

'Captain, you're not leaving us already, surely?' asked Mrs Drake, disappointed.

'Duty calls, dear lady,' he said, happy to be obsequious now that he was making his leave, 'duty calls. Mr Carter, you'll take care of our guests, I presume?'

'Of course, sir.'

'Good. Then I'll be on deck if I'm required.'

A thin balcony ran around the navigating room and it was the captain's custom to smoke a cigar there before retiring for the evening. He stood in a darkened spot where he would not be noticed, save for the bright red spark of his cigar. It was peaceful there and he could hear nothing except the muted sound of music from the steerage deck some distance away and the harmony of the waves as the *Montrose* crashed through them. About to turn in for the night, he noticed two passengers emerging from below deck, where he had dined earlier, and he watched as they huddled into the shadows, looking around themselves nervously.

'Let's go back to the cabin,' said Mr Robinson in a hushed tone. 'We can speak there.'

'In a moment,' said Edmund. 'I just need a breath of fresh air.'

Captain Kendall was going to signal them that he was aloft, for Mr Robinson had proved himself his favourite of the passengers so far. Not cursed with the crudity of Mrs Drake, nor the distance of her daughter, nor the colourful gallantry of Mr Zéla, nor the adolescent pinings of his nephew, nor the simpering nature of Miss Hayes, nor the cocky arrogance of Mr Carter, he was about the only one to whom he would have spoken in private. Had Edmund not been present, he might have even invited him to join him in a cigar, a replacement for Mr Sorenson.

'Are you really playing bowls with that girl tomorrow?' asked Mr Robinson.

'I didn't want her to be upset,' replied Edmund. 'I'm sure she's a pleasant enough sort underneath it all. Just a little self-centred.'

'She will try to seduce you again,' he said. 'Count on it.'

I knew it, thought Captain Kendall, strangely pleased that the implication was that the boy had rejected her advances.

'I don't think so,' said Edmund. 'She'll be too busy fighting off that DuMarqué boy. Did you see the way he was looking at her? I thought he was going to eat her alive. And he's only a child.'

'I barely saw him,' said Mr Robinson, pulling Edmund closer to him. 'My eyes, as ever, were locked on you.'

Silence lingered between them for a moment as they stared into each other's eyes. Captain Kendall leaned further forward, squinting in the darkness to make out what was going on. As he watched, his eyes grew wider and it was all that he could do not to let out a shout. Mr Robinson and Edmund were engaged in a passionate kiss, their lips locked, their hands pressed tight against each other's backs. He stared and could not believe what he was witnessing. It was too shocking, too outrageous, too—

Mr Robinson ran his hands through Edmund's hair and without warning it came loose, falling to the deck in a bundle. Captain Kendall gasped and thought he would be sick. What the—? he asked himself, before narrowing his eyes and noticing that what he had seen as the boy's hair was in fact a wig and that beneath it lay a tight pack of brunette curls.

'My hair,' Edmund whispered, reaching down to retrieve it. As he did so, the light caught his face in outline, and Captain Kendall saw the delicate profile and real hair for the first time. Edmund gave a quick glance around to ensure that no one had seen and replaced the wig on his head carefully. 'Let's go below,' he said, and they disappeared down the stairs towards the first-class cabins.

'A woman!' said Captain Kendall out loud, his face pale, amazed by what he had witnessed. 'Edmund Robinson is a woman!'

6

The Second Mistake

New York; London: 1893–1899

At first, the crowds of people in New York City intimidated Dr Hawley Harvey Crippen and he longed to return either to the less metropolitan world of Detroit or to the peace and quiet of Ann Arbor. He had been engaged by DeWitt Lansing Medical Suppliers as their sales representative in Manhattan and spent his mornings trawling from doctor's surgery to doctor's surgery, keeping appointments with men often younger than himself, trying to interest them in purchasing the latest tools or medicines for their practices. It was depressing work for him as he had never wanted to be the salesman, but to be the doctor instead. Their attitudes made him feel small; his clients glanced at their watches impatiently and cut him off in mid-sentence. Despite himself, he kept his anger inside and scraped a living. His afternoons were spent at DeWitt Lansing's warehouse near the South Street Seaport, where he filled whatever orders he had managed to obtain during the day and dispatched them. He received a small basic salary and earned a fifteen per cent commission on all sales. It was enough to cover the rent on a tiny one-room apartment in the East 50s; it was damp and depressing and the children from upstairs cried constantly. He could, in fact, have afforded something a little better but, rather than spend the money, he decided to save it for a real release from this life and had managed to amass almost six hundred dollars in a short period of time, and he hid it under one of the floorboards in his room.

The morning of 18 June 1893 found him standing outside the doors of Dr Richard Morton, a general practitioner located on the corner of Bleeker Street and the Avenue of the Americas. Dr Morton was a regular client; Hawley's predecessor at DeWitt Lansing, one James Allvoy, had booked his thrice-yearly appointments in the diary before leaving the firm for a career in the circus, where he was to be a lion-tamer. This was Hawley's first visit to the surgery, but he was aware that there was a good commission to be earned here if he played his cards right.

A middle-aged woman opened the door, and he offered her his most obsequious smile. 'Hawley Crippen,' he said, doffing his hat. 'From DeWitt Lansing Medical Suppliers. Here to see Dr Morton.'

'Have you an appointment?' she asked, blocking the entrance with her bulk. He nodded and explained that he was the new representative for the firm, and with a sigh, as if it was inconveniencing her tremendously, she allowed him in and showed him into a small waiting room, where three patients were already sitting. 'I'll tell the doctor you're here,' she said, 'but he has to see all this lot yet, so there might be a wait.'

'Perfectly fine,' said Hawley, waiting until she had left before pulling a face and glancing at his watch anxiously. It was one o'clock already and he had one final appointment at two thirty before he needed to go to the warehouse. He couldn't afford to be late for either and he glanced at the three patients gathered in the waiting room, wondering whether he could figure out their symptoms by simply looking at them. An old man stared at the ground with a miserable expression on his face; his wheezing breath could be heard from across the room. Asthmatic, Hawley reasoned. New prescription, five minutes at most. A young woman kept herself bundled together in the shade beside the curtains, trying not to be noticed by anyone. Single, pregnant woman. Ten minutes. A teenage boy with his arm in a sling, looking bored and shooting looks across at the young woman when he thought she wasn't looking. Probably just needed the cast removed. Fifteen minutes. All going well, that should take him to about one thirty. It would take about forty-five minutes to go through the new Autumn range, which would leave him just enough time to make it to his final appointment of the day if he hurried. He gave a sigh of relief and watched the door anxiously.

In the end, it was almost 2 p.m. before Dr Morton summoned him into his office, and Hawley was already perspiring with a combination of heat and anxiety. To his disappointment, the surgery appeared to be surprisingly well stocked already, the shelves and cabinets filled with supplies, some of which he did not immediately recognize. Dr Morton looked at him suspiciously and offered no apologies for his tardiness. After seeing the three patients from the waiting room he had taken a break for some lunch, and Hawley could smell the roast beef and pickle on his breath as he sat down beside him, a little too close to him for comfort. I must remember to show him our latest remedies for halitosis, he thought to himself.

'I haven't seen you before, have I?' Dr Morton asked. 'What happened to that other fellow who used to come here? Short chap. Bad skin. Always scratching himself.'

'Mr Allvoy?' said Hawley. 'He found a new position. I will be taking the orders for DeWitt Lansing from now on. Hawley Crippen.' He decided not to tell the doctor exactly what exotic career path Mr Allvoy had chosen.

'New position indeed,' he snorted. 'In my day a fellow took a job and stayed in it for life, working his way up. Nowadays it seems the young men only stick with things for a few years at a time. That's the life of a hobo, not a working man.'

'Indeed,' said Hawley, opening his folder and bag of wares, unwilling to be drawn into a conversation about the decline and fall of contemporary youth. The first rule of a salesman's life, he knew, was not to argue with the client. 'Now, Dr Morton,' he began with affected cheerfulness, 'I have a very exciting range of products to show you today, beginning with a revolutionary new—'

'Before you start, young man,' the other said, raising a thick, wrinkled hand to silence him, 'it's probably worth my saying that Jenson's been here and I've been doing a lot of business with him recently, so orders will be down. No point arguing about it. Let's have that out in the open from the get-go.'

'Jenson?' Hawley asked, on hearing the name of DeWitt Lansing's most serious competitor among the medical suppliers of New York. 'But you've been one of *our* clients for so many years.'

'And I still am, my boy, I still am,' he insisted. 'It's just that he's been able to undercut you on some products and I've bought them from him. Others I know you do cheaper, so I'm happy to take a look at them, but the chances are I'll be splitting my business between you both from now on.'

Hawley swallowed and tried to keep calm. He spied a surgical knife on a side table and considered making a grab for it and losing it between Morton's eyes. There was nothing he could do if the doctor wanted to use two different suppliers, but he knew that it would reduce his commission. He worked through his order book, demonstrating some of the new products which he had brought with him, describing others, and the doctor took some and informed him that Jenson was supplying him with some of the others at a third off. By the time he had finished, Hawley could barely contain his anger. The order was less than half what he had expected and it was already half past two, by which time he should have been visiting Dr Albert Cuttle on the corner of Sixteenth Street and Fifth Avenue.

'Your face is bright red,' Dr Morton observed as Hawley gathered his things together silently. 'Are you sick? Want me to give you the once-over?'

'Not at all,' he replied. 'I'm a little disappointed, however, that you didn't afford us an opportunity to improve our terms with you before using a different supplier, that's all. After all, we have a long-standing relationship.'

'I've only just met you,' said Dr Morton with a smile, unwilling to be chastised in his own surgery.

'You have a long-standing relationship with my firm,' Hawley insisted. 'At my last surgery in Detroit, we honoured such arrangements.'

'Your last surgery?' he asked, surprised. 'But you're a representative, surely. Not a doctor.'

'Actually I *am* a doctor,' Hawley replied irritably. 'I simply haven't yet found a position in New York suitable to my talents. The good people at DeWitt Lansing recognized an opportunity in the meantime.'

'Well, what sort of a doctor are you?' asked Morton, not believing a word of it and irritated that this young upstart should speak to him like this; after all, it was his decision how he spent his money. 'What medical school did you attend?'

Hawley licked his lips, regretting having said anything. 'I hold a diploma from the Medical College of Philadelphia,' he said. 'And another as an eye and ear specialist from the Ophthalmic Hospital of New York.'

Dr Morton thought about it. 'Correspondence

courses?' he asked. Hawley nodded slightly. 'Then, sir, you are not a doctor,' said Dr Morton with a satisfied smile. 'It takes many years of study, full time, at a recognized medical institution to earn the title. One cannot simply fill in a few forms and send off for a certificate. That may be how people join the priesthood today, but not the medical profession.'

'I am Dr Hawley Harvey Crippen,' came the angry reply.

'Don't be ridiculous, man, you're nothing of the sort.' He pointed a bony finger at Hawley and wagged it in his face. 'Make no mistake, if I was to hear of a fellow such as yourself practising medicine in this city without a degree, I would have no choice but to inform the authorities. There are laws about such things, you know.'

Twenty minutes later, a minuscule order in his folder, Hawley found himself out on the street, clutching his bags angrily. He knew that what Dr Morton had said was, strictly speaking, quite true, and he hated him for it. Although he always introduced himself to people as a doctor, he was aware that he was stretching the legal description somewhat. In fact, his diplomas served only to allow him to practise as a physician's assistant, as he had done with the older Dr Lake in Detroit. To pretend otherwise was to deceive.

He pulled his watch from his pocket and looked at it. Almost three o'clock. He was too late for Dr Cuttle who, he knew from experience, would refuse to see him now. He considered going there anyway and pleading for a later appointment, but he knew he would be turned down, for that man was a strict observer of punctuality. He also had the ability to anger Hawley, for he was only twenty-four years old and was already a fully qualified doctor with his own surgery, which Hawley envied enormously. He had heard that the man was a distant Roosevelt cousin, and they had funded it for him.

'Enough!' he thought finally, adrift in the Manhattan grid. 'Enough of this day!'

He spent the afternoon back in his room, lying on his bed and staring at the ceiling. He felt a sensation of great loneliness. He had no friends in the city, no family. His thoughts drifted to Charlotte from time to time, but he knew that he did not miss her tremendously, and that in itself bothered him. He wondered whether he was really as cold as that implied. As for Otto, he hadn't laid eyes on him since dispatching him to his grandparents' home after Charlotte's death. He had communicated with his in-laws by post for a little while but lately had grown out of the habit for he had nothing to say to them and could not pretend to have any paternal feelings. In his heart, he knew that he would never see his son again.

Unusually for him, he decided to go out for the evening and drown his sorrows at a local music hall. He had seen the show advertised on billboards many times, for he passed by the theatre every day as he left his apartment, but he had never gone inside. The girl at the ticket booth was chewing gum and barely glanced at him as he paid the ten cents entry fee, but still he felt a little self-conscious as he sat at a table on his own, drinking beer while comedy performers and dance troupes came out on stage and went through their routines with as much enthusiasm as they could muster for the few cents they earned. The audience paid as much attention to their own conversations as they did to the stage; the rows of seats were only about half filled, while a good many patrons remained standing or sitting around the tables by the bar. An hour or more passed and several beers were consumed before Hawley began to grow tired and consider returning home. However, before he could leave, his attention was taken by the dapper, middle-aged man in the paisley waistcoat and the elaborate moustache who strode on to the stage, clapping his hands to call the audience to attention.

'Ladies and *geeeent*-lemen,' he announced loudly, stretching out the words like elastic, ignoring the mocking sounds coming from various sections of the theatre, the catcalls, the whistles. 'I now have the very great pleasure, yes the very *great* pleasure in*deeeed*, of introducing to you one of the true stars of the New York musical stage. She's been a favourite here at the Playbill Showhouse for six months now. Six months, ladies and gentlemen, of refinement! Of artistry! Of elegance! Please sit back and prepare to enjoy the musical stylings of the delightful, the delicious, the deliriously delectable Bella Elmore!'

Hawley glanced up from his drink only for a moment as a buxom girl of about seventeen marched out to muted applause – sounds which were in deliberate contrast to her enthusiastic introduction – before doing a double take and looking at her more closely. She was not unattractive of face, but she had quite broad shoulders and was a little heavy set for one so young. Her dark hair was piled up on top of her head, a few strands escaping down her neck, while her cheeks were heavily rouged. She sang three popular songs in quick succession – one of which was a little bawdy for his liking – and performed them merely adequately, taking barely any notice that most of the audience were talking their way through her routine. Hawley, however, was transfixed. He watched her, hoping that she would notice him, and as she finished her last song he caught her eye, offering her a gentle smile. She stared back at him for a moment carefully, as if unsure of his intentions, but finally she smiled back and gave him a polite nod of the head. She disappeared off the stage eventually to make way for a juggler with a waxed moustache, and Hawley looked around to see whether she might reappear in the audience but there was no sign of her.

After ten minutes, sighing and disappointed, he stood up, preparing to return home alone once again.

'And there was me thinking you might buy me a drink.' A voice came from behind him and he spun around to see the young singer standing there, hands on hips, smiling at him suggestively.

'I'd be honoured to,' said Hawley, a little flustered, clicking his fingers to attract the attention of one of the waitresses.

'Bottle of champagne, Cissie,' she said, ordering for them both as she sat down. 'And two glasses.' Hawley smiled, mentally scanning the contents of his wallet, hoping that he had enough money on him to pay for such excess. He was not to know that, whenever this girl caught the eye of a patron, she made sure to order the most expensive drinks from the bar. The more bottles of champagne she could convince customers to buy, the more dollars she found in her pay packet at the end of the week.

'Hawley Crippen,' he said, extending his hand. 'And you're Miss Bella Elmore, is that right?'

'Cora Turner,' she said, shaking her head. 'Bella's just my stage name. It has an elegant air, don't you think? Thought of it myself, don't you know.' She affected an elaborate accent, as if she had been brought up in Buckingham Palace, and not as the daughter of Russian-Polish immigrants in a tenement block in the borough of Queens. Cora Turner itself was also a pseudonym; she had been born Kunigunde Mackamotski but had quickly discarded that mouthful of a name.

'Very elegant indeed,' he replied, anxious to please. 'I enjoyed your singing very much, Miss Turner. You have a beautiful voice.'

'I know,' she said. 'I'm the best singer here.'

'I'm sure you are.'

She accepted the compliment without a word and lit a cigarette, holding his stare all the time. Usually the men made all the moves, but she could tell that he was a quiet one and needed some help. 'And what do you do then, Hawley Crippen?' she asked after a few moments' silence.

'I'm a doctor.'

'A doctor, eh? Very posh.'

'Not really,' he said, laughing a little. 'I specialize in ophthalmology. It's not as glamorous as it sounds.'

'Ophthalmology?' she asked, wrinkling up her nose and experiencing a little difficulty pronouncing the word. 'What's that then when it's at home?'

'The study of the eyes,' he replied.

'And you make a living off of that, do you?' she asked, gulping down a mouthful of champagne now as Hawley sipped his carefully.

'Oh yes.'

'I've always been told that I have beautiful eyes,' she said, fishing for a compliment.

'Indeed,' he replied, disappointing her. 'Might I ask how long you have been in the music-hall business?'

'Three years,' she said. 'Ever since I turned fourteen. I intend to be one of the world's finest opera singers. I just need to get the right voice coach, that's all. Only, they cost money. The natural gifts are there though, they just need training.'

'I have no doubt of it,' said Hawley. 'And you are from New York originally?'

She narrowed her eyes and leaned forward, closing them into a quiet conspiracy of two. 'Do you know why I came over here?' she asked him, and he shook his head. 'I came over here because when I was on stage I could feel your eyes burning through me.' She reached her hand under the table and placed it softly on his knee. He felt his body grow rigid with desire and fear. 'And when I looked over towards you, I thought to myself: there's a respectable gentleman and one I wouldn't mind having a drink with. Much kinder looking than most of the men we get in here.' She sat back – she'd used this line many times before – lit another cigarette and waited for him to respond.

'I apologize for staring,' he said.

'Don't. I'm on stage, you're supposed to be looking at me. It's better than half the fools here who just carry on talking to each other while I'm trying to perform. What are you doing here on your own anyway?'

'I had a long day and felt I needed a little refreshment. I don't normally drink alone, but tonight—'

'Tonight you just felt like one, am I right?'

He smiled. 'Yes,' he admitted. 'That's about it.'

'And where's your wife then? She doesn't mind you going to music-hall shows on your own?'

Hawley bowed his head slightly. 'My wife died three years ago,' he said. 'A traffic accident.'

Cora nodded but didn't express any sympathy; all she was doing was collecting information, filing it all away in her head for future use or exploitation. They sat staring at each other, unsure where to go from here, while she made up her mind about something in her head. 'Are you hungry, Dr Crippen?' she asked, deciding.

'Hungry?'

'Yes. I haven't eaten yet and I thought about going out for a little dinner. Would you like to join me?'

Again, Hawley could only think about the contents of his wallet, but there was something wonderfully attractive about this girl and it had been so long since he had enjoyed a pleasant conversation with a woman – with *anyone*, for that matter – that he could not help but agree. 'Certainly,' he said. 'I'd be delighted to.'

'Wonderful,' she said, standing up. He rose as well, but she placed a hand on his shoulder to push him back down in his seat. 'Let me go change,' she said. 'I'll just run back to my dressing room. Won't be five minutes. You'll still be here when I come back?'

'I'll still be here,' he promised.

Pulling off her stage outfit quickly in the dressing room she shared with three other girls, Cora stared at herself in the mirror and wondered whether she needed to apply any more lipstick.

'What's got the wind into you?' asked Lizzie Macklin, one of the dancers, unaccustomed to seeing Cora move so quickly.

'I've got a date.'

'So what's new? You go home with a different man every night of the week.'

Cora threw her an angry look but continued to change. 'I don't know,' she said after a pause. 'I think this one might be different. He looks like he might have some money.'

'You thought that about that bloke last Saturday night. Had his way with you and all, didn't he?'

'He was wearing a silk waistcoat and had a gold watch. How was I to know he'd stolen them?'

'Well, you could start by getting to know the men a bit first. Or save up for your own voice lessons, seeing as that's all you're after. What makes you think this one's any different?'

'I don't know,' said Cora. 'Call it intuition. But I think this might be it. I know that sounds silly, but I really do. If he's got a few dollars in his pocket and no wife, why, he might be the one to help me become a famous singer.'

'Famous singer!' said Lizzie. 'Always wanting something more than what you've got. Why does anyone need to be famous anyway?' she asked. 'Can't you just be happy here? You think you're so much better than the rest of us, Cora Turner.'

'You just watch,' said Cora, ready now and spinning round with a smile on her face as she made for the door. 'One of these days you're going to be reading all about me in the papers and you'll turn to your husband and say, "Why that's Cora Crippen! Cora Turner as was. We

153

used to be in the music hall together. And look what happened to her. Whoever would have thought it?"'

Soon afterwards, Dr Hawley Harvey and Mrs Cora Crippen packed their belongings and moved from New York City to London, England, where Cora believed her star would finally rise. In her mind had always been the idea that a man would come along, a man with money, a man with ambition, a man who would take her away from being bottom of the bill at the music halls of New York to top of the bill in the opera houses of Europe. The great actresses and singers belonged in London and Paris, she believed, not in Manhattan. And certainly not entertaining drunks every night, wandering home for ten minutes' pleasure with every prospective husband who walked through the door. She had waited for the right man to come along. But she got Hawley Crippen.

Unlike his new, younger wife, however, he was entirely happy to stay in America. Although he did not like his job, his savings were growing and he had considered a long-term, part-time course in a training hospital in New York which might eventually lead to his being able to use the word 'doctor' for real. He did not want to leave, but a showdown between the two had ensured that she would have her way.

'You don't want me to use my talents, do you?' she screamed at him in their small room in the East 50s of Manhattan. 'You want to keep me caged up like an animal in here. You're jealous of me.'

'My dear, that's simply not true,' said Hawley quietly, hoping that his own hushed tones would encourage her to speak more quietly too. Only two evenings before, a rather large man from downstairs had banged on their door and told him that if he could not shut up the screeching of his crazy wife, then he would do it for him, an offer that Hawley was increasingly considering.

'It *is* true,' she screeched. 'Look at you, you jumped-up little nothing, prancing around pretending to be a doctor when all you are is a salesman. I can be a great singer, Hawley. I could be a sensation on the London stage. New York's too full of singers. Over there I'll be exotic. People will pay to see me.'

'But London . . .' he whimpered. 'It's so far away.'

'Oh good heavens, it's almost the twentieth century! We could be there in two or three weeks' time. Six months from that, we could be dining with Queen Victoria at Buckingham Palace.'

The arguments continued. Sometimes she chose a different tack, pointing out that they could start afresh in London and he might be able to afford to go to medical school there. 'I'll be earning so much money anyway,' she said. 'I could be one of the great stage singers and I'll pay for your medical education. Then you can set up a practice on Harley Street and we'll entertain every night. Think of the parties, Hawley! Think of the life we can lead.'

When she spoke like that, tender and encouraging, he was more inclined towards the idea, but her mood could change on the turn of a coin. Sometimes he wondered how he had got into this situation in the first place. Shortly after meeting Cora he had fallen for her. She was company for him. She was kind and thoughtful and demure. He pretended to be something he wasn't, exaggerating his wealth and position; she did the same, pretending she was nice. Soon they became lovers and he could not stand to be parted from her. Unlike his first wife, who was shy and innocent until her death, Cora knew what she wanted from a man and sought it out. Although only seventeen years of age, fourteen years his junior, she had experience and talents between the sheets that shocked and entranced him. He was her way out of the gutter, and she was someone who listened to him and said she believed in him. They married and were both disappointed with the results.

155

Although he visited the vaudeville most nights and enjoyed her performances, he could not help but feel at the back of his mind that it would take more than a decent voice coach to make his new wife into a singing star. She could hold a tune, there was no doubt about that – but then so could he when he tried; it didn't make him Caruso. Her voice travelled only about halfway across the theatre and sounded more like a bird twittering on a windowsill than a morning chorus preparing to greet the sun. She practised her scales in their room until the unpleasant man from downstairs threatened to break both their necks, but the higher notes remained discordant. Still she maintained that she had enormous talent which the whole world would soon recognize.

In London, they found a house in South Crescent, off the Tottenham Court Road, and took the top floor at a reasonable rent. Hawley enjoyed the fact that he could walk around Bedford Square, along Montague Street and into the British Museum, where peace and quiet reigned at all times, where no one stood at the window practising broken arpeggios, and where he could sit and read books about medicine without being disturbed. He became more and more interested in the new world of pathology and forensic medicine, and read as many articles as he could about autopsies and the dissection of the human body. The pictures, crude line-drawings scattered throughout these pages, fascinated him and he wondered how a visitor might arrange to see an actual autopsy in progress. The books described the various instruments used, the tools required to remove the organs, the thin blades of the scalpels that cut through skin like hot knives through butter, the saws that opened the chest cavity, the forceps that separated the ribcage. Reading about them, thinking about them, sent a ripple of excitement through his whole body. His eyes would grow wide, his mouth dry; he became aroused. The museum had a good stack of medical journals, and whenever he sat with a pile *of Scientific Americans* or copies of the *British Medical Journal* he was brought immediately back to his childhood and youth in Ann Arbor, remembering Jezebel Crippen's determination to turn him away from the sinful world of medicine and back on the road for Jesus. He had cut off all communication with his parents long ago and had no idea whether either of them was still alive; he almost never thought about them, and when he did it was with no emotion or human feeling whatsoever.

Before long, their savings began to dwindle and Hawley was forced to look for work. Strolling along Shaftesbury Avenue late one afternoon in early spring, he saw a sign in a window of Munyon's Homoeopathic Medicines looking for a 'man for a good position with this firm' and stepped inside, presenting himself as Doctor Hawley Harvey Crippen, late of Detroit and New York City, now happily residing in the West End of London, and available for suitable employment.

James Munyon, the ageing owner of the company, listened to the unfamiliar accent and peered at him over his glasses, taking in his rather shabby clothes and shoes at a glance. Munyon was in his seventies and had worked in the medical trade all his life; his hands were stained with the colours of the various potions he had mixed up in pharmacies over the previous fifty years. His voice was raspy from a lifetime of breathing in their fumes. In all respects he resembled something out of a gothic horror story, a man half skin and bone and half chemicals. Hawley swallowed but held his nerve as he addressed him; he had determined that he would not be treated with the same level of disrespect in London that he had been shown in New York. After all, he was an educated man, a man of medicine, and not one to be looked down upon.

'It's not a medical position,' said Munyon, presuming

that when Hawley declared himself a doctor he was telling the truth. 'I'm looking for an office manager. Munyon's is an agency for homoeopathic medicines, not a surgery of any kind. You do understand that, don't you?'

'Certainly,' said Hawley, aware that any income right now was better than none. Although he still had about half his savings left, some of which was deliberately hidden from both the eyes and the mind of his charming wife, he did not want to dip into them any further. And now that she was determinedly searching for a voice coach, he knew that a quick injection of cash was imperative; it was only a matter of time before she came demanding a handout. 'And homoeopathic medicine,' he began, struggling with the word and trying to recall the references to it he had read in the medical magazines at the British Museum. 'That's . . . ?'

'We deal with complementary medicines, Dr Crippen. Our clients prefer to treat diseases with minute doses of natural substances which, taken by a healthy person, would produce symptoms of disease. However, correctly applied to the ill, they can provide a remarkable cure. You are familiar with the advances in homoeopathic medicine in recent years, of course?'

'Naturally,' he lied. 'But in America, the market is currently small and medical attention to it has been slight.'

'It's still taking time to win over the disbelievers,' Munyon admitted. 'Many doctors won't have anything to do with it. They still prefer to treat everything with potions and lotions, knives and bleeding. Leeches, even. Archaic methods, if you ask me.'

Hawley was slightly surprised by the modern notions of Mr Munyon, for his frailty and age had made him believe that the old man would be a traditionalist. The offices had a close, unusual smell, the cabinets filled with rainbow-coloured cartons and packets of strangely named substances. 'The clients come here?' he asked, intrigued by the Aladdin's cave he had walked into. 'They seek medical advice here?'

'Sometimes, but mostly they collect prescriptions,' said Munyon. 'There are several homoeopathic clinics around London and we keep in close contact with them, of course. They prescribe certain treatments and we fill them. In that manner, we work a little like a pharmacy. However, we also advertise the non-prescriptive treatments for regular consumer use. The early days were difficult, but times have improved considerably. Which is why I'm looking to hire an office manager.'

'Well,' said Hawley, fascinated by all he saw, despite his natural inclination to be suspicious of anything that was not entirely scientific. 'If you will give me a chance, I'm sure that I won't let you down.'

Cora arrived home with a bag full of groceries under each arm and struggled to get her key into the lock of the front door without dropping any of them. After what she deemed a successful afternoon, she had decided to treat herself and Hawley to a more elaborate dinner than they were accustomed to. (Typically, she provided the ingredients and he prepared the meal.) It was a cold day and had started to drizzle while she was walking home from the grocer's shop. Her dress, which was slightly too long for her, had dragged on the pavement behind her, soaking up the rain from the puddles as she walked. Her hands were occupied, so she could not lift it, and she sighed in frustration, looking forward to getting back to their rooms where she could strip off and make herself a cup of tea. She had worn the dress, her best one, only because of where she had been going earlier in the day; but she regretted it now, for it would need washing. Upon entering the house in South Crescent, one came first to a small lobby area which led to the stairway; on the ground floor lived the Crippens' neighbours, the Jennings family, and although they were ostensibly polite to each other at all times it was clear that Mrs Jennings and Mrs Crippen could barely tolerate each other, desperately trying to outdo the other whenever they met. The Jenningses, Irish Catholics, had six children, aged from eight months to eight years, and they struck Cora as an unruly crew, forever smeared with the remains of their breakfasts or dinners, constantly staring at her as she passed by, like a bunch of suspicious cats. There was not an ounce of maternal instinct in Cora and, looking at the Jennings brood, she could not help but feel that these were children only a mother could love. Unlocking the door now and stepping inside, she was confronted by the smallest child, only ever referred to as Baby, crawling around the ground-floor area. Baby – Cora didn't even know whether the Jennings had ever bothered to give the child a name – stopped his/her movements and watched her as she closed the door.

'Good afternoon,' said Cora a little nervously, for something about the infant always unsettled her. When forced to converse, she spoke in adult tones and words, refusing to kowtow to convention by gurgling and cooing at the infant like a demented person. She made for the stairway, but before she could set foot on it Mrs Jennings emerged from her living room, her hands and cheeks dusted with flour from the bread she was baking, in search of her smallest child.

'Oh, good afternoon, Mrs Crippen,' she said, affecting the upper-class tones she used when addressing her, in stark contrast to the East End accent she employed when screaming at Mr Jennings, who was frequently inebriated. 'Look at you. Soaked to the skin.'

'I got caught in the rain,' Cora explained, irritated that she should be seen like this, her dress wet and dirty, her hair falling down in soaking strings from beneath her hat.

'You poor thing. Don't you look like a wet dish-cloth!'

'Oh, but you're covered in flour, Mrs Jennings,' Cora said sweetly. 'Hawley and I always buy our bread from the store. It must taste so much better when circumstances force you to make your own. A sense of achievement brings a smile to even the poorest faces.'

'Oh yes,' Mrs Jennings replied, more than capable of responding in kind. 'And it must be so much easier, bringing your shopping home when you're a muscular thing like you are. Why, the first time I saw you I thought you were a man with those broad shoulders of yours.'

Cora smiled. 'Good afternoon,' she said, gritting her teeth together but too wet and cold to continue the badinage. 'But you know what it's like, Mrs Jennings,' she offered, before continuing on her way. 'Once I start to shop I can't seem to stop myself. I can't bear to wear last season's clothes. Some people manage to do so and keep them amazingly fresh, but I just don't have that gift. That's a lovely blouse you're wearing, by the way. I used to have one just like it.'

Mrs Jennings smiled. For her part, her main reason for disliking Cora was the American accent which still poured through the affected upper-class tones.

'Not that I was just out shopping, you understand,' continued Cora, placing her bags on the ground now as their conversation continued. 'I had a meeting earlier with Señor Berlosci, my voice coach. The air in London is so vile that I need a little help to retrain my vocal cords.'

'Really,' said Mrs Jennings, her smile a frozen block of ice anchored to her face. 'I was always under the impression that singing was a natural gift. One could either do it or not do it. One didn't need to be trained for it. A little like motherhood in that way.'

'For the average person, yes. But I am a trained

professional, Mrs Jennings. Why, in New York I was the headline act in music halls throughout the city. Someone with my abilities needs to value their voice like a musician would a Stradivarius. That's a violin,' she added with a smile. 'Do you know, I spend almost a shilling a week on honey, just to lubricate my voice every morning and evening? Why, that's probably as much as you spend on feeding Baby.'

Mrs Jennings considered grabbing Cora by the hair and pounding her head against the wall until blood poured from both her ears, but she restrained herself. An uneasy harmony resided between the two floors on South Crescent and an unspoken feeling that those who were on the ground floor lived below stairs, while those above were the gentry. For their own parts, the ladies' husbands scarcely spoke to each other at all, being entirely different sorts. Hawley Crippen was as far removed from the drunken sloth that was Paddy Jennings as could possibly be imagined. It astonished him that the man's face was permanently covered in a thick stubble which he never shaved off but which never seemed to develop fully into a beard. He wondered whether this was a medical marvel and considered writing a paper on it for the *British Medical Journal*. They had met from time to time in the corridor or on the stairs, one in his vest and trousers, smoking a cigarette and reeking of body odour and alcohol, the other in a suit and tie, his moustache finely combed, a walking stick in hand, his face tired and weary. They had little to say to each other, and Hawley always moved away with only a nod of greeting, aware that he was being watched contemptuously.

'He's the kind of man I want to punch on the nose,' Mr Jennings said to his wife frequently, before doing the same thing to her. 'I don't know why, it would just make me feel better.'

Señor Berlosci lived not far from the Crippens in a

comfortable house in Tavistock Square which he had inherited from an aunt who had died childless. Cora had seen his services advertised in *The Times* and had visited him earlier in the week, when he had made an appointment for her to come back to see him that day. Seeking to make a good impression, she wore her finest dress and hat and was immediately taken by the opulent, if rather gaudy, surroundings in which Berlosci lived. An Italian, he had lived in London for almost eight years and coached many aspiring singers and actresses, considering it a personal failure if they did not find success within a year of completing his programme, which included breathing exercises, vocal techniques and seduction by Berlosci himself. A single man, he had fathered seven children that he knew of, but recognized none of them. His recent birthday, his fiftieth, had seen no decrease in his libidinous appetite; if anything, he saw age as a challenge to it and continued to seduce his way around the theatres and music halls of London shamelessly. Although he was not immediately attracted to Cora – her wide shoulders were always the first thing one noticed about her, followed closely by her grizzly dark hair and thin lips – he made it a personal rule not to reject a potential lover on the grounds of attraction alone. Personal pleasure was all that was important to him, both musically and romantically, and even ugly women could provide that.

'Mrs Crippen,' he said, exaggerating his Italian accent somewhat as he entered the room in a wave of lilac aftershave and hair tonic. (First impressions were also important to him.) 'Delighted to see you again. You are here to excite me with your talents, are you not?'

'I hope so, Señor Berlosci,' she replied, flattered and attracted at the same time. 'Honestly, I don't think I need too much work, just a little help, that's all. I was quite the star in New York, you know.'

'You sang in New York?'

'Oh yes. All over Broadway,' she lied. 'As Bella Elmore. I'm very well known there. I only came to London because my husband, Dr Crippen, is setting up his own medical practice in the city. He's gone to receive his English licence today, as it happens. But I want to sing in London.'

'And become a star, yes?'

'Yes,' she said determinedly.

'Well, London is the place for it,' he said, smiling coyly. 'New York is all well and good, but to the more refined person it can be quite cheap, quite tasteless. But London – and Paris and Rome of course – these are centres of excellence. The truly great singers must ply their trade there, don't you agree?'

'I do,' she said breathlessly. 'Oh, I most certainly do.'

Berlosci positioned her by the window and offered her a few instructions as to what she should do; he sat by the piano and played a middle C, to which Cora responded with an arpeggio C-E-G-high-C-G-E-C. He played a D and she moved up a tone, then an E and she moved up another. He stopped at G and turned around to stare at her. Cora gave a gentle cough, as if to suggest that she had a cold and might not be performing at her best, making excuses for herself already.

'Very beautiful,' said Berlosci in a quiet voice that suggested he had just listened to a soloist from the heavenly choir of angels. 'You have a fine voice.'

'Thank you,' she said, feeling relieved for, despite her confidence with others, she was never entirely convinced at heart that she had what it took.

'We have much work to do, however.'

'We do?'

'Certainly. The natural gifts are there, but they need refining. Your breathing is poor. You are singing from the throat and not from the diaphragm, where truly the notes are formed. But these are techniques. They simply take work to perfect them.'

'Well, I'm willing to work, Señor Berlosci,' said Cora. 'I'll do whatever it takes.'

'And, of course, work is expensive. I charge two shillings an hour, and we would need to meet for four sessions a week, for an hour each time. How are these terms to you?'

Cora made a rapid calculation in her head and swallowed nervously. That was a lot of money to be found, particularly on the salary Hawley was earning from Munyon's. 'All right,' she said, nodding forcefully. 'When can we start?'

Waiting for Hawley to return now, Cora said a silent prayer that he would not refuse her the money to attend the voice lessons. He had been a lot more short-tempered with her recently and she had begun to worry that he was not as much under her control as she wished. That was something she needed to beat out of him. Their relationship could never survive, she knew, if he had too much to say for himself. She would simply inform him that she needed the money – that *they* needed it if they were to have a successful future together – and he would turn it over, no questions asked.

She heard him come in and walk up the stairs quickly. He hated lingering in the hallway in case Mr Jennings saw him and, drunk, challenged him to a fight. Stepping through the door, however, she saw something different in his eyes tonight, a look of utter frustration, anger and even hatred. He nodded at her and threw his hat on the bed, walking straight into the bathroom without a word, and she heard the sound of water running in the sink. When he emerged, a few minutes later, his face was pink and his collar wet, as if he had been washing away the filth of the day relentlessly.

'What an afternoon,' said Cora, declining to ask him whether anything was the matter, even though something clearly was. 'I went to see Señor Berlosci for my first lesson.'

'Who?' Hawley asked, distracted.

'Señor Berlosci. I told you about him. The voice coach. Over on Tavistock Square. I went to see him.'

'Oh yes,' he said, looking away and frowning when he saw the condition of their flat. The dirty dishes were still in the sink from last night's dinner and clothes were hanging down to dry from a rope extended from wall to wall. He saw a pair of Cora's stage tights suspended behind her like a pair of amputated legs, and they disgusted him, made his stomach turn. One thing he could say in Charlotte's favour was that at least she had kept a tidy home. 'That was today, was it?'

'Yes. And he's a real professional, Hawley. He said that in fifteen years of teaching he had never come across a more natural singer than me. He said that with the right guidance I could be the most successful singer on the London stage.' Naturally, he had never said any such thing.

'That's good news,' he muttered, clearing away some of the debris from the armchair and falling into it heavily, covering his eyes with his hands. 'I, however, have the opposite.'

She narrowed her eyes and stared at him. For a moment – just a moment – she felt concerned for him, as if some great calamity might have occurred and a little personal feeling was for once emerging in her. 'Hawley,' she said. 'What's happened? You look so tense.'

He gave a bitter laugh and shook his head, looking away from his wife so that she would not see the well of tears forming like puddles in his eyes. He was afraid to blink in case they tumbled down his cheeks like waterfalls. She had never seen him cry before and he did not want her to witness it now. 'I went to the Medical Association,' he began.

'Of course. I forgot. I wasn't thinking. Did you receive your licence?'

'Ha!' he said. 'I did not.'

Her heart sank and she sat down on a kitchen chair, praying that this was just a temporary setback. 'Why not?' she asked, when it was clear that he was not going to expand on this. 'Was it money? Do you need to pay for it?'

He turned and looked at her now and she could tell that he was genuinely upset. 'The Medical Association say that my diplomas are not valid in England. They say that to practise as a doctor I need to attend medical school in London and pass their certified exams. Which would, of course, take several years and more money than we can afford.'

Cora gasped. 'No!' she said. Her husband merely nodded. 'But Hawley, that's ridiculous. You're a trained doctor.'

'They claim I am not. They claim that two diplomas earned by correspondence course from Philadelphia and New York are not enough to make one a doctor. Oh, don't look so amazed, Cora. I've come across this attitude before. You know I have. That fool Anthony Lake, he knew it. And that fellow Richard Morton, he said it to my face, like I was a dog without feelings. You've said it yourself on more than one occasion. I've been battling this for years now. And all because I could not afford to attend proper medical school. That . . . woman's fault,' he added bitterly, hissing the words.

Cora stood up and came towards him, then assumed a kneeling position by his side. She took his hand in hers and stroked it carefully. He looked at her, surprised. Was she actually going to offer him some wifely comfort at last? Was their sterile, bullying relationship about to change in the face of his disappointment? He could hardly believe it. 'Hawley,' she said finally in a quiet voice. 'Señor Berlosci will need eight shillings a week to train me. You have to find it somewhere. Will Munyon's offer you some more work, do you think?'

He blinked, unable to believe his ears. 'What's that?' he asked.

'Munyon's,' she repeated. 'At the moment, they pay you enough for us both to live reasonably comfortably, but to earn the extra eight shillings . . . well, you're going to need to work some extra shifts. Or perhaps Mr Munyon could increase your wages? You have to speak to him about it. It's important.'

Hawley loosened his hand from hers and stood up slowly, walking towards the window and breathing heavily, attempting to keep his temper under control. In the four years they had been married, he had never once raised his voice to his wife. He left that side of things to her. All their arguments were based around his inability to fund the lifestyle she felt she deserved. All their fights ended with her screaming at him, berating him, threatening him with frying pans and pots, while he agreed to do whatever she asked, anything so long as she stopped shouting at him. Now, however, he felt an anger grow inside him that he had never felt before. It consumed him from within, like a piece of burning coal smouldering at the base of his stomach, rising through his chest, and charring at his heart. He turned and looked at her while she stared back at him defiantly, aware of the sudden change of temperature in their relationship.

'How heartless you are,' he said, his voice rising. 'Everything is always about *your* ambition, *your* dreams. Never about mine. I receive yet another setback and all you can think about is where I can find an extra eight shillings to fund your singing lessons?' He was shouting now, but he had underestimated his audience, for she was able to give back as good as she got.

'It's our way out of this hovel,' she screeched. 'Don't you see? I can be a great star and make us thousands and thousands of pounds. We can—'

'Oh, stop deluding yourself, woman!' he cried. 'You'll

never be a star. You're only a passable singer at the best of times. Dogs in the street have a better chance of—'

She never found out what dogs in the street had a better chance of doing, because before he could finish his sentence she had stepped forward and slapped him hard across the face. Her lip curled in anger as she stared him down, but his fists curled too and he had to hold himself back from punching her face, an emotion he had never felt before.

'Don't you ever speak to me like that again, you worthless fool,' she said quietly, her voice several tones deeper than normal, like a sound emerging from the depths of hell. 'You're just bitter because I *will* be a great star, whereas you will never be a real doctor. And you will find me that eight shillings a week, Hawley Crippen, or I shall want to know the reason why. Do we understand each other?'

He stared at her, and a million different answers occurred to him. He sought through every corner of his personality to find the strength to choose the words he wanted to say; but as she stood before him, ready to strike again if necessary, if not with her hands then with her tongue, he felt himself collapse within and knew there was only one answer, two words, that would suffice. On this occasion he did not have the strength to stand up to her. He nodded and looked away.

'Yes, Cora,' he said.

7

The Smythsons and the Nashes

Mrs Louise Smythson and her husband Nicholas arrived in the dining room of the Savoy Hotel a little after four fifteen in the afternoon. Having arranged to meet their friends, Mr and Mrs Nash, for a birthday tea at four o'clock, they were both somewhat embarrassed to be late, but the last few days had been so busy and distressing that they were sure their friends would understand.

They had slept later than usual that morning. Five days earlier, on April Fool's Day, Nicholas's father, Lord Smythson, had died in his sleep. Nicholas had been beside himself with grief since then, but this was nothing compared to what was being endured by his wife – for a very different reason. Her misery was down to the fact that Lord Smythson's title had passed immediately to her brother-in-law Martin who, despite being forty years younger than his father, was just as sickly. It had been Louise's fervent desire that Martin would die young, preferably before Lord Smythson, to ensure that the title landed with Nicholas. However, that possibility had now passed and she simply had to wait and hope that nature would take its course.

The doorbell had rung a little after eleven o'clock that morning and Louise was surprised to be informed by the maid, Julie, that her sister-in-law Elizabeth had come to call. Elizabeth had married Martin six months earlier and had been embraced by all the family as a perfect English rose and a suitable wife for the eldest son. There was no question that her pretty features and quiet charm exemplified everything that the Smythsons had looked for in breeding stock; their disquiet when Nicholas had introduced his own choice of bride to them was still a sore point for Louise, but she had managed to win them over eventually by proving extremely proficient at hiding her lower-class origins – and her accent – and embracing all the social attitudes of the upper classes as if she had been born to it. Upon their introduction, Elizabeth had immediately sought to become friends with her new sister-in-law, and Louise allowed a deception to continue, that deception being that she actually liked her. In fact, Elizabeth was the enemy; a woman who, if she wasn't stopped, could provide an heir to the Smythson title and fortune. It was clear that she was passionately in love with her sickly husband, and any issue from the marriage would leave Nicholas and Louise for ever the poor relations. She had to be stopped.

'Elizabeth,' she exclaimed when the visitor walked into the room, still wearing black in mourning for their late father-in-law. 'How lovely to see you. And at such an early hour.'

'I hope you don't mind my calling around, Louise,' she said anxiously.

'Of course not,' the other replied, seeing instantly the look of worry in her face. 'Sit down. Julie will bring tea. Julie!' she snapped as if the maid was hard of hearing. 'Tea!'

The ladies sat together on the sofa and discussed the events of the previous few days. The funeral of Lord

Smythson. The passing of the title. The reading of the will. The constant coughing of Martin as they sat in the cathedral, listening to the service. 'He's so very ill at the moment,' said Elizabeth. 'The doctors fear it might be pneumonia. I'm beside myself with worry, my dear Louise, I truly am.'

'Only natural,' said Louise, ushering Julie away delightedly and pouring the tea herself. 'He shouldn't have attended the funeral on such a rainy day, you know. It was bound to make him ill.'

'I know. But you were right when you insisted that he come. After all, how would it look for an eldest son not to attend the last service for his dear father?'

'True,' she replied. 'Of course I was only thinking of his reputation. I do hope I haven't damaged his health by doing so.'

'But I almost forgot!' said Elizabeth, reaching into her bag for a small jewellery box. 'I brought you a birthday present. I knew you wouldn't want to celebrate so close to a family funeral, but I couldn't let the day pass unmarked.'

'How kind,' said Louise, snatching the box greedily. 'And don't worry, we're having tea with our friends the Nashes later anyway. Mrs Nash is a friend of mine from the Music Hall Ladies' Guild. Now let me see this better . . .' She opened the box and removed the earrings from within, holding them up to the light. 'Well, aren't they charming,' she said, not wanting to appear over-excited by the set of sapphire gems. 'Thank you so much, my dear.'

'You're welcome,' said Elizabeth, looking away before her face collapsed suddenly in pain.

Without warning she burst into tears and Louise could only stare at her, irritated and baffled. 'Elizabeth,' she asked, moved to put an arm around her in comfort, but resisting it, 'whatever's the matter? You're not still crying for our father-in-law, surely?'

Elizabeth shook her head. 'No, it's not that,' she said.

'Martin then.'

'Well, yes, partly. You see, I spoke to the doctor last night and he wants to move him into hospital today for tests and observation. He says it's the best thing for him.'

'But Elizabeth, surely that's a good thing,' said Louise, making a mental note to write to her brother-in-law's doctor and demand that his wishes to be left alone be respected and that, if he had to die, he should at least be allowed the dignity of dying at home. 'They can do their best for him in there.'

Elizabeth nodded but still looked miserable. 'I know that,' she said. 'I know the doctors there might be able to help him – but to look at him, Louise, is to break my heart. He's so thin and so pale. And he can hardly breathe sometimes. He's like a shadow of his former self.'

For this, and this alone, Louise felt some sympathy. The two women did not socialize together very often, and when she had seen her brother-in-law at the funeral a few days earlier she had been taken aback by his obviously unwell state. He had been brought to the front row of the church in a wheelchair, a blanket covering his pencil-thin legs, and she had pushed along the pew a little way to distance herself from him. Louise was not a woman who felt comfortable among the sick.

'We can only pray for him,' said Louise, reaching for something positive to say and failing. She glanced at the clock and wished that Elizabeth would finish her tea and leave. She had some letters to write before they left for the Savoy and a romance novel which had been thrilling her for days to finish.

'There is another thing, however,' said Elizabeth, her voice catching a little in her throat. It sounded as if she was afraid to say it but she needed a confidante.

'Something else?' said Louise, narrowing her eyes, sensing a secret. 'What is it?'

'I . . .' she began, before shaking her head and weeping some more. 'I shouldn't say.'

'Of course you should,' she replied greedily. 'Why, we're practically sisters, aren't we?'

'Well, yes . . .' said Elizabeth, unsure about this. Although she tried to hide the fact from herself, she often suspected that Louise did not like her.

'Well then. You must tell me everything. Just like I do you.'

'But you never tell me any secrets.'

'That's because I have none, my dear. Now go ahead. You'll feel better for getting it off your chest, whatever it is.'

'Well, I can't be sure about it,' Elizabeth began hesitantly.

'Yes?'

'Of course it's early days.'

'Just tell me.'

Elizabeth swallowed and looked her sister-in-law directly in the eyes. 'I think I may be with child,' she said.

Louise's eyes opened wide and she put a hand to her stomach as she felt it began to churn. This is it, she thought to herself. This is what it feels like when the blood literally drains from your face. 'A child?' she asked, barely able to get the hated words out.

Elizabeth nodded. 'I've made an appointment with my doctor to confirm it, but I'm almost sure of it. A woman can tell, you know.'

Louise gasped, unsure what to say. 'You're . . . you're not certain then?' she said. 'It might be a mistake.'

'Well not *entirely* sure, but—'

'Then don't worry about it for now. It might just be—'

'Louise, you don't understand. I hope I *am* pregnant.

174

I desperately want for Martin and me to have a baby together. I'm just worried that he'll be too sick to be a real father to it. Or worse. What if . . . what if . . . ?'

She could not bring herself to finish her thought and collapsed in further tears, and Louise had to restrain herself from picking her up and slapping her. This went on for another hour before Louise finally persuaded her sister-in-law to return home, seeing her to the door and apologizing after she stepped too close to her, almost pushing her down the wet steps outside. She didn't tell her husband of this distress, however, as Nicholas would have been delighted at the news. He didn't seem to care about the title, the attainment of which had been Louise's mission in life since their marriage. And so she had taken a longer bath than usual and was spoiling for a fight with him afterwards, proclaiming the necklace he had bought her to be gaudy and more suited to a woman from below stairs. By the time they finally left their home, it was almost four o'clock and they were bound to be late. Arriving at the Savoy, Louise was torn between anger and despair and a fervent hope that she could take it out on someone.

The Nashes were old friends of Nicholas Smythson, and it had been Margaret Nash who had seen to it that the newly married Louise was admitted to the Music Hall Ladies' Guild, a group which got together once a week to listen to performances, discuss the issues of the day or, more usually, simply to take tea together and discuss the latest fashions. From time to time they organized charitable functions to help the impoverished children of the city, but such events had become few and far between, being troublesome and involving the poor. Andrew Nash had attended Cambridge with Nicholas and he encouraged his wife to champion Louise after their marriage, a task she had taken to gladly. Although originally from quite different backgrounds, they had hit it off well together and became fast friends, for Mrs

Nash was every bit the social climber that Louise was and, like her, had married above her station.

'How are you now, Nicholas?' asked Margaret, who had not seen him since the funeral. 'Are you coming to terms with your loss yet?'

'Oh yes, quite,' he replied, although this was not entirely true. He had loved his father very much and already missed him greatly. He had barely slept in recent days, so racked was he with painful memories.

'He was a fine man,' Andrew said gruffly, affecting the elderly gentleman role to which he aspired, although he was still only in his early forties.

'And Martin, how is he?' Margaret continued. 'He looked simply dreadful at the funeral. He will be all right, won't he?'

Nicholas shrugged. He didn't like to think about it. Losing one family member was bad enough. He dreaded the idea of losing Martin too.

Louise's lip curled in distaste, unable to rid her mind of the prospect of Elizabeth's baby, and she changed the subject immediately. It might not be true anyway, she reasoned. Maybe it's a false alarm.

'My dear,' she said, reaching across and tapping Margaret on the arm gently. 'I never told you about my visit to Scotland Yard, did I?'

'No!' said Margaret. 'You mean you actually went?'

'Indeed I did.'

'What's this?' asked Andrew, puffing away on a cigar. 'What were you doing at Scotland Yard, for heaven's sake? Here, Smythson!' he said in too loud a voice across the table. 'What's this wife of yours been up to that we know nothing about? Not some sort of criminal mastermind, is she?'

'Stop it, Andrew,' said Margaret in a serious tone. 'You won't be laughing when you hear about it. Now tell me, Louise. What happened? What did they say?'

'It was about Cora Crippen,' Louise explained,

turning to her friend's husband, aware that he knew nothing about this. 'About what happened to her.'

'Cora Crippen? You mean that big, loud woman you're friends with?'

Louise sighed and recalled how Mrs Crippen had joined their group in the first place. A year or two after marrying Nicholas, she had been walking along Tavistock Square one afternoon when a woman had stopped and introduced herself as Cora Crippen in such a tone as to suggest that they were old friends.

'Cora Crippen?' she had repeated, trying to remember, although the face was a little familiar. 'I'm afraid I don't—'

'Oh, but you must remember me,' said Cora. 'I used to visit the Horse and Three Bells public house when I was performing at the Regency Music Hall. You worked there. Before your marriage.'

'Bella Elmore!' Louise said, remembering. 'That was your stage name, if I recollect.'

'That's right. But it's Cora Crippen by day.'

They spoke for some time, and for once Louise did not mind being reminded of her earlier, less exalted days. She and Cora had got along very well in the old days and, when it became clear that they were living not far from each other, it did not seem too much to imagine that they could be part of the same social set. Louise tried out a few names on her to make sure and Cora lied, saying she knew them all.

'And are you still singing?' asked Louise.

'But of course. I'm hoping to make my debut at the Palladium in the spring.'

'The Palladium? You never are!'

'Well, negotiations are at an early stage, of course, but fingers crossed. My agent is organizing it.' Naturally there were no negotiations, nor was there an agent, nor was there any risk whatsoever of her playing at the Palladium.

177

'Cora, you must join our guild,' said Louise on their second meeting, for tea at Louise's own house. 'We have some wonderful members. You must know Anne Richardson-Lewis? Of the Richardson-Lewises? And Janet Tyler? She's one of the Tylers?'

'Of course,' lied Cora.

'And Alexandra Harrington is a regular attendee.'

'Is she one of the Harringtons?'

'No. She's one of the other Harringtons.'

'Oh, better still. I've always preferred them anyway.'

'And Sarah Kenley. Margaret Nash. All wonderful women. I'm sure they'd be delighted for you to become a member.'

Louise had never before sponsored another lady for membership, and she had been on the lookout in recent times for a suitable candidate, the adoption of a new member being something of a status symbol in itself. It meant that within the group there was someone who would always be beholden to you, someone who, by your introducing them in the first place, became your natural inferior. And so, in time, she had brought Cora to a meeting, and she had been accepted by the other ladies. Cora introduced herself as a famous New York singer, now happily married to one of London's finest doctors, and the rich women, coated in furs and encrusted with jewels, opened their arms *en masse* and welcomed her into their society, like a school of whales embracing a minnow. It had been one of the happiest evenings of Cora's life.

'We saw that Crippen fellow at the theatre, didn't we?' said Andrew, looking at his wife.

'Yes,' she explained. 'That's where all this started. Remember, we were at *A Midsummer Night's Dream* and there he was, not a care in the world, despite the fact that his wife had just died only a few weeks before.'

'Well, a fellow has to get over things, doesn't he? Can't go on mourning the poor woman for ever.'

'But it's all a bit mysterious, Andrew, don't you see? Cora left London without a word to anyone, not even any of her friends at the Music Hall Ladies' Guild. She went to California for a few weeks to visit a sick relative.'

'That's what Dr Crippen said anyway,' said Margaret.

'And she wrote me a letter from there,' Louise continued, 'stating that she would probably stay in California for a few months as this relative, whoever he or she was, was doing very badly. And then, before any of us knew it, her husband announces that she herself has died in California and he's just received the telegram to tell him so.'

'Shocking,' said Nicholas, shaking his head and still thinking of his father. 'That poor woman. With so much to live for. She was a pretty thing too, wasn't she?'

'Well, not really,' Margaret Nash admitted. 'She had broad shoulders and coarse hair. But she was a wonderful woman nevertheless. Very kind and thoughtful. An excellent wife. Dr Crippen could hardly have found a more loving companion in this world.'

'So what's the mystery then?' Andrew asked, confused. 'Where does Scotland Yard come into all this?'

'When we saw Dr Crippen at the theatre that night,' said Margaret, 'he had another woman with him, don't you remember?'

'Here's the heart of it,' Nicholas said good-naturedly. 'Jealousy.'

'A common sort of woman,' said Louise.

'Hardly our sort,' continued Margaret.

'No name to speak of.'

'I don't remember her,' said Andrew. 'What did she look like?'

'A small woman,' said Margaret. 'With dark hair. And a scar above her lip. Quite unpleasant. What's her name, Louise? You know it, don't you?'

'Ethel LeNeve,' said Louise. 'If you please,' she added,

as if the possession of a name at all on Ethel's part was something of a presumption.

'That's it, LeNeve. Apparently she used to work with Dr Crippen at that mad medicine shop he runs in Shaftesbury Avenue. Well, she was there at the theatre with him that night. Wearing *her* jewellery. Shameless.'

Margaret and Louise both sat back in their chairs, as if a great jigsaw puzzle had been laid out before them, and the men nodded and thought about it, willing to amuse their wives if necessary by locating the corners for them.

'So it seems to me,' said Nicholas, 'that you're accusing this Crippen fellow of undue haste in finding a new lady, and her of poor taste in wearing a dead woman's jewellery. It's hardly something to bother Scotland Yard with, now is it?'

'We're *saying*,' said Louise, unwilling to be patronized after the day she had suffered, 'that a woman does not leave for America without telling her friends. We're saying that she does not go there and then suddenly die when there was not a thing in the world wrong with her before. And we're saying that she certainly does not leave her best jewellery behind for any tart or trollop to rifle through, the minute her back is turned. It just doesn't seem likely, and I don't believe a word of it for a moment.'

'You don't think the fellow's done her in or something, do you?' asked Andrew, laughing now. 'Oh really. I don't know what you ladies do at these meetings of yours, but it seems to me as if you are letting your imaginations—'

'Tell me what they said, Louise,' said Margaret, interrupting her husband. 'At Scotland Yard. What did they say to you?'

'I saw Inspector Dew,' she began.

'Dew?' said Andrew. 'I've heard of him. A top man, I believe.'

'Well, naturally he was very courteous to me, but to be honest I don't think he was particularly interested. Seemed to think I was worrying unnecessarily. Practically accused me of wasting his time.'

'Oh, Louise! And you the daughter-in-law of Lord Smythson!'

'Sister-in-law,' Andrew pointed out.

'I know, it's frightful, isn't it? Anyway, I told him in the end. I told him that this was all far from over and soon he would want my help and that of my friends in locating Cora Crippen, and where would he be then? Standing there with egg all over his face!'

'My dear, your expressions,' laughed Nicholas.

'I'm only saying what we're all thinking,' Louise insisted. 'And what Margaret and I think is that he did away with Cora. And how are we supposed to allow that when she's a friend of ours?'

'For a start,' said Andrew, 'if he has done away with her, as you put it, then he's hardly going to have been asking for your permission anyway. And secondly, the man's a doctor. He helps sustain life, not take it away. He's hardly going to get himself involved in something like that, is he? Your imaginations really are running away with you. Have you been eating cheese before going to bed? I read somewhere that that's a common cause of hysteria among the ladies.'

'Oh Andrew, you must find out though,' said Margaret.

'I? What can I do?'

'Well, you have that business in Mexico next month, don't you? The mining contract?' Andrew thought about it. She was referring to a trip he would be making to Central America in a few weeks' time to ensure that his company was keeping to their timetable on his mining project in Guadalajara.

'Yes, I do,' he said. 'But I fail to see how—'

'You could go to California afterwards,' she said,

'and find out exactly how Cora died. That's where it's supposed to have happened.'

'Oh yes, Andrew,' said Louise, clapping her hands together. 'You could do that.'

'But I won't have time,' he protested. 'I'll be too busy with my work.'

'You can spare one day to catch a killer, can't you?'

'He's *not* a killer.'

'But he might be. Oh please, Andrew. Say you'll do it.'

He sighed and shook his head. 'I don't know what you expect me to find out there,' he said eventually. 'But if it means that much to you . . .'

'Oh, you are wonderful,' said Louise, delighted. 'Now we'll find out the truth for sure.'

Having talked him into undertaking the task, they changed the subject to less morbid topics. Only as the evening progressed did Louise return to her unhappier state, remembering the news that her sister-in-law had given her earlier. Maybe I should introduce Dr Crippen to Martin, she thought to herself uncharitably. Maybe he could give him a few ideas.

8

The Dentist

London: 1899–1905

Six years after moving to London, in the winter of 1899, Dr Hawley Harvey Crippen finally set up his own medical practice, working as a dentist from a small office in Holborn. It was not a full-time job; he still worked during the day at Munyon's Homeopathic Medicines, where he had responsibility for every detail in the business since his employer had retired, from seven o'clock in the morning until four o'clock in the afternoon, with only an hour's break for lunch. Between four and six in the evening he would visit the Pig in the Pond pub in Chancery Lane, where he read *The Times* newspaper or one of his medical periodicals while eating his dinner. (There was nothing he enjoyed more than reading about the latest advances in autopsy procedures while carving the breast of a chicken or sliding his knife through a rare fillet steak.) Between six and nine he opened his surgery and treated those members of the public who needed a dentist but could not see one during the day because of their own work commitments. Between both jobs he made a decent living. The decision to specialize in dentistry came about when it became clear that he would never have the means to study for a medical degree and work as a real doctor; at thirty-six years of age he was becoming more of a pragmatist in that respect. And so he simply decided that he would call himself a dentist instead, opening the surgery without any degree or qualification whatsoever. It was a risky strategy, but there was less chance of his being discovered when operating only on people's mouths than if performing as a general practitioner.

Cora and he still lived in South Crescent in Bloomsbury and had settled comfortably into a life of mutual disharmony. Mrs Crippen had spent a year working with Señor Berlosci and had noticed only a small improvement in her talents during that time. She had, however, fallen in love with him, a passion that was not returned by her vocal coach. Naturally, he had seduced her, but talk of anything further was anathema to him.

'If I didn't have you,' she said one afternoon, lying naked on the divan in his living room while he got dressed and glanced at his watch carelessly to check the time that his next appointment would arrive, 'I believe I would go mad. You're everything that Hawley is not.' She made herself all the less attractive by lying there with her legs stretched apart, her breasts sliding down to either side of her body, while the sunlight poured through the window, highlighting her every flaw.

'My dear Cora,' he said, bored by conversation. 'You'll catch your death of cold lying there. Cover yourself.' He had a strange aversion to seeing women naked after he had made love to them, preferring that they dressed as quickly as possibly and left. When the sexual urge had left him, he had little need for their attention any more. Cora rose and padded across the floor towards him, pressing her body up against his and kissing him gently on the lips, hoping for a stronger reaction.

'When will you speak to Mr Mullins about me?' she

asked quietly, relocating her lips towards his ears and then down along his neck.

'Soon, soon,' he replied. 'You're not ready yet.'

'But it's been a year, Alfredo,' she reasoned. 'Surely it's time by now?' She continued to kiss him, hoping to arouse him once again, although she knew this was unlikely. Despite his lustful appetite, the ageing Italian behaved like a temperamental diva, refusing to perform more than once in an afternoon, and the curtain had already come down on the matinee.

'He is a very busy man,' Berlosci said, releasing himself from her grasp and picking up her undergarments from the floor where she had thrown them earlier and handing them to her while averting his eyes from her nudity. While making love to her, lying down on the divan or in his bed, he found Cora to be an altogether distracting partner. There were, perhaps, more parcels of flesh around the thighs than he would have liked, and her shoulders offered a certain masculine pleasure that bothered him, but all in all she was lustful and accommodating and had never refused him any favour. Standing up, however, his eyes were drawn only to her worst features. The way her breasts hung slightly askew on her frame, each a little too small when compared to her upper-body muscle . . . the porridge-like skin around her knees . . . the slight excess of body hair around the legs. She stood before him in the pose of a seductive Venus de Milo, but all he saw was a woman approaching her thirties whose body was self-destructing well before its time, due to unhealthy eating and a lack of exercise. 'Now, please. Get dressed, Cora,' he urged. 'I have a client in fifteen minutes.'

Cora breathed heavily in irritation and began to put her clothes back on. Mr Mullins was the owner of a small theatre in Shaftesbury Avenue (by coincidence, not far from where Hawley worked) and Señor Berlosci claimed that they were close friends. The man often produced variety shows and evenings devoted to particular singers and, in a moment of lust-fuelled madness some months earlier, Berlosci had promised Cora that he would arrange an audition for her. However, unknown to her, her teacher had sent so many prospective stars to Mullins over the years that the theatre owner knew it was just a tool to get these women into bed and had put a stop to it. He had informed his friend in no uncertain terms that he would only audition real talents and that if he suspected he was being used for any other purpose he would not see any more of his pupils. Because of this, Berlosci had sent only two of his students to Mullins during the previous year, both exemplary singers, and he knew that Cora epitomized the type of average hopeful whom Mullins would instantly reject.

'You promised me,' Cora said quietly, not wanting an argument but needing to make her point all the same.

'And I meant it,' he insisted. 'I will speak to him soon. But you are not ready yet.' He softened slightly and came towards her, reaching down and kissing her forehead like a proud father. 'Trust me. Some day soon you will be quite ready and Mr Mullins will see you then. He will fall at your feet and shower you with garlands, as the French did with Marie de Santé or the Italians with the great Sabella Donato.'

'Do you promise it, Alfredo?' she asked, trying to look coquettish, and failing.

'Promissio.'

Watching her leave that afternoon, Señor Berlosci decided that it was time for him and Cora Crippen to part company, both as teacher and student and as lovers.

There were usually two or three patients waiting for Dr Crippen when he arrived at his surgery in the evening, and each one had a look which combined a mixture of agonizing pain and total fear at the ordeal which lay ahead. In the twelve months he had been practising as a dentist he had come to realize that no one ever visited him when a dental problem first reared its head. Instead, they waited, praying that whatever it was would go away, and only when they had come to terms with the fact that things were only getting worse did they make the trip to see him. Mainly working-class people, they didn't notice the lack of dental degrees on his wall and never glanced at the two framed diplomas from the Medical College of Philadelphia and the Ophthalmic Hospital of New York which had pride of place in the surgery. They came there, wanting nothing more than an end to their pain, with an infliction of as little extra pain as possible.

On this particular evening, only two patients were waiting for Hawley when he arrived, both of whom claimed to have been there first. A woman of about fifty swore blind that she had been waiting since three o'clock that afternoon, while her companion, a boy of about fifteen, said that she had arrived only five minutes before Hawley himself and that he should be seen first. Unaccustomed to such disputes, he was forced to toss a coin for the right to be first in the dentist's chair and the young man won, looking at the woman with such an expression of triumph that Hawley felt like reversing the outcome.

Hawley had spent almost fifty pounds of his savings stocking the surgery with the proper dental equipment and a large lamp which hung down over the patient's chair, aimed at the darkest recesses of their pain. Peering into the boy's mouth, he could tell immediately what the problem was. One of the molars in the lower back six had been chipped and an abscess had formed. The nerve was almost exposed and the remaining half of the tooth had turned black. 'When did you chip it?' he asked, checking the rest of his mouth for similar problems.

'About a month ago,' said the young man, Peter Milburn, afraid to tell the truth – that it had been almost six months before – in case the doctor told him off.

'Right,' said Hawley, not believing a word of it. 'Well, it will have to come out, I'm afraid. There's no other choice.'

'I thought as much,' said Milburn, who had already resigned himself to this. 'Will it be painful?' he asked in a tiny voice, like a small child.

Hawley suppressed a laugh. 'Don't worry,' he replied. 'I've performed hundreds of extractions. It will be over before you know it.'

He went across to his surgical cabinet and filled a large needle with anaesthetic, testing the spray carefully over the sink. It was not a particularly strong anaesthetic but he was unable to purchase anything stronger without a licence and so had to settle for the next best thing, which invariably brought cries of pain from his patients. He had considered tying wrist straps to the chair to stop them flailing around so much, but he had decided in the end that this would make the whole thing seem more like a medieval torture chamber than a medical procedure and had decided against it. After all, repeat business was important to him.

Milburn flinched when he saw the needle coming towards his mouth, but Hawley assured him that he would not feel much pain from it, which was true.

'Now,' he said, when the injection was complete. 'Let's just wait for it to settle in a little and we'll have that tooth out.'

Beside the sink he kept a range of needles, forceps and pliers in a tray of sterile disinfectant. Each was of a different calibre and grading and was designed for different teeth, and he chose several different implements to lay on the white cloth which covered the empty tray beside the patient's chair. After a few minutes Milburn assured him that the left-hand side of his mouth was reasonably numb – *reasonably* being the operative word – and Crippen got to work.

To begin with, he took a sharp-pointed No. 6 needle with a narrow silver blade at the top and inserted it into the tip of the abscess, which immediately burst and leaked its fluid into Milburn's mouth. The second the blade touched the blister, the boy jumped as if struck by electricity and Hawley sat back, accustomed to this reaction. 'I have to drain the abscess first,' he explained. 'I'm sorry, this will be a little painful but it won't take long. You have to be patient.'

Milburn, who was not by nature a coward and already had aspirations towards joining the police force, nodded in resignation and sat back, his fists clenched together tightly on the armrests, his fingernails pressed deeply into the palms of his hands to counteract the pain over which he had no control. He closed his eyes when Hawley put the blade in his mouth again, but it was difficult to remain still while the doctor scraped out the abscess.

'Can't you give me some more anaesthetic?' he pleaded after washing out his mouth for the eighth time, his body trembling from the pain.

Hawley shook his head. 'That's the strongest one that I'm allowed to use,' he lied. 'It's just that the abscess is so far developed that it's bound to be painful. But it's nearly clear now, which means I can remove the tooth.'

Milburn nodded and sat back again. A thin line of perspiration had broken out across his forehead and he was trying to mentally remove himself from the proceedings by staring into the light and performing an act of self-hypnosis. The abscess now cleaned out, Hawley reached for one of the forceps and, urging the young man to open his mouth wider, clamped it around the dark remaining half-tooth, took a firm hold of it and, gently at first, levered it from side to side, attempting to urge it from its moorings. A cry of pain issued from the boy's mouth as throbbing and pressure combined to send jolts of pain through his body. His ears became more alert to the sound of the pliers wrestling the creaking tooth back and forth and, had Hawley not been standing over him with a knee on his chest as he pulled, he might have jumped up and run from the surgery in fright. A sharp crack sent Hawley tripping slightly backwards, pliers in hand, part of the tooth in its grasp as blood poured out of Milburn's mouth. He gave a yell of surprise and jolted forward in the seat, but the sudden pain of the tooth's removal was as nothing compared to his relief when he saw that the operation was over. He lay back, surprised that his mouth was still aching, and swore to himself that he would never wait so long again before going to the dentist.

Hawley told him to wash out his mouth several times at the sink and he placed some gauze where the tooth had been in order to stem the flow of blood and, when it had finally stopped, the doctor returned to his position and looked inside, frowning.

'Bad news, I'm afraid, Master Milburn,' he said, making the young man's heart flutter in terror. 'It's as I thought. The tooth was so bad that it cracked as I pulled it. The root is still planted in the gum and I'll have to remove it surgically.'

'Oh no,' Milburn sighed to himself, wondering whether it would be monstrous to start crying. 'Surely not. Can't it just stay there?'

'If it did, your whole jaw would become infected and you would end up having to have all your teeth removed within a month.'

Milburn nodded stoically and resigned himself to more pain. Surely, he reasoned, there could not be much left to endure. 'Go on then,' he said, lying back and closing his eyes.

'Unfortunately, no more of the tooth is left above the gum to pull, so I am going to have to cut open the gum and extract it from the inside. Not very pleasant, I'm afraid.'

Milburn stared at him and felt himself begin to laugh hysterically. Was this really a dentist who stood before him or some type of sadistic murderer, intent on producing as much blood and pain as possible? Still, he had little choice but to let the man finish the job he had started, and he lay back, his palms indented now with the sharpness of his fingernails, as Hawley took a sharper blade and, ignoring the boy's screams, sliced the gum open in a criss-cross shape, like a hot cross bun, thus exposing the root of the damaged molar. 'There she is,' he exclaimed in delight, using two implements now to push back both sides of the gum so that he could see the offending object. 'What a beauty!' It was difficult to remove with so much blood pouring into the cavity, but he quickly reached inside with the narrowest forceps he possessed and, quite oblivious to the squirming and screaming of the boy beneath him, reached in and took a firm hold of it, pulling it loose with his right hand while his left rested on the boy's chest, pressing him down into the chair lest he try to escape. With the sound of air being sucked into a vacuum, the remainder of the tooth came free and he stood back triumphantly, the forceps and his hand covered in blood while Peter Milburn held a palm to the side of his face in agony, one of the worst experiences of his life finally behind him, although he would never quite forget it. He sat up and tried to get out of the chair but his legs were weak beneath him and he was aware that a river of blood was pouring from his mouth.

'Look at that,' said Hawley, rotating the forceps in the light and admiring the tooth like a proud father. 'Rotten to the core. A thing of beauty in itself.' He glanced at the boy and nodded towards the sink. 'You'd better wash

your mouth out,' he said. 'Then sit back down and I'll
stitch you up.'

'Stitch me—?'

'Well, I can't leave you like that, now can I?' Hawley
asked, grinning from ear to ear. 'The blood won't clot
until I close the wound. A few stitches, and you'll be
right as rain.'

Milburn almost fainted and in his mind started
to run through all the terrible things he had ever
done in his life, wondering whether this was God's
retribution called back on him now. As a child he had
bullied his younger brother mercilessly and exposed
himself to every girl in his classroom for an apple.
He had recently been the driving force behind a rift
between his widowed mother and a gentleman she
had fallen in love with, a perfectly decent gentleman
but one who had threatened the boy's home life and
the selfish attentions he demanded. Two weeks before,
he had stolen twelve pence from the cash box on his
uncle's fruit stall where he worked after school and,
having got away with it, had resolved to take similar
amounts at irregular intervals until he could afford a
new bicycle. Perhaps all these misdeeds were coming
back to haunt him now, he thought as he leaned
back in the chair, his mind suddenly filling with an
image of himself in his coffin, and he lay there while
Hawley completed eight expertly applied sutures to
close up the hole which he had left in his mouth.
The anaesthetic had practically worn off by now, and
Milburn screamed throughout the whole procedure,
blood-curdling screams, the screams of the demented
and the hysterical; but Hawley hardly heard a note of
them, so intent was he on his work, so proud of his
abilities, so much in love with the art of medicine that
for him the music of pain was nothing more than a
melody to work by. Finally he placed more gauze in
the boy's mouth and told him to bite down on it for

ten minutes; when he removed it, it was soaked in blood, making him feel even more faint, but when he washed out his mouth the blood had indeed clotted and the procedure was finally over.

'You'll have to come back to me in a week's time,' Hawley said, 'so I can remove the stitches.' Milburn stared at him in horror. 'Don't worry,' he continued, laughing. 'That will only take about thirty seconds and you won't feel a thing.'

Handing over the two shillings which the operation had cost, the boy reeled out of the room and into the waiting area where, horrified by what she perceived to be the sounds of the young man's murder in the ghastly chamber beyond, Hawley's other prospective patient, the fifty-year-old woman, had fled into the night, determined to live with her pain rather than subject herself to the passions of a sadist.

Hawley didn't care. The hour he had spent correcting Peter Milburn's mouth, the use of the needles and forceps, pliers and stitches, had excited him considerably and he wanted nothing more than to close the surgery now and return home; and this, having washed the used implements and replaced them in the disinfectant for the following night's use, he did.

Cora was already in bed when he returned home, for her activities with Señor Berlosci that afternoon had exhausted her, and she barely glanced in his direction as he came in. It had been almost eight months since they had been intimate together, but tonight he had practically run down High Holborn and across Tottenham Court Road in order to return to his wife. She was surprised by the speed with which he removed his jacket, shirt and trousers – he normally waited until she was asleep before joining her in the marital bed – but when he came towards her and slipped under the covers, nuzzling his head against her breasts, it was all she could do to keep her dinner down.

'Hawley!' she exclaimed. 'What on earth do you think you're doing?'

He looked up at her as if that should have been obvious. 'Do not deny me, Cora,' he pleaded, although in truth he felt little attraction for this woman he had married six years before. She would merely provide him with some comfort now. He pressed himself against her and she felt his desire and pushed him away.

'Get off me,' she shrieked. 'Filthy man!'

'But Cora—'

'I mean it, Hawley. How dare you?'

He stared at her, his lust descending with each passing second, and he felt a sense of loneliness as never before.

'Honestly,' she muttered, rolling over and away from him, nervously hoping that he would not continue to display his emotions to her any longer that night.

He did not, rolling in the opposite direction, embarrassed and humiliated. It was several hours more before he fell asleep and, when he did, his dreams were filled with the memory of Peter Milburn's torturous evening. When he awoke, he was surprised to find himself as damp as a pubescent teenager and was forced to steal from the bed quietly before his wife awoke to clean away the signs of his dream, his desire fuelled by his memory of the pain and screaming he had inflicted earlier that night.

Business at Munyon's Homoeopathic Medicines was improving but the health of its owner, Mr James Munyon, was failing more and more every day. He had become increasingly forgetful and unable to work through the entire day without feeling exhausted by the end of it. Finally, on the advice of his own doctor, he agreed to retire, leaving Hawley to run the shop alone. It was almost a month before anyone responded to the 'Help Wanted' sign the younger man placed in the window. Several unsuitable applicants offered themselves for the job, but he rejected them quickly and began to worry that he would never find a suitable assistant. He had almost forgotten about the search when the bell above the door gave a jingle to announce the presence of a young woman in the shop. Hawley looked up from the accounts he was studying, but his new customer had her back to him and was examining a display of herbal medications in the corner of the store by the window, picking up a jar and carefully reading the instructions on the side. He looked back down at the invoices and receipts spread out before him, but within a moment he glanced up again for something about her drew him instantly. She was not very tall, no more than about five foot five inches, and with her back to him had an almost boyish figure: slim, narrow-hipped and healthy. Her hair was dark and cut short just above the shoulder. As he watched her, she sensed his eyes on her back and turned a little to the left so that he could observe her pale skin and the sharpness of her cheekbones in profile. He looked down at once, not allowing himself to glance up again even when he heard her walking towards him. Only when she gave a small cough to announce her presence did he tear himself away from his figures and stare at her as if he had not even heard another person come through the door.

'Good afternoon,' he said quietly, taking her features in at a glance. She was quite young and very pretty in a slightly androgynous way, as if God had been unable to decide whether to make her a surprisingly masculine girl or an unusually pretty boy. Somehow, however, even in His confusion He had managed to create something extraordinary. A small scar running from under her nose to her lip was the only noticeable flaw, but Hawley felt a sudden desire to touch it. 'How can I help you?' he asked, resisting.

195

'I saw your sign,' she said in a firm voice which suggested that it was taking some courage on her part to speak to him.

'My sign?'

'The sign in the window. The "Help Wanted" sign. I wished to enquire about it.'

'Ah,' said Hawley, putting his pen down and sitting back a little. 'Of course. The position.'

'Indeed.'

He nodded at her, unsure what to say next. He had interviewed several people for this job and he always wanted to appear authoritative but friendly, get things off to the right start. This was exactly where things had gone wrong with Helen Aldershot. Mr Munyon had hired her and, determined to make a good impression, Hawley had been too nice to her. By the time he needed to assert his authority it was already too late and she was walking all over him.

'To whom should I speak?' the woman asked after an uncomfortable silence had descended on them.

'Speak? About what?'

'About the position.'

'Oh, the *position*,' he repeated, as if this was an entirely new conversation. 'I do beg your pardon, miss,' he added after a moment. 'You're actually the first applicant I've seen in quite some time, so I was trying to think where I should begin.' He frowned at once, unsure whether he should have told her this. After all, it would not do to appear desperate. 'Let me find a fresh sheet of paper and take your details,' he said finally, flustered, and rooting in his desk before finding one. 'Your name,' he said. 'That's the best place to start.'

'Ethel LeNeve,' she replied. 'L-e-N-e-v-e,' she added, spelling it out. 'Capital L, capital N.'

'Miss LeNeve,' he repeated, writing it down. 'And that would be Miss or Mrs?'

'Miss.'

'Miss LeNeve. And your address?'

She gave it to him and he knew the street she was referring to, for he walked past it every evening on his way to his surgery. 'Quiet little place,' he told her. 'Very pleasant.'

'You know it then?'

'I run a small dental practice in the evenings in Holborn. I must walk past your home every day. You live with your parents, I assume?'

Ethel shook her head. 'I live alone,' she said; and this surprised him, for a single woman of twenty (which was her age) to be living alone could constitute a scandal. 'My parents are dead,' she explained. 'But they left me their small flat. A widow lives downstairs and I sometimes act as her companion. She's a nice lady, but she sometimes mistakes me for her son.'

'Her son?' he asked, surprised.

'Her mind isn't what it used to be. But she has a heart of gold and treats me very kindly.'

Hawley nodded, pleased that there was no suggestion of any impropriety and wondering whether the widow should be introduced to Mr Munyon. They could enjoy their senility together, mistaking each other for a lamp-post or a stick of celery. 'Well, Miss LeNeve,' he began. 'The position is one of general assistant and typist. Can you type?'

'Typing is one of my skills,' she said with a sweet smile. 'Forty words per minute at the last count.'

'Well that's fortunate,' he said. 'If I try to type fast, I inevitably mis-spell a word and have to begin again. I can go through reams of paper like that. Naturally, in a pharmacy it's very important that we do not make mistakes with what we type on our prescriptions. We don't want to end up killing anyone.'

'Naturally,' she said, looking around. 'But can you tell me, exactly what type of pharmacy this is? I'm afraid I don't know very much about . . . homoeopathic medicine,' she said, struggling with the word a little.

Hawley relaxed now, enjoying her comfortable presence, and he began the speech he had used on more than one occasion, explaining the birth of homoeopathy in Japan thousands of years before and its gradual reintroduction into western culture, its uses and benefits. He stopped short of expressing his own lack of belief in its healing powers, for that was something he had admitted to no one, not even to his wife; and Ethel seemed intrigued by all he said. She stared at him, listening to every word and watching his lips as he spoke. By the end, she was hooked.

'That's fascinating,' she said. 'I never knew there could be so many alternatives to visiting the doctor. To be honest with you, I'm always rather afraid to do so. Sometimes I wonder whether they know what they're doing at all. If you think about it, anyone could set themselves up in a practice and claim they have a medical degree and then kill half their patients by mistake. Or by design.'

Hawley gave a narrow smile and realized that he had not yet introduced himself. 'I'm a doctor myself, actually, Miss LeNeve,' he explained.

'Oh!'

'Hawley Harvey Crippen,' he said, extending his hand. 'Doctor Crippen, that is. I should have introduced myself earlier.'

'I do apologize,' she said, blushing a little. 'I didn't mean you, of course. It's just that one hears so many stories about—'

'Don't give it another thought, miss,' he said, raising a hand. 'It's perfectly fine. You're quite right, in fact. There are a lot of charlatans around on the streets of London these days and it can be hard to know who to believe. I myself, however, received my degrees from two medical colleges, one in Philadelphia and one in

New York, so you need have no worries about me in that regard.'

'From America,' she exclaimed breathlessly.

'Indeed,' he said. He had taken to renaming his diplomas as degrees these days; it made things simpler, he believed.

'So you're an American. I've always wanted to go there.'

'Really. I always wanted to leave,' he said, which was untrue but seemed witty to him. She smiled. Another silence descended but it was broken by the jingle of the bell as the door opened again and Hawley looked around, his face falling when he saw his wife striding towards him, her handbag clutched tightly in her hands in front of her, her eyes like thunder. 'My dear,' he began, before she interrupted him.

'Don't "my dear" me,' she snapped. 'Have you spoken to those Anderson fellows yet?'

He closed his eyes, his heart sinking as he remembered. 'I forgot,' he admitted, unable to think up a suitable excuse.

'You forgot? You *forgot?*' she cried, her voice rising. 'For heaven's sake, you useless creature. They're supposed to arrive tomorrow morning first thing, and they told me they would not come if you did not provide the inventory in advance. What use are you exactly? Can you tell me that? I give you the simplest task to perform and instead you just—'

'My dear, may I introduce Miss LeNeve,' Hawley interrupted her quickly, embarrassed by her coarseness and hoping to contain her a little by pointing out that at present they were not alone in South Crescent, where her tirades could run until she grew tired or became hungry, but were in a place of business, with strangers present. Cora looked quickly at Ethel, sizing her up in a glance.

'Charmed,' she said in a cold voice.

199

Ethel swallowed and said nothing.

'Miss LeNeve is applying for a position,' he explained. 'Miss Aldershot's old position.'

'Ha!' said Cora. 'You don't want to work for him,' she added, nodding in the direction of her husband. 'He's as useless as a sack full of rotten potatoes. If you take my advice, dear, you'll continue down the road and see whether more suitable employment can be found elsewhere.'

'Cora, really,' said Hawley, laughing a little as if to suggest that she was only joking, which she was clearly not.

'Hawley, the Andersons!' she insisted, not interested at all in the life and career of Ethel LeNeve. 'What's to be done about them?'

'I have the list in my coat pocket,' he said. 'I'll go round to their offices immediately after I shut the shop.'

'Oh, don't bother. Just give it to me and I'll take it around now. They might be closed later. Honestly, Hawley. I don't know why I bother sometimes. I really don't. If a stagehand in the theatre behaved with as much stupidity as you, they'd be dismissed immediately as an incompetent.'

'Yes, dear,' said Hawley, retrieving the list she wanted and handing it to her. She glanced at it to make sure it was the right one and seemed almost disappointed that it was; anything else and she could have attacked him again.

'You take my advice, Miss LeNeve,' she said, turning around and offering a parting shot. 'Find a different employer. Lord knows I wish I could find a different husband.' And with that she stormed out again, slamming the door behind her so hard that they both jumped in shock.

Ethel turned slowly to look at Hawley, embarrassed for him, wishing that the scene had never taken place.

'My wife,' he said with a gentle laugh, as if that

explained everything. 'She's under a little pressure at the moment. We're moving house tomorrow, you see, and the removal men needed the inventory. Otherwise they won't . . . they won't . . .' He lost track of his train of thought, wishing she would just leave him alone now to feel miserable.

'How lovely,' she said in a cheerful voice, aware of his embarrassment. 'And where are you moving to, might I ask?'

He looked up at her, encouraged by her kindness. 'Hilldrop Crescent,' he said, 'in Camden. We've been living in Bloomsbury for some time, but we were only able to afford the top floor of a house, so it will be nice to have a home to ourselves. We're very excited by it.'

'And so you should be,' she said. 'It's only natural that your wife's spirits would be high under the circumstances.'

Hawley nodded and knew instantly that he had found a new friend. And perhaps a typist too. 'So, Miss LeNeve,' he began.

'Please call me Ethel,' she said.

'Ethel, then. You're still interested in the position?'

9

Mrs Louise Smythson's Second Visit to Scotland Yard

London: 30 June 1910

Police Constable Peter Milburn glanced up when the front door to Scotland Yard opened and he saw two middle-aged women striding towards him like army officers, left, right, left, right in unison, clutching their bags in front of them with both hands, their hats set at identical angles, one wearing a dark-red dress, the other green, like a pair of conflicting traffic lights. He sighed and put his time sheets away, then looked up at them with a resigned smile.

'Good morning, ladies,' he said, and he would have offered more but the lady on the left in the red dress, Mrs Louise Smythson, interrupted him.

'We've met before, young man,' she said. 'Don't you remember?'

He blinked. He dealt with at least a hundred people at this desk every day and could scarcely remember any of them when they had gone from his line of vision, but on this occasion there was something about her that was familiar. 'How can I help you?' he asked, ignoring the question.

'You can help me by answering my question,' she demanded, never one to be put off. 'Do you remember meeting me before?'

'Of course, ma'am. It was in connection with . . . ?'

'I came to see you at the end of March. In connection with a missing person, Cora Crippen. I received no satisfaction then, but not today, I assure you. This is my friend, Mrs Margaret Nash.'

PC Milburn looked towards the companion, whose stern face broke into a three-second smile while she uttered the monosyllable, 'Charmed.'

'Mrs Nash,' said PC Milburn with a nod of the head. 'And Mrs—?'

'Smythson. Mrs Louise Smythson. Honestly, don't you have a memory in that head of yours? I don't know what kind of people we are employing in our police constabulary today, I really don't. Children. Idiots, most of them.'

Immediately a memory returned to PC Milburn of Louise's last visit. She had been particularly rude to him then, demanding to see one of the inspectors, despite the fact that her case was one entirely of supposition and guesswork. She had also made him feel a little uncomfortable, for after inviting her to sit in the lobby he had felt her eyes lingering on him relentlessly. Although he might often have felt flattered by such attentions, at the time he was particularly in love with a young florist named Sally Minstrel and had not enjoyed it. When he had finally allowed her in to see Inspector Dew, she had given him a suggestive wink and he had blushed scarlet.

For her part, Louise was pleased that PC Milburn was on duty again. In the three months since she had last visited Scotland Yard she had thought of him on more than one occasion. Although fifteen years her junior, he was exactly the kind of man who made her go weak at the knees. Tall with swept-back dark hair, deeply chiselled cheekbones and a uniform. Although she was very fond of her husband Nicholas, and was extremely fond of his house, his money and his potential title, he had never been the sort of fellow to inspire passion in a woman. Not like this ravishing lad. Or like Stephen Dempsey, the boy who tended the gardens for them at Tavistock Square and was not averse to visiting her boudoir when invited. Or like Jim Taylor, the young man who delivered the vegetables on a Tuesday morning and who could always be relied upon to fix a leak in her upstairs bathroom. Or like any of the other tradesmen and boys whom she had seduced over the years. Much though she desired membership of the upper class and would not have given it up for all the world, her passions tended to run to her more humble roots. And PC Milburn was exactly the sort of fellow she craved. It was beyond her, however, to show him any form of civility.

'Well, how can I help you this morning, Mrs Smythson?' he asked, offering her a gentle smile through which she could see a row of perfectly white teeth.

'We wish to see Inspector Dew,' she announced. 'I believe we have some additional evidence for the case.'

'Has the inspector been investigating the lady's disappearance, then?'

'No, not that I know of,' Louise admitted.

'Then there is no case at present,' he said.

'Don't play word games with me, you young pup,' she said in a loud voice. 'I won't stand for it.'

'Disgraceful,' Mrs Nash muttered in solidarity.

'Inspector Dew will want to hear the evidence, believe me. It is most incriminating. We can prove, in fact, that a murder has been committed!'

She stood back a little to allow the word to settle and Mrs Nash gave a slight gasp at the drama of the moment, even though she knew full well what they were there to say. She hoped that PC Milburn would jump to attention when the word 'murder' was used, perhaps call the entire troop of inspectors out to speak to them, but he appeared unmoved, as if this kind of thing happened every day. Which, in fact, it did. She admired his casual air; it made her want him even more.

'A murder,' he said, taking a piece of paper and writing on it. 'And who do you think has been murdered exactly?'

'Why, Cora Crippen of course. Just like I said last time. But this isn't a case for a boy like you. I demand to speak to Inspector Dew immediately.'

'The inspector is a very busy man, Mrs Smythson. He's—'

'Is he in the building?'

'I'm sorry?'

'Is Inspector Dew at Scotland Yard at this moment?' she demanded, and with a sigh he consulted his time sheets, hoping that the inspector was out on an assignment so that he could send her home again without having to resort to a lie. Unfortunately, this was not the case.

'He is,' he admitted. 'But he's—'

'Then send for him, Milburn, send for him. I won't be fobbed off this time. Not when a woman's life is at stake.'

'I thought you said she's been murdered,' said PC Milburn.

'And what if I did?'

'Well, it's just that if she *has* been murdered, then her life is not at stake, now is it? She's already dead.'

Louise leaned in closer so that he could smell the cheese-and-pickle lunchtime sandwiches on her breath. What lovely skin, she thought as she scrutinized him. What full lips. 'Young man, are you trying to be clever with me?' she asked.

'No, ma'am, I'm simply pointing out that—'

'There he is!' Louise cried, noticing a white-bearded,

kindly-looking man of about fifty passing through the office beyond. 'Inspector Dew,' she cried out, 'Inspector Dew.'

PC Milburn turned around and saw the inspector looking at the three of them suspiciously. He continued to examine some papers, but Louise was not going to be denied. 'Inspector,' she called. 'If I could just have a moment of your time, please.'

Sighing and making a mental note to instruct the young constable to keep the office door closed behind him in future, Inspector Walter Dew adopted a smile of resignation and stepped out towards the desk. 'Yes, madam,' he said, placing his hands firmly on the desk. 'And how can I be of assistance?'

'Inspector, I hope you remember me,' she said. 'Mrs Louise Smythson. Wife of Nicholas Smythson. Daughter-in-law of the late Lord Smythson. My brother-in-law Martin now has the title. For the time being.'

Dew stared at her, a memory of the early chapters of the Bible returning to him, in which the lineage of everyone in Christendom is traced from Adam to Jesus. 'We've met before,' he said, his voice not betraying whether this was a question or a statement.

'We have, Inspector,' she said. 'I came to see you at the end of March to tell you about my friend Mrs Cora Crippen. That she'd disappeared. Well, I have proof, conclusive proof, Inspector, that the poor woman has been murdered by her husband. It's imperative that we speak today. This instant in fact.'

Dew narrowed his eyes and considered the matter. He was aware that a large number of hysterics and madmen came into Scotland Yard each day and it was the job of the constables to sift through them, not his. He was a busy man with several cases on the go. However, when two well-dressed ladies appeared and mentioned their connections, it was difficult not to humour them for a few minutes. The chances were that she or one of her friends would be dining with the Police Commissioner later that night, and if she decided to complain about him he would have to go through the irritation of defending himself. Having only a vague memory of their earlier meeting, he looked across at Mrs Smythson's friend, who was staring at him fervently. 'And you are?' he asked.

'Margaret Nash,' she said quickly. 'Mrs. Charmed.'

'And you're a friend of the missing woman too?'

'Oh, a very good friend.'

'I'm her *best* friend,' said Louise, determined to keep some of the glory for herself. 'Really, Inspector. If you could just spare us five minutes. I promise it won't take—'

'Certainly, certainly,' he said, realizing it would be easier simply to hear them out and then send them on their way. 'Constable, let these ladies through, will you? Follow me.'

PC Milburn opened the hatch and Mrs Nash walked through first, followed by Mrs Smythson, who saw her opportunity to pinch the young constable's behind while he had his back to her. Turning around in surprise, he watched her disappear down the corridor, stopping only to give him another lascivious wink. The blood rushed to his face once again and he began to wonder whether he would not be better off simply making an honest woman of Sally Minstrel. After all, she was a decent, respectable sort and never caused him embarrassment like this. Some of these other ladies could be so crude, and he detested that. He sat back down at his desk, as confused as ever.

Inspector Dew's office was just as she remembered it. Once again he opened the window overlooking the Embankment when they stepped inside, but this time, as they sat down in the armchairs facing him, they dispensed with the small talk and moved straight to the matter at hand.

'So,' said Dew. 'Remind me of our earlier meeting.'

'I came to see you at the end of March,' said Louise, a little exasperated that he had not kept every detail of their earlier encounter lodged at the forefront of his mind since then. 'My friend Cora Crippen had gone missing but her husband had been seen at the theatre with his mistress wearing Cora's jewellery.'

'Her husband?'

'The mistress.'

'It was my husband and I who saw them together,' said Mrs Nash, determined to play her part. 'It was I who told Louise, Mrs Smythson, about it.'

'The woman had died, had she not?' asked Dew, recalling it a little better now. 'On a walking tour of Europe, if I recall. I remember it now.'

'It was in America, Inspector,' said Louise. 'She had gone to California to tend a sick relative, and then a telegram arrived for Dr Crippen, her husband, informing him that she had died. And that was the last we heard of her. Only I for one never believed it because a woman simply does not leave all her best jewellery behind when she goes away. Who knows what functions she might be invited to?'

'I thought she was looking after a sick person,' said Dew. 'What would she need her jewellery for under those circumstances?'

'Inspector, are you married?' Louise asked sweetly.

'No.'

'Well, surely you know the ways of women. Can you imagine any lady going abroad and leaving her finest necklaces and ear-rings behind in her home? Can you?'

He considered it; alas, he knew almost nothing about the ways of women and he could hardly imagine what their habits might be.

'As I told you last time, Mrs Smythson,' said Dew. 'If the lady died in America, then there's really nothing we can do. The American authorities would have—'

'But that's just it, Inspector,' said Louise, delighted to get to the point at last. 'We don't believe she did die in America. We don't believe she ever went there at all. We believe he done her in!'

'Who?'

'Her husband, of course. Dr Crippen.'

Dew smiled. 'Dr Crippen,' he said doubtfully. 'It hardly sounds like the name of a wife murderer, now does it?'

'Well, I don't expect they're all called Jack the Ripper, are they?' she asked.

'No, I suppose not,' he admitted. 'But what has changed to bring you back here? Where's your new evidence?'

Louise sat back and looked at Margaret Nash, who had agreed to take up this part of the story.

'My husband is Mr Andrew Nash,' she began. 'He owns the Nash Trading and Mining Company. Perhaps you've heard of him?'

'No,' said Inspector Dew.

'Well, he's very well known in business circles,' she replied, a little put out. 'Anyway, he had business in Mexico recently and agreed to travel on to California to find out the truth about Cora's death. When he got there he went straight to the authorities and told them the date she had supposedly arrived in the country and the date of her apparent death. It seems that visitors have to register with the police after they arrive. She never did. In fact there was no evidence of her arrival in California at all. Nor was there any record of her death. Andrew went directly to city hall and they checked the deaths register for the weeks surrounding the date that Dr Crippen said she died. There was no one answering her description whatsoever. Nothing at the mortuaries, nothing at the funeral parlours. Nothing anywhere to suggest she had ever been there, let alone died there.'

'Nor do we know the name of the relative that Cora was supposedly attending,' said Louise.

'She didn't even tell us she was going,' said Margaret. 'And we're her best friends.'

'I'm her *particular* best friend,' said Louise.

Inspector Dew sat back in his chair and thought about it, stroking his beard as he considered their story. 'These Crippens,' he said finally. 'What sort of couple are they? Do you know them well?'

'Oh, very well,' said Margaret Nash. 'Cora is part of our Music Hall Ladies' Guild. And she's a well-known singer. She was going to be a star, you know. Before he done her in!' she added dramatically.

'And Dr Crippen. What is he like?'

'He's a quiet sort of a man,' said Louise. 'Works as a dentist part of the time and in a pharmacy the rest of it. Sometimes you'd think he wouldn't say boo to a goose, but there's evil behind those eyes, Inspector. I can sense it.'

Dew smiled. He was accustomed to people running away with their stories in their imagination and attributing every unsolved crime on the streets of London to those they considered a bad lot. 'And did they get along?' he asked. 'Were they happy?'

'Not entirely,' said Louise. 'Although, really, Cora was the kindest, most gentle woman in the world. It would take a monster not to get along with her. Hawley Crippen was a lucky man, if you ask me.'

He nodded and made a few notes in his journal. In his heart he doubted there was anything to it, but nevertheless he thought he might just pay a visit to the doctor. 'Can you give me their address?' he asked.

'39 Hilldrop Crescent, Camden,' said Louise.

He wrote this down and stood up, ushering them towards the door. 'Well, I'll pay a little call on Dr Crippen,' he said. 'Don't worry. I'll get to the bottom of the matter. I'm sure there's nothing to it.'

'Well, we certainly *hope* there's nothing to it,' said Margaret Nash, although in truth she was quite enjoying the drama. 'I would hate to think of something bad happening to such a lovely woman.'

'You will keep us informed, Inspector, won't you?' asked Louise, walking down the stairs, irritated that he was not going to see them out.

'Yes, of course. Give your addresses to PC Milburn at the front desk and I'll let you know what happens.'

Louise and Margaret returned to the lobby and gave their details to the constable. 'I'm usually at home alone on Mondays between four and six,' Louise whispered in his ear.

Upstairs in his office, Inspector Walter Dew looked in his diary. He was pretty busy throughout the next week, but he had promised to look into the matter and he would not disappoint them. He turned the page to the following week, saw a free morning and scribbled the details down quickly:

'Dr Crippen. 39 Hilldrop Crescent. Missing wife. Supposedly dead. Pay a visit.'

10

On Board the *Montrose*

The sun broke early on Friday morning on board
the *Montrose*, but Mr John Robinson slept late in his
bunk. Edmund had woken around eight o'clock and
had gone to breakfast, finding the dining hall filled
with passengers for the first time since their voyage
had begun. The majority of his fellow travellers had
grown accustomed to the movement of the ship over
the previous few days and appetites had returned in
strength. All around him he could see the faces of first-
class passengers, the colour back in their fat cheeks,
filling their starving bellies with food as if a famine had
just ended and supplies had been delivered for the first
time in weeks. Not wishing to engage in conversation,
he searched the room for a place where he might sit
alone but he could not see a spare table. There were
at least ten people queuing at the buffet, however, so
he walked towards it, hoping that a seat might present
itself by the time he had been served.

Catching sight of his reflection in the mirrored wall
behind the food stands, it struck Edmund how easy it
was to make the transformation from female to male,

particularly when one was as small and slim as he was. People believed what was presented to them and rarely challenged it, which was how the deception had worked so convincingly thus far.

Their first conversation on the subject had taken place in Antwerp, on the afternoon that Hawley had bought the tickets which would gain them passage on the *Montrose* and, ultimately, bring them to their new lives together in Canada. He returned to their hotel room in the late afternoon, armed with several parcels, and laid them out on the bed with a look of anxiety on his face, barely able to look at his lover as he prepared his explanation. Ethel was accustomed to his mood swings by now; ever since his wife's death she felt that he had grown increasingly tortured by the memory of her. The fact that their own relationship had begun before Cora went to California seemed to weigh on his mind to the point where Ethel believed he actually blamed himself for her leaving. In their adultery lay the failure of the marriage, as opposed to Cora's unreasonable behaviour.

'What's all this?' she asked, turning around from the dressing table where she had been trying on a pearl necklace belonging to Cora which she had never worn before. Perhaps it was the light, but she didn't like the way it looked on her; the pearls were far too white, compared to the paleness of her own neck. Cora had enjoyed a darker complexion, which matched her moods. Ethel threw them aside with little ceremony. 'Hawley, you haven't been buying me presents again, surely? You're spoiling me. And we should be saving our money.'

'Not quite, my dear,' he replied, reaching over and giving her a gentle kiss on the forehead. 'Just a few things for the voyage, that's all.'

'But our bags are quite full already,' she said, standing up and going over to examine his purchases happily. Although she had never had a relationship with a man before, she was sure that no one alive was as attentive and thoughtful as Doctor Hawley Harvey Crippen. If there was one thing he knew how to do, it was how to make a girl feel valued. She poured out the contents of the bags on the bed and stared at them in surprise. 'I don't understand,' she muttered, turning to stare at him, bewildered. 'Is someone else joining us?'

Across the blanket lay a couple of pairs of boy's breeches, along with some shirts, a pair of braces, some boots, a cap and a black wig. They all appeared to be in Ethel's size but were clearly designed for a boy rather than for a girl.

'I should explain,' said Hawley, his face growing a little red with embarrassment.

'I think you should.'

Hawley sat down on a chair and held Ethel's hand as she sat on the corner of the bed opposite him. 'I think we need to be very careful,' he said, beginning the speech he had prepared earlier, not knowing whether she would believe him or not. 'You see, I have a friend who travelled to America last year with his fiancée, and a scandal was created on board when it was discovered that they were sharing a cabin in an unmarried state. They were shunned for the entire voyage. Almost two weeks. I'm worried that it would be the same with us. I thought it would be better if no one knew our true feelings for each other.'

Ethel stared at him in amazement. 'Hawley, you can't be serious,' she said.

'I'm perfectly serious,' he replied. 'You see, what I thought was that, if you were to dress as a boy, then—'

'A boy?'

'Just hear me out, Ethel. If you were to dress as a boy, then no one would give any serious thought to the question of our sharing a cabin. No one would care.'

Ethel held her breath; she could scarcely believe what she was hearing. She turned around and looked at the clothes he had bought for her and she couldn't help but laugh. 'Hawley, you're such a prude!' she said. 'This is 1910, for heaven's sake. Not 1810. No one cares about such things today, surely.'

'Of course they do. Don't be so naïve.'

'And if they do,' she added with determination, 'what of it? We're in love, aren't we?'

'Of course we are.'

'And we're adults?'

'Yes, but—'

'And we plan to be married when we reach Canada, don't we?'

'As soon as is humanly possible.'

'Then I ask you, Hawley, what business is it of anyone else how we choose to arrange our lives in the mean time? If we want to spend the voyage hanging out of the crow's nest, huddled up in a lifeboat, or howling at the moon, what does it matter to others as long as we have paid the fare?'

Hawley stood up and walked across to the window, pulling back the curtain a little with his fingers and looking down on the streets of Antwerp below. The market was closing for the day and he could make out a group of boys watching a grocery stall in earnest, waiting for the owner to turn his back so that they could each steal an apple. Their intent was obvious; he wondered why the stall owner failed to notice them. If it was mine, he thought to himself, I would keep a whip under the stall to dissuade thieves. 'Ethel,' he said in a quiet voice, 'I wouldn't ask you to do this if I didn't believe it was completely necessary. I've been married twice before, you know that.'

'Of course I do, but I don't see what that—'

'Both marriages failed. Oh, I know that Charlotte died and Cora left me for another man, but I was miserable with both ladies and that's the truth of it. With you, things are different. I believe we have a chance of true happiness. For the first time in my life, real affection and love. And the moment we set foot on that boat tomorrow, we begin our new lives. Away from Europe. Just you and me. And I want every moment to be perfect. This trip across the ocean is our pre-honeymoon, don't you see? If we have to put up with the comments of the other passengers or if we end up being snubbed by our peers, then what kind of voyage will it be? Eleven days of misery. And that's no way to begin our lives together. And what if the scandal follows us to Canada and we find it hard to make new friends there? I ask you, do we deserve that? Please, Ethel. For me. Just consider it.'

She shook her head slowly, not as a refusal but out of amazement at his ideas, and turned once again to look at the clothes, picking up a pair of the breeches he had purchased and holding them against her legs to measure the size. She examined her reflection in the mirror; they seemed like a perfect fit. She took the wig off the bed and, piling her own hair up on her head, placed it on top, settling it gently at the sides. She looked in the glass again and wasn't sure whether she should laugh or not. 'It would take some adjusting,' she said. 'I might need to cut my own hair underneath it.'

'But it will work. You agree to it?'

'People will see through it,' she said, exasperated.

'People believe what they are told. No one expects a grown woman to dress as a teenage boy. Why would they? It will work, believe me.'

She sighed dramatically. 'And who shall we say we are?' she asked. 'What pretence shall we give?'

'I've thought about that too,' he said. 'It will be a game for us. I will say that my name is Mr John Robinson and you're—'

'Mr John—?'

'You're my son, Edmund.'

'Your son,' she said in a matter-of-fact tone. 'Hawley,

this isn't some strange fantasy you've cooked up, is it? Because if it is, I can tell you now that—'

'It's a deception, that's all, and it might even prove an entertaining one for us. Please, Ethel. I truly believe that this will be the sensible way for us to escape from here and begin again.'

She considered it. It was the most ridiculous thing she had ever heard and she failed to understand why he was so determined about it. Of course, his point was a valid one. If their fellow passengers in first class discovered an unmarried man and woman sharing a cabin, they would naturally cause a scandal; but, unlike Hawley, Ethel did not particularly care. She was not a woman overly concerned with the opinions of others.

'And when we reach Canada,' she said, 'we can stop pretending? We can go back to being plain old Hawley and Ethel?'

'I promise it.'

She turned and looked at herself in the mirror once again. 'I make quite a good boy, really, don't I?' she asked.

Three days later, and she had not only grown accustomed to wearing her new outfit, but had begun to enjoy it. She felt a sense of great adventure and freedom pretending to be someone that she was not. Of course, problems had arisen along the way. Her basic prettiness, her wide eyes, her sharp cheekbones, her full lips, had made her into quite an attractive boy, and that had inspired the attentions of Victoria Drake who, she noticed happily, was not in the dining hall this morning. But everything about being Edmund Robinson, rather than Ethel LeNeve, offered a sense of danger and challenge which she had never felt before. She could walk differently, speak differently, act differently and think differently. She had boarded in Antwerp as a boy but, if nothing else, she believed that the trip across the Atlantic would make her a man.

Having helped himself to breakfast, the self-created Edmund Robinson stared around the hall, which still appeared to be filled to capacity. Running along the wall, however, was a row of tables set for two people and he saw an empty one at the very end, so he made his way towards it quickly, sitting down just as another passenger pulled out the opposite seat. He looked up to see the dark, scowling face of Tom DuMarqué as he planted himself at the other side of the table, his tray almost overloaded with food. He had the sense that Tom had been waiting for him.

'Tom,' he said, irritated to see him, for he had wanted to eat in peace this morning. 'How nice.'

'Edmund,' the other replied with a curt nod. 'You don't mind if I sit here, do you?'

'Not at all,' he replied, shaking his head. 'Please yourself.'

Tom sat down with a sudden heaviness and breathed in quickly, placing a hand under the table as if he was in pain.

'Are you all right?' asked Edmund, observing the scowl which had crossed his face.

'Fine,' he grunted.

'It's just that you look as if you've hurt yourself.'

'I'm *fine*,' he insisted, raising his hand back up and laying his breakfast out across the table: cereal, juice, toast, a plate of ham and eggs, two pastries and a cup of coffee – while Edmund stared at it with a smile. He himself usually preferred to eat nothing more adventurous than tea and toast in the morning, but today he had thrown caution to the wind and had taken a plate of scrambled eggs as well.

'Hungry, are you?' he asked.

'Yes.'

Although they had sat opposite each other at dinner the previous evening and had chatted amiably enough, Edmund could sense that there was little love lost between them. He had observed the longing glances that the boy had thrown in the direction of Victoria Drake and was more than aware that Tom could see the same looks being thrown from Victoria towards himself. It amused him a little but, although there was no possibility of the young girl succeeding in her flirtations, he suspected there was even less chance for Tom with the object of his own affections. Although he was a good-looking boy and his rude, worldly manner might have made him all the more attractive to some, he was little more than a child – and was not, he suspected, where Victoria's realm of interest lay.

'I was waiting for you, actually,' said Tom after a few silent minutes had passed, confirming Edmund's suspicion.

'Waiting for me?' he asked, looking up in surprise as his companion scoffed his breakfast. 'Really?'

'Yes. I wanted to talk to you.'

'All right.'

'About Victoria Drake.'

'Ah,' said Edmund, nodding his head.

'I'm giving you fair warning, Robinson,' the youngster said in a low voice.

'Fair warning of what?'

'Of what will happen if you don't keep your filthy hands off her, that's what. I'm giving it to you now and I won't give it again.'

Edmund smiled and put his cup down. Forthrightness was one thing. Passion was another. But threats were something else entirely, and he was damned if he would put up with them, even if they were groundless.

'Now just a moment—' he began, before being cut off.

'Just you listen to me, Robinson,' Tom hissed. 'I don't know what your game is, but I don't like it. I don't like how you follow her around all the time and try and get in with her.'

'How *I*—?'

'I saw that girl first and, given half a chance, I'll get her too. I'm twice the man you are, even if you do have a few years on me. So you'll just stop chasing after her if you know what's good for you.'

'Me chasing after her?' Edmund repeated with a laugh. 'That's rich. It's *her* who won't leave *me* alone, you idiot. She's been after me ever since we met on the first day.'

'Don't be ridiculous. A girl like that? She'd never chase after a scrawny thing like you. You're far from being a man, if you ask me.'

Further than you realize, Edmund thought.

'Skinny arms, weedy voice, you ain't even had to shave yet, have you? And *don't* call me an idiot or I'll take you outside and throw you overboard. Let the sharks finish you off.'

'Look, Tom,' said Edmund, putting his knife and fork down, exasperated that he was obliged to continue this conversation at all. 'It's no use speaking to *me* about this. If you have any interest in Victoria, then I suggest you—'

'I'm not interested in your suggestions,' said the boy, picking up his butter knife now and leaning forward. The knife-point was only a few inches away from Edmund's heart and he looked down at it nervously. 'You don't know anything about me,' said Tom. 'You don't know what I'm capable of. Where I grew up, I had to fight to survive. Don't think because my uncle struts around like the King of France, that makes me the Dauphin. I know how to get what I want and I'll tell you this, you piece of shit, I'll get that Victoria or crush you along the way, do you understand me? No one gets in the way of a DuMarqué. I come from a long line of fighters. My father died in the Boer War. My ancestors have killed for centuries. One was a highwayman. Another worked for Robespierre in the French Revolution, so I know a little about chopping the heads off the privileged. There has never been a coward among us.'

Edmund stared at him in horror. He may have been only fourteen years old, but there was a wildness behind those dark eyes that made him believe every word he was saying. The knife continued to point in his direction and it was held perfectly still; there was not a trace of nervousness in Tom's demeanour. For two pennies, he thought, the maniac would stab him right there and then. Slowly Tom turned the knife around so that it was facing himself, and Edmund watched as the boy ran the blade along the inside of his palm, a thin line of blood appearing as he did so, while Tom did not twitch or betray any symptom of pain whatsoever.

'I've lost my appetite,' Edmund said, standing up and pushing his plate forward. He was upset and scared, an emotion he was not accustomed to. 'I'm . . . I've got to . . .'

'Just you remember what I said, Robinson,' said Tom, turning the knife again and cutting it straight through the fried egg on his plate. The yolk exploded over the side, as if an artery had been cut, and he mashed the white into a piece of ham before eating it. 'And like I said, I don't offer warnings twice,' he added. 'You should think yourself lucky that I'm warning you at all.'

Pale, Edmund turned and walked quickly from the dining hall. His legs felt a little weak, his stomach sick. He wanted nothing more now than to return to his cabin. He wanted to cry. He hated violence and threats; they brought back too many bad memories. This business with Victoria Drake had struck him as something of a joke until now. The venom of Tom DuMarqué's words however had turned it into something more serious. He stretched his hand out before even reaching the door of the hall, needing to push it forward quickly so as to get some air into his lungs. How can I pretend, he asked himself, when I am not a man at all and never can be?

He sucked in the fresh sea air on the outside like a drowning man coming up for air. Spots floated in front of his eyes and he hoped that he would manage to reach the cabin without collapsing. He had never felt such a mixture of anger and fear in all his life. On the deck he tripped over a length of rope and fell into a pair of familiar arms, giving a slight shout as he did so.

'Edmund,' said Mr John Robinson, staring at him. 'What's the matter?'

'Haw—' he began, before realizing his mistake. 'Father,' he corrected himself quickly, staring from him to Martha Hayes and back again, trying desperately to recover his equilibrium. 'I'm sorry, I'm feeling a little unwell. I thought I might get some more sleep.'

'Perhaps you're hungry?'

'No!' he snapped. 'No, I've eaten already.'

'All right. Well, as you wish,' said Mr Robinson, his face looking perplexed and concerned. 'Would you like me to come downstairs with you?'

'No, I'm fine, I just need some peace, that's all.'

'Perhaps I could bring you some water, Edmund?' Martha asked, seeing the boy's features become even paler than usual and the line of perspiration bursting out along the hairline. 'It wouldn't be any trouble.'

'Really, I'll be fine,' he repeated firmly. 'I just need to rest, that's all. I'll see you both later.'

He rushed past them and they watched as he disappeared down the stairs. John Robinson frowned and wondered whether he should follow after all.

'He'll be fine,' said Martha, reading his mind. 'Let him sleep.'

'Of course,' he replied, sure that this was the sensible course. 'Shall we go on for breakfast, then?'

'Oh, let's wait a few minutes,' she said, linking her arm through his. 'I love this time of morning, don't you? Let's just sit and enjoy it for a few minutes. It sounds pretty crowded in there anyway.'

Not very hungry yet anyway, Mr Robinson agreed and they relaxed on two deckchairs, watching as the seabirds swooped down into the water and flew back out of sight with whatever they had caught. Mr Robinson had still not reached the point where he was enjoying the voyage, but Martha Hayes was loving every moment of it.

'I never imagined for a moment that I would end up crossing the Atlantic,' she said, staring at the sea with such delight and excitement in her eyes that Mr Robinson could not help but smile. 'It's so far removed from my expectations in life. And I was so unhappy in Antwerp. This morning I woke up and felt just . . . excited about my new life. Sitting here, I feel happier than I have in a long time.'

'I was born in America,' said Mr Robinson, who would have preferred to have returned to the cabin. 'I'll be glad to be back there.'

'Really? You have hardly a trace of an accent.'

'Well, I've lived in London for years. I imagine I must have buried it there somewhere. I didn't much enjoy the trip across in the first place, and I don't much care for it now either.'

'You'll stay in Canada then? You'll never come back?'

'Canada. Or the United States. But yes, I'll never return to Europe or England. I hate England. I hate the people. I found nothing but . . . misery there.'

Martha frowned; his tone was bitter and she found his manner slightly unsettling. 'Do you know what today would have been?' she asked, hoping to change the subject.

'*Would* have been?' he asked, surprised at the tense.

'It would have been my wedding day,' she said with a sigh.

Mr Robinson said nothing. He had been aware that there was more to Martha Hayes than she had let on so far, and he had not wanted to ask her any personal questions until she was ready to offer the answers herself.

'I have told you about my friend, Mr Brillt?' she asked. He nodded, recalling a few passing remarks. 'Mr Brillt and I met some eighteen months ago. He was a teacher in Antwerp, a very intelligent man. His grasp of history and literature amazed me. The things he told me, the books he introduced me to! Oh, Mr Robinson, I believe that man had read every word that had ever been written. From the Roman historians to the medieval poets, the Renaissance dramatists to the new novelists. Even the European novels in their original languages. He could speak six different languages, you see. A brilliant man. And I don't mind admitting that he opened my mind a lot to different possibilities. Oh, he wasn't the most handsome man in the world, but there was something else about him. Something magical. Something so intelligent that it was hard not to be amazed by him.'

'People like to pretend they're in love,' Mr Robinson suggested, 'but there's no such thing really. We all just use each other for our own ends. Don't you agree?'

'No, I don't,' she said. 'What a cynical attitude! I loved Mr Brillt as if love had never existed before in the world. And he said he loved me too. We spent so much time together. We went to the theatre together, the music halls.' He flinched at those hated words. 'Sometimes he took me boating and we would eat a picnic in the middle of the lakes. He knew all the best shops and made the sandwiches himself with exotic cheeses and cold meats. Tastes I had never imagined. Wonderful afternoons,' she added, drifting into a haze of memory. 'He asked me to marry him, you see. Six months ago we went to dinner and he got down on one knee and produced a diamond ring and said that I, Martha Hayes, would make him the happiest man

224

in the world if I would consent to becoming Mrs Léon Brillt.'

'And you agreed?'

'I did. I was thrilled. I couldn't believe that a man as cultured and intelligent as he would have any interest in a woman like me. Of course, I had hoped that he might propose one day and had already begun to daydream about the life we would lead together when we were married, but when he asked me I was still shocked. We set the date – today's date – and booked a church. I had already started planning our future together. And that's when it happened.'

Mr Robinson stared at her. He could see that she was setting her jaw firmly in anticipation of the difficult part of the story. 'Tell me,' he urged her. 'Or later, if you would prefer. If it's painful.'

Before she could continue, Tom DuMarqué emerged from the dining hall and began walking towards them awkwardly. He stared at them as he approached, like a vicious animal sniffing its prey before deciding whether or not to attack. Eventually he passed them by, dragging his leg a little, offering them just a nod, and Martha shivered involuntarily.

'There's something about that boy,' she began, but didn't continue the thought. 'And was he limping?'

'He has a strange air about him,' Mr Robinson agreed. 'As if he's very angry about something but isn't sure what. He's very different from his uncle. *He* doesn't seem to have a care in the world. And yes, he did seem to be dragging his leg a little. But please, Miss Hayes – Martha – tell me what happened with your engagement. Nothing tragic occurred, I hope? My own first wife died in a traffic accident, so I know something of such things.' The words were out before he could stop himself, but he immediately regretted having revealed anything so personal.

Fortunately, she did not react to them. 'It was a

Thursday afternoon, about two months ago,' she said, looking away from him. 'I had found the most beautiful wedding dress in a shop in Antwerp and was so excited that I thought I would go to Léon's school and tell him about it. I bought some sandwiches, thinking we could have lunch together. When I arrived, I went to his usual classroom but there was a stranger there, a man I had never met before. To be honest, Léon had never introduced me to any of his friends or colleagues, so I wouldn't have known the man anyway, nor would he have known me. Léon always said that he wanted to keep me all to himself. Anyway, this other teacher asked me who I was and I said that I was a friend of Mr Brillt's. He took me aside and said that Léon had suffered an attack in the classroom earlier that day, something to do with his heart, they thought, and he had been immediately taken to hospital. Naturally I was racked with worry, and I ran from the room and went straight to the hospital. It was difficult to track him down at first, but eventually I found him in a private room and ran inside, prepared for the worst. Or what I *imagined* would be the worst. He was sitting up in bed, looking pale and anxious, but he was talking so I immediately knew that he was not at death's door. But when he turned and saw me standing there, I thought for a moment that he might have another heart attack. "Martha," he said, swallowing hard. I looked around the room and saw that he was surrounded by six children and a large, middle-aged woman, who were all staring back at me without the faintest idea who I was. Of course they were his wife and children. I knew it immediately. I could tell.'

'And what did you do?'

'I did the only thing I could think of. I turned around and ran away. I only saw Léon once more after that, about two weeks later, when he visited me and tried to explain. He said that he and his wife led mostly separate lives and that there was no reason why we had to stop seeing each other. I was devastated, of course. I wanted to kill myself, Mr Robinson, I really did. And then one day I woke up and I thought that I would not allow this man to ruin my life any longer, that I had my own future to look forward to, and so I decided I would change my plans entirely. I went to the harbour and found out the details of transatlantic crossings and then I bought a ticket for Canada, for the *Montrose*, which is how you find me where I am now. But sometimes I think that had Léon not suffered the heart attack that morning, I could well have been marrying him today. He could have continued with his deception for ever. Some marriage. Based on lies.'

She sat back and looked at him with a trace of a smile but not an element of self-pity.

'I'm sorry,' he said quietly, knowing that his words would really be little comfort.

'Don't be. I'm better off without him.'

'Nevertheless. It's a terrible thing to do to someone.'

She turned around and looked him straight in the eye. 'You know what I think?' she said. 'That this was a man with one wife already, who was trying to marry another, knowing that it would be a fraud which would eventually ruin them both anyway. If you ask me, Mr Robinson, some men are simply not supposed to take wives at all.'

He looked away and thought about it. 'Are you hungry yet?' he asked.

Matthieu Zéla was lying on his bed in the Presidential Suite, reading a copy of *The Immoralist* by André Gide. One of the pleasures of a long journey such as this one, he believed, was the opportunity it afforded one to spend long periods of time with little else to do but read. The real world was so busy, and life so filled with affairs of business and money and romance, that there was precious little opportunity to enjoy more cultural pursuits. To this end he had brought several books with him for the journey to Canada. He'd wanted to read the Gide ever since he'd heard that the pope had publicly condemned its author. Such criticisms usually made him more eager to sample the books than even the most positive commentary in *The Times* newspaper. He had never met the present pope, but he had once been employed by one of his predecessors to construct an opera house in the city of Rome, a project which had ultimately failed to come to fruition, and he had spent long hours in the Vatican poring over historical designs and discussing plans for its construction. He knew from his experience there that the personal tastes of the occupants of the Vatican often ran to the exotic. To this end, alongside *The Immoralist*, he had brought copies of Voltaire's *Philosophical Letters*, Victor Hugo's *Notre-Dame de Paris* and a volume of Casanova's *Memoirs* to enjoy while he travelled to Canada, each of which had found a place on the Papal Index over the years.

The Presidential Suite was the largest single cabin on board the *Montrose* and in fact housed four separate rooms: the master bedroom, where he lay at the moment, a smaller one, in which his nephew Tom slept, a medium-sized bathroom and a sitting room for entertainment purposes. He had not planned on doing very much entertaining while travelling (his books were company enough for him, his nephew distraction enough) but he had had the misfortune of running into Mrs Antoinette Drake earlier in the day and she had enquired as to the comfort of his apartments, continuing her questioning *ad nauseam* until it became clear that she wanted to inspect them herself, at which point he had little choice but to observe etiquette and invite her for afternoon tea, an offer she had eagerly accepted. She was due at four o'clock; it was a quarter to the hour now, and Matthieu sighed, for he was enjoying the descriptions of Africa, which he had visited some twenty years before, and would have preferred to remain lost in them for another hour or two. Sadly, duty called and he placed the bookmark at the end of the chapter, preparing himself for the ordeal ahead.

Like Mr John Robinson, this was not Matthieu's first trip across the Atlantic Ocean, nor would it be his last. Throughout his life he had travelled far and wide and he scarcely considered himself to be a citizen of any particular country, so varied was his life experience. Born in Paris, he had fled thence to England with his younger brother at the age of seventeen, when they had been orphaned. It was on a boat much smaller than this that he had met the only true love of his life, one Dominique Sauvet, and where his adult adventures had begun, although the romance faltered. He had been fortunate enough to make a great deal of money at a youthful age and had invested it wisely, moving from city to city whenever boredom struck, living in glamorous surroundings while never actually living beyond his means. He wasn't sure how much he was worth exactly, but whenever he tried to make an account of his wealth it seemed to have grown once again.

He shaved quickly, barely glancing at the reflection in the mirror; he knew better than to expect any signs of ageing. His dark hair had a slight hint of grey running through it, but that had been there for so many years now without spreading at all that he hardly noticed it any more. Matthieu Zéla was an elegant man, the type of individual whose appearance suggests fifty years of good, healthy, athletic living. That this was quite contrary to the truth mattered little, for appearances, he had long grown to realize, were the most deceptive of all human traits.

The chiming of the clock in the sitting room indicated four o'clock, and by the fourth strike of the bell there was a sharp knock on the cabin door and he went to answer it. He imagined that Mrs Drake must have been standing in the corridor for several minutes, waiting for the hour exactly before appearing, and he could not help but smile to himself at her eagerness.

'Mrs Drake,' he said, standing back to allow her vast girth to come through the door unimpeded. 'How lovely to see you.'

'But Mr Zéla, how kind of you to invite me,' she said obsequiously, her head darting from side to side in a quick appreciation of her surroundings, as if the whole visit had been his idea all along.

'Matthieu, please,' he muttered.

'Of course,' she replied. 'And you must call me Antoinette. What charming rooms you have here. Poor Mr Drake was so apologetic when he informed my daughter and me that the Presidential Suite was already taken when he booked our tickets for us. He felt quite guilty. That's why we're only in the first-class cabin, you see. You got there before us, Mr Zéla, you naughty man. Matthieu, I mean.'

He smiled and closed the door behind her, aware that his decision to bring Tom to Canada had been a last-minute one and that he had only booked this suite twenty-four hours before leaving Antwerp. He doubted very much whether Mrs Drake's unfortunate husband had ever enquired about it at all; if he had, it would have been merely to check the price before deciding against it.

'Well, then I must apologize and try to make amends with tea,' he said gallantly. 'I hope your cabin is comfortable.'

'Oh, perfectly adequate,' she replied. 'I don't bother too much about these matters myself, of course. The important thing is that we arrive in Canada safely. I'm not a very material person, you see.' Matthieu nodded and glanced quickly at her expensive dress, her luminous jewellery and the fine hat she was removing as she sat down. 'But how lovely that you have your own facilities for making tea,' she added, watching as he boiled some water in a pan. 'What will they think of next, do you suppose?'

'I have no idea,' he said. 'But I look forward to being there when they do. Would you prefer tea or coffee?'

'Tea, I think. I feel coffee is an unsuitable drink, don't you?'

'For whom?'

'Why, for anyone. I don't know why, but it seems common to me. A little tea with lemon in the afternoon, and I'm a contented woman, Matthieu. If it's good enough for Queen Alexandra, it's good enough for me, and I know for a fact that she sits down to tea every day at four herself. I can't imagine the royal family sitting down to coffee, can you?'

'I've never thought about it.'

'Well, I'm sure you'd agree if you did. Anyway, it doesn't take much to satisfy me, you know. A simple cup of tea and I'm as happy as a lamb.' She flicked out her fan with these words and his eyebrows rose a little; he found that last statement somewhat hard to swallow. The tea made, however, he sat down opposite her in an armchair and allowed the pot to sit for a few minutes before pouring.

'It's so lovely to have made some acquaintances on board, don't you agree, Matthieu?' she asked.

'Quite.'

'My husband, Mr Drake, he travels a lot for his work and he can always strike up a conversation with another gentleman about business or politics or some such thing, I expect. But for a lady like myself, travelling with her daughter, one feels a little more cautious. One would not want one's fellow passengers to get the wrong idea about one.'

'And what idea would that be, Antoinette?' he asked.

'Well, I know you will think it a strange thing,' she

231

said with what she believed to be a girlish giggle. 'But I have heard that there are many women who use these transatlantic crossings as a way to ensnare a husband. Two weeks at sea and off to a new life, new money, new man. I've seen it myself, Matthieu. That first day, boarding the ship, all those poor unfortunate single women running around, trying to discover the unmarried men and reel them in with their harpoons. Surely you've noticed them. It's terribly embarrassing.'

'I'm afraid I kept myself to myself that first day,' he admitted. 'Slept through the whole thing. But I'm sure you're right.' Of course, Matthieu had been married himself, on a number of occasions, and he was more than aware of the admiration some ladies in society had for the institution. Few of his marriages had ended well, however, and he had turned against it, although he still found himself falling into the same trap time and time again. Had it not been for the many references she had made to Mr Drake, he would have believed that Antoinette was trying to become the next Mrs Zéla herself. As it was, he felt she merely wished to be associated with the richest man on board. Marriage or money, these were the important things to women like her, he reasoned. And preferably both.

'Take Miss Hayes, for instance,' Mrs Drake continued, oblivious to her companion's drifting away into his own dream-world. 'A charming woman, no one could doubt it. Friendly, thoughtful and a lovely conversationalist. Such a shame that she is a little plain, but not every woman can be a great beauty. Only some of us are fortunate enough to have been born with good genes, and my family comes from a long line of great beauties. No, I will say this of Miss Hayes: she is a very pleasant woman. There can be no denying it. But her attempts to trap Mr Robinson are, shall we say, a little obvious, don't you think?'

'Mr Robinson?' asked Matthieu. 'The fellow we dined with last night, you mean?'

'Of course. You must have noticed what was going on. She hangs on his every word.'

In truth he had noticed no such thing. A keen observer of human nature, he had examined each of his dinner companions in detail the previous evening and had already made up his mind on the characters of each. Miss Hayes, he believed, was no more interested in Mr Robinson than he was. She was simply a friendly woman, open to conversation and hoping to relieve the tedium of a voyage on one's own by making a few friends along the way. And as for Mr Robinson himself? Well, Matthieu could scarcely believe that that milksop of a man would attract any serious female attention. He was quiet, moody, dull and entirely lacking in social graces. He wore a beard without a moustache, an outdated look. He had made it clear throughout dinner that he did not want to be there, barely acknowledging any of his companions and uttering monosyllabic answers whenever questioned. Even if Miss Hayes was interested in finding a husband, which he doubted, her tastes would hardly run to the likes of Mr John Robinson.

'I think perhaps you do her a disservice,' he suggested.

'Do you, Matthieu?' she asked, leaning forward, using every available opportunity to use his given name. 'Do you really?'

'Yes. I think she sees him merely as a friend.'

'I think he's tiring of her attentions,' she replied, pursing her lips. 'The poor man seems to run in fright every time he sees me. I think he expects Miss Hayes to be two feet behind me, where quite frankly she often does seem to be. I wonder, is she looking for a position as a paid companion? Do you think so? If so, she's looking in the wrong place. I have my daughter for company and have never been short of friends.'

'And how is your daughter keeping?' Matthieu asked, keen to steer the conversation away from Miss Hayes. 'I hope my nephew isn't bothering her too much?'

'Your nephew? Gracious, no,' she said, shaking her head.

Mrs Drake herself was not immune to the attentions that Tom DuMarqué had been showing Victoria over the previous few days, and she was only disappointed that he was a mere child of fourteen. Had he been a few years older, then she would have seen him as a splendid match for her daughter, considering his lineage. And his potential bank account.

'You have no children yourself then, Matthieu?' she asked, looking around the room for any pictures which might contradict this hypothesis.

'None, I'm afraid.'

'But you have been married?'

'Yes.'

'But no children.'

'Still none,' he replied with a smile. Mrs Drake stared at him, expecting some additional information but nothing was forthcoming.

'Such a shame,' she said eventually. 'Children can be such a blessing.'

'Victoria is your only one?'

'Oh yes. After all, one doesn't need too many blessings in life. One shouldn't be greedy.'

'Indeed.'

'Perhaps one day?' she continued, unwilling to let the matter drop. Matthieu wondered whether she would simply prefer him to produce a copy of his will, in order to let her know to whom he intended leaving his money. If so, she would be disappointed. He had never made one. He'd never seen the point.

'Perhaps,' he said. 'The future is a little like the Mona Lisa. A mystery to all of us. You mentioned that you're planning on spending time with a relative in Canada?'

'Yes, my sister's family. I haven't seen them in so many years. I really can't wait. And of course Victoria will have the chance to meet some of her cousins, which should be exciting. To be honest, Matthieu, I'm hoping that she may find a suitable beau in Canada. Some of the fellows she associates with in Europe can be such crude creatures. And they're all down on their luck, more's the pity. They come from aristocratic families, of course, with ties back to the Borgias, most of them, but ask them to buy a meal in a restaurant and they can't even afford to look at the bill. Not so much as two shillings to rub together between them. That's the strangest thing about the wealthiest families of Europe: they're all penniless.'

'Well, there's always Edmund Robinson,' Matthieu suggested, interested in what her response would be to his suitorship. 'She seems very keen on him.'

'*Her* keen on *him*?' Mrs Drake said, appalled. 'I think it's the other way around, Matthieu. He can't seem to keep his eyes off her. If you ask me, young Master Robinson and your nephew will come to blows before this voyage is over.'

'I certainly hope not.'

'But Victoria's a beautiful girl.'

'Indeed she is, I wasn't suggesting otherwise. But Tom's too young for her, and Edmund—'

'Edmund what?' she asked, ready to be insulted if he said something which demeaned her daughter, such as a suggestion that he was too good for her.

'Edmund is unworthy of her,' he said tactfully. 'I think Victoria would be better with a more independent sort. With a little more maturity. Someone who has control over his own life. If you ask me, young Master Robinson is too old to be travelling so closely with his father. He should have struck out on his own by now. And he's such a delicate thing, too. No, Antoinette, I believe that Victoria has better fish than him to catch in Canada.'

Mrs Drake sat back and drained her tea, delighted by his observations. She had reserved judgement on Edmund until now, having adopted a high opinion of his gentle father but still unsure as to their financial position or anything else concerning their family. She knew nothing whatsoever of Edmund's mother, and that would be necessary before allowing any courtship to take place between the two young people. Relaxing in the Presidential Suite, she regretted that her husband had been so cruel as to deny it to her, insisting that she and Victoria settle for first class instead. It was a much more comfortable arrangement here and it said a lot about the cabin's occupant. Mr Zéla was clearly a gentleman and he had risen in her personal ranking system to the point where he was now her favourite passenger on board, surpassing even Mr Robinson, despite the fact that he was a Frenchman – which was surely just an accident of birth for which he could hardly be held responsible. And, she convinced herself, she was sure that he had not invited her to tea in his rooms just as an act of friendship. He had probably fallen in love with her a little; but no good would come of it as she was a faithful wife and would never consider giving in to his animal passions. Still, it was always nice to have an admirer.

Matthieu Zéla, for his part, collected the tea things and brought them over to the sideboard, amused by the discussion of Victoria's love life for, through his observations of the previous evening, several other things had become clear to him. First, that his nephew Tom had fallen hopelessly in love, and probably for the first time in his life. He recognized the desperate look in the boy's eyes, the longing for the girl's attention and company, for he had seen that look before, and usually in a mirror, many years earlier when he himself had loved Dominique. Secondly, that Victoria had no interest in his young nephew whatsoever, but that she in turn had fallen for the delicate charms of Edmund Robinson, who, he was absolutely sure, would never return those affections.

For Edmund Robinson, he had deduced within sixty seconds of meeting him, was clearly a woman in disguise.

At the other end of the ship, standing by the bow and looking into the distance at the open sea through his binoculars, stood Captain Henry Kendall, his mind filled with what he had observed the previous night. He was clear on one point: that Mr John Robinson and the boy he had presented as his son, Edmund, had shared a passionate kiss on the deck of the *Montrose*. And this was not a loving embrace between parent and child; no, indeed. This had been a true kiss of lovers, lips on lips, mouths open, bodies entwined. Absolutely outrageous. He had heard of such things happening, of course – in Paris usually – but this did not make them right. Naturally a husband and wife could share whatever foul intimacies their desires demanded of them; it was to be expected if children were desired of a union. No one could possibly enjoy the coarseness of the act, but that was the way of the world and he grudgingly accepted it. But a love between two men? Unconscionable. And between a man and boy? Disgusting. What would Mr Sorenson think of it, he wondered. Why, had he been present the previous evening, he would surely have voted to send them both overboard immediately and without the dinghy and compass that the traitor Fletcher Christian had given to William Bligh. For the first time Captain Kendall actually felt pleased that Mr Sorenson was not present on board this voyage, as such appalling behaviour would certainly have upset him. The captain thought of him, lying in his hospital bed in Antwerp, perhaps sporting the purple silk pyjamas which he had bought when they had visited the city of Quebec on their last voyage, and he gave a gentle sigh.

However, there was one other issue which negated his outrage and created a new sort for him to enjoy. While he had been watching the kiss take place, what he had thought was Edmund's hat had blown off his head, revealing the hair beneath. But of course it had not been a hat at all but a wig. He could not swear to it, but every facet of his mind and every element of logic pointed to the conclusion that Edmund Robinson was in fact a woman. Of course the idea was infamous. That an unmarried man and woman would travel as husband and wife defied logic and decency. But which was worse: the embrace of a man and another man, a love affair between a father and son, or a hidden romance between the sexes in which the woman, for reasons unknown, disguised herself as a boy? He could not decide; all three disgusted him. He needed advice. Oh, Mr Sorenson, he thought. My dear Mr Sorenson! Where are you when I need your counsel most?

'Captain?' A voice from behind him startled him and he spun around, a delighted smile rushing across his face.

'Mr Sorenson?'

'Er, no, sir,' came the confused reply. 'It's me, sir. First Officer Carter.'

'Oh yes,' he said, disappointed, and turning back to watch the waves. 'Of course. My mistake, Mr Carter. What can I do for you?'

'Just bringing you today's projections, sir. As requested. We're making steady time, I'm pleased to report. Good healthy wind behind us, engines working fine, still operating on four of the six tanks. We could pump them up, you know, if you wanted. With this weather and the good wind, we could make Canada a day ahead of schedule if we gave it some heave-ho.'

Kendall shook his head. 'To be a day ahead or a day

behind schedule is one and the same thing to me, Mr Carter,' he said.

'A captain's responsibility is to bring the ship into port exactly on schedule. We are not in a race. We are not trying to conquer the sea. We are simply trying to reach our destination safely and on time. We shall continue to run on four tanks for the time being.'

'Very good, sir,' said Carter, frowning. He had hoped that the captain would give the go-ahead to increase speed, knowing that the sooner they arrived in Quebec, the sooner he could get on a ship back to Antwerp, and the sooner, therefore, he would be back with his wife. He was counting the days down and could think of little else other than the imminent birth of his child. Although there was still plenty of time before it was due, he was constantly worried that circumstances would get in the way and he would miss it, something for which he would never forgive himself. Or Captain Kendall.

The captain read through the figures which his first officer had handed him and approved them all silently. 'Tell me, Mr Carter,' he began.

'Call me Billy, sir. All the other captains do.'

'Tell me, Mr Carter,' he repeated, refusing to utter the ridiculous name. 'How do you think the voyage is going so far?'

'So far? Very well, sir, I'd say. We're making good time, we haven't had any problems with—'

'How about the passengers? Any thoughts on them?'

'No, they seem like a lively bunch. We had a problem last night down below decks of course, but you probably heard about that?' Kendall shook his head and Billy Carter explained. 'Well, it came to nothing much in the end, thankfully,' he said. 'A girl down in steerage, about nineteen or twenty, sir, sitting out alone having a cigarette, and she says a chap came up behind her and dragged her into one of the lifeboats. Kept his hand over her mouth and tried to get fresh with her. She says he was ready to get serious about it but she managed to get her knee into the right position and do him a bit of an injury. Had his trousers around his ankles at the time and she said she heard an almighty crunch, so he got what he deserved, I suppose. Probably feeling the pain in his groin this morning. And he was winded, naturally, but somehow he found enough strength to pull himself out of there and run off before he could be recognized.'

Kendall frowned. This was the kind of animal behaviour he absolutely refused to tolerate on board. 'Did she describe him?' he asked. 'Can we catch him?'

'Unlikely. She said he wasn't very big; she thought he was only a bit of a kid maybe, but quite strong with it, which is how he overcame her. Anyway, she's all right now. She was a bit shocked last night, of course, but she's a game girl and seemed delighted that she'd managed to fight him off. She's turned herself into a bit of a heroine down there actually, as far as I can tell.'

The captain snorted. If these young girls insisted on sitting alone on deck late at night or, worse, smoking, well then, they were only asking for trouble. If the choice was his, he'd lock the pair of them up in the brig. 'Post an extra sailor to patrol the decks at night,' he said. 'And let me know if the doctor receives any passengers with, shall we say, sensitive injuries. That kind of thing is unacceptable.'

'Of course, sir.'

'Any other thoughts?' he asked in as casual a voice as he dared, not wanting to give away what he was really thinking.

'I don't think so, sir. Everyone else seems all right. No major troubles.'

'I had a pleasant dinner last night,' the captain lied, since he had hated every moment of it. 'Your idea, the guest list, was it?'

'Yes, sir. Just some of the first-class passengers. And Mr Zéla, of course.'

'Oh yes. The Frenchman. In the Presidential Suite. Something of a dandy, I feel.'

'A wealthy dandy, sir. My favourite sort.'

'I'm sure.'

'He's a pleasant fellow, sir. Always has a word for the crew as he walks around.'

'And Mr Robinson and his son,' Captain Kendall interrupted him. 'How do they strike you?'

Billy Carter pulled a face. 'Pleasant as well, sir,' he said. 'A bit quiet, the father especially. But they're all right. Haven't been any trouble, if that's what you're getting at.'

'I'm not *getting* at anything, Mr Carter,' he replied, irritated. 'I'm merely having a conversation with my first officer about the conduct of the passengers so that I can captain this ship as well as possible. I'm sorry if that bores you.'

'No sir, not at all, sir. I just thought you meant—'

'That will be all, Mr Carter,' he said, dismissing the man with a wave of the hand as he gave the papers back to him. 'I'll see you later this evening, I'm sure. I am already trembling with anticipation.'

'Yes, sir,' Billy said, walking away unhappily. He traced back over his three-day history with Captain Kendall and could not, for the life of him, understand where their relationship had gone wrong. He had never met such an abrupt captain before, someone who seemed to have nothing but contempt for his officers. He was like something out of the Navy archives. Only a few more weeks, he reasoned. Only a few more weeks and I'll be back home with Billy Junior.

Twenty minutes later, Captain Kendall found himself standing outside Cabin A4, the one which was occupied by Mr John Robinson and his son Edmund, with his ear pressed to the door, listening intently to the sounds

241

from within. A wild idea had occurred to him as he stood by the bow, an idea so shocking, so incredible, that he could scarcely bring himself to believe it. However, it had brought him here now and he cursed the designers of the boat for making the first-class cabins so airtight secure. The door was so thick he could hear only muffled sounds and snippets of conversation. He glanced up and down the empty corridor in case he was spotted, hoping that no one would appear before he could find some evidence.

'It's not a hotel,' came one voice from within, the younger one, the higher-pitched one, the *woman*'s one. 'They don't do room service.'

'Well, at these prices they should,' was the reply. Some more conversation went by unheard and he scrunched his face up and pressed it even closer to the woodwork, determined to hear something incriminating.

'She's a pleasant enough sort,' he heard. 'Better than that Drake woman.'

'I think she likes you.'

'The mother after the father, the daughter after the son. It's rather poetic, isn't it?'

'Only I'm not your son, am I?'

Kendall gasped. The truth at last. Pressing a hand to his mouth, he held his breath, praying for more.

'And you nearly called me Hawley when you ran into Miss Hayes and me this morning. You have to be careful about that.'

'I'm sorry, but I was feeling faint. That DuMarqué boy practically attacked me in the dining hall.'

'It's all right, she didn't notice, but just take more care in future.'

'What are you doing?' A voice from down the hallway made Captain Kendall jump, and he spun around in fright. 'Why are you listening at that door?'

'I . . . I . . .' He blushed from the top of his ears right down to his neck, and he was more than aware how ridiculous his red, swollen face would look, cast against his silver-white beard, the kind of beard he believed a seafaring captain was supposed to wear.

'What were you doing listening at that door?'

'I wasn't listening,' he stammered. 'I was . . . I was passing by and thought I heard some commotion from within. I was about to check that they were all right, but it seems to have stopped now.'

Victoria nodded, unconvinced. He gave her a brief smile and marched past, determined to return to his cabin as quickly as possible. He turned away and scampered off down the corridor. Running inside, he closed the door and locked it behind him, tossing his cap across the room on to the bed, then rummaged through a pile of papers on his desk.

'Where is it, where is it?' he muttered aloud, searching for what he had been reading the day they had left the port of Antwerp. He prayed that Jimmy, the young cabin boy, had not thrown it away and he was almost ready to give up when he saw its corner poking out from the very bottom of the pile. A newspaper from three days ago. He whipped it out, almost ripping it in the process, and ran his finger down the front page until he reached the article he wanted. If his face had been filled with blood after being discovered by Victoria Drake, it was drained of it now. 'Good Lord,' he said out loud. 'Goodness gracious me.' He dropped the paper on the floor and looked around the cabin nervously, relieved that he had locked the door behind him.

First Officer Billy Carter was sitting with two sailors in the navigation room, chatting away without a care in the world when he saw the captain striding purposefully along the deck towards them, and then climbing the steps. 'Caps on, lads,' he said, aware of Kendall's rules, and he had just managed to put his own on his head when the older man marched through, indicating with the tip of his finger that he should follow him.

'Everything all right, Captain?' he asked perkily, sensing a determined mood in the man that he had not seen before.

'Not exactly,' he replied. 'But it will be soon. Come with me.'

The two men went back down the steps and turned left, then down another flight and into the radio room, Carter practically having to run along to keep up with his captain. The room was empty and, when they were both inside, Captain Kendall locked the door behind them and ordered Carter to sit at the desk.

'You're familiar with the Marconi telegraph?' he asked, and the first officer turned around to look at the wireless machinery and equipment laid out before him.

'Certainly, sir,' he said. 'An amazing invention. Don't know how we managed before we had it.'

'I need you to send a message, ship to shore,' he said, not interested in idle conversation. 'I'd do it myself, but I need to think it out correctly. Can you send it?'

Billy Carter blinked. This was serious, he could tell. He took his cap off and placed it on the desk beside him. 'Yes, sir,' he said formally, with a quick nod of the head.

'And when we leave this room, you discuss this message with no one. *With no one,*' he repeated firmly. 'Do you understand?'

'Of course, sir. Strictest secrecy.'

'All right then,' said Kendall. 'Start her up.'

Carter flexed his fingers and pulled the Morse code device towards him, racking his brain to remember the signals of dots and dashes which he had learned many years before but which he had had to use on only a handful of occasions since. He thought them through and relaxed as they came back to him.

'The message is to be addressed to Scotland Yard,' said Kendall.

'Scotland Yard?' Carter asked, spinning around, but the captain pushed him back to his former position.

'Just send it,' he said firmly. 'No questions.'

Carter tapped away. 'To Scotland Yard. From Henry Kendall, Captain of the SS *Montrose*, of the Canadian Pacific Fleet.' He cleared his throat and waited for Carter to finish sending that before continuing. 'Have strong suspicions that Crippen, London cellar murderer, and accomplice are among saloon passengers. Moustache taken off, growing beard. Accomplice dressed as boy. Voice, manner and build undoubtedly a girl. Please advise.'

Billy Carter sent the message to the wireless receiver which Guglielmo Marconi himself had built at Poldhu in Cornwall before turning around and staring at his captain with a mixture of amazement and sudden respect.

Kendall looked at him and smiled coldly. 'Now we wait for a response,' he said, anticipating the younger man's question.

11

Losing Patience

London: 1906–1910

Cora Crippen stared out of the window of 39 Hilldrop Crescent, Camden, her face screwed up like a hungry rodent. Hawley had promised to be home by seven, and it was already ten minutes past and there was no sign of him. Useless man, she thought to herself, absolutely useless. It was Thursday evening and she never liked to be at home alone on a Thursday evening because that was the night when Mr Micklefield called around to collect the rent. They had been living in their new home for over a year now, and he had arrived promptly at seven thirty every week without fail; she didn't like to face him alone because he always flirted with her and she found both him and his manner distasteful; but, more importantly, she didn't like to be the one to pay him as it reinforced the fact that she was a mere tenant and not mistress of her own home.

It had been Cora's decision to move to Camden in the first place. She had finally grown weary of the constant noise from the Jennings family downstairs and had insisted that they find a place of their own. Ever since she had joined the Music Hall Ladies' Guild, renewing her friendship with Mrs Louise Smythson and acquainting herself for the first time with respectable couples such as the Nashes and the Martinettis, she had felt a little embarrassed by her living arrangements. None of the other ladies had to share a house; most of them not only owned their own, but they had servants working for them too. She could not possibly invite any of her new friends to tea, she reasoned, if there was the slightest possibility of their being attacked by a marauding bunch of children on the stairs below, or by that drunken oaf in his vest and underwear. She had gone house-hunting herself, telling Hawley nothing about it, and only when the deed was signed did she inform him that they were leaving South Crescent.

For his part, Hawley found the whole matter disagreeable. It meant a longer walk in the evenings to his dental surgery and in the mornings to his job at Munyon's. Of course this was balanced with the fact that their home was now bigger and so he and Cora could spend time there together without having to look at each other, but nevertheless it was too bad of her to simply rent a new home without consulting him. As he strode along the street that evening, perspiring slightly with the knowledge that he was late, he patted his pocket nervously to make sure the money was still there. He was not particularly fond of Mr Micklefield either, and he would have preferred to post the rent through his own front door every week; but the landlord insisted that it be so and therefore he had little choice. In recent times it had not been as easy as before to find the money. The dental surgery was not doing as well as it once had because a rival firm had opened only five minutes down the street. The dentists there, he was aware, were *real* dentists, with qualifications and everything, and he was gradually losing his patient base to them. Talk of the painful procedures that Dr Crippen performed, his cautious use of anaesthetic, his love of oral surgery, his incredible number of needles and pliers, had limited numbers anyway, and now they were dwindling to the point where he could often spend his three hours in the evening there and not see anyone at all. In the years he had been at Munyon's he had received steady pay rises, but they did not balance against this sudden loss of income, and money had become tight.

'At last!' Cora cried, looking up from her meal as he walked through the door. 'What time do you call this anyway?'

'I was delayed, my dear,' he replied quietly, 'but I'm here now.'

'You're here now at twenty minutes past seven. When I specifically told you to return on the hour. Honestly, Hawley, why must you continue to disobey me?'

He said nothing, merely taking off his coat and hanging it on the stand, taking the rent money from his pocket and laying it on the table.

'And *please* do not invite that man in here this evening,' she insisted. 'Just give him his rent in the hallway. I can't stand the way he looks at me. He makes me feel an object.'

'Easier said than done,' he said. 'You know what he's like.'

'Just tell him I'm indisposed. It's ridiculous, the way he looks in and pokes his nose around all the time. I won't have it, Hawley, do you hear me? And I need six shillings by the morning. Can you leave it by the bed, please?'

Hawley stared at her. 'Six shillings?' he asked. 'What do you need six shillings for?'

She laughed. 'I beg your pardon,' she said, sounding for all the world as if he had just insulted her grossly. 'Do I have to explain myself to you now?'

'Not explain yourself, dear. Of course not. I just wondered why you—'

'If you must know, there is a dress in the window of Lacey's which I want to buy. It's beautiful, Hawley. A

248

deep red, almost the colour of blood. It will be perfect for Tuesday night.'

'Tuesday night?'

'The Majestic, Hawley,' she sighed. 'I'm beginning a new repertoire on Tuesday and I want a new outfit to go with it.' Cora was performing two nights a week at a music hall in the Strand. Although it paid her eight shillings a week, she considered this to be her personal income and contributed none of it to the family finances.

'Six shillings though, my dear,' he said quietly, tugging at his moustache as if the money might fall out of it.

'Now, you're hardly going to begrudge me six shillings, are you? After all the work I do here for you? What kind of husband are you anyway?'

He stared around the room and raised an eyebrow. A pile of washing lay in a corner, untouched for days. The sink was filled with dishes, and a thin layer of dust had spread over the top of the bookcase since he had last cleaned it. 'Of course not, Cora,' he replied. 'But money is tight at the moment, you know that. New dresses might be an unnecessary expense.'

'It's tight because you refuse to work,' she snapped, standing up and adding her plate to the growing pile in the sink.

He looked around hopefully, as if there might be a plate waiting for him too, but he knew that this was unlikely; his stomach growled in disappointment.

'Honestly, Hawley, you live the life of a king, you really do. You put in a few hours at that pharmacy, *hardly* very taxing work, and sit around in your surgery in the evenings, staring at the ceiling. Perhaps if you found some more *productive* way to spend your time, then you would earn a little more and it wouldn't all be left to me.'

'I've explained why the takings are down, my dear,'

he said, referring to his surgical practice. 'Ever since that other—'

'I don't want to hear about it,' she said, raising a hand. 'The minutiae of your daily existence are of no consequence to me. But Hawley, I am your wife and will not be treated in this manner. The Majestic is my first step to stardom, you know that. I should have thought you would be delighted to be married to one of London's premier singing sensations. If I don't have that dress, then I may as well kiss my career goodbye.'

'For the sake of a *dress*?' he asked sceptically.

'Six shillings, Hawley. I mean it. Otherwise—'

He never heard what the alternative was for there was a sharp knock on the door, indicating the arrival of Mr Micklefield. Without waiting for an answer, his key was in the lock and he was entering the room, even as Hawley rushed towards the door. One of his pet hates was the way his landlord never gave them time to open it before entering himself. It was his private belief that the man was hoping to catch Cora in a state of undress, and for this reason Hawley usually planted himself beside the door at seven thirty so he could open it before Mr Micklefield did. However, with the onset of tonight's argument, he had forgotten entirely and their obese landlord was moving between them like a shot.

'Evening, all,' he said, pulling out a notebook and licking the top of his pencil. 'Nice night for it. How are you, Mrs C?' he asked, winking lasciviously at her. She sighed in exasperation and turned away from them both, two of her least favourite men in London.

'Here you are, Mr Micklefield,' Hawley said, picking up the envelope and passing it to him quickly while steering him back towards the door. He noticed unsightly sprouts of hair growing in tufts along the man's neck and stared at them in disgust. We'll see you next week.'

'Everything all right here?' the landlord asked,

stopping and looking around, his eyes darting from item to item like a rat searching for cheese. 'No problems at all?'

'None, Mr Micklefield. We'll let you know if there are.'

'Water running all right? Gas? Floorboards not creaking too much?'

'Everything's fine, Mr Micklefield. Mrs Crippen and I were just having a conversation though, so if you wouldn't mind . . .'

'Looking gorgeous as ever, Mrs C,' he yelled across at her, trying to stay in the room a moment longer. 'If you ever tire of the doctor here, you know who to call.'

'*If?*' she replied, giving a quick snort. 'That's a joke.'

'Thank you, Mr Micklefield,' Hawley insisted, pushing him through the door. He closed it behind him and stared at the wood for a moment, not wanting to turn around. He closed his eyes and for a moment felt almost at peace.

'Six shillings, Hawley,' Cora repeated when he turned around. Her face was determined and he knew there were no two ways about it. 'Six shillings by the bed tomorrow morning. Or there'll be hell to pay.'

He nodded and said his two most commonly uttered words: 'Yes, dear.'

If Hawley thought that his wife was impervious to their financial difficulties, if he thought for a moment that she believed she could simply continue to spend at will and the money would always be there, he was quite wrong. Cora was more than aware that belts would have to be tightened – or, more specifically, that *Hawley's* belt would have to be tightened – if she was to continue to lead the lifestyle to which she aspired. Naturally, the six shillings did appear on the bedside table first thing the following morning before Hawley left for work – no lunch for him for the next few days – but there was not an infinite number of six shillings waiting for her in her husband's shallow pockets, she knew that. It was pointless waiting for him to do something to improve their situation, however. It was up to her. And even before the night had ended, an idea, and a very attractive idea at that, had occurred to her.

The following Tuesday was one of those now rare days in the dental surgery when Hawley had seen more than one patient. Arriving at 7 p.m. he had been confronted with a terrified-looking child, a small girl who was being held there entirely against her will by the firm hand of two fierce-looking parents. Her teeth were rotten and two extractions were called for, and the child had convinced herself that Dr Crippen was going to murder her in the chair, for two of her classmates had already had the misfortune to visit him and had lived to regret it, entertaining the schoolyard with tales of his sadism for days afterwards. In her case, however, the teeth emerged from her mouth with little difficulty and she had nearly burst into tears when it was over, so grateful was she for the lack of pain inflicted (not that this would alter the gruesome story she told her friends the next day). After her there was a teenage boy who had chipped a tooth in a fight with another boy, and then a middle-aged woman who needed a filling. All in all, it had been a prosperous night and there was a slight spring in his step as he made his way home, his pennies jingling in his pocket as testament to his hard work. Maybe the good people of Camden had grown weary of the new surgery, he thought, not really believing it but enjoying the fantasy. Maybe they'll all come back to Dr Crippen now.

He entered the house and put his hat and coat in the hallway before walking into the living room with a sigh. Inside, he could hear Cora singing, but only quietly, as if she was engaged on some unlikely task, such as washing the dishes. Entering the room, however, he froze, believing for a moment that he might have entered the wrong house, before realizing that such a thing was impossible. Sitting in the middle of the room, in the armchair he always sat in himself, was a young man, smoking a cigarette and reading a newspaper, which he lowered slowly as Hawley stood before him, looking him up and down arrogantly. 'Evening,' he said in a deep voice, nodding his head slowly.

Hawley looked past him at his wife, who was – mysteriously – busying herself in the kitchen and coming towards him now with a smile, the like of which he had not seen in a long time. 'Oh, Hawley dear,' she said, welcoming him home with a kiss on the cheek. (He flinched back in surprise, as if worried that her lips were coated in strychnine.) 'You're home. How lovely. Dinner won't be long.'

'Cora,' he said, glancing from her to the young man. 'Yes,' he muttered, trying to make sense of the situation. 'May I ask—?'

'Oh, you haven't met Mr Heath, have you?' she asked, knowing full well that he hadn't. 'This is Mr Alec Heath, Hawley. Our new lodger.'

'Our new what?'

'Lodger, darling. You remember I told you about him?'

Hawley blinked in surprise. He knew for a fact that Cora had never mentioned anything to him about a lodger, and he found it outrageous that she would select one without discussing the matter with him first.

In fact, she had come up with the idea of a lodger long before Mr Micklefield's last visit and had been working on it ever since. In truth, the house in Hilldrop Crescent was a little too big for just the Crippens, something she had originally thought to be necessary when impressing her friends with their new accommodation, and the top floor had a third, decent-sized bedroom which was lying entirely to waste. She had decided that such a

253

room would be best sub-let to another tenant and had known immediately whom to ask.

'I don't recall,' Hawley replied miserably.

'Oh, you must,' she said with a laugh. 'Alec, this is my husband, Dr Hawley Harvey Crippen.'

Slowly, as if every movement was irritating for him, Alec Heath folded the newspaper – *Hawley's* newspaper – and placed it on the side of the armchair, pulling himself up and standing before his new landlord, extending his hand. The new man's presence immediately intimidated Hawley. Alec was about six foot tall, broad and muscular, with a shock of unruly dark hair falling down his forehead in definite contrast to Hawley's balding pate. He had dark skin, as if he spent a lot of time at sports or outdoor activities, and he had not shaved that day, leaving a rough line of stubble around his jaw. The shirtsleeve of the extended arm was rolled up, revealing a powerful forearm and bulging bicep that amazed Hawley. This was the sort of fellow whom ladies looked at twice in the streets, but he had grey, cold eyes, which suggested he had little time for romance. 'Hey,' he said, by way of a greeting.

Hawley shook his hand. 'Good evening, Mr Heath,' he replied.

'Alec works with me at the Majestic,' Cora explained. 'He's an assistant stage manager. He's only nineteen years old and already has one of the most responsible jobs in the music hall. Isn't that something?'

'Nineteen?' Hawley asked quietly.

'He's from Wales originally, aren't you, Alec?'

He nodded, not taking his eyes off Hawley for a moment, and the older man could sense that he was sizing him up for any potential conflict between the two and realizing happily that he would surely have the upper hand.

'Cardiff,' he said.

'The poor boy's been living in a hovel for the last

year. Some rat-infested flat in Collier's Wood. The distance he had to travel to work is ridiculous and his landlady was apparently a nightmare. Anyway, he was looking for new lodgings and we were looking to fill the spare room on the top floor, so naturally I thought of him.'

'Naturally,' said Hawley.

'I'm sure we'll all get along famously,' she continued, her cheerful air unlike any he had seen since just before their marriage. 'Now, why don't you two men sit down and get to know each other while I finish dinner.'

'You're cooking?' Hawley asked, amazed.

'Why, of course I'm cooking,' she said, laughing as she glanced towards Alec. 'Don't I always have a lovely dinner ready for you when you come home in the evenings?' He thought about it. 'No' was the correct answer, but he assumed the question had been rhetorical. 'Ready in ten minutes,' she added, practically dancing away.

Alec sat back down in the armchair, leaving Hawley the sofa, and they stared at each other suspiciously. For a few moments they had nothing whatsoever to say, but it was only Hawley who felt uncomfortable as he sized up the well-built boy opposite him and felt himself to be puny and almost feminine in contrast to him. Alec was not threatened at all. He had been concerned earlier in the day as to how he would get on with his new landlord but, meeting him now, he realized that his worries had been misplaced. He pulled another cigarette from a silver case and lit it without either asking whether he could smoke or offering one to Hawley. The case seemed expensive as it caught Hawley's eye and he used it as a means to break the silence between them.

'What a fine case,' he said. 'Was it a gift?'

Alec shrugged. 'A woman I knew in Chelsea gave it to me,' he said with a quick wink. 'Nice, eh?'

'Yes, very nice,' Hawley admitted.

'I earned it, believe me.'

Hawley nodded. 'You worked for her, then?' he asked. 'Were you employed by her before you joined the music hall?'

'I didn't work for her,' Alec said in a disgusted tone. 'Not likely.'

'But you said you earned it.'

He put the cigarette between his lips and drew on it heavily, exhaling a thin line of smoke which he watched evaporate into the air before bothering to answer. 'I did,' he said quietly.

'Hawley, could you open this for me, please?' Cora asked, returning to them and handing her husband a jar of preserves whose top she could not budge. 'I can never open these things,' she said with a laugh.

Hawley struggled with the jar, but he knew instantly that he was not going to be able to manage it. The top felt a little greasy and his hands kept slipping. His face grew more and more red as he tried to open it, but it was useless; without a word, Alec reached across and took it from him. He placed his large hand around the lid and opened it effortlessly, almost by merely glancing at it and frightening it into coming undone. Hawley's heart sank. Sitting on the sofa, shrinking into its vastness while Alec Heath relaxed in the armchair, he realized that he was no longer master in his own home – if he had ever been in the first place.

'Thank you,' Cora said, taking it back from him. 'Hawley, won't it be wonderful having Alec in the house?' she cried from the kitchen. 'He'll be able to do all those little jobs that neither of us can manage. Such a help!'

'Indeed,' said Hawley, unconvinced.

'Anything you can't manage,' Alec said to Hawley with a smile.

'I'll bear it in mind.'

'It'll be so useful having a man about the place,' she called out, returning to the living room.

'I am a man, my dear,' Hawley pointed out.

'A young man,' she corrected herself. 'After all, you're not fit for all the manual work you once might have been, now are you? It would be unfair to ask you, even. No, things will be better now that we have Alec with us.' She reached forward and ruffled the boy's hair gently, letting her fingers linger in the thick black thatch for a little longer than was appropriate; Hawley gazed at the boy's face to see whether he was smiling, but it was slowly disappearing behind a cloud of smoke and all he could make out were those cold, grey eyes staring back at him contemptuously.

It was a Tuesday evening in late summer and Hawley was alone in the back garden at 39 Hilldrop Crescent, strolling around with his hands in his pockets, disturbing the soil with the toe of his boot. Cora had left for the Majestic a few hours earlier for her regular performance there, wearing the red dress that had cost him six shillings a few months earlier. Recently, he had taken to closing the dental surgery on Tuesdays and returning straight home after Munyon's closed. It wasn't as if his practice made much money anyway, although that wasn't his reason for the night off. In fact, this was the only evening in the week when he had the entire house to himself and he valued the peace and quiet which it afforded him. Over the past twelve weeks his life seemed to have gone further and further downhill, to the point where he could hardly wait for sleep to come at night, since it gave him some sweet relief from the daily grind. Only the first few seconds in the morning were peaceful for him as he slowly awoke, before he remembered how wretched his life really was. Although his marriage to Cora had been a failure from the start, he could scarcely remember a time when he was as miserable as he was at this point. Her life seemed to revolve around only two things: the music hall and taking care of Alec Heath. He was not so jealous of the Majestic, because he knew it was still something which made her believe that she had a future in show business, something he himself had long believed to be a pipe dream. Alec, however, was a different matter. The boy seemed intent on being a constant annoyance to Hawley, being everything that he wasn't and presenting such an obvious contrast to her ageing husband, so that he made him seethe with anger and jealousy.

Mornings were the worst. Alec would sit at the kitchen table, smoking a cigarette, shirtless, with no thought for decorum or manners. His muscular body provided an unspoken rebuke to Hawley, who cowered in his own chair, nibbling at a piece of dry toast and sipping his tea nervously, a stranger in his own home. Alec seemed to relish the attention that Cora paid to him, and the manner of her flirtations was obvious when she spoke to Hawley while resting a hand on one of the boy's bare shoulders. He desperately wanted to order him to cover up or stay in his room until he was dressed, but he was afraid that he would be laughed at and that then he would have nothing left to say in his own defence. And so he stayed mute, quietly seething, wishing that the boy would simply leave or find another couple to intrude upon.

From the back garden, he heard a distant knock on the front door and sighed. He glanced at his watch; it was only eight fifteen. Neither his wife nor Alec should be home from the Majestic yet, unless one of them was ill and had forgotten their front-door key, a double co-incidence. He hoped not. Tuesday evenings were all he had; surely fate would not deprive him of this small luxury?

To his surprise, the small figure of Ethel LeNeve was standing on his doorstep, looking neat and prim in a new coat she had purchased the previous day. 'Ethel,' he said, surprised to find himself so pleased to see her. 'I wasn't expecting you. Is anything the matter?'

'Nothing, Hawley,' she said. 'I'm sorry for calling around, but when I went home I realized I'd taken your shop keys with me. And of course you're in first thing in the morning so I knew you'd need them.'

Her small hand fished into her pocket and retrieved the set of keys for Munyon's front door and she offered them to him. 'I never even missed them,' he said, shaking his head. 'I must be getting old and forgetful. Will you come in for a moment?'

'No, I shouldn't,' she said, shaking her head. 'I don't want to disturb you or Mrs Crippen. I just wanted to drop the keys round. I'll leave you both in peace.'

'Well, Mrs Crippen isn't here right now, and you're not disturbing me. Not in the least. Please come in. I'll make some tea.'

Ethel considered the offer and looked up and down the street nervously. 'Well, if you're sure,' she said doubtfully and Hawley stepped out of the doorway to let her through.

'Of course, of course,' he said. 'Please. Come in.'

Ethel walked through into the living room and took her coat off, laying it over the side of the armchair. 'What a lovely place you have here,' she said, looking around. For once, their home was fairly neat, for he had cleaned it himself the previous night after Cora had handed him a mop and bucket. 'You're sure I haven't disturbed your work?'

'Not at all. I was only in the garden, pottering around. Cora performs at the music hall every Tuesday night, so I have the place to myself.'

'Of course,' said Ethel, remembering him telling her this before. 'How glamorous. I'm surprised you're not there, though, cheering her on from the audience.'

Hawley smiled regretfully. 'I'm not really one for

the music hall,' he admitted. 'And to be honest, I don't think Cora would thank me for coming. She has her friends there, you see. And her audience. The last thing she needs is me worrying her.'

'But you're her husband.'

'Exactly.'

He boiled some water in a pan on the stove and made a pot of tea for them both, laying it out carefully on the table with some cups. It was pleasant, he realized, to entertain a friend. It crossed his mind that he had never done such a thing before and that Ethel was, perhaps, his best friend. In the year they had been working together at the pharmacy they had formed a close alliance, trusting the other entirely and enjoying each other's company and humour. Although he tried not to dwell on the fact for very long, he knew that her presence in his life was one of its few bright sparks.

'It seems strange to see you here,' he remarked. 'Sitting at my table, drinking tea. I don't think we've ever seen each other outside the shop before, have we? We're like fish out of water.'

'That's true,' she said, taking a sip and almost burning her tongue. 'But I suppose we must both have lives outside of Munyon's. You're a married man, after all. That's a whole life in itself.'

'You never wanted to marry?' he asked her, the first time he had ever broached such a personal topic with her. Somehow it seemed appropriate in this setting for him to do so.

The question, however, was a slightly odd one, as she was only twenty years old and had hardly been left on the shelf just yet. She blushed, however, and looked down at the tablecloth. 'Not yet,' she said. 'No man seems to want to fall in love with me.'

'I find that hard to believe.'

'It's true,' she replied. 'Sometimes a young fellow speaks to me at a dance or in a public place, but . . .'

She drifted off, the tips of her fingers touching the scar above her lip self-consciously, as if this was the impediment to romance for her. 'Somehow it never seems to come to anything,' she concluded.

'One day,' he said. 'Very soon. I have no doubt of it.'

'I hope so,' she said, her face bursting into a smile at the thought of it, and he couldn't help but smile back. 'It must be quite something to be married as long as you and Mrs Crippen have been. And such a comfort for you both. How long has it been now, anyway?'

'Eleven years,' he said with a sigh. 'For my sins,' he added.

'Such a long time. I was only nine at the time. Just a child.'

'Good Lord, but you're just a child now!'

'Hardly.'

'Of course you are! With time and beauty and intelligence on your side. Really, Ethel. You mustn't put yourself down like this. It's too bad.'

She stared across at him, cocking her head to the left slightly, feeling flattered by his kind remarks. She had always been glad that she had had the good fortune to walk into Munyon's that day when she saw the 'Help Wanted' sign. She could scarcely imagine a better employer and friend than Hawley. Of course, in the early days they had been a little more reserved; it had taken time for them both to get to know and to trust each other, but with familiarity grew affection and these traits were as important to her as she knew they were to him. She was about to risk everything and tell him just how fond of him she really was when a door outside the living room slammed – the front door – and, like a tornado arriving unannounced over a peaceful town, Cora Crippen swept into the room, flinging her hat across it.

'Damn it all to hell!' she screamed, her voice piercing

through the air with such venom and volume that windows might have smashed. Hawley jumped in fright, while Ethel simply stared at her, her mouth hanging open in horror at the lunatic woman who'd just appeared. 'Damn it!' she repeated, even louder than before, clenching her fists together and screeching like a rabid dog.

'Cora,' said Hawley, jumping up and running over to her. 'What on earth's the matter? What's happened to you? Have you been attacked?'

'Attacked? *Attacked?*' she asked through gritted teeth. 'Worse. I have been insulted beyond anything that a person should have to suffer. I tell you, Hawley, I will take a box of matches and burn that music hall to the *ground* before I allow such a thing to happen again.' Her voice rose in decibels as the sentence progressed and Hawley could only stare at her, transfixed, forgetting his guest. He had seen her angry before, but never anything like this. Although he knew that nothing he had done could be to blame, he was sure he would have to pay the price for it.

'For heaven's sake, Cora. Tell me. What has happened?'

She glanced past him and spotted Ethel sitting at the table, one hand gripping the arm of her chair nervously as she watched the older woman, wondering whether she would suddenly pounce and bite her head off. 'Who's that?' Cora asked, looking at her husband before turning to stare at Ethel again. 'Who are you?' she snapped.

'This is Miss LeNeve, Cora,' Hawley explained. 'I've told you about her. You've met once before. My assistant at Munyon's.'

'*Miss* LeNeve?' Cora asked contemptuously. 'I thought you were a boy. Stand up and let me get a good look at you.' Ethel stood up obediently and stared at the ground, holding her hands tightly before her. 'Hmm, maybe you are a miss after all,' Cora said. 'Well, what of it? What are you doing here?'

'Ethel was bringing round my keys,' said Hawley. 'It hardly matters. You must tell me what's happened.'

The reminder that *something* had happened made Cora scream in anger once again, and Hawley jumped back, shocked, wondering whether she might be in need of a doctor. A *real* doctor. 'It's *insufferable*,' she shouted.

'Perhaps I should go,' said Ethel, not wanting to be around for any more of this scene.

'Yes, yes, perhaps,' said Hawley, going over to her and taking her arm, leading her to the door. 'I do apologize, Ethel,' he whispered as he let her out. 'I don't know what's come over her. I promise you she doesn't normally act like this.'

'I'm sure,' said Ethel, unconvinced. 'I'll see you tomorrow anyway, Hawley.'

'Yes, and once again I am sorry for all the commotion. Thank you for the keys.'

Their glance lingered in the open doorway for a few moments, and she felt an urge to touch his cheek. The skin looked pale and tired and she wanted to place her hand over it and warm it up. Instead she turned around reluctantly and began to walk home, feeling nothing but sympathy for the poor individual who had the misfortune to be married to such a harridan.

Similar sentiments were being felt by Hawley Harvey Crippen, who marched back into the living room, torn between anger and fear, and stared at his wife, who was pacing up and down the floor like an expectant father.

'Now for heaven's sake, Cora,' he shouted. 'Tell me what's happened.'

'That *bastard*,' she shouted.

'Cora!'

'I mean it, Hawley, that *bastard*!'

'Who? Who are you talking about?'

'That son of a bitch who runs the Majestic, that's

who I'm talking about,' she screamed. 'That shit-eating monster. I'll kill him. I'll rip his insides out and make him swallow them, I swear it.'

'Cora, you must relax,' said Hawley, taking her by the arm nervously and leading her to the sofa. 'You're hysterical. Breathe. Just breathe for a minute.'

For once she did as he suggested and took in great gulps of air before rolling her eyes and snorting in disgust once again. 'Mr Hammond,' she said finally. 'The manager of the music hall.'

'Yes? And what has he done?'

'He invited me into his office this evening,' she explained. 'Before the show started. He was all smiles, of course. All friendly, like he always is. Then he tells me that he's found this great new talent, some young girl called Maisie Something-or-other. It seems he's heard her sing and he thinks she's the best thing he's ever heard. He's giving her a spot on the bill, he says. Thinks all the punters will love her, he says. "I don't care", says I. "Why should I?" Then he tells me that there's only room for one singer in the second half of the show and that her voice is better than mine and he's sorry but there's nothing he can do about it.'

'Oh Cora,' he said sorrowfully, knowing what a blow this must be to her.

'Next thing I know, I'm being run out of the office, collecting my final wage packet, and I'm off the bill. Out of a job. Me! The singing sensation Bella Elmore! And of course when I get a look at this new girl, naturally she's some little blonde thing with big dimples and bosoms out to here. No wonder he wanted to be rid of me,' she said, standing up and pacing again, this time heading for the kitchen. 'It's an insult, an insult!'

'There'll be other jobs,' he reasoned. 'Other music halls.'

'There won't be,' she shouted, lifting up a pan from the dresser for something to grip and press tightly in her frustration. Before he knew it, she was marching around, holding on to it like a gun.

He tried to reason with her. 'Cora, please. You're a wonderful singer. You know you are.'

'Oh don't bother, Hawley. You think I'm useless. Just like everyone else does. You've never supported my career.'

'That's not fair! It's *all* I do.'

'Ha!'

'I do,' he said, angry now. 'I work every hour of the day for you. I feed you, I clean for you, I support you.'

'I do everything,' she muttered, ignoring him. 'Absolutely everything.'

'And if Mr Hammond has found a better singer, then it just means you have to work harder to improve your voice. That's all.'

She turned around slowly and stared at him. 'What did you say?' she asked quietly.

He thought about it. 'I said, you have to work harder to—'

'No. Before that.'

'I . . . I can't remember.'

'You said she was a better singer than me.'

'I didn't mean *better*,' he said, backtracking, aware of his error. 'I meant fresher. Newer. Someone he hasn't heard before.'

'You said better,' she screeched.

'Cora, please. I—'

He didn't get to finish his sentence. Turning away from him for a moment, Cora summoned all the strength and anger she had left in her body and funnelled it into her right arm. Swinging back, she raised the frying pan in the air like a tennis racket and, without giving him any opportunity to anticipate the blow, she slapped it against the side of his face, knocking his spectacles off and sending them crashing into the wall while he was flung back, his entire left cheek feeling numb for a moment before bursting into flames of pain, his eye momentarily blinded as he fell over and landed on the floor. He lay there, stunned, a hand pressed to his cheek, and through his one good eye he saw the avenging figure of his wife standing over him, the frying pan still in her hand, wiping a line of spittle from her mouth as she looked down at him in disgust.

'You – said – better,' she stated in slow, flat tones.

12

Beginning the Chase

Liverpool: Saturday, 23 July 1910

Inspector Walter Dew got off the train in Liverpool and looked around anxiously for Police Constable Delaney who, he had been promised, would be waiting with a car to take him to the port. He glanced at his watch and exhaled loudly in frustration; it was nine forty in the morning, twenty minutes before the *Laurentic* was due to set sail, and his driver was nowhere to be seen. He had made it clear when he contacted the Liverpool authorities before leaving London that it was imperative that someone meet him at the station, but he could tell that whoever was at the other end of the telephone line had little regard for Scotland Yard inspectors, probably resenting and disliking them in equal parts. He counted to twenty slowly in his head, deciding that if no one had appeared by the time he reached the end he would simply go outside and hail a hansom cab himself. *One . . . two . . . three . . .*

Captain Kendall's message had come through to Scotland Yard late the previous evening, just as he was preparing to leave for the day. It was his sister's birthday and he was due to visit her home in Kensington for a celebratory dinner and he had intended stopping for a drink *en route*. He needed sustenance before he went there, as she had eight children, none of whom were over the age of nine, and their screams and hysteria drove him to the very edge of dementia.

'Inspector Dew,' PC Milburn said, as he was exiting the building, 'I was just coming up to see you.'

'Heading off,' he replied, tapping his watch. 'It's been a long day. See you tomorrow, Milburn. You should try to get some sleep tonight, too.'

'I think you should read this,' the PC said, holding out a telegram.

Dew frowned. 'Can't it wait?' he asked.

'I don't think so, sir. I think you'll want to see it.'

Hesitating only for a moment, the inspector reached across and took the paper, reading it through quickly, his eyes opening wide as he did so, before going back to the beginning of the page and reading it again.

'When did this come through?' he asked.

'Just a few minutes ago, sir. On the Marconi telegraph, transmitted from Poldhu. Like I said, I was just about to bring it to you. That's three days he's got on us, sir!'

Dew looked at his watch again and made a quick decision. 'Right,' he said. 'Find out the quickest way for me to get across the Atlantic.'

'What?' Milburn asked, amazed.

'You heard me.'

'But sir, that's—'

'Get in touch with the shipping lines,' he insisted, unwilling to be questioned. 'Find out what ships are going to Canada and when. I need to get on the next available boat.' He leaned forward, looking around to make sure that no one could hear him. 'It's Crippen,' he said. 'He's been spotted.'

Milburn nodded quickly and picked up the telephone. Within fifteen minutes he had confirmed that a passenger ship, the SS *Laurentic*, would be departing from Liverpool at ten o'clock the following morning, bound for Canada, and he had booked a ticket in the name of Inspector Dew. He also confirmed that the first train to that city would arrive at around half past nine in the morning, leaving little time for delay. Dew himself had phoned Liverpool police station and demanded an escort to take him to the port. In the mean time he sent a message back to Captain Kendall, informing him that he was giving chase and instructing him to share his discovery with no one until he received further instructions.

Dew's count had reached fifteen and he was picking up his bag to walk out of the station when he noticed a young constable running in his direction. They were all the same, it seemed to him: lazy, unpunctual, sloppy in their habits. Not like when he was a lad. Sometimes he wondered what would become of the Yard when his own generation had retired and their successors were in control. Mayhem, he presumed. 'Come on,' he shouted at the young man without bothering with any formal introductions. 'There's no time to waste. The ship will sail without me if I'm not there by ten. I told your sergeant that last night.'

They ran outside and jumped into the waiting car. 'Sorry I'm late, sir,' said the police constable, one Jeffrey Delaney, as they drove off.

'I specifically said I needed someone here by nine thirty,' Dew insisted irritably. 'If that ship sets sail without me—'

'It's only a few minutes away,' the young man replied forcibly, willing to apologize but not to be told off by some big shot from London. 'Don't worry. I'll get you there on time.'

Dew grunted a response and stared out the window as the Liverpool streets passed by. He had never been in this city before, but there was little time for sightseeing. He pulled Captain Kendall's Marconi message from his bag and read it again, intrigued. 'Accomplice dressed as boy. Voice, manner and build undoubtedly a girl.' Shaking his head, he could scarcely believe the gall of the man. He had seemed such a quiet, personable fellow when they had met. But the memory of what he had discovered when he'd visited the cellar in Hilldrop Crescent had changed all that. He closed his eyes and tried to block it out, but it was a very difficult thing to do. In all his years in the force he'd never seen anything quite so vile. He imagined he would never forget it. And Ethel LeNeve had hardly seemed the sort to involve herself in something like this, either. She had appeared to be the mousy sort. He was disappointed in himself, too; it was unlike him to be so easily deceived. Perhaps I'm getting old, he thought, before dismissing the idea. Or perhaps they're just getting better. His life was Scotland Yard, he had known no other and was interested in no other. But if he let Crippen escape, if he made it to Canada without being captured, questions would be asked concerning his own abilities.

'Here we are, sir,' said PC Delaney, skidding to a halt a few moments later. 'Told you we'd make it.'

'With five minutes to spare,' said Dew, opening the door and stepping outside as the foghorn of the *Laurentic* signalled that she was preparing to depart and any remaining people on board who were not passengers should disembark immediately. He looked across at her, impressed and intimidated at the same time by her size. She was over a hundred and eighty feet in length, with a beam span of seventy feet. The name of the ship was emblazoned in massive black letters along the side. Dew swallowed nervously; he had never crossed the ocean before and in truth was not a fan of sailing. Like Tom DuMarqué on the *Montrose*, he felt secure only when his feet were rooted firmly on solid ground. He grabbed his bag now and, muttering a grudging 'Thank you' to PC Delaney for politeness' sake, made for the ship.

A crowd of men was gathered by the gangplank and he gave them only the briefest glance as he walked towards it; however, when he was no more than ten feet away, one of the men turned around, stared at him, pointed a finger and then let out a roar, shocking Inspector Dew and making him turn to check whether someone famous had appeared behind him. 'There he is,' the man called. 'That's him!'

At this, the others all gathered together – about fifteen men in total – and rushed towards him, notebooks and pens at the ready, firing questions rapidly while three photographers almost blinded him with their flashbulbs. Dew could barely register what they were saying, so surprised was he by this sudden attention.

'Inspector, is it true you're on your way to capture Dr Crippen – ?'

'Did he really chop up his wife – ?'

'Do you think you can catch up with the *Montrose* – ?'

'Who's he going there to see – ?'

'Do you want to see him hang – ?'

'Who's the woman he's travelling with – ?'

'Have you found the head yet – ?'

'Gentlemen, gentlemen!' Dew cried, holding up his hands in surprise and irritation. 'One at a time, please. One at a time.' He turned around and glared at PC Delaney, who had followed him to the ship. 'Reporters,' he hissed. 'Who leaked this story?'

'No one said it was a secret,' the younger man said with a detached air. 'Sorry.'

'You will be if this goes awry.' He turned back to the gathered press and smiled at them. 'Just one or two questions, please,' he said. 'I have to board.'

'Inspector Dew,' one of them said, stepping forward from the pack as their representative. 'Can you tell us why you're boarding the *Laurentic*? Is it true you're chasing the wife-killer, Dr Crippen?'

Dew licked his lips and thought about it. There was

no chance that anyone on board the *Montrose* could possibly find out what was happening on land. Nor could they know that he was giving chase as long as Captain Kendall kept his mouth shut. Surely there would be no harm in telling the truth now. It might even present a good impression of Scotland Yard – the fact that he was willing to travel halfway across the world in order to get his man.

'It has been brought to our attention,' he said, 'that a man and woman travelling on board the SS *Montrose* towards Canada answer the description of Dr Hawley Harvey Crippen and Miss Ethel LeNeve, who are wanted for questioning in connection with the murder of Cora Crippen. My task is to apprehend them before they reach their destination and bring them back to England for justice.'

'Sir, the ship has been gone for three days now. Do you really think you can—?'

'That's all for now, gentlemen, I'm afraid,' he said, making his way up the gangplank just as the sailor at the top was preparing to close the doors. 'I'll be telegraphing back to Scotland Yard news of our progress, so stay in touch with them if you want to follow the story.'

They continued to shout questions at him as he disappeared out of sight, but he had no more time to answer them. The sailor checked his ticket and nodded at him quickly. 'Inspector Dew,' he said. 'Yes, we've been waiting for you.'

'Thank you. I was afraid you'd sail without me.'

'The captain requested that you go directly to see him, once you boarded. We're about to set sail now, but if you walk towards the deck and take the steps up to the wheelhouse, you'll find him there.'

Dew nodded and walked in the direction indicated, brushing past the crowds of passengers who were standing at the side of the ship, waving to the people gathered below to see them off. For a moment he had the strange idea of leaning over and waving to the reporters, when they could perhaps take another photograph as he set sail in search of the killer, but he decided against it. That would involve leaning over the side, and it was entirely possible that some unruly child might rush past him and knock him over, which would make a terrible front-page story.

He found the wheelhouse without much difficulty and knocked on the open door, announcing himself to the crew members gathered inside. 'Inspector Dew,' he said. 'Scotland Yard. Here to see the captain.'

'Inspector,' said a tall, bespectacled fellow, who was younger than he had expected and who was walking towards him. 'Pleased to meet you, sir. I'm Captain David Taylor. Welcome aboard the *Laurentic*.'

'Thank you.'

'Good trip from London, was it?'

'Long and tiring. I'll be glad of a rest in my cabin, to be honest.'

Taylor laughed. 'You're lucky,' he said. 'We had a cancellation at the last minute for one of our state rooms, so I've put you in there. One of the nicest cabins on board, in fact. Nicer even than my own.'

'Excellent,' he said, pleased that if he had to travel by sea then it would be in some comfort. 'I'm grateful for your help, Captain.'

'No trouble, no trouble at all. I see there was a reception committee waiting for you down below. Sorry about that.'

Dew nodded, shaking his head as if he disapproved of such things, even though in truth he quite enjoyed the publicity. 'Damn scoundrels,' he said. 'One sniff of a story and they're all over it like a bee around honey. You can't keep a secret in a police station these days, it seems. Not like in the old days. Don't know what the world's coming to.'

'Well, this will be a front-page story for the next week or so, I would imagine,' said the captain. 'They'll be following this voyage carefully. I had a bunch of them asking me questions earlier on, too. Told them nothing, of course. I'll leave that to you.'

'Captain Taylor,' Dew asked, leaning forward, 'realistically, what chance do we have of catching up with the *Montrose*?'

'I've made some calculations,' he replied, reaching for a pad of paper. 'It's certainly possible, but we'll have to make very good time. The *Laurentic* runs at sixteen knots, the *Montrose* at only twelve. But we're a slightly heavier ship. Still, we have the advantage of leaving from Liverpool, whereas they left from Antwerp. They have three days on us, Inspector, and will probably dock in Quebec on 31 July. We're due to arrive the following day.'

'Captain, it's imperative that we capture them before they reach land. If they disembark in Canada, it will be the devil's own business trying to get them back again.'

'And the Canadian authorities?' the captain asked. 'Couldn't they simply arrest them when they arrive?'

Dew shook his head. 'The crime is outside their jurisdiction,' he explained. 'If Dr Crippen sets one foot on Canadian soil, then he has escaped. We have to catch him before then.'

Taylor nodded. 'Well, as I say, Inspector, it's possible. But we have a full day to make up. I'll do everything I can to get you there, though. I promise you that.'

'Thank you, Captain. Perhaps I'll go to my cabin now and arrange my things.'

The captain called over one of his crew members and asked him to show the inspector to the state room. 'One last thing, Inspector,' he said as they left the helm, 'what exactly did the man do? I've heard rumours, but nothing for sure.'

Dew hesitated. Of course he was innocent until

proven guilty, but nevertheless the evidence was overwhelming. 'He murdered his wife,' he explained. 'He killed her, chopped her up and buried pieces of her under the stones in his cellar. Then he covered the bones with acid to dissolve them. We haven't recovered the head yet.'

Taylor, a squeamish individual at the best of times, gasped. 'I'll give you your day, Inspector,' he said with determination. 'If I have to push the *Laurentic* to full capacity, I'll give it to you. If we're not in sight of the *Montrose* by the end of the month, I will consider it a personal failure.'

Dew smiled. He was pleased to have the man on his side. 'Thank you, Captain,' he said. 'I'll put my faith in you then.'

13

The Dinner Party

In various parts of London, ten people were preparing for Cora Crippen's dinner party with varying degrees of excitement. In the upstairs bedroom of a house in Tavistock Square, Mrs Louise Smythson was sitting in front of her dressing table, applying perfume to her neck while examining the skin beneath her eyes for signs of ageing. Some small lines were definitely developing just below the eyelash, hardly visible at all, but nevertheless she sighed, knowing that this was just the beginning. Soon they would spread out while her cheeks sank in. Her hands would become gnarled and liver-spotted, her legs thick-veined and pale. Her breasts would lose their weight and would sag, and the mirror would become a previously close friend whom she no longer wanted to visit. She could hear her husband Nicholas whistling while he got ready in his dressing room next door.

She had been surprised to receive the invitation to come to dinner. It was a special occasion, Cora Crippen had said: her fifteenth wedding anniversary, and she wanted to celebrate. The invitation had been issued at a meeting of the Music Hall Ladies' Guild the previous week and she had accepted immediately. During all the time she had known Cora, she had met Dr Crippen only on a handful of occasions and she scarcely knew him at all. She considered him a dry stick, unequipped for social conversation and hardly a suitable dinner companion at all; but he was Cora's husband, so she could hardly criticize too loudly. Naturally she would have preferred to be invited to a posh restaurant, but Cora had insisted on doing the cooking herself, and Louise had considered such strange behaviour to be part of her friend's eccentric charm, not knowing that it was merely financial necessity that made her do so. She checked her watch and went next door to fetch her husband. It was time to leave.

Hawley Crippen himself had been busy all day, preparing for the meal. Cora had only told him about it two nights before, when she had issued her instructions. He had been a little surprised that she had either remembered or wanted to celebrate their wedding anniversary at all, but he had not questioned it. He knew very well that it was merely a way of impressing her friends and insinuating herself further into the society she coveted and had nothing at all to do with him. It was obvious that by inviting couples such as the Smythsons or the Nashes to dinner, they were ultimately obliged to return the invitation. And since neither he nor Cora had ever been invited to dine with either couple in their home, it would be a considerable coup for her to achieve this.

He stood still in the middle of the kitchen and worked his way through the checklist in his mind. The table was set, the wine was on the dresser, the lamb was cooking in the oven, the potatoes were boiling gently, the vegetables ready to be thrown in a pot at the right moment. The carpet had been thoroughly cleaned by him that morning, a task which had taken almost two hours – and one which was not helped when Alec Heath had walked through it in a pair of muddy boots, ignoring his prostrate landlord, who was scrubbing away at it carefully. He was sure that something was missing but could not think what. Even if he was wrong, Cora would find a way of complaining about it; but he was accustomed to that and, much as it wore him down, at least it never came as a surprise any more. He opened the oven door and stepped back before looking inside when the hot air quickly escaped. The juices of the meat were running down nicely; it smelled wonderful. There was only one thing left to do before he could relax. He took two solid carving knives from the dresser and began to sharpen them, making sure that their blades would slide through the meat without any difficulty. He was reminded of his early days in the McKinley-Ross abattoir.

Fifteen minutes' walk away, Ethel LeNeve was putting the final touches to her outfit, taking off a simple silver necklace which she had bought a month earlier in an effort to cheer herself up and replacing it with her late mother's pearls. She had hardly slept the night before, so excited was she by the prospect of a dinner party, although she had been totally amazed to receive the invitation. What she didn't know was that Cora Crippen had spent an evening racking her brain in an attempt to think of a single woman to invite, for without one the numbers were unbalanced. However, all her female friends were married and she could not think of any other suitable choice. It had been Hawley's suggestion that he invite Ethel along, and she had been initially reluctant. 'Who?' she asked. 'Ethel who?'

'Ethel LeNeve,' he replied patiently. 'My assistant at Munyon's. You've met her, my dear, on any number of occasions.'

'What, that little boyish-looking thing with the bloody great scar above her lip?'

'My assistant,' he repeated, unwilling to answer that question. 'A delightful woman.'

278

'Oh, I hardly think she's suitable,' said Cora. 'Isn't she a bit common?'

More common than you, who picked me up in a music hall? he wondered. More common than Louise Smythson who used to work as a bar girl? 'No,' he said. 'She's excellent company.'

'Well, I suppose she is single,' Cora said doubtfully. 'I mean, who'd have her, the ugly little creature.'

Hawley had felt a deep rush of hatred for his wife when she said this but he kept it inside him for now. Finally, she had given her permission and he had invited Ethel the next day at work. Naturally, she said she would be delighted to come. Strolling down the street now towards their home, her umbrella beside her tapping on the pavement, she hoped that tonight she would get along with Cora Crippen a little better than she ever had before. She'd only met her a handful of times; once, several years before, on the morning when she had first walked into Munyon's and met her darling Hawley for the first time. Once, a little over a year ago, when she had to return some keys to the dear man and had the misfortune to be interrupted by a furious Cora who had suffered some career setback, she had found out later. Once in Battersea Park on a Sunday afternoon, when she was sitting on a bench reading a book and the Crippens had passed her by. And once when Cora had come to the pharmacy to demand money off her husband and had looked as if she was going to have apoplexy if she didn't get it immediately. She was a strong-willed woman, there was no question of that. And Cora didn't like her.

Passing Ethel in a hansom cab, unaware that she was another dinner guest, Andrew and Margaret Nash chatted amiably to each other as they approached the Crippens' home. Like the Smythsons, they had been somewhat surprised to be invited to the wedding anniversary, but decorum meant they had to accept.

'Let's make sure we leave by eleven,' Andrew said as they pulled up. 'I have a meeting in the morning quite early and don't want to be overtired.'

'Of course, dear,' Margaret said. 'I'm sure the party will have ended by then. What a charming house,' she added, looking at the exterior.

'Seems a bit cramped to me,' he muttered. 'Are you sure these people are our sort?'

'Well, I don't know *him*,' she admitted. 'But Cora's a delightful woman. You couldn't hope to meet a more refined, elegant lady. Perfect manners. Charming. I'm sure you'll like her. And he is a doctor, after all.'

'I hate doctors,' said Andrew. 'Always looking at you as if you're going to fall over and collapse in front of them. I don't hold with it. If you're going to die, then you're going to die. Nothing you can do about it. No point trying.'

'Of course, dear. Oh, would you look at that poor unfortunate woman,' she added, glancing at Ethel, who was now only five or six doors away. 'The scar on her lip. I bet she drinks.'

'Why?' Andrew asked, baffled and amused.

'She most likely drinks and fell over one night when inebriated, cutting her lip open. She looks quite common, don't you think?'

He turned to look, but she was already upon them and surprised them by announcing herself as one of their fellow guests.

Alec Heath dragged himself off his bed and stood up, yawning loudly. He had fallen asleep an hour or two earlier, although he had intended to have a bath before dinner. He had stayed out late the night before with one of the chorus girls from the Majestic, an action which had caused Cora some serious injury. She had waited up until two o'clock in the morning for him to return but, exhausted, had given in then and had gone to bed, where she lay awake, waiting to hear his key in the lock, which she eventually heard, some two hours later. He had gone for some beers with a girl, and she had taken him to a late night bar where she knew they served distilled whisky at twopence a glass into the small hours. Afterwards, drunk, she had allowed him to drag her down a dark, wet lane and he had made rapid love to her under the street lamp before returning home. He'd been back at work by eleven that morning, as they were building a new stage set, and he had ignored the girl when he had seen her again, for what need had he of her now? His plan had been to have a long bath before dinner which would refresh him, but instead he had fallen asleep. No matter, he decided, buttoning the cuffs of his shirt and reaching for his tie as he examined his rough appearance in the mirror. He stroked his stubble, which was a little too obvious for decorum, but he decided against shaving. They could take him as he was or not at all. However, he did throw a little water over his face from the rose bowl and decided that was enough preparation. His stomach was growling. He wanted his dinner.

Cora descended from the heavens into her living room only when she knew that all her guests had arrived. It had been up to Hawley to entertain them until then, and he had done so to the best of his abilities, such as they were, while she had sat at the door of her bedroom, counting them in. She had read somewhere that the hostess should not appear at an intimate dinner party until all the guests had arrived and she was reluctant to go against this in case the Nashes or the Smythsons noticed it and despised her for it. She walked downstairs slowly in a brand-new dress, her hair piled on top of her head, revealing bare, masculine shoulders, far too wide and muscular to be on public display, a fact to which she was always oblivious. The sound of chatter from inside delighted her and she wondered why she had never thrown a party like this before. Now I am a society hostess, she thought to herself in delight. She pushed open the door and, with a fixed smile, stepped inside.

The dinner was delicious; Hawley had proved to be an excellent cook. Cora dominated the conversation, chatting amiably with all around the table for the first hour, until more wine entered her system and she began to grow a little more lively.

'Mexico,' she cried, after hearing of Andrew Nash's plans to build an underground pipe there linking the mines. 'How exciting.'

'It will be,' he said, 'although it will be another eight months before work actually begins.'

'And have you been there yet?'

He shook his head. 'Not yet. The company has sent scouts and engineers out there. They're working on the plans at the moment. Not much for me to do at the moment, I'm afraid. I'd only get in the way.'

'Andrew isn't really one to get his hands dirty,' Margaret laughed.

'No point in it,' he said. 'I'm an ideas man. I leave the hands-on work to the hands-on people. No, I shall most likely go over there sometime around next April or May. Make sure the work is being completed on time, kick a few workers around if necessary. It's damnable but we'll have to employ a lot of Mexicans to do the work.'

'Oh, surely not,' Cora said, appalled.

'Well, of course. It will take hundreds of men. We're hardly going to send a shipload of Englishmen over there to do it. Easier to work with the Mexicans. Although I must admit I'm a bit worried about it. I hope they're up to the task. Cheaper than the English, of course.'

'You need to send an Englishman over there to keep an eye on them,' Alec Heath said. 'Someone who can keep them all in line.'

'Indeed. Of course there are a few company men who—'

'I mean someone who isn't afraid to kick those little bastards around. Not a bunch of upper-class layabouts.'

'Alec,' Hawley cautioned him from across the table. 'There are ladies present.'

'Oh, don't mind us,' said Louise Smythson. 'Young Mr Heath is right. Company men are surely all about facts and figures. They'll sit in their offices all day, running through lists of figures, adding them up, down, inside and out, and never making sure that the men outside are doing their jobs properly. Then, of course, the costs rise.'

'You're quite right, of course,' said Andrew. 'I'll give it some thought.'

'I know what I'd do if they didn't pull their weight,' said Alec, leaning forward and suddenly pounding his right fist into the palm of his left hand. 'That.'

There was nervous laughter from around the table, except from Ethel who, sitting beside him, had jumped at the power of his punch. Small as she was, she felt quite dwarfed by this muscle-bound boy who had all but ignored her for the last hour except, she noted, to stare down the front of her dress when he thought she wasn't looking. He was attractive, she could see that, but there was something about his manner that scared her.

'Perhaps I'll make some coffee,' Hawley suggested, but Cora waved him down.

'No coffee, you boring man,' she said, laughing. 'Fetch another bottle of wine, why don't you? Make yourself useful for once in your life.'

'Of course, the other problem with these foreigners,' Margaret Nash explained, 'is that the slightest head-ache, and they down tools for the day. They're so lazy they just pretend to be sick and expect to get paid for it.'

'I haven't been sick a day in my life,' said Alec. 'What's

the point in it? Just get up and get on with your day and stop being a baby, that's what I say.'

'Some people can't,' Hawley explained. 'If they are truly sick, that is, and not just hung-over.'

Alec glared at him. 'And what would you know?' he asked.

'Hawley *is* a doctor,' Ethel said, defending him. 'He treats many patients. You should see him in our pharmacy some days. Even though we are supposed to be selling the homoeopathic cures, there are many customers who come in with a complaint and Hawley just takes them aside and gives them a little advice, and then off they go to follow it and we never see them again.'

'Maybe they die,' Cora suggested. 'Maybe that's why you never see them again. And if he'd let them alone to buy whatever they wanted, they would have lived.'

'They don't die,' said Ethel, pinning her down with a stare. 'Hawley knows exactly what he's doing.'

'Here, here,' said Andrew Nash, lighting up a cigar and offering one to Nicholas and Alec but, for reasons unexplained, ignoring Hawley. 'I think you have an admirer here, Crippen. Say, Cora, you'd better watch out.'

Ethel blushed deeply and stared at her plate, feeling the eyes of the entire table upon her. Hawley, aware of her discomfort, thrust his hand out and deliberately knocked over his wine glass, spilling the dark-red claret across the linen tablecloth, thus diverting everybody's eyes back to him.

'Oh, Hawley, look what you've done,' Cora cried in exasperation, as Alec moved his chair around a little, closer to Ethel, rather than have the spilt wine on his trousers. She didn't like him coming closer to her. His massive girth was blocking her view of Hawley; she thought the young man like an eclipse, the moon suddenly covering and blocking out the sun.

'No matter, no matter,' Hawley said, mopping up the mess with a few napkins. 'It's only a little wine.'

'On the good tablecloth, though,' she moaned. 'Oh, you are useless. Good for absolutely nothing.'

He sighed and threw the soaking napkins into the washing basket, returning to the table and wondering how much longer they would all have to sit there, pretending to be interested in each other's lives. 'Shall I make coffee?' he asked again.

'Oh, you and your coffee,' Cora cried, exasperated. 'Anyone would think you had shares in a plantation. Fine, then. Make your coffee if it means that much to you.'

He stood up and put the water on, aware of the uncomfortable silence which had greeted her loud remarks. Looking back into the living room, he could see Alec leaning down and whispering something in Ethel's ear. She looked back at him fearfully.

'Ethel,' Cora said, observing their private conversation and remembering how the young woman had defended her husband a few minutes before, an unforgivable sin, 'I was so happy you were able to come tonight.'

'I was pleased to be invited,' she replied.

Cora smiled. 'Well, it would have been awful to have been one person short. And I couldn't think of any single women. You're the only adult woman I know who isn't married or engaged.' Ethel nodded and tried not to look insulted. 'You must be on the lookout though, surely?'

'I . . . I hadn't thought about it,' she said quietly.

'Margaret, Louise, don't you know any single men who might be looking for a wife? We can't allow the poor girl to remain a spinster all her life, now can we? Margaret, didn't you mention that you had an under-gardener who was widowed with a small child?'

'Yes indeed,' said Mrs Nash, nodding happily, remembering. 'Dempsey is his name. Not sure what his first name is, he's always just been Dempsey to us. I mean, he's pretty old, about fifty, but his daughter's only an infant. He certainly needs someone to take care of his house and look after the child. Should I arrange an introduction?'

'No!' Ethel snapped, wishing that Hawley would return soon with the coffee. Her wish was answered, for he came back into the room at that moment. 'No, please don't bother,' she added in a more polite tone. 'I'm perfectly fine as I am.'

'What's this?' Hawley asked.

'Margaret's going to arrange a meeting between Ethel and one of her under-gardeners. The man might be in need of a wife.'

'I really couldn't,' said Ethel.

'Too old for you?' Alec asked with a smile.

'Really, Cora,' Hawley said, frowning. 'I don't think this is suitable at all.'

'Marriage, my dear,' Cora said quietly, leaning across and placing her hand on top of Ethel's tiny one, 'is a blessing. If you only knew how happy my dear Hawley and I have been these past fifteen years, then you would hope for nothing else. No, it's arranged,' she said, taking her hand back. 'We'll set it up.'

'I'd rather you didn't,' Ethel said in a firm voice. 'Really, Mrs Crippen. I absolutely cannot.'

'I believe she has a sweetheart,' said Louise Smythson, watching her carefully and breaking into a smile. 'I believe the poor girl has a hidden romance that she's not telling us about.'

'Do you?' Cora asked, surprised. 'I shouldn't imagine so, Louise. But do you really?'

'No,' said Ethel.

'Cora!' said Hawley.

'Oh, Hawley, we're just teasing. Look at her. She's gone quite red. Her heart has been given to someone. But he doesn't know it. It's not Alec, is it? I wouldn't bother, my dear. He's the "love them and leave them" sort. You'll never find a husband from the likes of him.'

'Will you excuse me a moment?' Ethel asked, wiping her mouth with her napkin and standing up.

'It's just upstairs. Room on the left,' Cora said, grinning as she left, humiliated. That'll teach her to defend my husband, she thought. Horrid little creature!

Ethel stood in the bathroom, weeping quietly and trying to stop her tears before her eyes and cheeks grew too red. Her feelings for Hawley had grown without her even realizing it. She had never intended to fall in love with him; from the start she had seen him as more of a father figure than a lover, to replace the father she had never known. He had died when she was just a baby and her mother, a violent drunk of a woman, had inflicted the scar above her lip when she punched her in the face as a child when wearing a sharp ring. Like Jezebel Crippen, she had claimed to be a religious woman, and had brought her daughter up to fear God, but her actions stood in stark contrast to her words. As an adult, Ethel had never looked for love, never considered it much, until the kindness of Hawley Crippen had overtaken her. And working together, side by side, had provided her with a new sense of security and happiness. When he was cheerful at work, she found herself happy throughout the day. But sometimes he arrived in one of his black moods, and on such occasions he was impenetrable, even a little scary in his manner towards her. She knew one thing for sure: that Cora Crippen was a heartless, evil, nasty, manipulative bitch. And a perceptive one. Because she was right, of course. Her heart did belong to someone. But she could hardly announce her love for Hawley in the middle of his wedding anniversary dinner. She pulled herself together and resolved to return to the living room for no longer than another twenty minutes, when she would make her excuses and go home alone.

And then she would never return to this house while Cora Crippen still lived in it.

She opened the door and jumped, startled, for blocking her way to the stairs was Alec Heath.

'Hello,' he said, winking at her.

'Mr Heath,' she said, surprised to see him there, standing so close to the bathroom door.

'What's your hurry?' he asked. 'You're not going back downstairs, are you?'

'For a little while,' she said. 'It's been a lovely evening, hasn't it?'

'Don't try to fool me. She hates you, and you probably can't stand her either. It's not worth your while.'

Ethel frowned. He was right, of course, and she would love to have admitted that, but she couldn't. He was crowding her now too and she hoped he would get out of the way.

'For what it's worth,' he said, 'I wouldn't pay any attention to Cora. She's all right really, but she can be a right bitch when she wants to be.'

'I'm sure I—'

'But she was right about one thing,' he continued, turning now so that she was pressed against the wall. 'You shouldn't be on your own like this. You're a pretty thing, you know. Even with that scar.' He reached forward and his thick fingers traced a line along it, while she shivered nervously, unable to break free from him.

'Mr Heath, please,' she begged.

'Ssh,' he whispered. 'Just enjoy it.' His right hand moved from her scar down to her neck and he slowly ran his finger along the skin, while his left stretched down towards her breasts.

She struggled against him. 'Get off me,' she cried. 'Please, Mr Heath, get off me.'

'Just shut up for a minute,' he hissed and pressed himself against her. She could feel him growing excited

288

and looked at the stairs, wondering what would happen if she simply launched herself down there, whether she would even survive the fall. He relented for a moment, however, stepping back to adjust his trousers, and in the moment where there was a gap between them, just as she was ready to run, Hawley appeared on the stairs below and looked up at them in surprise.

'Ethel,' he said. 'Is everything all right?'

'Fine, Hawley,' she said, pulling herself together and struggling free of Alec Heath as she made her way nervously downstairs.

Alec's lip curled in anger as she walked away. 'Ethel, come back. Let's finish our conversation,' he said.

'No thank you, Mr Heath,' she shouted without turning around.

Hawley stared up at him, wondering what had taken place, but the younger man, unimpressed, ignored him.

'Lovely to have met you,' she called up to him. 'Hawley,' she whispered in a quieter voice. 'I need to leave now.'

'But Ethel, we—'

'Hawley, I'm going,' she insisted.

They stared at each other for a moment and he wished he could take her hand and they could both run as fast as their legs could carry them away from 39 Hilldrop Crescent. 'Of course,' he said, nodding. 'I do apologize. I'm so very sorry.'

'It's not your fault,' she said, taking her coat off the stand. 'Please say goodbye to the others for me. And thank you for a lovely evening.'

'Ethel, what can I say to you?'

'Say nothing, Hawley. I must go.'

He leaned forward, wanting to get all his pain off his chest, but Alec was walking down to the hallway and he stopped in front of them, not allowing them a moment's privacy. 'I'll see you tomorrow at work,' he muttered as she opened the door and disappeared through it, closing it quickly behind her, leaving Dr Crippen alone and shaking with fury and hatred.

The shop had been particularly quiet for a Monday, traditionally their busiest day of the week. Hawley had spent the morning going through the accounts with Mr Munyon who, he believed, was not long for this world. His humpbacked figure had become even frailer in recent times and he seemed to be having difficulty with even the simplest arithmetic. Although he visited his shop only twice a week now – on Monday mornings and Friday evenings – Hawley liked to keep the old man informed of even the most minor matters that took place. This he did out of respect for him. Once his faculties began to slow down, it was only a matter of time before the rest of him did, and as a doctor he wanted to prevent that happening.

'Takings are up, Crippen,' Mr Munyon said, running a bony finger along a list of figures.

'No, sir. Takings are down,' he replied. 'Not by much, though. And today's been a busy day.'

'Hmm,' he grunted, irritated that he couldn't tell the difference any more. 'And how's the new girl working out? Any use, is she?'

'New girl?' Hawley asked, confused. 'But we haven't hired a new girl.'

'Her out there,' the old man said, lifting his stick and waving it in the general direction of Ethel, who was serving a customer at the counter.

'You mean Ethel?' Hawley asked. 'Miss LeNeve, I should say. Why, she's not new, sir. She's worked here for two and a half years.'

'When you're eighty-seven years old and have spent sixty-two years of them building a business, that will seem pretty new to you,' Mr Munyon retorted, squinting at her but pleased that he'd come up with a good excuse for his forgetfulness.

'Quite,' said Hawley.

Mr Munyon stood up and gathered his things together while Hawley put the ledger and bank books away. 'What happened to your eye?' he asked after a moment.

'What's that?'

'Your eye, Crippen. What happened to it?'

Hawley placed a finger over the deep cut above his eyebrow and touched it tentatively. 'It's the silliest thing,' he said. 'I got up in the middle of the night and wasn't watching where I was going. Before I knew it, I was walking into the door. Cut myself pretty badly.'

Munyon nodded. 'You're always having accidents, Crippen,' he said. 'Never known a man like you for it. Every week it seems you have a new cut or bruise. You want to pay more attention to the world around you. I'm half blind but I don't seem to walk into as many things as you do.'

Ethel glanced around as they passed her on the way out, and she wished her employer a polite 'Good afternoon'. She said nothing to Hawley when he returned and didn't even look up at him; he wondered whether he had done something to offend her. She had been quiet with him from the start of the day, answering him whenever he spoke to her but never beginning a conversation herself. He racked his brains for anything he might have said to upset her, but he could think of nothing. It had been over a month since the disastrous wedding anniversary party, and since then relations between them had been awkward. So much affection had grown between them that it had become difficult for them to approach each other simply as friends. If only he wasn't married to Cora, he felt he could say something to her about the feelings he had developed for her, feelings that he was convinced were reciprocated, but he was married and they both

291

knew that, and he would not insult her by suggesting anything immoral while that state remained.

He waited until the end of the day when the shop was empty and the door was locked before attempting to engage her in conversation again. 'A busy Monday,' he began, employing small talk. 'This week might be busier than last.' He looked across at her, but she merely nodded, saying nothing. He sighed. 'Ethel?' he asked.

She turned to look at him. 'Yes, Hawley?'

'I said this week might be—'

'Yes, I heard you. I'm sorry, I was lost in thought. I think it might be, yes.'

'You're angry about something.'

'What?'

'Ethel, you're angry. You've hardly said two words to me today. What's the matter? Is it something I've done? Something I've said?'

She laughed it off. 'Of course not, don't be ridiculous. What *could* you have done?'

'I don't know; that's why I'm asking.'

'It's nothing, Hawley. Don't mind me. I'm just pre-occupied.'

He nodded and let it go for now, but finally he could bear the silence no longer and went around the counter to stand in front of her. 'Tell me,' he said. 'What is it?'

'Hawley, I—'

'Ethel, I consider us friends. If there is something annoying or upsetting you, I would consider it hurtful if you felt you could not confide in me. Is there some problem in your home life that you wish to talk about?'

'It's not *my* home life I'm worried about,' she said finally, unable to look at him.

'Not yours?' he asked, confused. 'Whose then?'

'Whose do you think? *Yours*, Hawley. It's *you* I'm concerned for.'

He laughed. 'Me?' he said, surprised. 'But why, for

292

heaven's sake? Why do you need to be concerned about me?'

She thought about it and looked down, closing her eyes for a moment, before looking him directly in the eyes. 'Hawley, a moment ago you said that you considered us friends.'

'And I do.'

'Of course I do too. And you said that if there was a problem you would want me to tell you about it. Well, I feel the same way towards you.' He stared at her, unable to decipher her meaning. 'Hawley,' she said finally. 'What happened to your face?'

His heart skipped a beat and he looked away, biting his lip. This was not a subject he wanted to talk about. 'My face?' he asked. 'Why? What's wrong with it?'

'I'm talking about your eye, Hawley. No, don't walk away from me,' she said, taking his arm. 'I want you to tell me. You have a deep cut over your eye. It looks terribly painful. I'm surprised you didn't need stitches.'

'I am a doctor, Ethel.'

'How did it happen?'

'It's the silliest thing. I woke in the night and—'

'No,' Ethel said firmly. 'I heard you say that to Mr Munyon earlier, and I'm sorry but I simply do not believe you. It's possible for someone to walk into a door once in a blue moon but not as often as you do. You are constantly coming in to work covered in scars. You say you've walked into doors or fallen downstairs. You've opened bottles of wine and had the cork fly out into your eye. You've been hit by hansom cabs and ended up with so many bruises that you can barely walk. Now, either you are the most accident-prone man in England or there is more to this story than meets the eye. And I want to know what it is. I am not Mr Munyon and I want the truth.'

Hawley licked his lips. He could see the concern in her eyes and he loved her for it. 'Really,' he said finally.

293

'You're letting your imagination run away with you. I'm just clumsy.'

'It's her, isn't it?' she said, determined to say what she believed. 'She does this to you.'

'She? Who?'

'Your wife, Hawley. That harridan you're married to.'

'Ethel, I—'

'I'm sorry, Hawley. I hate to say such things or use such words, but there are no others for it. I've seen the way she treats you. I've heard the way she speaks to you. And I do not believe that it ends at that. She beats you, doesn't she? She treats you no better than she would treat a dog in the street, and you sit back and take it.'

'Ethel, it's not like that. She gets upset, she—'

'*Upset?*' she cried, growing upset herself now. 'I'm sure *you* get upset, but you don't beat her black and blue, do you?'

'Of course not. I've never laid a finger on Cora in anger.'

'That's because you are a gentleman.'

'It's because I'm *afraid*,' he shouted, causing her to take a step back. He swallowed and felt the tears start to form. 'I'm afraid of her, Ethel,' he said. 'Does that make me sound weak? Maybe it does. Does it make me sound like half a man? Perhaps I am. She has such mood swings, you wouldn't believe it. I wake in the morning and the first thing I think is, what kind of mood will she be in today? We sit together in the evening, listening to music on the phonograph, and I'm afraid to make a comment, to say anything about anything, because no matter what I say she'll contradict me and pick a fight. It seems to me that all she ever wants to do is fight. That it's the only way she can have a relationship with me at all. By reducing me to nothing.'

'That's because *she* is nothing,' said Ethel fiercely. 'Because she has nothing in her own life. This nonsense about her being a singer. It's never going to come to anything. You know it, I know it, and she knows it. She's so frustrated with her own life that she takes it out on you. You're the easiest target. Because you're kind. And you're gentle. And you're a man of peace. You're everything that she is not.'

'What would you have me do?' he asked her, beseechingly. 'It's been too long now. Maybe if I'd stood up to her all those years ago—'

'It's never too late, Hawley. Admit it to me. She hits you, doesn't she?' He nodded. 'She beats you.' He nodded again. 'What does she use? Frying pans, pots, her *fists*?'

'All three,' he admitted. 'And more.'

'*I* don't think you a lesser man,' she said quietly, shaking her head, close to tears. 'I think you're in a horrible relationship and you need to break free from it. You need to get away from her. Before she kills you. And she will, Hawley. If things go on like this, she will kill you one day.'

'I'd be better off,' he said in so low a voice that she only just heard him.

'You would not,' she shouted, bursting into sudden tears. 'Oh, Hawley, how can you say that? How can you even suggest it? What about me? How could I possibly survive without you?'

Hawley looked up at her, shocked. 'You?' he asked. 'But what—?'

'I couldn't,' she said firmly. 'It's that simple. I've never loved a man like I love you, Hawley. And to see her treat you like this. It makes me want to kill her.' She stepped forward and, before either of them knew what they were doing, their lips had met and they were kissing. It didn't last long, only a few moments, and then they broke apart, staring at each other with a mixture of panic and love. Ethel looked as if she was ready to collapse. 'I must go,' she said, grabbing her coat and unlocking the door.

'Ethel, wait. We should—'

'I'll see you tomorrow, Hawley,' she cried, not turning around. 'Just don't let her hurt you any more. Please. For me.'

And then she was gone. Hawley exhaled and sat down on a chair, scratching his head in amazement. She loves me? he thought. It was too unbelievable for words. He took his coat from the stand and locked the shop behind him, hoping that she might be still on the street outside, but she had vanished from sight. It was not the right time to follow her anyway, he thought. Now was the time to go home. The time to tell Cora how things would be from now on. That she would not be allowed to treat him as she had any more. That there would be no more shouting, no more violence, no more trouble. He picked up his stride, enlivened by what Ethel had said and her feelings for him, and he felt nothing but anger, directed mainly at himself for having allowed himself to be treated like this in the first place. Normally at this time he would have gone to the dental surgery, but not tonight.

Back home in Hilldrop Crescent he expected to find his wife lying on the sofa, eating fruit and reading a book, her favourite early evening occupation. She wasn't there but somehow he could sense that she was in the house. Two half-empty cups of tea were sitting on the table and he touched the side of one; it was still warm. He stepped into the kitchen, not really expecting to find her there, and he was not surprised. Nor was she in the bathroom, whose door was swinging open. He walked through to the bedroom but she was not to be found there either. He stroked his moustache and was about to return downstairs when a sound caught his attention. It was coming from upstairs, from the room where Alec Heath lodged. He listened carefully and wasn't sure whether he had imagined it. But no – there it was again. Slowly, he walked outside the bedroom and placed a foot on the steps. He had not been up there since Alec had moved in, over a year ago, and had no idea what condition the room was in; in truth he no longer considered it a part of their home. Trying to make as little noise as possible, he went up the stairs, and as he did so the sounds grew louder. Moans and grunts, single syllables uttered as cries, while bed springs provided their music. He reached the top, the door was ajar, and he placed his hand on it, the pressure pushing it further open without any noise. Before him, on Alec's bed, was a sight which at first his brain failed to comprehend, so strange was it to him. Lying down on top of the sheets was the boy they had rented this room to; he was naked as the day he was born, his long legs stretched out, his eyes half shut in pleasure as he moaned Cora's name. Above him, sitting perched across him, was his wife, also naked, her breasts hanging down, a trickle of perspiration tracing a path between them, while her hand pressed down on her young lover's face, forcing him further and further into the bed, pushing him down as far as she could while she sighed in pleasure.

On the evening of 19 January 1910, Mr Henry Wilkinson, a twenty-four-year-old chemist, was working the late shift at Lewis & Burrow's Pharmacy in Oxford Street. He was yawning incessantly as this was his eighth working day in a row, owing to the continued illness of Mr Tubbs, his employer, and he was thoroughly exhausted. He knew that if Mr Tubbs was ill again the following day, he would need to close at lunchtime or risk mixing the wrong prescriptions. He could barely keep his eyes open as it was, and that would never do.

The chime above the door sounded and he looked up to see a man enter; he was wearing a hat, spectacles and a heavy coat, with the collar turned up around his neck. He sported a black moustache and walked quickly to the counter, handed across a prescription, and looked away without a word. Henry opened it and read it, raising an eyebrow in surprise.

'Hydro bromide of hyoscine,' he said. 'This is powerful stuff. Your doctor explained the dangers of it?'

'I *am* a doctor,' came the reply.

'Oh. Right you are,' said Henry. 'It'll take me a little while to prepare it, though. I don't often get orders for poisons like this.'

'How long?' the man asked in a muffled voice.

'About ten minutes, sir,' said Henry. 'Would you like to wait or come back later? We're open till ten.'

'I'll wait.'

Henry walked into the back room, from where he could still see the front of the shop, and consulted a manual before taking the ingredients down from the shelf, pouring them carefully through a pipette into a medium-sized prescription bottle. There was something curious about the man out front, he thought. He was acting very suspiciously, looking at all the shelves but making sure of keeping his back to him at all times.

'Nice night for it,' Henry called in an attempt at conversation. 'Heading home for your dinner?' The man said nothing but continued to pace the floor, tapping his walking stick as he did so. 'Suit yourself,' Henry muttered.

Ten minutes later, the mixture prepared, he stepped outside and put it in a bag.

'Now,' he said, 'I don't have to tell you to be careful with this, sir. Make sure you dilute one capful with five capfuls of water or you'll know all about it. Says so on the label.'

The man extended a one pound note and Henry took it, getting the change from the till. 'I have to ask you to sign for this, sir,' he said, producing a large black folder and skimming through it until he found the appropriate page. 'That's one of the drugs we're not allowed to issue without a signature and address.'

The man nodded, fully aware of this, and wrote carefully on the page: James Middleton, 46 The Rise, Clerkenwell. Henry glanced at it and nodded. 'Thanks very much, Dr Middleton,' he said. 'Mind how you go now.'

Outside, he took the bottle out of its packaging and read the instruction label again. One capful to five capfuls of water. Once a day. His heart beating fast within his chest, his lips dry, his legs a little weak, he put the bottle in the pocket of his coat and headed home.

14

Inspector Dew Visits 39 Hilldrop Crescent – Several Times

London: Friday, 8 July – Wednesday, 13 July 1910

FRIDAY, 8 JULY

Inspector Walter Dew walked along Camden Road towards Hilldrop Crescent, irritated that he had to make this visit at all. Making rash promises was part of what being a Scotland Yard inspector was all about; in the course of any given day he was forced to deal with so many hysterics and fabulists that if he was to investigate all their wild claims he would never have time for actually solving any real crimes. He had planned on sending a police constable to the house to take any details which were necessary. A phone call from the London Police Commissioner, however, had put an end to that idea.

'Dew?' he asked, shouting down the phone as if he had still not grown accustomed to its use. 'What's all this about some Crippen fellow you're supposed to be investigating?'

'Crippen?' he asked, surprised that the name had reached his superior. 'There's nothing to investigate

there, sir. Just a couple of women with overactive imaginations believing the poor man has murdered his
wife. That's all.'

'That's all, eh? You think murder's not a serious thing,
do you?'

'Of course I don't, sir. I meant that their claims don't
sound too serious. It seems to me they just have a little
too much time on their hands and have been reading
too many mystery novels.'

'Well, that's as may be,' grunted the commissioner.
'But look here, I've just had a phone call from Lord
Smythson, who says that one of these women is his
sister-in-law and that she's upset because you haven't
done anything about it yet. So she got on to him about it
as she knew we were in the same club. Now Smythson's
a weak fellow, but he's asked me to look into it and I can
hardly say no. And I'll have to tell him something soon,
just to shut him up. So call round there and find out
what's going on, will you, there's a good fellow.'

'But sir, I have a lot on at the moment. I can't just
drop everything because some—'

'Just do it, Dew,' the other said, exasperated. 'And
don't question me.'

'Yes, sir,' he replied, replacing the receiver with a
sigh.

The internal politics of the Yard were a source of
constant irritation to the inspector. There were real
crimes and murders taking place daily among the working classes but no one gave them any thought the
moment something troublesome happened among
the rich. That very morning he had received a report of
a body floating in the Thames near Bow and a woman
who had been stabbed at her flower stall in Leicester
Square. And instead he was stuck with this.

He rang the bell of 39 Hilldrop Crescent and turned
around as he waited for the door to be opened, staring
at the dying flowers in the front garden which had not

been watered in some time. A group of children were running along the street, chasing a small dog. The malnourished mutt was barking weakly and seemed to be lame. He frowned and watched as they caught it and lifted it in the air, and he was about to go over and intervene before they did the animal any further harm when the door opened behind him and he turned around quickly instead.

'Can I help you?' Hawley asked, adjusting his pince-nez to look more closely at the smartly dressed middle-aged man who was standing before him, holding his hat in front of him in his hands. Somehow, before even a word was said, he knew that this someone was here on official business.

'Dr Crippen?' asked Dew.

'Yes.'

'Inspector Walter Dew,' he said. 'From Scotland Yard.' Dew was well aware that one of the most important moments in any investigation was the one taking place at that very moment. Typically, a person would either look frightened when confronted by an officer of the Yard, or they would look confused. He could generally tell in an instant whether someone had anything to hide. On this occasion, however, there was no perceptible difference in Dr Crippen's face, a rare feat for anyone.

'And how may I help you, Inspector?' he asked, his arm blocking entry into the house as they stood there.

'I wonder if I could take a few moments of your time,' Dew replied. 'Inside.'

Hawley hesitated for only a moment before opening the door wider and inviting the inspector in. The house was deathly quiet and dark, and Dew looked around uneasily as he stood in the hallway.

'Please. Come into the living room,' Hawley said in a relaxed tone. 'I'll make us some tea.'

'Thank you,' he replied, looking around. He was trained to observe his surroundings quickly in case they might be of use in solving a crime. The room was spotlessly clean and a bowl of fruit stood in the centre of the table. The cushions on the sofa and chairs were arranged at neat angles and the fire place had been recently cleaned. It struck him how orderly the house was in comparison to the garden. 'I hoped I'd find you at home,' said Dew, raising his voice so that Hawley could hear him in the kitchen. 'I wasn't sure whether you'd be at work or not.'

'Normally I would be at this time,' he said, coming back into the room and laying out some cups on the table. 'I haven't been feeling very well this week, however, and my assistant has taken over.'

'And where is that?' asked Dew.

'Where is what?'

'Where you work?'

'Oh. Munyon's Homoeopathic Medicines,' Hawley replied, pouring the tea. 'Perhaps you know it? A pharmacy in New Oxford Street.'

Dew nodded. He had seen a number of such stores popping up around London but he didn't hold with them. The type of man who had never been sick a day in his life, he wasn't interested in miracle cures and eastern medications.

'I confess, I have never been visited by a member of the force before,' said Hawley, as they sat down. 'I hope it's nothing serious.'

'Nothing too serious, I hope,' said Dew, removing a notebook from his pocket and licking the top of his pencil out of habit. 'I just wanted to ask you a few questions, that's all.'

'Certainly.'

'About your wife.'

Hawley blinked and hesitated for a moment. 'My wife?' he asked.

'Yes. We've had a complaint brought to us and—'

'About my wife?' He appeared to be amazed.

'Your wife died recently, did she not?' Inspector Dew asked, preferring to put the questions rather than answer them.

'Sadly, yes.'

'Can you tell me about that, please?'

'Of course. What would you like to know?'

'The details surrounding her death, mainly. When it took place. Where. Anything you might want to tell me in fact.'

Hawley thought about it. He'd been aware that a moment like this might arrive and had prepared a speech for the occasion, but the unexpectedness of it now had made him a little forgetful.

'Cora,' he began, 'Mrs Crippen, that is. She had a relative in America. In California. An uncle. And he wrote to say that he was very ill and had only a month or two left to live. This was some months ago, of course. She had been very close to him as a girl, and naturally she was very upset.'

'Naturally,' said Dew.

'So she decided to visit him.'

'All the way to America?' he asked. 'It seems a long way to go for just a brief stay. Didn't he have any family closer to home?'

'None at all. He had never married, you see, and was entirely alone. And as I said, Inspector, they had been very close once, and so he contacted her. She couldn't bear to think of him dying without anyone to comfort him at the end. So she decided to go herself.'

'I see,' he said. 'And where was this exactly?'

'California.'

'So she went to California to look after him and then – ?'

'I believe she caught a virus on board the boat and was feeling ill when she arrived in New York. She cabled me from there to tell me about it but said she was sure she would feel better once she got to her uncle's.'

'Do you still have that wire?'

'I'm afraid not. I usually throw things like that away. I had no idea I might need it.'

'Quite, quite,' he said, making a note. 'Go on.'

'Well, then she had to travel across the States, from the east coast to the west. That must have taken it out of her further, I expect. I didn't hear from her for about a week or two after that, but then the Californian authorities wired me to tell me that she had died suddenly. Her uncle had outlived her by only a few days and they were buried together.'

Inspector Dew nodded and continued to make notes, even though Hawley had fallen silent. The inspector didn't want to say anything yet; it was his habit to let the person he was interrogating say as much as possible in the hope that they might incriminate themselves. Sometimes the pressure of the silence made them say more than they had intended. The ploy worked, for after a whole minute and a half with neither man speaking, Hawley finally found his voice again.

'It was quite devastating for me,' he said. 'I never would have let her go if I'd known what would happen. I have heard those transatlantic boats can be death traps. I travelled on one once myself, when I left America for London, but I would not want to do so again.'

'You're an American?' Inspector Dew asked, surprised.

'I was born in Michigan.'

'I'd never have guessed it. You don't have any trace of an accent.'

Hawley smiled. 'I've lived here a long time,' he said. 'I think it's faded.'

'It's been reported that there is no record of your wife being in California,' Dew said after a moment, licking his lips and watching Hawley's face for any perceptible change.

'How's that?' he asked.

'Foreigners are obliged to report to the authorities on arrival in a state,' the inspector explained. 'It seems there is no record of a Cora Crippen arriving in California.'

'No record,' Hawley repeated, thinking this through.

'Nor, for that matter, is there a death certificate. Or any evidence of a funeral.'

'I see,' he said, nodding his head.

Silence ensued again for a few moments, but on this occasion it was Inspector Dew who broke it.

'Perhaps you could shed some light on that,' he said.

'I assume, Inspector,' Hawley said, 'that what you are saying is there is no record of a Cora Crippen arriving in, or dying in, California.'

'Just so.'

'The thing is, my wife was a rather unusual case in that she had a number of, how shall I put this, pseudonyms.'

'Really?' Dew said, arching an eyebrow. 'And why would she do that? Was she a novelist?'

'No, certainly not,' Hawley said with a laugh. 'She was a performer. A singer in a music hall. And in the world of the stage she called herself Bella Elmore. So it is possible she used that name in California. Or even her maiden name, Cora Turner. Or there again, it is entirely possible that her passport had her listed as Kunigunde Mackamotski.'

'I beg your pardon?'

'Kunigunde Mackamotski,' he repeated. 'Her birth name. She was of Russian-Polish descent, you see. She changed her name to Cora Turner when she was about sixteen as she felt that such an ethnic name would hinder her chances in life. Perhaps she was right, I don't know. But it's perfectly possible that that was the name on her passport, since it would have necessarily been the name on her birth certificate. Unfortunately, I never saw the document so I can't be sure. But there we are, you see. She could have been using any of those names over there. To tell the truth, Cora Crippen is one of the less likely.'

Dew nodded and closed his notebook. 'I believe that was the only name which was looked for,' he said, satisfied with Hawley's answer. 'I think that's probably all I needed to know, so I'll take my leave of you. I'm sorry to have disturbed you and had to ask you such personal questions. I'm sure you're still in mourning for Mrs Crippen.'

'It was no trouble at all, Inspector,' Hawley said, standing up and ignoring the second part of Walter Dew's comment.

'And my condolences too, of course, on the death of your wife.'

Hawley acknowledged this with a handshake. 'Thank you,' he said. 'But can I ask you a question?' Dew nodded. 'What brought you around here to ask me these questions in the first place? How had Scotland Yard heard about Cora's death?'

'I'm afraid I can't go into that, Doctor,' he replied. 'All I can say is that a certain party or parties were worried that Mrs Crippen might have come to harm. But rest assured, I will be speaking to the parties concerned later today and I doubt if we will be taking the matter any further.'

They walked to the door and Hawley opened it, amazed that it had been as easy as this.

'Just one last thing before I go,' said Dew, before stepping outside.

'Inspector?'

'The wire.'

Hawley stared at him. 'I beg your pardon?'

'The wire from the Californian authorities. Informing you of your poor wife's death. I just need to take that with me for the file, to prove there was no funny business. You understand.'

307

'The wire,' Hawley repeated, his face growing a little paler as he licked his lips and thought about it. 'I'm not sure if—'

'Oh come, come, Dr Crippen,' Inspector Dew said in a friendly tone of voice. 'I can understand your disposing of your wife's wire from New York informing you that she had got there safely. But surely you would have held on to such an important document as this.'

'Yes,' he said. 'I suppose I would.'

'Then if you could just get it for me,' he said, closing the door again so that they were standing in the darkness of the hallway again. For the first time, Dew realized that there might be more to this than met the eye. They stood there together for a moment before Hawley raised his eyes from the carpet and looked the inspector in the face.

'I think,' he said slowly, 'I had better tell you the truth.'

'Yes, Doctor,' he replied, a frisson of surprise running through his body. 'I think you'd better.'

'You've caught me in a lie, you see.'

'Perhaps we should go back inside,' suggested Dew, his interest picking up somewhat now. Had she really come to mischief? Was there to be a sudden and unexpected confession?

They went back into the living room and sat down. Hawley had never thought through his fiction up to this point before, but, sitting there now, an idea sprang into his head and he scrambled through the implications in his mind to make sure it made sense before saying anything. For his part, Inspector Dew was watching him with some sympathy. Although he had only been in his company a short time, he had already appraised the doctor in his mind. He seemed a harmless, polite and mild-mannered fellow, far removed from the degenerates whom he had to deal with on a daily basis. He doubted that this man would be capable of what

Mrs Louise Smythson and Mrs Margaret Nash had suggested.

'My wife,' Hawley began, taking a deep breath before continuing. 'You see, Inspector, my wife is not dead at all.'

Dew raised an eyebrow and took his notebook out of his pocket again. 'Not dead,' he said in a flat voice.

'No. In fact, she is very much alive.'

'Correct me if I'm wrong, Dr Crippen,' said Dew. 'But weren't you the one who told her friends that she had died?'

'Just so.'

'Perhaps you can explain, then?'

'Cora has indeed gone to America,' he said. 'Although whether she is in California or not, I do not know. If I had to make a prediction, I would be inclined to think Florida, but that's pure guesswork on my part.'

'Florida? Why on earth Florida?'

'Because that's where he was from, you see.'

'He?'

Hawley bit his lip and looked away, shaking his head sadly. 'It's scandalous, Inspector,' he said. 'Which is why I didn't want anyone to know.'

'Please, Doctor, if you could just tell me the truth, it would make things a lot easier.'

'She left me for another man, you see. As I told you, my wife was a music-hall singer and she met this fellow at a show one evening. He was a wealthy American and had been travelling the world. England was his last stop before going home. Anyway, she betrayed me with him and fell pregnant.'

'I see.'

'And then she told me that she was in love with the fellow and that he was taking her back to America with him. Naturally I was devastated. I loved my wife very much, Inspector. Truly I did. Although I think she found my lifestyle not as exciting as the one she

309

craved. She often accused me of holding her back. This other fellow offered her something more, I expect. Money, glamour, a new life in America. I said I would forgive her and bring up the child as my own, but she wasn't interested. One evening she was here, Inspector, and the next morning she was packing her bags and left London entirely. I didn't know what to do. If the news broke, there would be a scandal. I am a doctor and need my patients in order to make a living. If they heard about this, well, my practice would disintegrate overnight. And . . .' Here he wiped a tear from his eye as he looked more and more bereft. 'If I am to be truly honest with you, I will admit that I was embarrassed. I felt it made me look like only half a man. I couldn't bear it, Inspector. To be cuckolded by a man from my own country. It was more than I could deal with.'

Inspector Dew reached across and patted Hawley on the elbow; the last thing he wanted was to be drying the man's tears, but he could see how sorrowful this fellow was, and he was not immune to another's suffering.

'I'm sorry, Dr Crippen,' he said. 'I can see this is painful for you.'

'No, it is I who am sorry,' he replied, shaking his head quickly. 'I should never have come up with such an elaborate story in the first place. It was wrong of me. I think that in the back of my mind I actually wished she had died rather than left me. Does that sound a terrible thing to say?'

'Completely understandable, I think,' said Dew.

'No, it's unforgivable. Perhaps I didn't make her happy.'

'You can't blame yourself.'

'But I do, Inspector. And now look at the trouble I've caused. I have Scotland Yard interrogating me, and now the truth is bound to come out. Everyone will find out. I'll be pitied and despised in equal parts. And I have only myself to blame.'

'I'm afraid the truth always outs, Doctor,' Dew admitted. 'But the fact is that some of your wife's friends have not entirely believed your story anyway. Perhaps it would be best if you told them yourself? Remember, you are the injured party here, not the victim. Perhaps they will show you sympathy.' He scarcely believed his own words but thought they had to be said. He glanced at his watch. It was almost one o'clock. 'I was planning on having a little lunch before returning to the office,' he said. 'Perhaps you'd care to join me?'

'Really?' Hawley asked, surprised at the inspector's friendliness. 'Are you sure?'

'Certainly. I don't care for cases like this, if I'm to be honest with you. Prying into another fellow's domestic arrangements. Makes me feel shabby.'

Hawley thought about it. Given the choice, he would have preferred for Inspector Dew to leave Hilldrop Crescent immediately and never return, but that didn't seem to be an option. The only way out of this mess appeared to be by seeing his deception through to the end.

'I don't like leaving you in this condition either,' said Dew, real concern showing in his voice.

'All right, Inspector,' he said finally. 'Thank you, I'd be delighted. I'll fetch my coat.'

He left the room and Dew stood by the window, looking out into the street. The children had disappeared now, and so had the lame dog, and he wondered whether he should have intervened earlier in their game of torture. The poor creature was probably dead by now. His stomach grumbled a little and he glanced around to see where his companion was. The poor man, he thought. Having to reveal all that to a total stranger. He thought about Mrs Louise Smythson and Mrs Margaret Nash and despised them a little; if they had simply kept their noses out of Dr Crippen's business, he thought, then this innocent would not have had to reveal such

311

personal information. It was too bad. He wished for a moment that he could charge them for wasting police time, but he knew that such a thing was impossible.

'Are you ready, Inspector?' Hawley asked, opening the front door.

'Ready,' he said, following the man out of Hilldrop Crescent and into the street, the darkness and silence within guarding the secrets that the house contained.

They dined at a small restaurant not far from Hawley's Camden home and quickly discovered that they had a great deal in common. For one thing, Inspector Dew – who was only a year older than Dr Crippen – had struggled to join the police force in much the same way as he had struggled to become a doctor.

'My parents were the problem,' Dew told him, cheerfully eating a piece of rare steak with mushrooms and fried potatoes, sweeping the whole thing up with a slice of bread and leaving white portions of plate visible beneath. 'Well, my mother in particular. She was convinced that it was not a suitable job for a respectable young man. She wanted me to go into the law as a barrister or join the clergy, neither of which appealed to me. Didn't like the outfits, you see. Wigs for one, skirts for the other. I didn't think so. So I stood by my guns, and here I am today. Inspector Dew of the Yard, if you please. She never fully approved, though. Even when I started to get promoted through the ranks, she was still disappointed in me.'

'My mother was much the same,' Hawley admitted. 'But she considered the medical profession an insult to God. She thought anyone who attempted to cure a disease was tampering with His will. "God's glorious work," she called it. She never took any medicine herself, wouldn't even stem a cut with a bandage. She used to burn my copies of *Scientific American*, you know.'

'Good Lord. But she must have been proud of you

when you graduated, surely? It's not every man has the brain power to become a doctor.'

He thought about it. 'I don't believe she was,' he replied, ignoring the rather obvious fact that he had never actually graduated as a doctor. (This was, however, something he had long ago convinced himself had actually happened. If he tried hard enough, he could even remember scenes from the day. Collecting his degree. Shaking hands with the head of the university. They were all there in his imagination, feigning reality.) 'Actually, we haven't spoken in many years.'

'You shouldn't let that be the case,' said Dew. 'I mean, I still have lingering resentment towards my mother for putting so many obstacles in my path along the way, but by God I wouldn't be without her.'

'She's still alive then?'

'Oh yes. Eighty-four years old and the constitution of an ox. I have dinner with her once a week and she still acts as if she could put me over her knee if I don't finish my vegetables.' He smiled a little and shook his head. 'And I never did much care for them, either. Still, I wouldn't have her any other way,' he said.

'I expect mine is still in Michigan,' Hawley said, unmoved by the memory. 'At least, I haven't heard anything to the contrary.'

'And aren't you interested at all? Don't you want to stay in touch?'

'It seems to me, Inspector, that most of the people in whom I have ever put any trust in life have let me down. Particularly the women. If I am to be honest with you, I believe that my own character has been formed by these people and certain incidents associated with them, and my character is not one that I am always proud of.'

Dew frowned, intrigued by what the other had said. 'How so?' he asked.

'I think I am a weak man,' Hawley admitted, amazed that he could speak so openly to the inspector, but sensing in him a kindred spirit. 'I find it difficult to stand up for myself in difficult situations. My first wife was a kind soul, but had she lived – '

'Your *first* wife?' Dew asked, surprised. 'I was not aware you had been married before.'

'Oh yes. Back in America. Many years ago now, when I was a young man. Charlotte Bell was her name. A pretty girl and perfectly pleasant. We were only married a few years, however, when she was taken from me. A traffic accident. It was quite tragic really.'

'I'm sorry.'

'Don't be. It's a long time ago and I have no lingering feeling. I mention her merely to point out the fact that, had she lived, I believe she would have dominated me very much. She was very different from Cora, but she would have made certain . . . demands, I think. I don't know what would have happened between us in the end, but I've often thought it might well have ended badly.'

'As it did between you and Cora?'

'Indeed,' Hawley said, finishing his meal and pushing the plate away. 'Although I should, of course, have expected it. Can I tell you something, Inspector? Something just between you and me?'

Dew nodded. He forgot, for a moment, that he had originally met Dr Crippen with his professional hat on and he felt that during this short afternoon they had become something close to friends. 'Of course, Hawley,' he said, employing his Christian name for the first time. 'You can trust me entirely.'

'This American fellow she ran off with,' he said. 'He wasn't the first one, you see. I know of at least three other people that Cora had enjoyed affairs with. An Italian music teacher for one. An actor she met once at a party. A boy not yet twenty who lodged with us for a time. And I'm sure there were others too. She had an active social life. She worked at the music hall, you see.'

'Yes, you mentioned that.'

'I think she used the stage name Bella Elmore because Cora Crippen wasn't good enough for her. She had to sound grand. She always had to be someone she wasn't. That was her problem, you see. She couldn't stand for a moment to think that she might be just a regular, common human being. No frills. No adornments. Nothing special. Just a run-of-the-mill person whose dreams get shattered and crushed in the gutter like everyone else's.' His tone had changed to one of bitterness and Inspector Dew noticed it, but he felt only sympathy for him, not suspicion.

'You've been very honest with me, Dr Crippen,' he said. 'I appreciate that.'

'I apologize if I'm embarrassing you. It's just that, having told so many people that she had died, it's something of a weight off my mind to tell the truth for once. It's remarkably liberating.'

'You haven't embarrassed me at all. Quite the contrary.'

Hawley smiled. He wondered for a moment whether he should consider a career in fiction writing; not only had he managed to invent a credible story on the spot, one which could fool a successful inspector from Scotland Yard, but he seemed to have gained a friend out of it too.

'Actually,' Dew said, considering the matter, 'and I'm sorry to go on about it, but there is just one other thing I need.'

'Yes?'

'The name of the fellow she ran off with. And where he was staying in London. Just to close the file, you understand. I'm sorry, but my superiors can be terrible sticklers about these things.'

Hawley blinked. Had he fooled Dew, or had Dew fooled him with his friendly air? He considered the matter quickly; there was no way out of it.

'Well, I don't have it on me, of course,' he said.

'Naturally, naturally, but at home?'

'I think so,' Hawley said hesitantly. 'Yes, I believe I might have it written down somewhere for emergencies.'

'Then if you could just give that to me, we can let the matter drop.'

'Yes,' he replied, nodding, barely listening to the inspector as he thought the matter through. He thought about the house, about the letter. He looked at Dew and wondered what he would say when the policeman realized how much he had embellished the story once again, and how much he had invented. 'Shall we go then?'

'Certainly.'

The two men rose and Inspector Dew paid the bill at the counter, refusing Hawley's offer to share the expense. They stepped out of the restaurant, and it had started to rain. Neither man had an umbrella with him and Dew cursed under his breath suddenly as he looked at his watch. He spotted a hansom cab approaching and hailed it immediately. 'I'm sorry, I'd forgotten I have an appointment at three,' he explained. 'And in this weather I think I'd better take a cab or risk being late. Can I call around in a day or so and collect those details?'

'Certainly, Inspector,' Hawley said, relieved, stretching out his hand. 'In the evening preferably. After work.'

'Of course. Well, I'll see you then. And again, Dr Crippen – '

'Hawley.'

'Again, *Hawley*, I do apologize for having to put you through that ordeal. And I appreciate your frankness with me. Let me assure you I will be as discreet about the matter as possible.'

'Thank you, Inspector. I'll see you soon then.'

'Yes. Goodbye.' He jumped into the waiting cab and

drove off, waving a hand out the window as he left, as impressed with Hawley Crippen as he had ever been with any suspect in his career. Standing in the rain, however, watching him as he drove away, Hawley was less sure. 'This,' he muttered to himself as he turned around and made for home, 'is all far from over.'

MONDAY, II JULY

It was three days before Inspector Dew was able to call back at 39 Hilldrop Crescent, and he had left it until the evening, not just because Dr Crippen had suggested that this was the best time to catch him at home, but because his own working day was over by then and he hoped to interest Hawley in a drink at the local pub. His life contained few friends and he believed that he might have discovered one in this pleasant fellow. It was totally unlike him to encourage a new friendship, but their conversation at lunch had energized him and stirred memories. In the intervening days he had set about putting the minds of his most recent tormentors at rest regarding the supposed disappearance of Cora Crippen, and for the first time in his career he did so without discovering any evidence to prove the suspect's innocence first. To his irritation, the police commissioner who had so insisted in the first place that he call around to investigate scarcely seemed to remember the original query when he contacted him.

'Crippen?' he shouted down the phone. 'What Crippen? What on earth are you talking about, Dew?'

'*Doctor* Crippen,' he replied. 'You asked me to investigate the matter of his wife's disappearance?'

'I asked you? When did I? Have you gone mad?'

'A few days ago,' he said with a sigh. 'Lord Smythson had spoken to you about it.'

'Smythson? Oh yes, rings a bell somewhere,' he grunted. 'Well, what of it? Did he do it or didn't he?'

317

Dew laughed. 'He's no more guilty of murdering his wife than I am,' he said. 'He's a perfectly pleasant man in fact. A few personal troubles, but nothing to push him to that extreme.'

'And where's the wife, then? Back home already, is she? Come to her senses?'

'Not exactly, Commissioner. It seems she ran off with another fellow. He was a bit embarrassed about it, so he told everyone she'd died. Not clever, but not criminal either.'

There was silence on the other end of the line; his colleague had not reached such an elevated position without some sleuthing abilities of his own. 'He told you that, did he?' he asked. 'And you believed him?'

'Yes, I believed him,' Dew replied.

'Why?'

'Because I can read a man, Commissioner. I've been in this game long enough and I can promise you that Dr Crippen is absolutely innocent of any wrongdoing. He knows he's made a stupid mistake and I gave him a good telling-off for it,' he lied. 'I don't think he'll be doing anything like that again.'

'Right,' said the commissioner, not entirely convinced. 'Well, get on to that woman and let her know that everything's all right, will you?'

'What woman?'

'The Smythson woman. The one who started this whole thing off in the first place. Tell her we've investigated thoroughly and there's no case to answer. Hopefully she'll stop bothering us all then.'

'Yes, sir,' he said, irritated that he had to perform this task when it had been the police commissioner who had agreed to her request that he should investigate in the first place. He was about to suggest, humorously but hopefully, his idea of arresting her for wasting police time, but the line had already gone dead. He flicked through the small file he had created on Dr Crippen and picked up the phone again to call Mrs Louise Smythson.

Hilldrop Crescent was a lot quieter than it had been the last time he'd seen it. The children were nowhere to be seen and the street outside Hawley Crippen's home was almost deserted. He looked at the row of neat, terraced houses and wondered for a moment why his own life had not led him to a home like this.

He paused at the window of number 39 and peered inside, and he was surprised to see the figure of a young boy in the distance, tidying up in the kitchen. He squinted his eyes for a better look, but it was difficult to make him out. Did Dr Crippen have a son he hadn't mentioned? he wondered to himself, stepping up to the door and knocking.

When it opened he was surprised, and a little embarrassed, to see that it was not a young man at all who had been inside, but a young woman with a slim, boyish build standing before him. She was wearing a pair of Hawley's old trousers, their turn-ups rolled up, and they hung baggily on her, giving her an urchin-like appearance that Dew found strangely appealing. 'I beg your pardon, ma'am,' he said, doffing his hat and blushing a little at her strange appearance. 'Sorry to disturb you. Inspector Walter Dew. Scotland Yard. Is Dr Crippen in, do you know?'

'I'm afraid not,' she said. 'He's at his surgery tonight. Can I help you at all?'

'Oh,' Dew said, disappointed. 'And you are . . . ?'

'Ethel LeNeve,' she replied, breaking into a wide smile that made him notice for the first time the scar above her lip. His policeman's mind made him wonder where she had acquired it. A childhood accident? A violent father? An argumentative lover?

'Oh, Miss LeNeve,' he said, nodding. 'Yes, of course. I've heard your name mentioned.'

She cocked her head to one side in surprise and stared at him. 'Really?' she said. 'Might I ask where?'

That had been less than tactful of him and he regretted it. He could hardly tell her that there were certain ladies in society who considered her to be a harlot and a thief; that would hardly be polite. For once he was lost for words, but she saved him by not waiting for an answer. 'Perhaps we should go inside,' she said. 'Rather than talk in the street.'

'Certainly,' he agreed. 'Thank you.'

She ushered him into the living room where he had talked with Dr Crippen a few days before. He waited for her to sit down before taking the same seat he had used on that occasion.

'You'll have to forgive my appearance,' she said, looking down at her manly clothes and more than aware of the dirt and perspiration on her face. 'I decided to do some cleaning and borrowed some of Hawley's old things. I must look a fright.'

'Not at all, Miss LeNeve,' he said. 'On the contrary. Hard work never makes anyone look any the worse.'

She smiled, put at ease by his manner. 'Hawley told me you'd been to see him,' she said after a brief silence, ready to set aside the small talk and get down to business. 'Actually, he was quite taken with you, I think.'

Dew felt pleased and encouraged that he did not have to hide the reason for his visit. 'Really?' he said. 'Well, I'm delighted to hear it. I must admit that in all my years in the force I never felt quite so foolish as I did when I understood the kind of man Dr Crippen is. I was only following instructions to follow up the lead, you understand.'

'Of course. But might I ask – who suggested such a monstrous thing in the first place?'

The inspector thought about it. Strictly speaking he should not tell her, but already he had developed an idea that he and the Crippen–LeNeves were going to become fast friends. He recalled the conversation he had endured with Mrs Louise Smythson over the phone and knew that he could barely tolerate her.

'Innocent?' she had cried, horrified when he told her the case against Dr Crippen was closed. 'Hawley Crippen innocent? Presumably only in a language where "innocent" actually means "guilty". For heaven's sake, he killed her, Inspector Dew. As sure as eggs is eggs, he slit her throat from ear to ear and drank her blood. I'm sure of it.'

'I don't think so, Mrs Smythson,' he replied, part of him trying to keep his temper in check, the other part trying not to laugh at her lurid fantasies. 'I've spoken to Dr Crippen and he has assured me that—'

'Oh please,' she said interrupting him. 'He's assured you that he didn't do it, so that's an end to the matter, is that it? So tell me, Inspector, if you fellows ever manage to catch Jack the Ripper slashing up some poor tart, his arms dripping in blood, and he says, "honestly, it wasn't me," then you'll set him free? Is that the way Scotland Yard conduct their business these days? Oh my! Maybe he *is* Jack the Ripper!'

'Mrs Smythson, we have strict guidelines to follow when undertaking an investigation,' Dew said. 'Unfortunately I am not at liberty to outline them to you at this time. However, rest assured that I have spoken to Dr Crippen and have learned a little more about this case than you might currently know, and I am simply informing you that he has no charges to answer. Also, I think perhaps you are letting your imagination run away with you a little and that, I promise you, can be a dangerous thing.'

'Inspector, from the day I met that man I knew there was something fishy about him. It's in his eyes! The way he looks at you! It's clear he can't be trusted.'

'Nevertheless—'

'Ha!' she said, exasperated with him and not a little disappointed that there was not going to be a more gruesome end to this tale.

'Nevertheless, Mrs Smythson, if you require any further information, I suggest you talk to Dr Crippen himself and not to the police authorities.'

'I wouldn't dare,' she said haughtily. 'He'd probably come after me with a bread knife if he knew I'd been talking. Heavens!' she added, startled. 'You didn't tell him, did you? You didn't say it was I or Mrs Nash who came to see you?'

'Of course not,' he said, wishing he had. 'Such conversations as the ones that we have had are always kept strictly confidential. And when you went above my head and asked your brother-in-law to speak to one of my superiors, that's kept confidential too, so you needn't worry.' He had thrown that in as a reprimand and to prove that there was solidarity of a sort among officers. 'However, that's an end to the matter now, once and for all.'

'It's an end to Cora Crippen,' she said. 'You haven't heard the last of this, Inspector.'

'I believe I have, Mrs Smythson. Now I must urge you to let the matter drop. Any spurious allegations on your part could lead to criminal proceedings.'

'But that's exactly what we're looking for!'

'Against *you*, Mrs Smythson. You can't just go around accusing innocent people of murder whenever you feel like it. There are laws against slander, you know.' There was a silence at the other end of the phone for a few moments and eventually he was forced to say 'Hello?' to discover whether she was still there or not. When she finally spoke, her voice was deep and angry.

'I hope you're not threatening me, Inspector Dew.'

'Certainly not. I'm simply trying to help you by pointing out – '

'You *are* aware who my brother-in-law is?'

'Only too well. However, the facts are the facts and I'm afraid that's all I can offer you now.'

'Very well,' she said. 'But when you find that you were wrong and I was right and that conniving miscreant is swinging at the end of a rope, perhaps you'll see your way to offering me an apology. You've let me down once too often now, Inspector Dew.'

'I'll bear it in mind,' he replied, exhausted. 'And thank you for your interest, Mrs Smythson. Goodbye.' He hung up promptly, stepping away from the phone lest it jump up and bite him.

'Let's just say,' said Inspector Dew, choosing his words carefully, 'that certain members of Cora Crippen's circle of friends disapprove of Dr Crippen.'

Ethel smiled. 'I thought so,' she said. 'I said as much to Hawley. I said it would be someone from that chattering bunch of idle women. Nothing else to do, so they make up ridiculous allegations and waste everyone's time pursuing them.'

'Obviously it would be wrong of me to say that I agree heartily with every word you say,' he replied with a smile, 'so I won't say so.'

Ethel laughed and looked down at the table, chipping away a small candle-wax smudge with the nail of her finger. 'I think we understand each other, Inspector,' she said. 'Would you like some tea?'

He shook his head. 'I won't stay long,' he said. 'What time do you expect Dr Crippen home?'

'Any time now,' she said, checking her watch. 'Oh, do stay. I know he'd be sorry to have missed you.'

'Perhaps a few more minutes,' he said. He licked his lips and wondered whether it would be forward of him to ask the question which was hovering around in his mind. He decided in favour of it; after all, they were getting along well and she appeared to have nothing to hide. 'Tell me it's none of my business if you like,' he began, 'but what exactly is your position in this household?'

'My position?'

'Yes,' he said, feeling himself begin to blush a little at the personal nature of the question. 'Have you been helping Dr Crippen keep his house in order since his wife left him?'

She thought about it and decided on honesty. 'Hawley and I have worked together for many years,' she explained. 'At Munyon's, you know.'

'Yes, I'm aware of that.'

'I was his assistant there, you see. Well, I still am in point of fact. And we've become fast friends. And since Cora left, well, it's true that we've built on that friendship.'

'You're living here then?'

'I care for him very much, Inspector.'

'Of course. I wouldn't have suggested otherwise.'

'I think I can make him happy,' she said, shrugging her shoulders. 'And he can do the same for me. Although, considering the relationship he's just got out of, it wouldn't take much to be an improvement.'

Dew raised an eyebrow. 'You knew Cora Crippen well then?' he asked.

'Not very well,' she replied, regretting her last comment. 'But well enough. Well enough to know that she was the devil's own hound. And that she was only put on this earth to make poor Hawley's life a living nightmare.' Inspector Dew nodded and pursed his lips. 'I'm sorry, Inspector. I know it sounds as though I'm going too far and becoming melodramatic, but you didn't know her. She made his life a misery. Every moment of every day she mistreated him.'

'He seemed quite fond of her when he spoke to me,' Dew said doubtfully.

'Well, that's Hawley for you,' she explained. 'He won't be rude about her to anyone, not even to me. He's that kind of a man. The old school. No matter what she did, he forgave her. She cheated on him, she insulted him, she beat him – '

'She *beat* him?'

'Many times. I saw the scars myself. On one occasion I was sure he needed stitches on his face, but he wouldn't hear of it. It took months for the wound to heal properly. Oh, this is him now, I think,' she added, straining her neck to see out of the window and spying Hawley walking down the street towards them.

Dew shook his head. 'I hadn't realized,' he said. 'He had confided in me something about her . . . infidelities, but nothing about the violence.'

'Of course if we want to be Christian,' said Ethel, 'we could suggest that there was something wrong in her head, something that made her behave like that despite herself. But I'm not sure I do want to be Christian, Inspector. Does that make me sound hard?'

'You care about him,' he said. 'It's understandable.'

'The truth is, I don't believe that it's the case anyway,' she said. 'I think she was just so frustrated in life that her only way to survive it was to cause misery for someone else. All she wanted was to be a star, you see. A singing sensation, as she kept telling everyone. Her biggest ambition in life was to see her name splashed across the front pages of the newspapers. To go down in history. To have people write books about her. She was deluded.'

'And you don't believe it will ever happen.'

'Of course not, Inspector. She was a second-rate talent. She could hold a tune, but I can draw a little. It doesn't make me Monet.'

Dew laughed and looked around, wondering why the front door had not opened yet. 'He's on his way?' he asked.

Ethel looked out through the window again, but she couldn't see her lover anywhere in the street. 'Oh!'

she said, a little surprised. 'I was sure I saw him. I must have been mistaken. But please do wait, Inspector. I'm sure he'll be along soon.'

He glanced at his watch and shook his head. 'I tell you what,' he said. 'Why don't you tell him from me that I'll call around again on Wednesday evening. Say about eight o'clock? If he could be in then, I'd appreciate it.'

He stood up and reached for his hat, and she walked ahead of him to the door. 'Certainly,' she said. 'I'll make sure he's here. He'll be very sorry he missed you.'

'It's fine,' he said. 'But if he could be here then, I'd appreciate it.'

'Of course.'

He walked down the steps and was about to step out into the street when she stopped him. 'Inspector?' she called, and he looked back at her, waiting for her to continue. 'You do see it, don't you?' she asked. 'You see what a good man he is? What a gentle man? It's not just me, I mean.'

He thought about it and envied Hawley the love of this woman. Hesitating for only a moment, he smiled and nodded. 'Yes, Miss LeNeve,' he said. 'Yes, I believe I do.'

She smiled now, relieved, and stepped back into the house, closing the door behind her. Her heart was pounding in her chest. She considered returning to the garden but it was getting late now and she was feeling too tired to work, so she went upstairs to change instead.

Within five minutes she heard the front door open and stepped out on to the landing. 'Hawley,' she said, delighted to see him. You've just missed our visitor.'

'Really? Who?' he asked.

'Inspector Dew from Scotland Yard. Such a nice man, too.'

'Oh yes?'

'He came back for that information you were to give him.'

'That's right,' he said quietly. 'I said he would, didn't I?'

'He said he will be coming back on Wednesday night,' she said. 'Eight o'clock. He wants to talk to you then.'

Hawley nodded and went into the living room and sat down in the armchair, trembling slightly. He was cold, for he had been standing under a tree for the past fifteen minutes across the road, hidden from both Ethel and Dew, watching them in the window and waiting for the inspector to leave. Wednesday night, he thought. That doesn't give us much time.

WEDNESDAY, 13 JULY

The afternoon of Wednesday, 13 July 1910, dragged along slowly for Inspector Walter Dew. He sat in his office overlooking the Embankment and found himself staring out of the window for long periods of time, unable to concentrate on his work. Three folders lay before him, begging to be studied, and to each one he had attempted to give some attention, but he was failing with all three. The first contained the details of the woman who had been found floating in the Thames near Bow, a week earlier; the autopsy suggested that she had been strangled before being thrown into the river, as her lungs held no water. She was sixty-two years old, and he suspected the husband. With older women, it was always the husband who had finally snapped after years of nagging. The second folder contained a report on a series of robberies around Kensington, all late at night, with each disturbed house showing no sign of forced entry. The last concerned a young man who had been a victim of a hit-and-run attack perpetrated by a high-class horse and carriage, one which – according to the victim – carried the insignia of the Prince of Wales. He had placed this folder last in line as it would doubtless be the most difficult. He would require all his diplomatic skills for that one. None of them mattered right now, however, for he was shortly to leave for another visit to 39 Hilldrop Crescent. He had put on his best suit that morning and even bought a flower from a young girl in the street which he intended to put in his buttonhole as soon as he left the office. During the day he had kept it in a small glass of water on his desk in order to keep it fresh; looking down on it now, it seemed quite forlorn, standing there on its own, a clipped fragrance trying desperately to stay alive against the odds. He examined his reflection in the mirror and was pleased by what he saw. He looked lively and alert, a welcome dinner companion should he be invited to stay for a while by the Crippen–LeNeves, which was his fervent hope. Afterwards, perhaps, he would take a stroll down to the local public house with Hawley Crippen while Ethel washed the dishes, and they would talk men's talk, setting aside their mutual difficulties of the past and finding more things in common upon which they could build their friendship. He checked his watch again. He didn't want to be early, but it was now seven fifteen and if he took it slowly he would arrive exactly on time.

'Going somewhere nice, Inspector?' PC Milburn asked as the inspector came through the lobby.

'What's that?' Dew said gruffly, barely heeding the remark.

'I asked whether you were going anywhere nice,' he repeated. 'Only, you're all done up in your Sunday best and even have a buttonhole there to boot. You're not usually so well turned out, sir.'

'Not usually so – ?'

'Oh, I don't mean any offence, Inspector Dew,' PC

Milburn said hastily. 'I only meant you don't normally wear as expensive a suit as that. Obviously you always look well.' He took a deep breath. 'You're a very handsome man, sir,' he added in confusion before immediately regretting the words.

'Get back to your work, Milburn,' said Dew.

'Yes sir,' he replied, sitting down again.

'As it happens,' said Dew, turning around after a moment to inform the constable of his plans – something he did not usually do. 'I intend to dine with some close friends of mine tonight. A Dr Crippen and his lady friend. I thought it a respectable thing to do to make an effort. You should learn something by my example, Milburn, in case you and that young lady of yours ever get invited anywhere.'

If Dew was surprised to find himself giving Milburn this information, it was as nothing compared to Milburn's surprise at hearing it. The inspector never made small talk with him; perhaps, he wondered, he has me in mind for promotion? That would be a welcome bonus. 'Dr Crippen?' he asked, wrinkling his nose as he thought about it. 'The name rings a bell with me, sir. Where have I heard it before?'

'Nowhere, I shouldn't think,' said Dew, unwilling to share his new friend with a lowly constable.

'No, I remember now,' the PC said, recalling the various visits of Mrs Louise Smythson. 'He's the fellow that woman said had killed his wife.'

'Oh, don't be ridiculous, Milburn. The man's a perfect gentleman. He didn't kill his wife, I can assure you of that.'

'But that lady—'

'That *lady*, if that is indeed a term we can apply to the likes of her, came in making a spurious allegation that has since been proved wholly ridiculous. I myself am personally acquainted with the doctor and I can assure you he is a man of the very highest calibre.'

329

'Oh yes?' Milburn asked suspiciously. 'And how's his wife, then? Still alive?'

'Alive and residing quite comfortably in America. Florida, to be exact. It was an error on the Smythson woman's part and the case has been closed.'

'Glad to hear it, sir,' Milburn said with a wide grin as Dew turned around to leave. 'You have a nice evening then, sir.'

Inspector Dew waved a hand as he left the building and he breathed in the fresh air outside, filling his lungs with happiness and anticipation of the evening's entertainment which lay ahead. It was mid-July and the streets were quite bright still; he passed a park on the way and saw a group of young men playing cricket on the lawn, their voices carrying cheerfully through the trees, and he felt a great joy with life, a surge of excitement for his fellow men, a desire to love and be loved by all. Such emotions were foreign to him and he revelled in his new state. Passing by the Thames, he had an unlikely urge to jump on to an empty bench and burst into song, but he resisted lest he be dragged away to the asylum before he reached the bridge.

He tripped along quite casually, throwing a penny to a homeless man camped out on the corner of Mornington Crescent, and tipping his hat to the ladies he passed. His stomach grumbled slightly and he hoped once again that he might be invited to stay for supper. He had decided earlier in the day that he would not ask Dr Crippen for any more information about the man who had cuckolded him. As far as he was concerned, Cora and her lover could reside in Florida for the rest of their lives, and it was no business of his. He would tell Hawley when he arrived that the matter was now closed and he need not give him the name or address after all. Surely then he would be rewarded with their company and friendship. 'You need never think of the name Cora Crippen again,' he would say. He felt as a man might feel when he is about to give another the best news of his life and who knows that he will be rewarded for it in some way. When he had told Police Constable Milburn that the case was closed, he had meant it.

The children were out in force tonight along Hilldrop Crescent, but for once they were playing happily with each other and not tormenting any animals. He was pleased to see that; the last thing he needed in his present mood was to have to discipline wayward children. 'Good evening,' he said to them, and they stared at him in disbelief, for it was rare for such a well-dressed gentleman to notice them at all, let alone speak to them.

'Evening, sir,' one of them muttered in response, incurring the mocking glances of his friends.

To his surprise and disappointment, the lights were off in the living room of 39 Hilldrop Crescent, but as he stood on the street outside he told himself that his friends might be upstairs dressing for dinner, or perhaps relaxing in the back garden. The appointment had been made, after all, and it was just eight o'clock now. It was not as if they would not be at home. He practically danced up the steps to the door and rapped on it three times and, as his knuckles made contact with the wood for the third time, he was surprised to find the door give way gently and creak open a few inches, a shaft of light from the street pouring through into Dr Crippen's dark hallway.

He blinked and waited for any sounds from within; when none came, he reached out and pushed the door open slowly. The hinges creaked like those in a gothic horror story – he was instantly reminded of Jonathan Harker's first arrival at the castle of Count Dracula – but he stayed outside, leaning forward and calling out: 'Hawley? Miss LeNeve?'

There was no response and he looked around the street nervously. Although he was a senior inspector with Scotland Yard, he could imagine that someone seeing him enter a house that was not his own might call their local constable out to arrest him, which would be embarrassing for all and would surely irritate his hosts. However, no one seemed to be watching at that moment so, with an agile movement, he slipped inside and closed the door quickly behind him.

The darkness returned and he shivered. It was cold in here, even though it was midsummer. 'Hawley?' he cried again. 'It's Walter Dew. From Scotland Yard. Miss LeNeve?' His words seemed to carry through the air and lose themselves in the distance, and he frowned, his disappointment buried for a moment in the mystery of their absence. He opened the door of the living room where he had sat on a couple of occasions, and he looked inside. It was spotlessly clean as ever, but there was something different about it this time. He walked through quickly and into the kitchen, where he put a hand to the side of the teapot. Cold. He looked in the sink and it was entirely dry, implying that it had not been used in at least a day. Biting his lip, he went back to the hallway and strode upstairs, opening doors until he found what appeared to be Dr Crippen's bedroom, where he opened a wardrobe. It was half filled with clothes still, but there was a number of empty hangers on one side, while those which remained were pushed up close together on the other. His mind began to calculate reasons why this should be so as he went back downstairs to investigate further. He didn't want to imagine for a moment that there could be any sinister reason for it, even though it was clear that something unusual was going on.

He stood in the hallway with his hands on his hips, wondering what to do for the best, when his attention was attracted by a door under the stairs which he had not noticed before. He stared at it for a moment, before walking towards it and gripping the handle tightly, as if afraid it would come loose in his hand. Opening it, he saw a staircase leading to the cellar and he walked down carefully, switching on the single light bulb which hung near the bottom and which offered some small amount of brightness to the room. 'Hawley?' he said again, in a whisper this time, although not expecting an answer for a moment.

The cellar was slightly damp and it had a musty air about it. It was filled mainly with rubbish and he stared at the ground, noting the filthy stone floor. The room chilled him, and he considered leaving for the time being when his attention was taken by the state of the floor in the corner of the room, about ten feet away from him. Although the rest was dusty and the stone flat, here it was broken and clean, as if someone had taken it up, set it aside for a while so that for the first time in years it had a chance to dry out, then laid it back in its home. He swallowed nervously and walked towards it, crouching down as he got closer.

The smell hit his nose even before his fingers gripped the stone, and he gagged, disgusted. Nevertheless, turning his head a little to one side, he reached down under the cracks and managed to prise the stone away; it came out in three sections and he pushed them to the side of the room and peered at what lay underneath. It smelt dreadful but looked perfectly normal; there was a thick, brown, sandy substance which, he presumed, came between all the stone on this floor and the concrete under it. He poked it with the tip of his shoe, expecting to feel the hardness of the floor, but instead it landed on something soft and juicy, something that made a squelching sound, something that sounded *unnatural*, and he stepped back quickly, looking around the cellar in fright. Holding his breath for a moment, he knelt down on the floor and, using his hands, cleared away the sand carefully. Underneath, he found a number of newspaper-covered packages, thickly wrapped and bound with twine. They smelt foul and his mouth curled in distaste, but he had come this far and could not stop now. His stomach churning, he lifted one out – it slid away easily – and put it on the floor a few steps away. Taking his pocket knife out, he cut the twine and pushed it aside before placing his fingers on either side of the newspaper packaging, prising them slowly apart.

What he saw inside the parcel was about a square foot of human tissue, bone and congealed blood, carefully dissected and chopped up and placed in a neat fashion within the thick layers of paper, which now began slowly to ooze thick, blackish liquid. At the side was what appeared to be a thumb. It was a very tidy package and, like the others, which contained separate parts of a human cadaver, was already beginning to rot.

15

The Chase

Captain Taylor of the *Laurentic* sat with Inspector Dew of the Yard in the radio room of the ship, having just sent another message to Captain Kendall of the *Montrose* via the Marconi Telegraph. Four simple words, saying little but telling everything: 'Giving Chase – Keep Mum'. Afterwards, they went to the captain's private dining room, where they ate smoked salmon served with a selection of vegetables and potatoes prepared by the *Laurentic*'s cook.

'I always insist on having him aboard,' Taylor explained to his guest. 'These voyages can be very messy sometimes, and one of the few consolations is having a damn good chef on board. First thing I do when I receive the crew log is check who's cooking, and if it's not someone I approve of the ship stays in port.'

'I'm sure your passengers appreciate it,' said Dew, who had enjoyed the meal immensely.

'Passengers?' the captain repeated, spluttering in surprise. 'Damn the passengers, man. You don't think I'd waste his talents on a rabble like that, do you? He's worked in Paris, for heaven's sake. He's cooked for Sarah

Bernhardt, you know. No, I keep him strictly for the officers and myself. The company thinks he cooks for others as well as us, but we keep mum about that too.'

'You're a fortunate man,' Dew said, laughing. 'I have to look after myself most evenings.'

'And your cabin,' the captain asked. 'Comfortable enough in there?'

'Extremely. Thank you again for putting me in such a fine room.'

'*Cabin*, Inspector. *Cabin*.'

'Of course.'

'So this Crippen fellow we're after,' Taylor said after a moment, picking his teeth with his fingers for a bone from the fish so that his words came out a little muffled. 'I read about him in the papers before I left Liverpool. Killed his wife, they say.'

Dew nodded. 'So it would seem,' he admitted. 'A shocking business. It was I who discovered the remains.'

'Oh yes?'

'Chopped her up and buried her in the cellar. It was beyond anything I'd ever seen before.'

'Do tell, Inspector,' said the captain, who had a taste for the macabre.

Dew sighed. He had become something of a celebrity in the few short weeks since Crippen's disappearance, but he disliked having to talk about the matter to others. After finding the first parcels containing Cora's body hidden under the stone in the basement of 39 Hilldrop Crescent, a crew of police doctors and scientists had come in and ripped the place apart. Further on in the cellar, most of the flooring had been removed and more packages were discovered there. A gruesome jigsaw puzzle was assembled in the mortuary of a local hospital, and within a few days more than two hundred pieces of her body were laid out on a table for the doctors and policemen to examine.

'It's a messy job,' Dr Lewis, the chief pathologist, had

told him when he came down to examine the grizzly sight himself. 'If he really was a trained doctor, you'd think he'd have a better understanding of the way the human body works. Some of the limbs are torn away in the most difficult places. Like a novice carving up a chicken. Mrs Crippen was surely dead before he began the procedure, and that's a blessing in itself. It's not been easy putting the pieces back together, although I rather enjoyed the task, if you want to know the truth. Took me back to my days in medical school. My Lord, some of the pranks we pulled there. This one time, my friend Angus and I—'

'It's hardly something to take pleasure in, Doctor,' Dew cautioned him, in no mood to listen to stories about medical school high jinks.

'Quite, quite. I must admit, though, I've brought some of my students in here to take a look at her, and even a few of my colleagues too. I believe the man used to work in an abattoir, is that correct?'

'I only know what I've been reading in the newspapers,' Dew replied. 'The same as you.'

'Well, it just surprises me, that's all. Believe it or not, an abattoir is an excellent place to learn the craft of dissection. Some of those fellows could open an office in Harley Street if they put their mind to it.'

'Presumably he was nervous. That would account for his lack of precision.'

'I expect so.'

'And she's reassembled now?'

'Almost entirely.'

'Almost?'

Lewis looked at him, surprised. 'Well, you do know they still haven't found the head, don't you?' he asked.

The head. Over the last few weeks the London newspapers had become obsessed with discovering the whereabouts of Cora Crippen's head. It was the only piece of her which had not been discovered in the cellar of 39 Hilldrop Crescent, and it had become the final piece in the jigsaw which was needed before her remains could be scooped into a coffin and buried. Every child and urchin in London was opening dustbins and looking in sewers for signs of it, and a gang of men was scattered along the banks of the Thames, waiting to see whether it would float to shore. It was rumoured that the *Express* was offering £100 to the man, woman or child who could find her head first and bring it to them, and a crowd of Cockney Salomes had answered the call.

'I keep the smelling salts by my side throughout the day,' Mrs Louise Smythson said to her husband Nicholas and her friends, the Nashes, as they sat, having tea in the Savoy, a few days later. 'Every time I think of it, I feel quite faint. When I remember how we all sat there in that house, eating dinner. Why, he could have killed us all.'

'Louise, don't,' Margaret Nash begged.

'I can't help but wonder what he put in the food,' Nicholas Smythson said. 'Do you think it might be some slow-acting poison, and we'll all wake up one morning dead?'

'Oh, Nicholas!'

'Well, it's hard not to think about it,' he protested. 'What if he'd killed other people and buried them somewhere too? What if he was making soup from their bones? What if that's what he had in store for all of us?'

'Cream of Smythson,' said Andrew Nash with a guffaw. 'Not for me, thanks. I'll stick to the consommé.'

'I shall be sick,' said Louise. 'Nicholas, if you don't stop that kind of talk this instant, I shall be sick.'

'My dear,' Margaret said, leaning across and patting her hand. 'The strain on you has been terrible. And all those awful reporters.'

'They plague me,' she admitted with delight. 'Every time I open my door there's another one standing there.'

'Did you see that letter in *The Times* yesterday, Andrew?' Nicholas asked, laughing, as he looked across at his friend. 'Some fellow writes in and says isn't it about time we let the ladies join the constabulary. And while we're about it, why not make Louise Smythson an inspector at Scotland Yard! Seems as if she's more than a match for the ones they have.' He nearly choked with laughter at the absurdity of it.

'I say, that's rather good,' said Margaret Nash. 'Inspector Smythson. Can you see it, Louise?'

'What, and go around London discovering headless bodies in cellars?' she asked, shivering. 'I don't think so.' In truth she was extremely proud of her actions and was loving every moment of the publicity which was being heaped on her. She was being hailed a hero by everyone, from her local grocery shop owner to the Princess of Wales, who had made some off-the-record comments praising her and which had been duly reported in a newspaper.

'Still, he struck me as a very pleasant, very affable fellow,' said Inspector Dew.

'Pleasant?' Captain Taylor said incredulously. 'A man who chops his wife up into little bits and eats her? What on earth would you call rude?'

'Well, I didn't know at the time that he'd done that, did I?' Dew replied defensively. 'He seemed quite meek really. And he didn't *eat* her.'

'It's always the quiet ones you have to look out for.'

'Actually, it rarely is,' said Dew. 'It's not easy for a man to disguise his personality to that extent. I believe he just snapped one night, that's all. He'd had enough of her tormenting ways.'

'If he just snapped, Inspector, then he would hardly have bought the poison in advance, would he? Doesn't that smack of premeditation? I mean, that's what the papers say. That he bought a bottle of hydro something or other from a chemist in Oxford Street.'

'Of course, of course,' Dew admitted. 'I just think she pushed him too far, that's all. He couldn't find a way out. And it was hydro bromide of hyoscine, one of the most effective and quickest-acting poisons available.'

'You sound almost sympathetic towards him.'

'Do I?' he asked, surprised. 'No, I don't mean to, really I don't. What he did was a terrible thing. But still, I can't help wondering what's going through his mind now. Whether he regrets it at all. Whether he's having difficulty sleeping. It can't be easy to do a thing like that and then simply forget about it. To kill someone and dispose of them like that. It's terrible.'

Dew himself had been unable to think of anything else for the previous three weeks. He had scarcely slept for days after discovering Cora's remains and had been racked with a mixture of self-doubt and unhappiness ever since. The doubt came from his realization that he might not be the expert sleuth he believed himself to be. Never in his entire career had he felt so duped by anyone, so entirely deceived. And yet the misery came from knowing that Dr Crippen had in fact done this terrible thing. He tried to believe that he hadn't, that it was all a mistake, but there was no denying the truth. And a man with whom he had hoped for a friendship, a man with whom he had felt such a human connection was now somewhere in the middle of the Atlantic Ocean, unaware that someone who had respected him until recently was not far behind, chasing him, desiring nothing more than to bring him back to London and see him dangle at the end of a hangman's rope. What kind of a man did this make him?

'I think,' said Margaret Nash, finishing her pastry, 'that the only people in the world right now who are *not* discussing the infamous Dr Crippen are those who are closest to him, and it's *them* I pity the most. The first-class passengers on board the *Montrose*. God only knows when he'll strike next. The man has a taste for blood now. And he'll never give up,' she added dramatically, her eyes flaring, a trail of spittle hanging off her scarlet rouged lips.

The two messages came through on the Marconi Telegraph within fifteen minutes of each other. Ever since that afternoon a few days earlier when Captain Kendall had brought him to the radio room to tell him what he had deduced about Mr Robinson and his supposed son, from the moment he had asked him to send the message to Scotland Yard informing them of his suspicions, Billy Carter had spent more and more of his working day in the wireless room, and not a small portion of his free time as well. The captain had made it clear in the intervening days that no one else was to be told what was going on, not even the other officers. And so at any given moment of the day, either the first officer or the captain was to be found in this cabin, crouched in front of the Marconi, waiting for it to hiss into life and begin its bleeping signal. Their continual presence there confused the other members of the crew, but they were too well trained to ask any questions.

As things turned out, Billy Carter found that he quite liked the wireless room. It was peaceful and private, warm without being stuffy, unlike his own cabin, which was poky and without a porthole, Captain Kendall having refused to allow him to use Mr Sorenson's regular berth. He could sit in the wireless room for hours at a time, his feet up on the desk, drinking a mug of coffee, reading a book or daydreaming about life back home and how things would change once the little one arrived. Privately, he was grateful to Mr Robinson for chopping up his wife. It meant that there would be no delay whatsoever since the *Montrose* and the *Laurentic* were scheduled to meet before the end of the month as they both approached Canada; the importance of sticking to this schedule meant that he could catch the 3rd of August ship back to Europe and family life.

The first message came through at 6.15 p.m. and was a reply to the message Captain Kendall had sent, late the previous evening. Carter received it and scribbled it on a pad of paper, frowning and wondering how to break the news to the old man. He paced the floor, running a hand through his curls as he considered the likely reaction, and he was about to set off for his cabin to inform him when the captain himself opened the door of the wireless room and stepped inside.

'Mr Carter,' he boomed. '*Sans* cap again. I believe I told you—'

'Not when I'm in here, surely,' the younger man protested. 'It's not as if there are any passengers here to notice.'

Kendall raised an eyebrow. They were all the same, these young people. They always had a flippant remark, an easy comeback. They never simply did as you told them; that would be too easy. 'As you were,' he sighed, unwilling to pursue the point.

'Actually, Captain, I was on the point of coming to see you,' Carter said, biting his lip nervously.

'Yes?'

'A message came through a few moments ago.'

'Well, what of it?' he asked, eyeing his first officer suspiciously. What was the matter with the man? He was bouncing from foot to foot like a constipated kangaroo. 'What does it say? Do they want us to lock him up?'

'Lock who up?'

'Who? *Who?* Are you stupid, man? Who do you think? Jimmy the cabin boy? Crippen, of course! They said not to do anything for now in order not to cause a panic, but what's happened? Have they changed their minds?'

Carter shook his head, realizing that the captain had got hold of the wrong end of the stick. 'No, sir,' he said. 'It's nothing to do with Mr Robinson, sir. It's to do with Mr Sorenson.'

Kendall gasped and froze in his tracks. He looked startled, like a great actor whose lines have suddenly been taken away and he finds he has nothing left to say. 'Mr Sorenson?' he asked breathlessly. 'What of him?'

'It's a reply,' he said, 'to the message you sent last night. Enquiring after his health.'

'Just read it, man,' Kendall hissed, barely able to contain himself.

Billy Carter looked down at the pad of paper and read it aloud, exactly as it had come across the Marconi. 'Sorenson critical,' he said. 'Unexpected complications. Next few days vital for recovery. Comatose at present but doctors hopeful.'

He looked up at the captain nervously.

'Go on,' Kendall said sharply.

'That's it, sir,' he replied. 'That's the lot.'

'That's *it*?' the captain asked, ripping the pad out of the man's hands and staring at the words, willing them to change, to expand, to give him more information, anything that might set his mind at ease. 'This is all they've said?'

'Sir, you know they have to keep the telegraphs short.'

'Short? Short!' he shouted. 'An important member of this crew is dying and they keep their messages short! This is outrageous.' He turned away and read it again, afterwards putting his thumb and forefinger to his eyes and pressing them there tightly. Mr Sorenson in a coma, and here he was, his closest friend, thousands of miles away, stuck on a ship in the middle of the Atlantic Ocean with an idiot for a first officer and a murderer

343

and his transvestite companion on board for added company. Captain Bligh never had to suffer this, he thought.

'I'm sorry, sir,' said Carter. 'I know he's a good friend of yours, but—'

'Friend?' he barked. 'I'm his superior officer, Carter, and that's all there is to it. There's no question of friendships in the mercantile marine.'

'But you're obviously upset.'

Kendall leaned closer, his face grown so red that it contrasted vividly with the whiteness of his beard. 'I am not at all upset,' he said. 'I simply like to be kept informed as to which crew members I can expect to see in the future, that's all. This is not my last voyage, you know, Mr Carter. Even if it might be yours.'

Billy Carter stared at him in amazement. He had never seen anyone grow so close to hysteria in such a short time, and he wondered exactly what the relationship between Captain Kendall and First Officer Sorenson was. Could they perhaps be related in some way? Had they gone to school together, perhaps? He was about to ask such a question when a squeal from behind alerted them to another incoming message, and both men spun around quickly.

'It's them!' Kendall shouted, launching himself forward towards the receiver. 'He's dead. I can tell. He's succumbed without a friend in the world by his side.'

'Captain, please,' Carter begged, trying to wrestle the receiver from him. 'Let me take the message. I'll give it to you instantly.'

Kendall relented and slumped on the small sofa which ran along one wall, burying his face in his hands as the first officer scribbled away again on the pad directly below the message which had come through earlier. The captain's mind filled with images of his and Mr Sorenson's time together on board the *Montrose*. How they ate together, talked together, played chess of an evening. The nights they would sit on deck near the wheelhouse and watch the stars, each one telling the other how the sea and only the sea could be their mistress, for neither had ever met the woman who could steal him away from her. Were those nights gone for ever? Was this the untimely end of their friendship? He watched Billy Carter through a haze of tears and waited for the dreadful news.

'Steady on, sir,' said Carter, turning around and looking at him, a little embarrassed by how emotional he was growing. 'It's not from the hospital.'

'It's not?'

'No, it's from the *Laurentic*.'

'The what?' His mind was elsewhere now and he had little time for new business.

'The *Laurentic*. The ship carrying Inspector Dew.'

Kendall nodded slowly, remembering. 'Oh yes,' he said. 'Of course. Well, what of it? What does this one say?'

Carter read through it again as if he did not already know what it contained, but this time he paraphrased, rather than reading it out verbatim. 'It says they've picked up speed and should pass us by the 27th. They might send Dew over then or they may wait a while. In the mean time we're to sit tight and continue at the rate we're going. Give nothing away. Keep mum, he says again.'

'Keep mum,' Kendall said, disgusted. 'That's the second message he's sent saying that. Well, what the bloody hell does he think we *have* been doing for the past few days? We've been keeping so much mum we could open a home for elderly widows.'

Carter stared at him, wondering whether there were any more theatrics to come.

Kendall stood up and pulled himself together, wiping his eyes and tugging on his jacket, straightening out the creases. 'All right, Carter,' he said, coughing a little and unable to catch his eye. 'Very well, carry on. If there are any more messages, you may bring them to my cabin. Immediately.'

'Of course, sir.'

'Don't worry about the hour.'

'No, sir.'

'I stay up late, you see.'

'I understand, sir.'

'Probably be reading a book,' he muttered, opening the door. 'Or writing in my journal. Either way, I'll be awake.'

'At the first sign of news I will come to you directly.'

Kendall nodded and closed the door behind him, leaving his first officer to lean back in his chair and shake his head in amazement. Then he burst into laughter for a moment, before stopping himself and simply shaking his head, baffled.

Something on the sofa caught his eye and he looked towards the door but it was firmly closed now, the captain gone.

'Here,' he said out loud, to no one in particular, 'you forgot your cap.'

'You wanted to see me, Captain?' Mr John Robinson stood beside the wheelhouse of the *Montrose* and peered inside to see a worried-looking Captain Kendall standing there, clutching a pair of binoculars in his hands. Kendall himself was lost in thought over his sick friend but he drifted back to the present when he saw the man he believed to be the infamous Hawley Harvey Crippen standing before him.

'See you?' he asked, a little dazed for a moment.

'One of your crew came to my cabin. He said you needed a word.'

'Oh yes, of course,' he replied, inviting him in. 'I do apologize. I was daydreaming.'

Mr Robinson smiled. He had been a little surprised

when the crewman had passed on the message, and he began to worry immediately. Had they discovered the truth? Was the captain about to confront him? He trembled slightly as the older man approached him.

'Hello?' A voice from behind made them both turn around and they saw Mrs Drake bustling towards them. 'Mr Robinson,' she said. 'I saw you coming up here and thought I'd follow. I hope you don't mind.' She turned to the captain, whose face betrayed a wan smile.

'Of course not, Mrs Drake,' said Kendall. 'I had just invited Mr Robinson to take a look at the helm. I thought it might interest him.'

'Oh, how delightful,' she exclaimed.

'You thought it might interest *me*?' the passenger asked, a little surprised.

'Yes. You're a man's man, aren't you? Show me a fellow who isn't interested in the way machinery and engines work and I'll show you one who's looking for a horsewhipping, that's what I always say. Not that we administer horsewhippings in the navy any more, of course,' he added. 'More's the pity.'

'But, Captain, this isn't the navy anyway,' Mrs Drake interjected. 'It's a commercial vessel.'

'Indeed it is. Good of you to point that out, Mrs Drake.'

His intention in inviting Mr John Robinson to the wheelhouse of the *Montrose* had been twofold: first, he wanted to get his own mind away from the events taking place back in Antwerp where, for all he knew, priests were administering the last rites to Mr Sorenson and the undertaker was measuring him for his coffin; secondly, he hoped to prove the truth about Robinson in his own mind by trapping him in a number of lies. Ever since the second wire had come across via the Marconi telegraph from the *Laurentic*, it had occurred to him that he had based his theory on some very simple clues that could easily be misinterpreted:

Edmund Robinson's hidden nature . . . the passionate embrace between father and son . . . the fact that the physical description he had read in the newspaper was roughly similar to that of Mr Robinson. If, however, it turned out that he had made a mistake and there was some more innocent explanation for their ruse – but where could innocence lie in such a thing, he asked himself – *if* this was the case, however, he would be humiliated and perhaps arrested by Inspector Dew for wasting police time. What if the man refuses to return to Scotland Yard without a prisoner? he thought. *Any* prisoner? He would never get back to Antwerp if that were the case. Anyway, he was here now and he would ask his questions, regardless of Mrs Drake's presence.

'Isn't it interesting,' she said, looking over the machinery and controls with a greedy eye. 'I don't know how you keep track of it all. So many buttons and colours and levers. I'm sure I'd forget what to do.'

'It becomes second nature,' he said, reaching over for a guide to the ship he had left on the table, and then making a grab for his shoulder, crying out in pain.

'Captain, are you all right?' Mrs Drake asked.

'It's my shoulder,' he said. 'It's an old injury. I strain it every so often.'

'You should have a doctor look at it.'

'We have a doctor on board, but he can never seem to fix it. I just put up with the pain for a day or two, and then it calms down.' This was all a lie, of course, but he had hoped that Mr Robinson would enquire after his symptoms; he watched the man hopefully but was disappointed. The other seemed more interested in staring out through the window than discussing an invented medical condition.

'You like the sea, Mr Robinson?' he asked after a moment.

'Not very much,' he admitted.

'Oh no? Have you spent much time sailing? You're from London, aren't you?'

'Yes, I am.'

'Were you born there?'

'Yes.'

'Lived there all your life?'

'Yes.'

'Right,' he said. No joy there either. 'And your son?' he asked, spitting out the word, almost offended that he had to pretend at all. 'Your son is from London too?'

Mr Robinson turned around and stared at his interrogator, raising an eyebrow. Why were there so many questions, he wondered. Was the captain trying to get him to admit that Edmund was not his son after all? Was this his ploy?

'I've always enjoyed the sea,' a voice piped up from between them. 'Mr Drake owns a yacht, which he parks off Monaco.'

'Moors,' said Captain Kendall.

'I beg your pardon?'

'He moors it off Monaco,' he said. 'One parks motor cars. Or bicycles. Not boats.'

'Oh, of course,' she said, giggling. 'Silly me. But I do so enjoy our days out on it. And Victoria does too. I find the sea air so refreshing. Now these long trips can tire one out a little, of course, although I must admit it's strange because, as exhausted as I get on board, I seem unable to sleep very well. Isn't that an unusual thing?'

'Do you take any sleeping tablets?' the captain asked.

'From time to time. But they don't always work very well. Sometimes I wake up with the most terrible headaches because of them.'

'I prefer more natural remedies myself,' said Kendall, deliberately not catching Mr Robinson's eye. 'Herbal cures. Eastern medicines. Homoeopathic remedies,' he added.

'Really?' Mrs Drake asked, the sides of her mouth

curling up in distaste, as if she had just drunk sour milk. 'How unusual.'

'They can be very productive, actually,' said Mr Robinson, joining in the discussion, wholly unaware of the fact that the line had been aimed at him. 'And they're becoming more and more popular with people these days. Not everything needs to be cured by drugs and tonics, you know.'

'You're interested in homoeopathy then, Mr Robinson?' Kendall asked.

'A little.'

'Do you know much about it?'

'A little.'

'Have you ever taken any?'

'A little.'

Kendall felt his fists clench in anger. This man either had the cunning of a fox or was as innocent as a lamb. He couldn't decide which.

'Captain, are we on time, do you suppose?' Mrs Drake asked. 'Will we reach Canada by the end of the month?'

'Oh yes, I expect so,' he said. 'I've never brought a boat in ahead or behind time in my life, and I don't intend to start with this voyage. No matter what happens.'

'No matter what? Why, what do you expect to happen?'

'Nothing at all. I just meant that one is always prepared for any eventuality and ready to face it.'

'Of course.'

Just then one of the sailors handed the captain a note which stated that Billy Carter needed to see him in the wireless room. His heart skipped a beat; perhaps this was the dreaded or longed-for news. He was disappointed that he had not got more out of Mr Robinson; if only that confounded Mrs Drake hadn't insisted on tagging along. 'I'm sorry,' he told his guests. 'I have to leave you now.'

'Well, thank you for showing us round this area of the ship,' said Mr Robinson, still a little baffled as to why he had been summoned. 'It was most interesting.'

'Yes, thank you so much, Captain,' said Mrs Drake.

'You're very welcome. I'm sure I'll see you later today.' He made to turn away but then stopped and looked back at Mr Robinson. 'Such an unusual beard you sport,' he said. 'With no moustache. Is that the latest trend in London?'

'Not at all,' he said. 'Just my own peculiarity.'

'It's almost like the Amish folk in America. You're not Amish, are you?'

Mr Robinson gave a rare laugh. 'No, Captain,' he said. 'No, I'm not.'

'Have you always worn it like that?'

'No.'

'Do you plan to grow a moustache again?'

'No.'

Are you lying about being Mr John Robinson and in fact are actually Doctor Hawley Harvey Crippen, the man whom half the civilized world is after for murdering his wife, chopping her up and burying her without her head in the cellar of your house?

'Captain, you look as if you have one final question,' said Mr Robinson with a smile. 'Do you?'

He thought about it. A silence lay between them, one that Mr Robinson swore he would not be the first to break. He held Kendall's eye with a strength of purpose he had rarely felt. 'No,' the captain muttered finally, walking away.

Later that night, Mr Robinson, Miss Hayes and Mr Zéla were seated together at a small table in the billiards room, nursing some brandies and enjoying each other's company. They had managed to shake off Mrs Drake and the young people, and had spent an hour playing rummy for pennies, Martha Hayes winning the most.

'I believe Mrs Drake sees scandal everywhere she looks,' said Martha. 'It's almost as if we can't so much as have a conversation without being accused of getting engaged. I've been linked to you too, Matthieu, you know. So you'd better watch your back. Apparently I'm out for all I can get and am determined to find a husband before this trip is over.'

'Really?' he asked, amused. 'And whose charges are these?'

'The daughter's. Honestly, they're such a frustrating pair. Have they nothing better to do with their time than gossip and create scandal?'

'I don't think so,' said Matthieu. 'Believe me, I've met women like Antoinette Drake many times in my life. Their lives are fairly empty because they have nothing to aspire to. They have all the money they need, so they have no ambition. Their marriages have long since become devoid of passion. Their children despise them, as they do their children. I was married to a woman once quite like that. A long time ago. She made me so frustrated that I often felt like strangling her.'

'And did you?' Martha asked, smiling.

'Oh no. I divorced her instead. It involved less prison time.'

'It's not an answer, you know,' said Mr Robinson, unaware how drinking on an empty stomach was affecting him. 'Killing your wife. It doesn't solve anything.'

'Of course not, John,' said Martha. 'We're only teasing.'

'People do it all the time, though,' he said. 'And they get away with it.'

'I don't like violence,' Matthieu Zéla said, lighting a cigar and leaning back in his armchair. 'In my life I've seen too many people die at the hands of others, and it never gets any easier.'

'What do you *do* exactly?' Martha asked him, intrigued. 'You allude to so much but tell us so little.'

'I work in the arts,' he said with a smile. 'It has varied over the years. Theatres, opera houses, arts administration. You might call me an international artistic mercenary. People in positions of power seem to know my name and they contact me when they have a task that needs doing. Let's just say, I keep myself busy.'

'And what of you, Martha?' Mr Robinson asked. 'When you get to Canada, what are you going to do?'

She smiled. 'I don't know yet,' she said. 'I think I might like to go into the law.'

'The law?' he asked, surprised.

'Yes. I've always been interested in being a barrister. I'm not sure why. I never had the opportunity before. But Mr Brillt, for all his faults, did open my mind to the fact that I am capable of anything. I'm still a young woman, after all. I believe I will get a job and then put myself through university.'

'Well, I hope you succeed,' said Matthieu. 'But remember, you still have to make your choice before the voyage is over.'

'My choice?'

'Well, if Mrs Drake is so convinced that you intend to marry either myself or John here, then you will have to choose which one.'

She laughed and shook her head. 'An impossible choice, gentlemen,' she said, 'although I know which one she would choose for me.'

The two men stared at each other in surprise before looking back at her. 'Who?' they asked in unison.

'Why, you, of course, Matthieu,' she said. 'After all, you're in the Presidential Suite. And I am the world's premier gold-digger. In Mrs Drake's fantasies, you would have to be my number one choice. I'm sorry, John.'

'That's fine,' he said, aware that she was joking but somewhat offended nonetheless.

'You've both been chosen in a different way, of course,' said Martha after a moment. 'By Victoria Drake. The choice between your son and your nephew,' she said, looking from one to the other.

'How is your son today?' Matthieu asked, looking across at Mr Robinson. 'I haven't seen him around. He's not ill, is he?' Ever since deciding that Edmund Robinson was in fact a girl he had been observing his movements around the deck and had missed him during that afternoon. He was also intrigued by the relationship between the two but was not prepared to bring his findings out into the public domain just yet.

'He's fine,' said Mr Robinson. 'Around somewhere, no doubt.'

'If you ask me,' said Martha. 'You should encourage both boys to stay away from Victoria. She's not a pleasant girl.'

'For what it's worth, I think she should be equally encouraged to stay away from my nephew,' said Matthieu. 'I've only taken him in hand recently, and the edges are still, shall we say, a little rough.'

'Edmund has no interest in her,' Mr Robinson said sharply. 'It's ridiculous, the very idea.'

'I agree,' said Matthieu with a smile. 'Somehow they do not seem a likely pairing to me.'

'Then we're agreed,' said Martha. 'The Drakes are not our sort at all.'

'Agreed,' said both men, clinking glasses.

'Only a few days to go anyway,' she added. 'Then we'll be on dry land again. It's not as if Victoria can cause too much friction between them in that period of time, can she?'

Matthieu Zéla raised an eyebrow. Although he did not know his nephew very well, he could judge his character – and had enough experience of his lineage – to believe that trouble was always on the horizon. He decided he would be very happy if the *Montrose* managed to dock in Quebec without any further incident but he doubted, somehow, whether this would be possible.

Inspector Dew felt their eyes burning into his body as he wandered around the deck of the *Laurentic*, the passengers staring at him and whispering, looking at each other and asking, 'Is it him? Is that Dew?' He began to feel like a celebrity, a famous actor from the theatre or even a member of the government, and he found that he quite enjoyed the sensation. The relative anonymity of a Scotland Yard inspector's job had been replaced, if only for a short time, by excitement and glamour. He wondered whether he was a disappointment to them. Whether they had expected someone taller, younger, more handsome. Or whether he was exactly what they wanted: a reassuring presence, an older gentleman with a finely tuned mind and the desire to see justice served.

It was the children who watched him most. He could feel them scurrying around the deck like rats, hiding behind lifeboats, crouching behind deckchairs, excited and terrified at the same time. Sometimes he would stop suddenly and spin around, to see three or four of them gathered together, and he would bare his teeth and hiss; their eyes opened wide in terror and delight whenever he did this, and they ran screaming along the deck in fright. Their young minds could not differentiate between the man who had committed the killing and the man sent to find him; to them, they were both part of a sinister double act that would keep them awake at night.

One of the crewmen had leaked the news of Inspector Walter Dew's presence on the *Laurentic*, and it had taken very little time for it to circulate among all the passengers. Most of them had been following the story of Dr Hawley Harvey Crippen and his murdered wife Cora in the newspapers over the previous few weeks. It had turned into a nationwide manhunt, and for them to be suddenly involved in the climax of the action was exciting to them. At first Inspector Dew had been irritated by their obsessive interest, worried that it might interfere with the arrest, but this had soon worn off. After all, Dr Crippen and his accomplice were on another ship in the middle of the Atlantic Ocean and he knew exactly where; there was no chance of them escaping, even if they knew they were being pursued. The only reason he had told Captain Kendall not to do anything in the mean time was to prevent any trouble breaking out on the *Montrose* before they reached Canada, but there was no harm in the passengers of his own ship knowing. After all, the whole world was now following this chase and he was turning into a celebrated figure.

'Have you seen this?' Captain Taylor asked, tracking Dew down in the small cabin they had assigned him as an office. The walls were covered with pages from the Crippen file which he had pinned up as reference points. In the centre was a police cameraman's photograph of the table in the mortuary where the various parts of Cora Crippen they had unearthed had been reassembled; the captain had made the mistake of looking at it the previous day, trying to make out what the picture was. As it had slowly dawned on him what he was looking at, he felt his legs give way beneath him. Today, he studiously avoided looking in that direction. 'It's a telegraph from London. Seems you're quite the hero. The newspapers are all leading with the story.'

'Really?' Dew asked, surprised and pleased. 'What do they say?'

'*The Times* say this is the most adventurous manhunt in history. They're recommending you for a knighthood if you get your man. The *Star* calls you the finest member of England's police force for your daring.'

'Daring, eh?' he said, stroking his beard, pleased. 'I suppose it is rather daring.'

'*Le Monde* have said that you are going to be invited to address their own police force on your return, to instruct them on how to capture escaped murderers.'

'A free trip to Paris. Lovely. I shall enjoy that.'

'The *Michigan Daily Record* is running long features on us because Crippen was born there, apparently. They seem to be taking some pleasure in the hope that we're not going to catch up with him in time.'

'Of course we'll catch up with him. You promised me as much, didn't you?'

'We will, don't worry. And the *Quebec Gazette* is devoting pages and pages to the story. They have diagrams explaining where and when you'll catch him. They seem to think it's a great honour for Canada. A whole police force is being mobilized to stop the crowds at the port from creating a riot when either the *Laurentic* or the *Montrose* arrives.'

'Thank you, Captain,' Dew said, delighted. 'It's good to know this is not all in vain then.'

'Let's just hope you have the right man,' the captain said, an off-the-cuff remark that filled Dew with apprehension.

'Of course I have,' he said. 'It has to be him.'

Increasingly, as they got closer and closer to their prey, Dew was haunted with the worry that the man claiming to be Mr John Robinson was not the man he had developed a friendship with at 39 Hilldrop Crescent in Camden. And, thrilled as he was by the worldwide interest in the story, the humiliation which would ensue if it turned out to be someone else would be almost too much for him to bear. He would almost certainly be instantly demoted by the police commissioner for making fools of the Yard in the eyes of the public. Of the *world*. His knighthood would not appear. The invitation to Paris would be rescinded. And he would have to endure a trip back to England, being mocked by his fellow passengers rather than applauded. I'm simply chasing a suspected murderer, he thought, and yet my whole career seems to depend on it.

In order to feel closer to the heart of the action, several passengers had already approached him with ridiculous enquiries. Some wanted details of how the case had been handled so far, which of course he was not at liberty to tell them, although he threw out a few crumbs to keep the hungry blighters eager for more. Some were eager to hear the more lurid accounts of how Dr Crippen had chopped up his wife. Others still had various suggestions as to where the missing head might be found.

'Have you checked the dustbins?' one asked. 'That's where I'd put my wife's head if I knocked it off.'

'Or the oven?' another asked. 'Perhaps he's cooked it in there.'

'How about the chimney?'

'Or buried under a tree?'

'I heard that he ate it,' announced one particularly macabre woman. When her fellow passengers stared at her in amazement, she held her ground. 'Think about it,' she said. 'It's the only way to ensure it would never be found. If he can chop up a woman's body into little pieces without a care in the world, then he can certainly do the same to her head and boil it up into a stew and eat it. There'll be good iron in a head, too, you mark my words.'

'Really,' said Inspector Dew, his stomach turning at the very idea. 'I think you're all letting your imaginations run away with you now.'

Eager to spend time with the inspector and be painted by association with a little glamour, several people reported minor crimes on board the *Laurentic*; necklaces disappeared, coats were taken from deckchairs, money went missing from wallets.

'Not my department, I'm afraid,' Dew said whenever

someone reported any such occurrence to him. 'You'll have to speak to Captain Taylor.'

'But you're from Scotland Yard,' they protested. 'Surely you can do something about it.'

'I'm on a manhunt,' he announced firmly. 'And other than that, I have no jurisdiction for anything else on board this ship. I'm afraid I can't help you.'

This satisfied no one, but he held his ground. A late-night visit to see Captain Taylor on the evening of the 25th, however, provided him with some happiness.

'We'll make it all right,' the captain confirmed, studying his charts. 'Seems to me that we'll pass by the *Montrose* some time on the evening of the 27th. Should we telegraph ahead to Captain Kendall and tell him you'll be coming aboard?'

Dew thought about it. 'How would I do that?' he asked.

'We could lower a boat and one of my men could row you across to them. Then you board the other ship.'

Dew considered this and shook his head. 'I don't think so,' he said. 'As long as we pass them by, that's all that matters. The last thing I need is to have to spend three days on board that ship as she approaches Canada, before having to turn around again. I think it's best to leave Dr Crippen ignorant of what's going on until the last possible moment.'

'So what would you have us do?'

'We'll wait until the day they would be coming into port. And that morning, before they do, I'll ask Captain Kendall to come to a full stop while I board. I'll arrest him then, and after we dock I'll take the 3rd of August boat back to England.'

Taylor nodded. 'I'll use the Marconi to let them know,' he said. 'If that's permitted.'

'Indeed, indeed. But reiterate to them that no one should be told anything until the very last moment. Dr Crippen may be capable of anything and I do not want him vanishing into thin air or taking any hostages before I can get to him. And the last thing I need is another dead body on my hands.'

Taylor nodded and switched on the telegraph apparatus.

At night-time on the *Montrose* fierce music could be heard coming from the steerage deck of the ship while elegant violins played in the dining hall attached to first class. Most evenings, Ethel would have preferred to visit the former in order to see how the lower classes enjoyed themselves; it certainly sounded a lot more entertaining than the dirges to which she was otherwise subjected. Victoria Drake, on the other hand, was only just aware that there *were* people living in that part of the vessel. She had heard of the poor, naturally. And she was sure that it was all very unpleasant, but it had hardly anything to do with her, had it?

It was eleven o'clock and Mr Robinson had retired to his cabin with an improving book. Mrs Drake had gone to bed, claiming a headache after Matthieu Zéla had spun her around the dance floor one time too many and she had felt her dinner returning to upset her, a deliberate move on his part to get rid of her for the rest of the night. Her departure had meant that he and Martha Hayes could talk in peace, without having to watch their every move or announce their engagement at the end of the night.

Growing weary of playing the role of Edmund, a couple of nights before Ethel had found a quiet spot where she liked to sit alone and watch the stars, and she sat there tonight, still dressed in her male garb, her legs stretched out in front of her, her back leaning against a lifeboat, enjoying the sound of the waves crashing against the sides of the boat. She thought of Hawley Crippen, not John Robinson, and shook her head, laughing a little as she looked at the clothes she had been forced to wear for love. It had always shocked her that such a good man could be treated so cruelly and with such contempt by a woman not fit to shine his boots, let alone call herself his wife. She wondered how Cora had tricked Hawley into marrying her in the first place. But she was gone now, Ethel thought with a smile.

Victoria Drake had decided that tonight she would finally conquer Edmund's resolve or perish trying. They were drawing closer and closer to Canada now, and it would be outrageous if she arrived there, having practically thrown herself at a man and been rejected at every opportunity. It had never happened before in her life and she was damned if she was going to allow it to take place now. Why, once one person got away with that, any number could. And what if Edmund told people? Her reputation would be shattered. She might never have the upper hand again.

Going to bed the previous night, she had spotted Edmund sitting alone in his new secret hideaway by the lifeboats and had spent the day plotting her move. It was an entirely different ploy: she would win him over by subverting her true nature entirely and being everything she suspected a sensitive fellow like him wanted in a girl. In short, she would be nice. The idea revolted her, but there was little else she could do.

She made her way towards him carefully, picking her footsteps with caution for she did not want the glasses to clink together. Only when she was practically beside him did he look up, startled out of his daydream, and notice her standing there.

'Victoria,' he said. 'You gave me a shock.'

'Sorry,' she said. 'I did call your name but you didn't hear me.' A lie.

He glanced at the bottle and glasses she was holding in her hands and he sighed. Surely she was not going to make another attempt at romance between them.

'I'm not disturbing you, am I?' she asked gently.

'No,' he replied, without much enthusiasm but willing to observe social decorum. 'No, you're welcome to join me. Sit down. I see you brought some drinks.'

She laughed. 'It's been one of those days,' she said. 'And I fancied some champagne on my own, away from everyone. I thought I'd hide myself away here for a little while. I didn't expect anyone else to be here.'

'But you brought two glasses.'

'I told the wine steward they were for my mother and me. Otherwise he might not have given me the bottle. But here,' she added, handing him one, 'you might as well have one.'

Edmund thought about it for a moment and finally smiled, accepting the glass from her. The bottle she had brought with her was a large, two-litre bottle of champagne, a veritable magnum. 'When you bring a bottle, you really bring a bottle,' he said. 'You weren't going to drink all that on your own, were you?'

She shrugged and looked away from him, into the dark, black sea, the waves glinting in the moonlight. 'I thought I'd have a glass,' she told him. 'And then I'd have another. And if I felt like it, I'd have another. And then see how I got on from there.'

Edmund laughed. 'Well, let's start then,' he said. He reached down and popped the cork and held it away from himself while a little foam poured over the top.

Victoria loved champagne. It had been her favourite drink in the world from the age of fourteen. Edmund poured two glasses full and set the heavy bottle down behind him in a groove cut out by the holding bays, which prevented it from falling over. 'Cheers,' he said, clinking glasses.

'Cheers,' said Victoria. 'To Canada.'

'Canada.'

Silence fell between them for a few moments while

they watched the water and listened to its rhythmic melody crashing against the hull. Edmund felt pleased that Victoria was in a quiet mood for once. It didn't look as if she was going to start attempting to seduce him again, and this made him relax and enjoy his champagne even more.

'If you could change any one thing about this voyage,' she said finally, 'what would it be?'

Edmund thought about it. 'It sounds like a strange answer,' he said, 'but I think I'd change the captain.'

'The captain?' she asked, surprised. 'Why ever would you do that?'

'I don't know,' he replied. 'There's something about the man that I don't trust. Every time I turn around, he seems to be standing there, watching me. I come out of my cabin and he's lurking around, I sit in the dining hall and he's ten feet away from me. I take a walk on deck, look up towards the wheelhouse, and he's up there with his binoculars pointing in my direction. The second I look, he turns away of course, but nevertheless I find him unsettling.'

Victoria raised an eyebrow and brushed some strands of hair away from her face. 'I've barely noticed him, to be honest,' she said. 'Although I did see him in the corridor outside our cabins one day, acting very oddly indeed.'

'I'm probably being paranoid,' said Edmund. 'But what about you? What would you change?'

'Easy,' she said. 'I'd have my own cabin. Believe me, you haven't had sleepless nights until you've heard my mother snoring.'

Edmund laughed. 'That's a pleasure I believe I will be able to live without,' he said.

'Honestly, I asked for a separate cabin originally, but she said it was too expensive. And that's a joke because she asked my father to book us the Presidential Suite, which is almost twice as expensive as ours anyway, but he refused because *he* said *that* was too expensive. I come from a long line of skinflints, Edmund.'

They drank their champagne and for the first time he felt an attachment towards Victoria. He refilled their glasses and reflected that she wasn't such a bad girl really, just a little too keen to get her own way all the time. Was he any different? He thought not. After all, when he considered his own actions in recent times, it put Victoria's deeds in the shade.

When Victoria had been spying on Edmund earlier that evening and choosing her moment to make her presence felt, she had been unaware that she herself was being watched. Tom DuMarqué, freshly bathed for the first time in days, had been observing her from a distance and wondering why she was behaving as she was. She had a bottle and two glasses, but she was hovering in the shadows, watching something or someone in the distance. How he wished that he was sharing that bottle with her. When eventually she had made her move, he had followed her, but on the other side of the lifeboats, and when she settled down with her back to one of them, he had settled in on the other side, listening to her every word. It appalled him to see who she had gone to meet, and it was all he could do not to march around and break up their party. His hand reached into the inner pocket of his jacket where he kept his pocket knife and his fingers touched it with relief. If Edmund Robinson tried anything underhand, he would put an end to his Lothario ways once and for all. He had been warned.

'I think I owe you an apology,' Victoria said, inwardly almost gagging on the word.

'An apology? For what?'

'My tiresome attempt at seduction in your cabin the other day. I don't know what was wrong with me.'

'Really, Victoria, don't give it another thought.'

'I thought you were playing hard to get, you see.'

'No.'

'That's a tactic I've not seen very often.'

'Of course.'

'And the thing is, I'm not used to rejection.'

Edmund turned to look at her. In the moonlight, her pale beauty seemed a lot more vulnerable, especially when taken alongside what she had just said. 'I wouldn't imagine you are,' he said. 'You're too beautiful to be rejected.'

'And yet you did.'

He sighed. 'If you're not used to being rejected,' he said, 'trust me when I tell you that I'm even less used to having beautiful girls throw themselves at me.'

'Now I find that hard to believe,' she said, laughing.

'Well, it's true.'

'You underestimate yourself, Edmund. I was drawn to you the moment I saw you.'

'*Really?*' It amazed him to hear this, but intrigued him as well. 'Might I ask why?'

'Fishing for compliments, are we?'

'No,' he said, flustered. 'No, I just meant—'

'It's all right. I'm just teasing you. But since you ask, you have a sensitive look that many boys don't have. Your skin is so soft and your bone structure . . . listen to me,' she said, blushing in the darkness, amazed to hear herself carry off her deception so well. 'I sound like a romance novel.'

'You surprise me,' he said. 'And it surprises me to feel so flattered.'

'You do have a girlfriend somewhere, don't you?'

'Me?' he asked, shaking his head. 'No.'

'You must have had one once, though. You can't be . . . I mean surely you're not . . . you have *had* a girlfriend at some point in your life.'

'I've been in love, if that's what you mean,' he admitted. 'Once. I was lucky, really. I met someone very special. Someone damaged. Someone who had been hurt by another. And I helped this person out because I found feelings within myself I had never known before. I didn't realize the things you could do for love.'

'And what happened to her?' asked Victoria. 'She didn't die or anything, did she?'

'No,' he said, smiling. 'No, nothing like that. Let's just say, we have great hopes for the future.'

Victoria nodded. Edmund continued to confuse her, but their closeness on deck made her flesh tingle.

'This champagne is starting to go to my head,' he said, pouring a fourth glass for each of them. 'I'll be drunk soon.'

'There's half a bottle to get through yet,' she said, smiling, pleased that her plan was coming to fruition. It was a cheap trick to get him drunk in order to seduce him but it would be worth it. At least when the deed was done he could no longer act in so superior a way towards her.

From his vantage point a few feet away, Tom DuMarqué pressed the nails of his fingers into the palms of his hands and had to restrain himself physically from crying out in anger. Listening to Edmund speak, he grew to despise his rival even more; his fruitless talk of beauty and love and *feelings* disgusted the boy. This was the talk of a silly, romantic girl, not of a healthy young fellow. Had he and his friends cornered this popinjay back home on the streets of Paris, they would have known what to do with him. And as for her! Bone structure indeed. I'll give you bone structure, he thought. What a cruel world it was that wasted a beautiful girl like her on a useless fool like Edmund Robinson when he, Tom DuMarqué, strong, virile and athletic, was willing to take her on. It was almost too much for him to bear, but he could neither walk away nor interrupt their conversation.

'The thing about this boat,' said Edmund, beginning

to slur his words a little, 'is that it's too slow. Now I bet that fifty years from now they'll put bigger engines on these things and they'll speed across the ocean in a couple of hours.'

'Do you really think so?'

'Of course. It's inevitable. Technology always progresses. If you think that by the end of the twentieth century, transatlantic boats will still be going at this speed . . . well, you'd be crazy to think that because it just won't be so.'

'You should be an engineer,' Victoria murmured, nestling closer to him and desperate to run the tip of her finger along his jawline. 'Or an inventor.'

'Maybe I should,' he said.

'I'm sure you'd be very good at it,' she continued, encouraging him. 'You're so strong-willed and filled with ideas. I can see myself opening a newspaper in a few years' time and finding out that you've discovered some wonderful new idea that's changed the world. I'd be so proud of you then.'

'*You'd* be proud of *me*?'

'Of course.'

'But why? You scarcely know me.'

'I'd be proud that I knew you at all,' she said, and her words filtered gently into his ear, warming him, intriguing him. 'I'm proud I know you now.'

Edmund turned his head slowly and looked at his companion. His head was a little light and he felt as if he didn't have full control over his body any more. It had been so long since he had drunk this amount of alcohol that it was in danger of overwhelming him. He stared into Victoria's face and wondered how he could ever have found her annoying. The things she was saying to him were so thoughtful, so gentle; he almost never received encouragement like this, not even from Hawley.

'You're so kind, Victoria,' he whispered, but she

shushed him by putting a finger to his lips and holding it there for a moment. The sensation of touching those full red lips sent waves of desire through her body and she had to restrain herself from jumping on him, but she had succeeded this far and she was determined not to spoil it at the end.

'Don't say anything else, Edmund,' she whispered, taking her finger away and positioning her face so close to his that there was nothing else he could do now but lean forward and kiss her. Their lips met and, as they did so, Edmund closed his eyes, losing himself in the moment. The champagne ran through his system, exciting his nerves, stimulating his senses, and they continued to kiss, their mouths opening wider as their tongues explored each other's mouths.

They continued like this for the best part of a minute, before Edmund's eyes opened and he realized what he was doing. Surprised and startled, as if he had not even been part of the moment but a mere spectator, he leapt back, scrambling along the deck slightly, staring at Victoria in amazement.

'Edmund,' she said, her lip curling a little now in pleasure, having finally succeeded in gaining the upper hand. 'What's the matter?'

'I'm sorry,' he spluttered. 'I . . . I shouldn't be doing this.'

'Why not? There's nothing wrong with it.'

'There's *everything* wrong with it,' he said, standing up and brushing his trousers down, then putting a hand to his forehead in amazement. 'You don't understand. I shouldn't be . . . I can't explain it, it's—'

'Edmund, what on earth's the matter?' she asked, growing angry. This was ridiculous. She had never seen anyone react like this before to an intimate moment. What on earth was wrong with him? Was he religious or something? 'For heaven's sake, we were only kissing,' she said.

'Yes, but I shouldn't be kissing you,' he insisted. 'I'm not . . . you're not my type,' he said.

'It didn't seem like that to me. It felt like you were enjoying it.'

'I was. I mean I wasn't. I couldn't. I'm—' He stared around in bewilderment before stepping over her and striding off as he tried to get as far away from her as possible. 'I'm sorry, Victoria,' he said. 'I have to go.'

'But you can't,' she cried, growing angry at his foolishness. 'We've only just begun. There's no one around, no one can see us. I could make you very happy, Edmund,' she purred, 'if you'd just let me.'

'I *have* to,' he insisted. 'I'm sorry.' He turned so that she could not see his face and almost tripped over a coil of rope as he ran along the deck, his boots banging down sharply on the wood as he went.

Keeping almost perfect time with his footsteps, however, was Tom DuMarqué, who had heard and seen all that had happened and had been ready to leap over the lifeboat and beat Edmund to a pulp when he had broken free of Victoria and ran for it. They'd left her behind now, however, and he wasn't going to let him get away with it. As Edmund turned left in order to make for the central deck which led to the steps to the cabins, Tom intercepted him and jumped in his way.

Edmund stopped running in surprise when he saw him there, realized who it was and was about to run on; but the younger boy was too quick for him and grasped him by the throat, pushing him back along the deck until he had him pinned against the side of the wooden superstructure surrounding the first-class cabins.

'Tom,' Edmund squeaked, his words impeded by the boy's hands cutting off his supply of air. 'What are you—?'

'You can't say I didn't warn you,' Tom hissed. 'I told you to keep your hands off her.'

'I didn't—' he began, struggling to get the words out but failing to get any further.

Tom loosened his grip on Edmund's throat but the presence of his body kept Edmund standing there, facing him.

'Did you think I was joking when I gave you that warning? Did you?' he asked, pulling his knife out of his pocket and opening it, waving the blade in the air in front of Edmund's terrified face. 'Well, now I'm going to teach you a lesson,' he said. His right hand reached out between Edmund's legs; his intention was to grip him by the testicles and hold him against the wall while he sliced open the small piece of skin at the base of the nose connecting the nostrils, a trick he had learned from an early reading of *Tom Sawyer*. Reaching out, however, his hands clutched at the space between the legs and, finding no purchase there, he searched further before realizing there was nothing to grab. Surprised, wondering what was wrong, he looked up into Edmund's face, his eyes opening wider as his mouth fell open and his hand loosened on the knife for a moment, long enough for it to be ripped out of his hand and thrown across the deck.

Within a second, before he could realize what was happening, he was being dragged across the deck of the *Montrose* towards the railing. His feet scrabbled on the wooden deck beneath him, trying to find enough grip to stand up straight, but it was impossible and, before he knew it, his entire body was being forced backwards. He turned his head in terror to see the water rushing along below them, and he quickly turned away to stare imploringly into the face of Mr John Robinson, who had found an unexpected strength as he held the boy close to his death.

'Please,' Tom cried, almost unable to utter the words, so afraid was he that he was going to be thrown into the sea. 'Please. I'm sorry . . .'

'Sorry?' Mr Robinson shouted, turning around to look at Edmund, who was sitting down now and nursing his throat, while coughing loudly. 'I'll show you how sorry you'll be. You won't do that again, I assure you.'

He reached down to grasp the seat of the boy's pants, ready to lift him up and hoist him over the side, but now he was stopped by a hand on his shoulder, snapping him out of his rage and pulling him back towards sanity.

'Let him go, Mr Robinson, please,' Matthieu Zéla said anxiously. 'Let him go. Let me deal with him.'

Spinning around, he saw Martha standing near by, a look of horror on her face, and he relented, turning back to Tom and pushing him across the deck instead towards his relative. 'He was going to kill him,' Mr Robinson said, looking at the boy's uncle. 'He held a knife to Edmund's throat.'

Tom was shivering on the deck, bewildered by what had happened and newly terrified of the water again. 'I'll sort him out, don't worry,' Matthieu said, staring at his nephew with contempt. 'He won't bother either of you again.'

'He's not natural,' Tom said, pointing at Edmund, who was trying to fight back the tears. 'There's something—'

'Be quiet, boy,' Matthieu said. 'I'm sorry, Edmund,' he added, looking across at him. 'Let me apologize for him.'

'It's fine. I just want to go to my cabin,' he whispered, his throat still sore from the boy's hands. He ran down the steps with Martha following, leaving only Mr Robinson, Mr Zéla and Tom DuMarqué behind.

'If you touch him again,' Mr Robinson said, 'I'll cut both your hands off. And don't think I won't. Do you understand me?' His voice was so clear and so intense that Tom had no option but to nod quickly. Matthieu's eyes narrowed in surprise at the man's strength. 'Just as long as we understand each other,' he added, before himself turning and walking away slowly.

'You idiot,' Matthieu muttered, lifting his nephew up off the deck. 'You're as bad as your father. What did you think you were doing?'

'There's something . . . that Edmund . . . he didn't have any . . .' He couldn't seem to finish his sentences, his thoughts were so confused.

Matthieu took him by the elbow and led him back to the Presidential Suite in disgust.

And, just as Victoria had been watching Edmund, and Tom had been watching Victoria, from his perch in the wheelhouse Captain Kendall had watched and heard all of them, never intervening once, and he had been most pleased by the discovery that Tom DuMarqué had made, a discovery which only confirmed what he already knew to be true. Not long now, he thought to himself, smiling as he turned away.

Edmund ran into his cabin, ignoring the presence of Martha Hayes, who was following a few feet behind, and locked the door. He collapsed on the bed and buried his face in his hands, his head swimming from the alcohol. He kicked off his shoes like a child having a tantrum and ripped the wig from his head, throwing it across the room before shaking his natural hair out.

'Edmund,' Martha Hayes cried, knocking on the door, 'please let me in.'

'I just want to be left alone for a while,' he cried.

'Are you all right though? You're not injured? He didn't hurt you?'

'No.'

'Are you sure? I can find a doctor for you if he did. You looked in great pain on deck.'

'I'm fine. I'll *be* fine,' he said, correcting himself. 'Please, just . . . just let me be for now.'

There was silence outside for a moment as Martha

considered this. 'Well, you know where I am if you need me,' she said. 'I want you to call me if you do.' She felt sympathy towards him; it must have been humiliating for him to have been so overpowered by a fourteen-year-old boy, and it surprised her too. For although Edmund was small and slim, she had suspected that he had a wiry strength which would come to the fore in such a situation. Apparently not.

Alone now, Ethel burst into tears and felt as if they would never stop. The night had gone by so quickly and so eventfully that she could hardly bear to think about it. The fight with Tom was one thing, but the kissing with Victoria was another entirely. She wasn't sure whether the girl had deliberately got her drunk or not, but, even if she had, Ethel had still kissed her. And enjoyed it. It was shocking. She couldn't imagine how she would be able to look Victoria in the eyes the next time she saw her. She could imagine the supercilious smile she would be wearing, delighted that she had finally got her way with Edmund. Ethel wouldn't tell Hawley, that was for sure. And then there had been that final moment when Tom's suspicions about Edmund's true gender had been raised. What would come of that? Would he say anything? Would he even be believed?

A key turned in the lock and Hawley opened the door a little, sidling into the room through a crack in case anyone outside should see Ethel in her true state. She looked up in fright for a moment, as if suspecting that this might be Tom DuMarqué coming back to finish the job, but was relieved to see that it was not.

'Are you all right?' Hawley asked anxiously, sitting down beside her on the bed and placing an arm around her shoulders. 'What happened out there?'

'I'm fine,' Ethel replied, pulling herself together now and resisting the urge to collapse completely and break down in unending tears. 'I was just a little shocked, that's all.'

'But what happened? Why did he attack you like that?'

'I don't know,' she replied, lying. 'I was sitting, talking to Victoria—'

'Ah,' he said angrily. 'I might have known that little minx would be involved in this business somehow.'

'It's not her,' Ethel said, defending her. 'We were just talking. It was nice. And in the end I said I was coming back to my cabin. I was nearly here, too. That's when he jumped on me.'

'That awful boy,' Hawley hissed. 'I should have pushed him over the side.'

'You couldn't.'

'I could have. I would have liked to see him drown for what he did to you.'

Ethel shook her head. 'You could never kill anyone, no matter how angry you were,' she said. 'I know you, Hawley, and your nature would never stand for it. Remember, you're a doctor. You're in the business of saving lives, not taking them.'

He frowned and said nothing.

'My throat hurts,' Ethel said after a moment.

'Let me see,' he replied, examining her neck under the light. 'It's just a little bruising,' he said. 'You'll be fine.' He sniffed the air, surprised by the smell. 'Have you been drinking?' he asked.

'Just a little champagne.'

'A little? It smells like a lot to me.'

'It wasn't. Anyway, it doesn't matter. Something far more important has happened,' she replied. 'I think he knows.'

'Who knows what?'

'Tom. He knows that I'm not a boy at all. He knows I'm a girl.'

Hawley's mouth dropped open in surprise. 'He knows?' he said. 'You told him? Why?'

'No, of course I didn't tell him,' she hissed. 'But he

374

held me against the wall and I don't know what he was intending, but he reached between my legs and he was only there a moment before you pulled him off me, but nevertheless I could see it in his eyes.'

'Surely not.'

'Hawley, I'm telling you, he could tell.'

He stood up and paced the room, considering this new complication. 'This is terrible,' he said. 'What if he tells his uncle?'

'He might do. But I don't think so.'

'Why not?'

'Tom DuMarqué's whole trouble is that he is obsessed with Victoria Drake, who seems to be unable to keep her claws off me. That's why he hates me so much. No, if he tells anyone, I believe it will be Victoria.'

'Who will tell her mother.'

'Exactly.'

'Who will tell the whole ship.'

'Indeed.'

'But this is too bad. He has to be stopped.'

Ethel shrugged. 'I don't know how,' she said. 'He seems like an unstoppable force to me. I think he wants to get me, one way or the other. Especially now. Especially after tonight. He'll be out for my blood.'

Hawley thought about it. 'Maybe I should speak to Mr Zéla,' he said. 'Tell him there's been some sort of misunderstanding.'

'Do you think he'll believe you?'

'I don't know. Would you?'

She considered it. 'I think I'd take some convincing,' she admitted. 'But I don't think Mr Zéla has any motivation for hurting us. He doesn't seem the sort. He acts like a gentleman and is very much a live-and-let-live sort. Not the type to pry into other people's business. But even if he does, we have no one to blame but ourselves. This whole thing was wrong from the start. It was pointless, my dressing up like this.' She grew more and more frustrated as she thought about it. 'I mean, *why* couldn't we have just travelled as husband and wife? Changed our names by all means, but *this* deception . . . 'She shook her head in frustration. 'Something like this was bound to happen sooner or later.'

'I told you,' said Hawley. 'There are social mores to be considered. An unmarried man and woman would never be allowed to share a cabin as we have. We would have been shunned for the entire voyage. And as it is, we've had a rather pleasant trip, haven't we?'

'What, with the exception of my having to constantly fend off a man-eating girl and stop myself getting murdered by a teenage thug? Well yes, other than that it's been a dream holiday.'

'We couldn't have avoided it. Think of the conventions.'

'Oh, those stupid conventions,' Ethel said angrily. 'They're infuriating.'

'Nevertheless they are as they are. I've told you before, once we get to Canada we can return to our proper identities and all will be well. No one will care whether we are husband and wife or not there.'

Ethel sighed. 'That's all I want,' she said quietly. 'I just want us to be happy. Together.'

'And we will be,' he replied, sitting down beside her on the bed. 'I promise you.' They kissed and Hawley held her in his arms for a long time, comforting her, encouraging her, promising her that their new life would bring an end to the misery of recent times. Ethel wasn't so sure. Canada was getting closer, but there were still a few days to go.

Some twenty feet away, in the Presidential Suite, Matthieu Zéla was having something of a set-to with his nephew Tom.

'You stupid boy,' he shouted. 'You do realize that if

I hadn't been there, he would almost certainly have pushed you over the side?'

'No, he wouldn't,' Tom said, feeling humiliated at having been overpowered. 'I can look after myself.'

'Not at the bottom of the ocean you can't.'

'I could have taken him.'

'Oh, don't be ridiculous. Another moment, and he would have had you over. If I hadn't come along, that would have been the end of you. Another pointless death in your family. You haven't done anything recently that you shouldn't, have you?'

Tom raised an eyebrow. 'Such as?'

'Are there any girls back in Antwerp that you've got a little too close to?'

He looked surprised, unsure why his uncle was asking him this. 'No,' he said. 'I don't understand. What are you talking about?'

'It doesn't matter,' Matthieu said gruffly, shaking his head. 'It's just that when I agreed to take care of you I assumed that you might have some measure of civility within you, that's all. And what do I find? A roughneck child who gets so angry when he can't have the girl he wants that he tries to slit the throat of someone who can.'

'Listen to me, Uncle Matthieu,' the boy said. 'There's something you should know.'

'I know everything I need to know, believe me,' he shouted. 'And I promise you, Tom, that if this kind of behaviour continues in Canada, I will cut you off immediately. I have my own life to lead and I will not be dragged down by any of you DuMarqués, do you hear me? I'm too old to put up with dramas like this.'

'Yes, I hear you,' he said calmly. 'But will you please just listen to me for a moment? There's something else I have to tell you.'

'What? What else could there be?'

Tom thought for a moment and licked his lips, wondering how to phrase it so that it didn't make him sound insane. 'That Edmund,' he said. 'There's something odd about him.'

'Something odd? How do you mean?'

'He's . . . I can't explain it. He doesn't seem to have what everyone else has.'

Matthieu stared at him, wondering whether his nephew had discovered what he himself had observed days earlier; he was surprised if he had. 'Meaning?' he asked.

'He doesn't have any balls!' Tom cried, standing up. 'I swear it. I know it sounds weird, but there's nothing between his legs at all!'

'Listen to me, Tom,' Matthieu said, laying a hand tightly on his shoulder. 'People who go around poking their noses between other people's legs uninvited often find nasty shocks awaiting them. Which is why it is impolite to do so.'

'This isn't a joke, Uncle Matthieu.'

'I know that. But you can't be certain.'

'I *am*.'

Matthieu considered it. 'Well, as it happens, so am I,' he said finally in a quiet voice. 'I worked that out days ago.'

'You?'

'Yes. I just didn't feel the urge to say anything.'

'Well, what happened to him? Did he have them chopped off?'

Matthieu laughed. 'No, you foolish boy,' he said. 'He didn't have them chopped off. He never had them in the first place.'

Tom frowned. He didn't understand. 'How could he not have—?'

'He's not a "he",' said Matthieu. 'He's a "she". Edmund Robinson is not a boy at all. Your competition for the hand of Victoria Drake comes from another girl.'

Tom's eyes opened wider and his mouth fell open. He was surprised at feeling himself becoming aroused; the memory of the kiss between Victoria and Edmund earlier in the night came back to him.

'You can't be serious,' he said finally. Matthieu shook his head. 'But why?' he asked. 'Why would anyone—?'

'I don't know,' he replied. 'But there's something strange going on between those two that I haven't sorted out yet. Although I will, I can assure you of that. In the mean time you must promise me that you won't say anything to anyone about this.'

'Oh, I promise you,' the lad said, rubbing his hands together gleefully. 'I won't say a word.'

16

The Killer

On the night of 31 January, 1910, Cora Crippen dressed for the last time and looked at her reflection in the mirror miserably. The dress she was wearing was over two years old; it had been a present from Hawley for her thirty-fifth birthday and she had quite liked it at the time, but now it seemed dated and overly familiar. 'Why do I always have to wear the same things?' she asked herself. 'Why can't Hawley provide for me like other husbands do for their wives?' It was a continuing sore point with her, despite the fact that she had amassed a considerable amount of savings of her own. However, she simply refused to spend this money on herself, preferring to indulge her gentlemen friends instead. It was Hawley's job, she believed, to pay for the things she needed. Cora was convinced that Louise Smythson would notice how often she had worn this particular dress in the past and would despise her for it. She had often heard the woman make unflattering comments behind the backs of other women when they were seen in the same outfit one time too many and she had joined her in mocking them. Although she felt in her heart that she was superior to Louise in every way

– *she* had never had to work behind the bar of a public house, for example – she could not argue with the fact that Louise was married to a member of the aristocracy, while her own husband was a mere part-time dentist and shop assistant.

Her friendship with Louise had been suffering recently, and she was aware that she was being pushed further and further outside the other woman's social circle. Many of the ladies had begun to consider her coarse and affected, looking at her contemptuously and making it clear that they were disappointed in her constant inability to improve herself. Of course she had brought a lot of this on her own head by her behaviour in recent times. Two weeks before, she had attended a recital by the famous pianist Leopold Godowsky at the Music Hall Ladies' Guild; she had drunk too much wine and had fallen asleep during the performance, snoring so loudly that one of the elderly members had poked her in the back with a jewel-encrusted finger and shushed her loudly. A week after that, at one of their regular cocktail evenings, she had once again become inebriated and had flirted with a young waiter, who was eventually forced to inform her, in front of a crowd, that he was recently married and was not at all interested in her attentions, eliciting embarrassment for her and admiration for him.

Since then, the invitations to tea had dried up and her presence at Guild meetings had become more and more awkward. She was aware that Nicholas Smythson was having a birthday dinner soon, and even more aware of the fact that no invitation had arrived for her. If she was not careful, she would be evicted from the Music Hall Ladies' Guild altogether, and then where would she be? At home with Hawley, that's where.

In the light of these events, she had invited the Smythsons over for a bridge night, despite the fact that she didn't particularly want another night alone with them. As Mrs Louise Smythson had been her sponsor when she had originally been accepted into the Music Hall Ladies' Guild, it was up to Cora to impress her once again with a display of exemplary behaviour, hence the invitation to Hilldrop Crescent for the evening.

'They're such an awkward couple,' Nicholas complained as they approached the house. 'Every time we see them, they end up having an argument. It's highly embarrassing.'

'Of course it is, darling,' Mrs Louise Smythson agreed. 'But it's almost impossible to say "No" to the woman. She does insist so. Between you and I, I think she is going to be eased out of our group quite soon.'

'Really?'

'Yes,' she said, nodding her head. 'But don't say anything about it to anyone. Margaret Nash and I have been talking, and some of the others too, and we think she's just too crude.'

'Well, you were the one who invited her into your society in the first place, my dear. You have only yourself to blame.'

'I invited her in when I thought she really was somebody. She made so many extravagant claims. But it was a miscalculation on my part. Clearly the woman is mad. She has delusions of grandeur which she will never achieve. This nonsense about her being a singer, for example. She's always just about to gain international stardom, and does it ever happen? No. It's ridiculous. She told me once that she was going to be singing at Buckingham Palace in front of the Queen. Sheer fantasy on her part. No, I'm afraid the time has come to remove Cora Crippen and her dull husband from our lives for good. I promise this will be the last evening like this.'

'So why are we going there tonight, then?' Nicholas asked irritably. 'Why couldn't the new policy have begun yesterday?'

'Because it takes time, Nicholas, that's why. Only two ladies have ever been expelled from the Guild before, and their behaviour was just as bad. Obviously, we can't just throw someone out without a reason, however. It has to come through the medium of suggestion. But I can be a lot more subtle than you realize. I intend to begin by not inviting her to your birthday dinner next weekend, which she knows is taking place, and she has been hanging out for an invitation to it. I believe that's what this card evening is all about, if I'm to be honest with myself. She's hoping I'll reciprocate, which I will not do. Why, she'd probably get drunk and try to seduce Alfred.'

'My dear, he's just a child.'

'You haven't heard the stories I have heard, Nicholas,' she replied knowingly. 'Just watch. She'll spend all night desperately trying to get back into my good books.'

Nicholas nodded. He didn't care much whether she came to his birthday dinner or not. He was immune to the charms of most of his wife's friends and had little interest in socializing with them. If they were there, fine. If not, well that was fine, too. Usually he spoke only to the husbands anyway. Not that Hawley Crippen was much of a conversationalist. Damn fool hardly ever opened his mouth unless you asked him a direct question, and even then he was always knocked down by that wife of his. Nicholas couldn't understand a man letting himself be pushed around in that way.

'Don't slouch like that when you're walking, Nicholas,' Louise chided. 'You'll get a hunchback if you're not careful.'

'Cora, how lovely to see you,' Louise said when they arrived, kissing her on the cheek as they stepped inside. She gave a quick glance at Cora's dress and raised an eyebrow but said nothing; her hostess caught the look, however, and cursed her husband again for not buying her a new gown.

'Louise,' she said. 'Nicholas. I'm so glad you could make it. Hawley and I were just saying that we don't see enough of each other any more.'

'Really?' Louise asked, looking at Hawley, who chose neither to confirm nor to deny the allegation. 'Well, we're all so busy, I expect.'

Cora took their coats and they went to the living room, where she had laid out some snacks and drinks. They settled down for a game of bridge but the cards were a mere background to their conversation, which was awkward from the start.

'Where's that handsome boy who used to live with you?' Louise asked. 'What was his name again? Your lodger?'

'Alec Heath,' Hawley said quietly, not looking up from his cards.

'Yes, that's the one. Whatever happened to him? Did he move out?'

'He's gone to Mexico,' Cora explained. 'Andrew Nash gave him a job out there.'

'He didn't!' she exclaimed, surprised. 'I didn't know they knew each other.'

'Well, they didn't really,' Cora said. 'They only met here on a single occasion, but they talked about Andrew's work over there, and a few days later Alec went to see him and offered himself for a position in his plant. They must have hit it off somehow, because before I knew it he was packing his bags and off he went. We haven't seen or heard from him since, have we, Hawley?'

'No,' he said. Naturally, he had been pleased when Alec had left Hilldrop Crescent; although the lodger had seduced his wife, he had not felt the strength to confront him about it, nor had he ever raised the matter with Cora. And despite the fact that there was no question of intimacy between Hawley and Cora any more, he could not stand the idea of her being with another man. It raised his levels of humiliation even further when he was cuckolded by a mere boy. Cora, however, had no shame about the incident. She had tried neither to explain it nor apologize for it. In fact, she looked back to her afternoons with Alec Heath as some of the most pleasurable of her life.

'He was so useful to have around the house,' she said, refusing to let the matter drop, enjoying the fact that this conversation strand was probably annoying Hawley intensely. 'He was always ready to help me out when I needed something.'

'Indeed,' said Louise.

'Naturally, being younger, he was able to attend to some things that Hawley wasn't. Isn't that right, darling?' He shot her a look of contempt but she was enjoying her *doubles entendres* and wasn't ready to finish yet. 'He managed to take care of things around this house that hadn't been seen to for years. Cleared out a lot of cobwebs, so to speak. I must admit I miss him.'

'My wife finds my company infinitely less stimulating than that of her younger friends,' Hawley said quietly.

Nicholas Smythson shifted uncomfortably in his seat; here was the start of it. He'd seen it several times before. The moment Hawley got involved, it was offering *carte blanche* to his wife to attack him.

'Forgive me if I find it difficult to get worked up over the extraction of someone's molars,' she said, not looking at him but smiling fixedly at the Smythsons instead. 'This is what I have to listen to when he comes in of an evening, you see. Detailed descriptions of the dental health of half of London. He's such a romantic. Is it any wonder we've never had children?'

'Had a problem with my own teeth a few years back,' Nicholas said, trying to steer the conversation away from their hosts insulting each other. 'Easiest thing for it was to get them all pulled out and a false set put in. I haven't looked back since, have I, Louise? It was painful at the time, of course, but not a twinge since.'

'Nicholas,' Louise said quietly, putting her hand on top of his. 'I really don't think the Crippens want to hear about that.'

'Really?' he asked, looking from one to the other in surprise, as if the rules of decorum had only just dawned on him. 'Sorry,' he added, noticing his wife's irritated look. 'We fellows, eh?' he said to Hawley, looking across at him and attempting to draw him into a conspiracy of two. 'We can't do right at all, can we?'

'Hawley can't, that's for sure,' said Cora. 'He's useless. Worse than useless.' She said it with a set smile on her face, as if the whole thing was a terrific joke, only nobody was laughing.

Nicholas coughed to break the silence. 'I thought that Alec was going to pursue that little thing who was here last time,' said Louise. 'He seemed to take a shine to her after all.'

'What little thing?'

'That girl who works with Hawley. The mousy creature. With the ugly scar above her lip. What was her name?'

'Ethel is a decent, respectable sort,' Hawley said in a flat tone. 'I very much doubt whether she would be interested in the likes of Alec Heath.'

'My husband has taken that wretched creature under his wing,' Cora said in exasperation. 'I think he believes it makes him appear kind and generous to allow a nobody like her to associate with us. Do you know, he even suggested that we invite her to join our Music Hall Ladies' Guild.'

'Oh, I don't think so,' Louise said quickly, eager not to have another lower-class person in on her recommendation. She was still having to pay off her apologies for Cora.

'And why not?' Hawley asked, offended. 'Would she not be a worthy addition to any society?'

'I just don't think she's the type of woman we're looking for,' said Louise, unwilling to be bullied. 'Nor are we hers, probably.'

'She's not our sort, Hawley,' said Cora.

Louise licked her lips and saw a rare opportunity. 'Of course, if you feel strongly about it, Cora, perhaps you and she could organize your own chapter. A new society, if you will.'

'But I don't feel strongly about it. I entirely agree with you. As I said, she's not our sort at all.'

'Certainly not *our* sort,' said Louise. 'Obviously she's not the type I could introduce to my brother-in-law, Lord Smythson.'

'Louise,' Nicholas cautioned her, seeing where she was going with this.

'But *I've* never met Lord Smythson either,' Cora pointed out.

'No, indeed you haven't.'

'And Ethel LeNeve and I are hardly in the same class.'

Louise nodded and said nothing for a moment. 'Of course she does work with your husband,' she said eventually. 'They have the same position in life. Which would imply that your attitude to her might be a little condescending, all things considered.'

Cora could feel the blood draining from her face. Although she was well aware of the increasingly frosty relationship between her and the members of the Music Hall Ladies' Guild, she had no idea why Louise was deliberately provoking her. Of course, she had behaved badly in recent times, but that was only because she had enjoyed too much wine; she had apologized and had promised there would be no further incidents like that. She looked at Nicholas, who instantly stared down at his cards, and then at Hawley. For her part,

Louise was a little surprised to hear herself being quite so provocative this early in the evening. The words had seemed to come out of her mouth before she could do anything about them.

'Aren't you going to say something?' Cora demanded after a moment, staring at Hawley as if he was the cause of the insult – which, by his association with Ethel LeNeve, she believed him to be. 'Aren't you going to defend me?'

'Indeed I am,' he said in a firm voice, leaning forward and pointing a finger at Louise. 'I think that's a very unfair thing to say, Louise, I really do. I'm sorry. I realize you're a guest here, but I have to say it.'

'Now,' Cora said smugly, pleased with him.

'To suggest that Ethel LeNeve is a lower-class person is simply wrong. For your information, she is an educated, intelligent, witty, and extremely personable young lady.'

'Ethel LeNeve?' Cora cried, outraged. '*Ethel LeNeve?* You're defending *her*? What about me?'

'Now really, Cora,' Louise said, laughing gently. 'There's no need to get upset about it. I didn't mean any offence. I think perhaps you're reading more into what I said than I actually meant.'

'Well, what did you mean then?' she asked. 'It's hard for me not to feel offended when you mention me in the same breath as that guttersnipe. *And* you suggest that I'm not good enough to meet your precious family. *And* I might as well tell you now, don't think I haven't felt myself being excluded from social functions.'

'Social functions? Such as?'

'Nicholas's birthday party. I still haven't received an invitation and I know for a fact that many of the other ladies are going.'

'It's a small party,' Louise protested, willing to give her enough rope to hang herself. 'For family and close friends only.'

'And what am I then?' Cora screeched.

'A very close friend,' Louise said, relenting a little in the face of her hysteria. 'And of course you must come. You'd be very welcome. Both of you would.'

Nicholas agreed, although internally he sighed.

This seemed to calm Cora down a little and they continued to play cards, but the atmosphere had been spoiled and the silence between them all was deafening.

Finally, believing that all was lost anyway, resentment built up inside Cora too much and started to bubble over. 'Of course, it isn't me at all that you're embarrassed by,' she said finally, the alcohol hitting home again. 'It's Hawley. He's the one you want to be rid of. He's the one dragging us all down. Obviously I don't need to bring him with me. I could leave him at home if you prefer.'

'Cora!' said Hawley, offended.

'No, I will say my piece. I've had to put up with this long enough. Being dragged down by the likes of you,' she said, snarling at him, 'a useless halfwit without an ounce of respectability in his body. Is it any wonder I can't advance in life when I have you hanging round my neck all the time, weighing me down like an albatross.'

'Cora, please. Our guests—'

'They know I'm right,' she screamed, looking to them for support, but it was not forthcoming. Both Smythsons sat there, stony-faced and rigid. 'The fact is, I'm in this position because of you. My career has suffered because you have never shown me any support. And you do know why Alec Heath left, don't you?' she asked, turning around to stare at Louise. 'He left because he got tired of listening to Hawley's whining all day and all night. He loved me. We used to make love all night, you know, when Hawley had gone to sleep.'

'Cora!'

'It's true,' she said, her words beginning to slur. 'You know it's the truth and you just won't face up to it.'

She giggled and leaned closer to Louise. 'He caught us once, you know,' she said, winking at her. 'Stood in the doorway while Alec had me, and just watched. Probably couldn't even get it up then. He fails even as a voyeur.'

'I think we should leave, Nicholas,' Louise said in a sharp voice, standing up. 'Please fetch my coat.'

'No, you should stay,' Cora said, staring at her as if she had no idea why she could possibly want to go. 'It's you who should leave, Hawley. Go on, get out. Louise, Nicholas, you both have to stay. I promise that Hawley won't spoil anything for us again.'

'We *are* leaving, Cora,' said Louise. 'And I think this is a disgraceful way to behave in front of respectable people. I've never had to listen to profanity like that in my life.'

'As if I could care less what you think, you jumped-up tart,' said Cora, changing tack. 'For God's sake, I remember you when you were pulling pints down the Cock and Three Bells and dropping your knickers for anyone with a few shillings in their pockets.'

'Nicholas! My coat! *Now!*'

'That's right. Run away from it. You all run away from the truth. Well, you can all just get out, then, get the hell out, the lot of you,' she screamed.

The Smythsons wrenched open the front door and stormed through it, Louise pushing Nicholas forcibly down the steps.

'And you can forget your membership of the Music Hall Ladies' Guild,' Louise said as she stood in the street, trying to pull her coat on but putting her right arm into the left sleeve by mistake and becoming confused. 'Consider it revoked.'

'Go on, you old tart,' Cora shouted. 'There's probably an old drunk in a gutter somewhere willing to shell out for you. You can earn the money for your cab home.'

She turned back into the living room, wiping a trail of spittle away from her chin, and spied her husband standing there, trembling visibly. 'And what are you still doing here?' she asked, going over and hitting him viciously across the head. 'Go on. Get out. *Get out!*' She continued to slap him and punch him until he too was out through the front door and down in the street, looking back at her in dismay. 'And don't come back,' she shouted. 'I'm finished with you.'

She slammed the door shut and collapsed on the floor. She hated her life. She hated her husband. She hated London. But everything would change now. She had probably lost all her friends. Well, it didn't matter. Tomorrow morning, she determined, she would get up and pack her bags and leave Hawley for ever. Get out of London and move to somewhere where her talents would finally be appreciated. She marched up the stairs to bed and lay there, unable to sleep for quite some time through her trembling anger.

She had placed a glass of water beside the bed because she always woke in the middle of the night in need of a drink. She was not to know that she would not live to see the morning.

At three o'clock in the morning a light drizzle was falling over London and he was dressed in the same long coat and hat that he had worn the afternoon he had purchased the poison. Since then he had bought some gloves to match his outfit in case this moment ever arose; in truth, he could hardly believe that he was going to go through with it now; it had seemed like a strange but necessary notion when he had planned it originally, but to actually see it through? That was something else. Until the moment came, he wasn't even sure that he would. But his heart was in the job ahead. Too much had happened to change his mind. Matters had gone too far. The beatings, the screaming matches, the humiliation. And, having found true love for the first time, he didn't want to lose it now. How could they ever be together while that woman stood in their way? There was only one option. He had to get rid of her.

Something about his aspect as he walked slowly towards 39 Hilldrop Crescent made even the late-night dogs in the street stop their barking and stand still, watching him, as if his demeanour told them that they would do wrong to provoke him with their noise. He was determined; there was no question about that. He felt in his pockets; the left-hand one contained the bottle and a handkerchief; in the right were three solid, sharp knives to finish the deed. His heart beat fast within his chest but somehow he wasn't afraid. Despite a religious upbringing, he didn't fear God and he wasn't worried about retribution. Cora Crippen, he reasoned, was a demon in her own right and had no business remaining on this earth. The happiness of two people depended on her death. Her life brought only sadness and misery to those who surrounded her. Surely, therefore, he was doing a worthwhile thing removing her from the world.

He paused only briefly outside the house and that was to check that the lights were all off inside. The keys were already in his hand, and at first he inserted the wrong one in the lock, struggling with it before finding the one that fitted correctly and opening the door. He held it ajar for a moment without going inside, listening for any sound from within, but there was none to be heard so he stepped in and closed the door gently behind him. He considered taking his coat off and hanging it up in the hallway – after all, this could take some time – but decided against it. The less noise he made right now, the better.

He walked slowly up the stairs, able to hear the sound of his own breathing as he did so, convinced that it would wake the house, and he stopped out-side the bedroom door. Taking the bottle out of his pocket, he took the lid off, making sure not to breathe in too deeply as he held it firmly in his grip. Then, placing a gloved hand on the handle of the door, he opened it slowly and stood in the darkness, waiting for his eyes to adjust to the dark and staring at the figure within.

Cora was lying in bed, the sheets half pushed off her to reveal her upper body, tossing and turning and murmuring something in her sleep. The drama of the earlier part of the evening had given her difficulty in sleeping at first, and she had only drifted off half an hour before and was still in a fretful doze.

A sliver of moonlight was coming in through the slightly parted curtains and its arc ended on the pale, ghostly skin of Cora's right elbow. This was it, the last moment when he could turn around and change his mind. Creeping forward, he saw the glass of water beside the bed, half empty, and he poured the entire contents of the bottle into it. Replacing it on the night table, he returned to the doorway and coughed out loud, in order to disturb her sleep.

Her eyes opened slowly and she rubbed at them be-fore raising herself up in the bed and, squinting, looked towards the figure in the doorway.

'Hawley?' she asked in a sleepy voice. 'Is that you?' His reply was a mere grunt, a clearing of the throat, and before she could focus her eyes on him, he walked away, hiding on the landing, out of sight. 'Don't make so much noise, you fool,' she grunted, her last words. 'I'm trying to sleep.'

Before settling back on the pillows, she reached across for the glass of water and swallowed its contents in one go. He heard her suddenly wheeze for air, the stop-start sounds as she tried to breathe and failed, and he turned back into the bedroom while she clawed at her throat in pain. Her eyes opened wide as she saw him standing over her and she shook her head, amazed and confused by his presence, while the life slowly drained out of her. Emotionless, he watched as she fell back against the pillows and gave a few more fitful gasps before lying still, her eyes open and staring at the ceiling, a small trickle of water running from the side of her mouth down her right cheek. He gasped in amazement that it was actually over – that she was finally *dead* – and he felt great strength emerge from within. Nervous, amazed at his own audacity, he reached down and, taking a deep breath, placed his hands beneath her body, lifting her up.

She was heavier than he had ever imagined she would be, and it was a struggle getting her down the stairs. On more than one occasion he thought he was going to slip and drop her and watch her tumble to the ground, where she might break her neck; for a moment he considered throwing her. After all, she was already dead and he could do her no more harm. He reconsidered, however, thinking that the noise of her falling body might wake the neighbours, who could come to investigate. The stairs were narrow, and by the time he reached the downstairs floor he was perspiring heavily and had to put her carefully on the ground in order to recover his breath.

Stepping over to the cellar door, he opened it and peered down, searching for the switch for the single light bulb that showed the way down to the basement. It didn't offer much light, so he found some candles in the living room and brought them downstairs first, standing them at the back of the cellar, and lit them, creating a circle of light around the area where he was planning on working. Returning to the ground floor, he picked Cora up once again and felt the muscles in his arms cry out in pain as he negotiated the stone steps to the cellar and finally reached the chosen place. He dumped her there in a corner and took a moment to recover his breath.

Removing his jacket, gloves and hat, he took out a small chisel from his pocket and began prising the stone slabs up from their base. There was a layer of sand beneath them and then a grid of wooden slats which led down to a cement base below. In between, however, was an empty area about three inches thick. He lifted up enough panels until he had what he considered to be enough room, and then he returned to the body of Cora Crippen.

He laid her down flat on the ground over the now cleared area and wondered where to begin. He amazed himself by feeling no sense of horror, just urgency. He removed several knives from his pocket and laid them out on the ground. As he did so, a slight murmur seemed to emerge from her mouth and he stared at her in fright. Had he imagined it? Her lips seemed to move and whisper something, so, without giving it any thought, he reached for the sharpest of the knives and slit her throat open, watching in surprise as an empty wound sprang out, before suddenly filling with blood which poured down either side of her neck. A sucking noise came from her epiglottis as her body appeared to make a final desperate bid for air, but it ended quickly. He held her there for several minutes until her throat had bled dry and then he began the task he dreaded most, the necessary task, the only way to get rid of the body once and for all.

He gathered piles of newspapers from the other side of the cellar and left them at a little distance from the body, ready to wrap around their gruesome contents, and then set about amputating her arms and legs. It was a difficult task as the bones and muscles at the hip and shoulder were tougher than he expected them to be. They took some sharp cutting and a strong arm. Nevertheless, within about an hour Cora Crippen's torso lay there with her limbs in a pile at her side. To his surprise, after the first arm separated, the grotesqueness of the situation no longer bothered him and he worked industriously, rather than with any sense of dread.

Next to go was the head. The throat had already been slit, so a few well-chosen deep stabs around the neck separated it from the body quite easily and he set it aside for the moment. The ground under the body was covered in blood but it was seeping quite easily through the gaps in the flooring and collecting in a pool on the cement below. The cellar floor was perfectly flat, so it settled there, leaving only a thin, dark-red covering behind.

He separated the arms and legs and the elbow and knee joints and then sliced off the hands and feet, wrapping each part in a parcel of newspapers before placing them carefully in the ground. Soon afterwards, there was only the matter of the torso. He sliced through it in an 'X' fashion and pulled back the skin, revealing the viscera of the body. Using a serrated-edged knife, he cut out the major organs – heart, liver, kidneys – and laid each of them in its own neat package, which also went underground. The rib cage came next, and it had to be broken and squashed in as otherwise it took up too much space. All that was left then was what remained of the torso, which he carved into four equal pieces, wrapped up carefully, and buried. Finally, he took a bag of sand from the other side of the cellar and poured it over the packages, covering the bloodstained newspapers thoroughly before replacing the panels and stepping heavily on them to press them back into place. Within a few hours of arriving at 39 Hilldrop Crescent, the greater part of Cora Crippen was safely buried in the cellar, which itself looked as if it had hardly been touched at all.

He blew out the candles and took them away, then

switched off the single light and closed the cellar, eventually locking the front door of 39 Hilldrop Crescent behind him.

He took the head in a bag with him.

'Well, that's that,' he muttered as he walked away down the street.

17

Ships That Pass in the Morning

The Atlantic Ocean: Wednesday, 27 July 1910

It was estimated that the *Laurentic* would pass the *Montrose* at eleven o'clock on the morning of 27 July, and every soul on board Captain Taylor's ship was hoping to catch a glimpse of the infamous Dr Crippen. From the moment Inspector Walter Dew had set foot on the *Laurentic*, four days earlier, the ship's passengers had been obsessed with the unfolding drama and they found that the manhunt was by far the most entertaining element of their voyage. Their reaction to it, however, was split along gender, age and class lines. Men in the first-class cabins had placed wagers on the exact day and time that the ships would pass each other, betting thousands of pounds on the outcome. The women had cautioned their troublesome children that, if they did not behave, they would be sent over to Dr Crippen on the other ship for punishment the moment he was in sight. The children in steerage played horrific games in which they pretended to carve one another up and bury the pieces in the lifeboats. Rachel Bailey, a young newly-wed travelling on her honeymoon to a new life in Canada, where her husband Conor was to take up a post as a teacher, was among the most intrigued of all and seemed to take a sadistic delight in questioning Inspector Dew whenever she saw him.

'It was you who found the dead body, was it not?' she asked, her eyes wide as she took his hand and dragged him down on to a deckchair, continuing to hold it so he could not escape.

'Indeed,' he admitted. 'Although it was hardly a body any more when I came across it.'

She gasped and put her other hand to her mouth. Her innocent air, combined with her absolute need to know the grizzly details of Dr Crippen's crime, amused and shocked him in equal parts, but he had grown fond of her, much fonder than he was of the older and more salacious passengers, because she had the knack of making him feel important.

'How brave you must be! But that poor woman,' she added. 'Do you suppose they were happy once, Inspector?'

'Happy?'

'The Crippens. I mean, they married, so they must have loved each other at one time.'

He considered it. 'The two do not necessarily go hand in hand,' he said. 'Although in your case I'm sure that's not so.'

'Of course it isn't,' she said. 'I would never have married had I not been in love. After all, my parents wanted me to marry another man two years ago and I refused point-blank. He was the son of a merchant banker and my father thought it would be good for his business to join the two families, but I couldn't do it. After all, the fellow was only five feet tall and had warts on his face. How could I marry him?'

'How indeed,' Dew said, smiling a little, for he had seen her new husband and he was a tall, dashing lad with perfectly clear skin, who was keeping a daily diary of life aboard ship. 'You were right to wait.'

'But didn't you want to run away?' she asked.

'Run away? From what?'

'From the cellar. When you found her. Was it not too disgusting for words?'

'It wasn't pleasant,' he admitted. 'But I am a trained officer,' he explained, enjoying the air of bravery he gave off. 'I've been with Scotland Yard for many years. There's precious little can shock me these days, my dear.'

'And the blood,' she asked. 'There must have been a lot of blood.'

'Most of it had congealed into the sand. It smelt foul, of course. But really, Mrs Bailey, this is hardly an appropriate topic for discussion. You won't sleep tonight.'

'I must admit that the very idea of it shocks me,' she told him, deciding not to add that it excited her too. 'But imagine if Conor grew tired of me and cut me up into little pieces and buried me in the cellar. I'd never forgive him.'

'I'm sure there's no chance of that happening,' he said, suddenly concerned that a spate of copycat dissections would break out in London, if not the world, and he would be called upon to solve them all. 'I'm sure you're quite safe.'

She wasn't so sure. Along with several of her fellow-passengers, she was finding it hard to sleep, the closer they got to the *Montrose*. One fellow, a sixty-year-old civil servant, went directly to the captain to protest their route.

'Look here,' he said, his face choking in a kind of withered frown. 'This isn't good enough. The ship has a set route to take and we're veering off it to catch this Crippen fellow. That's hardly right, is it?'

'I'm afraid we don't have any choice, Mr Bellows,' Captain Taylor explained. 'We're acting under direct orders from Scotland Yard. And we're not veering very far off the route, just a little. We'll still make Canada on time. You have my word for that.'

'But it's hardly safe, is it?' he asked. 'We're just a group of passengers travelling somewhere. We can't be expected to go around capturing crazed killers. We're being dragged into something entirely against our will.'

'Only *one* crazed killer, sir,' the captain corrected him. 'And he may not even be crazed.'

'He killed his wife, didn't he? Chopped her up into little bits and ate her heart, I heard.'

Captain Taylor opened his eyes wide in surprise. He had grown accustomed to hearing exaggerations concerning what Dr Crippen had done, but the cannibalism story seemed to be one that was gaining hold. 'I don't think he did that,' he said doubtfully. 'But even if he had, all the more reason to capture him, wouldn't you agree?'

'No, I do not agree,' Bellows insisted. 'The fellow's a devious psychopath. He must be captured, by all means, but I do not like the idea of this ship taking it upon herself to do the capturing. There's every chance the fellow will turn around and kill the lot of us.'

'There are over sixteen hundred people on board the *Laurentic*,' said Taylor. 'It would be most difficult for him to accomplish that.'

'You say that now,' the other said. 'You have no idea what the man is capable of.'

'Perhaps not. But sixteen hundred murders . . . ?'

'I must protest, Captain Taylor. And I'd like it entered in the ship's log.'

The fellow had been reading too many gothic novels, Taylor could tell. Nevertheless, he agreed to do as he was asked, and the man went away, still unhappy but appeased for the moment. Despite the varying degrees of excitement and horror at what lay ahead, no one would be able to prevent the *Laurentic* from pursuing her current course, and on the afternoon of the 27th hundreds of passengers gathered on the deck of the ship, lining the railings for their first sight of the *Montrose*, filled with a mixture of fear and excitement.

'Do you think this is wise?' Captain Taylor asked the inspector as they stood in the wheelhouse, taking turns to look through a set of binoculars at the sea ahead. 'I could always confine the passengers to their cabins if you preferred.'

'That would look worse,' Dew said. 'We would then seem like a ghost ship to anyone looking across at us. No, as it is they will simply think our passengers are waving to them. It's not as if anyone on the *Montrose* will be able to hear anything across the waves.'

'No,' said the captain, 'that's true. And you're absolutely sure you don't want us to lower a boat for you to go across to them?'

'Absolutely sure. I'll wait until they're just short of land,' he said. 'The less intrusion on the *Montrose* for the moment, the better. I don't trust this fellow Crippen. He's capable of anything. There might be panic on board if they knew who he was.'

A seaman approached the captain with a pile of papers. 'Captain,' he said, holding them aloft. 'Through on the Marconi over the last hour. Seems like every newspaper in the world wants to know what's going on. And they all want to speak with you, Inspector.'

Dew smiled, enjoying the sensation of celebrity. 'I'll wait until we've passed them by,' he said. 'Then, Captain, perhaps you would assign a wireless operator to me and I could relay some messages back to the newspapers. And to the Yard, of course.'

'Certainly, certainly,' he said gruffly, before tapping the inspector's shoulder and pointing into the distance. 'Look,' he said quietly, a sense of dread and horror unexpectedly filling him now. 'There she is. The SS *Montrose*.'

A cheer, interspersed with some hysterical screams, was heard from the deck of the *Laurentic* as more and more passengers began to spot the other ship. Captain Taylor intended bringing his ship a little closer before passing the other by, and he gave instructions to his helmsman as to the course to take.

'Well, Inspector,' he said, passing the binoculars across to him. 'You still think he's on board?'

'He'd better be,' said Dew, 'or I might as well throw myself in the ocean right now, rather than return to London. I'd be a laughing stock the world over.'

The passengers enjoying the morning sunshine on the deck of the *Montrose* were surprised to see the other ship on the horizon. 'Look, Mr Robinson,' Martha Hayes said, shielding her eyes from the sun with her hand as the *Laurentic* began to come closer. 'It's another ship. What a surprise.'

'Another ship?' he asked, waking from his doze and looking out to sea. 'Impossible.'

'It is. Take a look.'

He squinted in the sunlight and realized she was right. 'Heavens,' he said. 'I'm surprised it's travelling so near to our path. You wouldn't expect to see another boat out here in the middle of the ocean. Still, I suppose these transatlantic crossings are becoming more and more numerous these days.'

'Indeed,' she said. Quite a few of their fellow-passengers began to gather along the railings as news of the *Laurentic* began to spread, and soon the deck was a mirror image of that on board the other ship. After more than a week at sea, it was a diversion for the passengers to see other signs of life, and they waved their handkerchiefs in the air and shouted greetings, although not a word they said could possibly be heard across the rush of the waves and the noise of the engines.

'It must be a faster ship than ours,' said Mr Robinson, considering it. 'After all, it's been behind us all this way and looks as if it's about to pass us by now. It will probably make Canada a day or two before us.'

'Lucky them,' she said, considering it. 'I can't wait to set foot on land again, Mr Robinson. Can you?'

He said he agreed with her, but secretly he had begun to enjoy life on board the *Montrose*. There was a simple schedule to his days here and no question of trouble. He and Edmund had managed to spend many happy moments together and, despite the events of the previous evening when he had nearly tossed Tom DuMarqué overboard, all in all it had been quite a pleasant voyage. He didn't know what future Canada held for him. With two wives behind him, he had begun to question whether he was even the marrying sort after all, although (unlike either Charlotte or Cora) he believed that Ethel was in love with him.

'Look at all the people on deck,' Martha Hayes said, surprised to see the hundreds of people gathered at the railings, waving to them. 'Don't they have enough cabin space?'

Mr Robinson narrowed his eyes and thought about this. 'They must be even more bored than the people here are,' he said. 'Any sign of new life has brought them all out. I don't like being watched like this. It makes me feel as if I'm on a stage.'

'They seem very excited, don't they?' she asked.

'Can you see him?' asked Captain Taylor. 'Can you make him out on deck?'

'No,' said Inspector Dew, staring through the binoculars and shaking his head. 'No, I can't, but I didn't expect to, really. It would be hoping for too much. There are too many people on board.'

'That's close enough, helmsman,' Taylor shouted. 'Keep her steady and straight ahead.'

'I'll wait for my moment,' Dew said, nodding. 'He's

on there somewhere. I can sense it. He won't escape me. I'll catch him yet.'

'I've never seen such excitement,' said Martha Hayes, marvelling at the bodies jumping up and down and behaving as though they had never ever seen anyone else before. She noticed that quite a few of them appeared to be making hanging motions with their hands, stretching their necks and lolling their tongues out of their mouths as if suspended at the end of a noose. 'The oddest thing,' she said. 'They look like a ship full of lunatics, if you ask me. Have you seen this?'

'The sea has made them all mad,' said Mr Robinson, settling back in his deckchair and closing his eyes to return to his doze. 'The best thing to do is to ignore them. They're like animals in a zoo. The more attention you pay them, the more outrageous their behaviour will become.'

'Hmm,' Martha Hayes said, unconvinced. 'It's most peculiar, though. I've never seen anything quite like it.'

'I wouldn't worry about them, my dear,' he replied. 'They'll pass us by and that'll be the last we'll see of them. Now, do you suppose one of the cabin crew could bring us some drinks?'

Captain Henry Kendall watched the passing of the *Laurentic* from the wheelhouse with First Officer Billy Carter by his side. Steering the *Montrose* was Crewman Mark Dawson, who had been a regular sailor for fifteen years with the Canadian Pacific fleet and had applied for promotion on eight occasions, each time having been rejected. This had made him somewhat bitter towards authority, and he resented Carter particularly for taking over the ill Mr Sorenson's position which, he believed, should rightfully have been his. Most days of their voyage he had maintained a sullen silence in the navigation room, refusing to speak to his immediate superior in any other than a series of grunts. Today, however, was a different matter, for he was more than aware that it was peculiar for two ships to pass so close to each other during a transatlantic crossing unless there was a very particular reason for it. The sea was a wide and empty space, and each vessel was given specific routes to follow in order to avoid collisions. Both the *Montrose* and the *Laurentic* had veered off their natural course and he wanted to know the reason why.

'Can't be right, sir, can it?' he asked, turning around to face Captain Kendall, rather than the first officer. 'Why do you suppose she's steering so close to us?'

'I have no idea, Dawson,' Kendall said, disdaining to confide in him. 'But I shouldn't worry about it; they're maintaining their distance. It's not as if we were going to collide. Just keep her steady, and things will be fine.'

'But maybe they're trying to get a message to us,' Dawson objected, fishing for information. 'Do you think we should check the Marconi?'

'Just steer the ship, crewman,' Billy Carter said irritably. 'And less of your questions.'

Dawson gave him a killer look that suggested he would like to string the younger man up, but he pressed his lips together and turned away from them both instead. After a suitable pause, the captain touched Carter's arm and indicated that he should follow him back to the wireless room.

Locking the door behind them as they entered, Kendall looked at the machine hopefully, but there was still no message from the hospital about the condition of Mr Sorenson. The captain had had a dream the night before that his former first officer had died, alone, in his bed and that he was being buried without a single friend to attend the funeral. He'd woken up shortly before six o'clock that morning, tears streaming down his face, his sheets damp with perspiration, his mouth dry and head aching. Why don't they send a message? he asked himself. He himself had sent seven.

'Inspector Dew contacted me earlier on the telegraph,' he said, sitting down and indicating that Carter should do the same. 'He's going straight on to Quebec, so the *Laurentic* can dock there and disembark her passengers.'

'Right,' said Carter. 'And he's going to be waiting for us when we arrive?'

'I think so,' the other said. 'Although he seems a little concerned about the crowds.'

Carter raised an eyebrow. 'Crowds?' he asked. 'What crowds?'

'Apparently we're front-page news all over the world.'

'You're joking!'

'Well, this Crippen story was already big news when we set sail from Antwerp. The manhunt was getting larger. Once the inspector boarded the *Laurentic*, it seems that every newspaper in the world has been following us. You must have noticed the crowds on deck as they passed us by?'

'I did, as it happens,' Carter admitted. 'But I thought they were just excited to see another ship. Like our passengers were. Some people find the sea quite isolating.'

'I suspect it was more than that. We've done a pretty good job of keeping this information to ourselves, but that will have to change soon. I think we'll need to tell the other officers before we dock in Canada.'

'Right.'

'Just so they can be prepared for the reception committee.'

'Of course. Do you want me to take care of that?'

'If you would.'

Silence reigned between them for a few moments. In recent days their relationship had improved somewhat. The older man had grown resigned to the loss of Mr Sorenson and the prospect of Mr Carter being more or less a permanent fixture on board the *Montrose* for some years to come. Although this was not an idea that pleased him particularly, he had little choice but to make the best of the situation. His had always been a happy ship and that must not change. Also, he had entrusted Carter with his beliefs about Mr John Robinson and his supposed son, and he had not been mocked for them. On the contrary, Carter seemed to have gained some respect for him. The first officer had also proved that he could be trusted, as so far there had been no leaks to either the crew or the passengers. But did he play chess? This was the important factor. Would he be prepared to stay up late at night with him? Could they ever have as intimate a friendship as the one he had enjoyed with Mr Sorenson?

'I want you to know, Mr Carter,' Kendall said, finally finding his voice but unable to look the younger man in the eye, 'that I think you've done a fine job on this voyage. Under somewhat difficult circumstances.'

'Thank you, sir,' he said, surprised.

'I'm aware that we didn't get off to the best start, but your work has impressed me since then. And I'm not a man who lets these things pass by unacknowledged.'

'Kind of you to say so, sir, but really there's no need. I know it can be difficult having a trusted colleague replaced by a newcomer.'

'Yes,' the captain muttered, wanting to point out that he hadn't replaced him as such, he had merely filled in during an illness.

'Any word on Mr Sorenson yet, sir?'

He shook his head. 'Nothing,' he said. 'However, you will doubtless be looking forward to returning to your wife,' he added, feeling that a friendly comment was required in return.

Carter's face burst into a wide smile at the mention of her. 'Yes, I was hoping to catch the 3rd of August ship back to Europe, sir, if that's convenient. Now that we're definitely going to be there on time, I mean.'

'That's fine, yes.'

'I should be back a month or so before the kid arrives, but it's best to be on the safe side.'

Kendall stood up, unwilling to pursue this topic any longer; family life interested him no more than it did Inspector Dew. They were both men whose careers were the only thing of importance to them. 'Don't tell the crew till tomorrow night,' he said. 'That should give them enough time to get used to the idea before we reach Canada. And make sure they know that they mustn't tell any of the passengers or there'll be pandemonium. If this gets out, I'll track down whoever it was, and they'll never sail with the Canadian Pacific fleet again.'

'Understood, sir,' said Carter, standing up and making for the door. He was pleased that the captain had finally offered him some sort of olive branch, for he had made every effort to live up to the man's exacting standards ever since he had come on board. It was hardly his fault that Mr Sorenson's appendix had exploded. 'You never can tell, sir, can you?' he said, turning around to look at him before he left.

'What's that?'

'I said, you never can tell. About people. The types they are. I mean, that Mr Robinson, well, he looks as if he wouldn't say boo to a goose. And as for Edmund . . . I mean, in the right light she really does look like a boy. Put a man's coat and hat on her and you'd be completely convinced she was a man. Do you suppose she knows what he did?'

Kendall shrugged. 'Hard to tell,' he said. 'If she does, she's a worse fool for staying with him. What kind of woman would want to stay with someone who chopped his last wife up? She'd be afraid to look at him in the wrong way in case he got the knives out. And if she doesn't know, then she could be in danger too. You're still keeping a close eye on them both, I hope.'

'Oh yes.'

'Well, only a couple of days to go. Then we'll know the truth for sure.'

He turned away from the first officer, who took this as his cue to leave. Alone in the room, Kendall stared at the Marconi machine and willed it into life. Send a message, he thought. Anything at all. Just send a message.

Having sat in his deckchair all that morning, Mr Robinson returned to his cabin to wash before lunch, feeling a little sick inside. The skin on his face felt rough and dry because he had sat in the sun for too long that day, and he resolved to stay indoors for the rest of the afternoon. He had a brief wash and changed his shirt, and he was about to leave the cabin to meet Edmund in the dining hall when a sharp knock on the door distracted him. He stared at it in surprise. This was not the deferential tap of a member of the crew or a steward, passing on a note from Edmund or a piece of information about the passage. Nor was it the urgent rap of the steerage children who regularly played tricks on the first-class passengers by knocking on their doors and then running away, screaming with delight. This was something more serious. This was a policeman's knock, the sound of someone who will ram the door down if it is not opened immediately. Hoping for the best, he opened it nervously and was surprised to see Mrs Antoinette Drake standing in front of him, her hand raised to knock again, her knuckles white as she clenched her fist, her cheeks startlingly red.

'Mrs Drake,' he said. 'What can I—?'

'Mr Robinson,' she announced, pushing past him and entering the cabin. 'I need to speak to you immediately. Please shut the door.'

He stared at her in surprise. 'I beg your pardon?' he said.

'Mr Robinson, I think you should shut the door or you will allow every passenger on this boat to hear what I have to say. And let me assure you that you do not want that to happen.'

Intimidated by her abrupt rudeness, he closed the door and remained standing by it. 'Would you like to sit down?' he asked.

'I'd rather stand.'

She didn't seem to be in any hurry to tell him what was on her mind, and they stood there for the best part of a minute, sizing one another up, each waiting for the other to speak.

'Mr Robinson,' she said finally, her voice betraying only slight nervousness. 'I realize that I am a woman travelling alone without her husband, but let me assure you that this does not make me a target for insults and abuse.'

'Of course not,' he said, still no wiser as to what she was referring to.

'And let me further assure you that, if Mr Drake was here, it would be he who was standing before you now, and not I. And the question of violence might even be raised. Mr Drake was a junior boxing champion when he was a younger man, you know. And he's still handy with his dukes,' she added, leaning forward, her eyes popping, her vocabulary betraying the fact that she had been brought up in the East End of London before marriage forced her to fictionalize her past.

'Mrs Drake, I'm not sure what has happened, but—'

'*Have* the decency to allow me to finish, sir,' she said, raising one palm in the air to silence him. 'I will have my say, and then you may offer whatever apology you like, but I warn you, the matter may yet be referred to the captain.'

'Mrs Drake, I think you should sit down. I'm really at a loss to know what you're so upset about.'

She sat down heavily in a chair and Mr Robinson sat opposite her, although still maintaining some distance.

'Now perhaps you'd like to start at the beginning,' he said.

'It has become clear to me over the last few years,' she began, 'as my daughter Victoria has blossomed towards womanhood, that she has become the object of many a young man's affections. True, she is a beautiful girl – but then she comes from a fine lineage that has produced many beautiful girls. Why, when I was her age I was quite the débutante and had to fight off a wealth of suitors, so I am fully aware of the difficulties she faces.'

'Quite,' Mr Robinson said, trying to imagine this heavy-set, pushy woman as a flower-like virgin, nobly retaining her virtue in the face of the lust-fuelled young men of London. He found the image difficult to visualize.

'In London and in Paris, Victoria has enjoyed a number of suitors, but she has of course behaved with impeccable dignity at all times, never compromising herself for a moment, despite the fact that any number of beaux have attempted to take liberties with her. But she is a decent, respectable girl, Mr Robinson. Make no mistake about that.'

'Of course. I have no doubt of it. But what, may I ask, has this to do with me?'

'Last night, Mr Robinson, Victoria returned to our cabin quite late. I must confess that I was asleep at the time, having taken a medicinal brandy earlier in the evening to counteract the effects of a slight chill I've developed on board. I *told* Mr Drake to book us the Presidential Suite, you know, but did he listen? No. He insisted that the suite had already been taken, which I am now unsure about.'

'Mrs Drake, this is about an illness you're suffering? Would you like me to summon a doctor?'

'I would not!' she cried. 'And it is *not* about an illness, as you must be well aware. Victoria returned to our cabin and woke me up with her crying because of an event which appears to have taken place on the deck of this boat last night.'

'Ah,' he replied, recalling the incident. He had awoken that morning with the hope that it would all have been forgotten by the afternoon. It seemed necessary that he would have to speak to Mr Zéla at some point during the day, but he hoped that that hideous nephew of his would be confined to his quarters during the conversation. He himself had left the cabin quite late the previous night, having expected Edmund to return half an hour earlier, and had gone in search of him. When he came on deck and his eyes adjusted to the darkness, he noticed what at first he took to be an embrace between two young people but which he slowly realized was the exact opposite of that. Recognizing Edmund's voice, he saw the glint of the knife in the air and had reacted without any thought, grabbing Tom DuMarqué's hand and pulling him away from his intended victim. Holding him over the side of the boat had not been a premeditated act; he was simply so consumed with anger at what he had seen that he could not help himself. He felt sure that had Mr Zéla not appeared when he did, then Tom DuMarqué would now be lying at the bottom of the Atlantic Ocean and he himself would have committed an unconscionable crime. Still, the incident had ended without any injury, and it had been his fervent desire since then that the matter would be dropped.

'You may well say "*ah*",' Mrs Drake said, anger forcing flecks of spittle to form at the sides of her mouth. 'But I would like to know exactly what you are going to do about it.'

'Victoria has told you then?' he asked.

'She has told me very little. She was too upset. She *remains* too upset. But I have a good idea what it is. From the moment we boarded this vessel, Mr Robinson, your son has been making inappropriate advances towards my daughter. He has followed her around, chased her like a little puppy-dog, and from what I do know of last night he has taken an unforgivable liberty.'

Mr Robinson could not help but smile at the very idea of it and he wondered what story Victoria had concocted to save herself.

'You are smiling, Mr Robinson,' she said angrily. 'You find this amusing?'

'No, Mrs Drake, of course not,' he replied. 'It's an unfortunate situation. But I believe you might, as they say, have got your wires crossed.'

'Might have *what*?' she asked, ignorant of the idiom.

'I think you have got hold of the wrong end of the stick,' he explained. 'Edmund has certainly not had any interest in Victoria other than as a friend. I can assure you of that.'

'I'm afraid my eyes have led me to a very different conclusion, sir,' she said haughtily. 'Surely you cannot have failed to notice the time they spend together, the cosy chats, the strolls around the deck?'

'Yes, but I believe they have been mainly at Victoria's suggestion.'

'What an insulting remark!'

'I don't mean to suggest anything inappropriate, you understand. Only that your daughter is the one who has taken a shine to my . . . to Edmund. And if she believes he returns those romantic affections, I'm afraid she is very much mistaken. In fact she could not be more wrong.'

Mrs Drake's mouth opened and closed several times in amazement. She truly believed she had never been so insulted. The suggestion that her daughter was the person making all the running was an outrageous one, but the idea that, having done so, she might be rejected by the object of her affections? Well that just beggared belief.

'Mr Robinson,' she said finally, trying to control the emotion in her voice. 'I am forced now to tell you something unpleasant which I must ask you to keep between these four walls.'

'Of course,' he said, intrigued.

'My daughter has told me very little of the events that took place last night, but there is one thing I do know for sure. And that is that the two young people . . .' She searched for the right words, horrified that she had to find them at all. '. . . the two young people shared a moment,' she said finally, closing her eyes in shame.

'A moment? I don't understand. I know they were talking, but—'

'They grew closer, Mr Robinson.'

'Well, I expect they have some things in common. It's not unusual for two young people to—'

'Oh, for heaven's sake,' she cried, throwing her hands in the air. 'They *kissed*, Mr Robinson. Your son Edmund kissed Victoria.'

He stared at her in disbelief, not knowing what to say under the circumstances. 'They kissed,' he repeated in a flat tone.

'Yes. It dishonours us both, of course, but there is no reason why this needs to go any further. However, it must be made clear to Edmund that he cannot take liberties like that again. It's simply unacceptable.'

'You think Edmund kissed her?' he asked, trying to imagine how such a thing could possibly have taken place.

'Yes,' she shouted. 'Oh, do wake up, Mr Robinson. You're acting as if you've been asleep for the last few hours. Surely it is not such an alien concept to you? You did father the boy, you must have some idea of the lusts

415

that drive men. From what I can gather, he kissed her quite passionately and she was forced to break free of his licentious advances, which is when she returned to our cabin in tears.'

'I see,' he said, standing up and forcing her to do the same. 'If Edmund has done what you say, Mrs Drake, let me apologize on his behalf and assure you that it will not happen again. However, I happen to believe that this is not necessarily the way the events of last night developed.'

'Are you calling Victoria a liar, Mr Robinson?'

'No, because, as you so clearly pointed out, she has not actually told you what happened. Therefore, how could she lie? However, you are also not in full possession of the facts. Indeed, you are merely piecing them together from your own rather vivid imagination.'

'Well, it hardly takes a great imagination to work it out, does it? We are both people of the world. We know what goes on in the minds of the young.'

'Of whom your daughter is one, just as much as Edmund.'

'My daughter is a lady!'

'And so is Edmund!' he roared in anger, unwilling to have the character of his beloved besmirched any more.

Mrs Drake took a step back and raised an eyebrow in surprise.

'A gentleman, I mean,' he corrected himself. 'Edmund is as much a gentleman as Victoria is a lady, and there is no reason why you should assume his guilt over hers.'

'I can see you are not willing to be reasonable about this,' she said, grunting like a hungry pig as she opened the door and pushed past him. 'But let me say now that if there is another incident of this type, I will not be coming to see you about it but will visit Captain Kendall instead. And I shall insist upon that so-called *gentleman* being put off this boat.'

'In the middle of the ocean?' he asked with a smile.

'Don't toy with me, Mr Robinson,' she snarled. 'Just tell Edmund to stay away from Victoria. Or I promise you there will be hell to pay.' And with that she stormed off down the corridor and returned to her cabin, slamming the door behind her in anger.

He stared after her for a moment, before shaking his head and stepping back inside. As he made to close the door, however, Ethel appeared and entered the cabin, looking at him in surprise.

'I came down to find you,' she said. 'I thought we were having lunch. What's the matter? You look upset.'

'I have just had a visit from Mrs Drake,' he replied. 'About last night.'

'Oh no. Is she after Tom DuMarqué's blood, then? I wouldn't much want to be in his shoes this morning.'

'On the contrary, my dear,' he replied in a calm voice. 'She's after yours. She seems to think it would be a good idea if you were thrown overboard and fed to the sharks.'

Ethel blinked and thought about this for a moment. 'Me?' she said eventually, removing the boy's wig she wore. 'Why me? What have I done?'

'Apparently, you kissed Victoria.'

Ethel's mouth fell open in surprise. That incident was one she had blocked from her mind all morning. The memory of it, the length of the kiss, the fact that she had rather enjoyed it. 'Hawley . . .' she said, shaking her head.

'It's outrageous, of course,' he said. 'I mean, the idea is beyond preposterous.'

'You *know* she's been after me since the day we left Antwerp,' Ethel protested.

'Yes, I know that.'

'The truth is that she cornered me last night. Gave me a little champagne and made one final move. She tried to kiss me, but naturally I rejected her. That's why she ran off so upset.'

'Ethel, it's not as if I believe her,' Hawley said. 'You don't have to defend yourself.'

'As long as you know the truth,' she replied, lying through her teeth. In the few moments she had had to think about it, she considered being honest about the events of the previous night, but she realized that there was nothing to be gained by doing so. It was all for the best to stick to this simple lie.

'Anyway, she wants you to stay away from Victoria for the rest of the voyage,' he continued. 'And I think that's the sensible thing to do, all things considered. As far away as possible.'

'Of course. But did you tell her about Tom? Did you tell her how he attacked me?'

He shook his head. 'There's no point in going into all that with her,' he explained. 'She's going to believe whatever she wants to believe anyway. I see little reason for her to know every detail. But here's the thing: when we came on board, we agreed that we would keep as low a profile as possible. And instead, we seem to have become embroiled in a series of unpleasant incidents on this ship, with far too many people claiming association with us, and I for one have had enough of it. Now we've only got a few days to go; can't we just keep ourselves to ourselves in the mean time?'

'Of course,' Ethel replied, taking him by the hand and sitting with him on the corner of the bed. 'Of course we can. We'll stay here if you like. We can eat here, sleep here. Make love here. No one else matters, you see. Just you and I.'

Hawley nodded, but he felt saddened. 'I want to understand you,' he said quietly. 'And I want to be a good husband to you. Truly I do. But there can be no more of this unpleasantness.'

'I know you do. And of course you're right.'

'I don't want there to be any secrets between us. Sometimes I think that if I had tried to understand Cora a little better from the beginning, then we might have been able to be happy together.'

Ethel frowned; she didn't like to think about the previous Mrs Crippen. 'She was a horrible woman,' she said. 'You know that. You have nothing to reproach yourself for when it comes to her.'

'Perhaps I made her the way she was,' he said. 'Perhaps I drove her away. If I did, then I am at fault. And I don't want to do that to you. I couldn't bear to lose you.'

'Hawley, you never could,' she said, taking his face in her hands. 'You could never drive me away. I'm nothing like Cora.'

'Oh, I know that. But at first she swore she loved me too.'

'But I mean it. And I won't change.'

'In the end she hated me. That's why she left me. And even though I could hardly bear being around her either, it still hurts to think that she left me for another man. Does that sound ridiculous?'

Ethel swallowed and glanced away, unable to look him in the eye. 'It's perfectly reasonable,' she said. 'But you have to stop thinking about her. What she did was unforgivable.'

'We don't have any secrets, do we?' he asked.

'Of course not, Hawley.'

'Because you know you can tell me anything,' he insisted. '*Anything*, and I would be able to forgive you. No matter how dreadful it was.'

Ethel swallowed and looked away. 'I have no secrets from you,' she said in a flat tone.

Hawley nodded and looked a little disappointed. 'She'll probably make that other poor devil's life a misery now, too,' he said eventually, laughing a little but wiping a tear from his eye at the thought of it. 'Serves him right. Still,' he said, standing up, 'I wish her happiness. I really do. I've found it with you. So why shouldn't she find it elsewhere?'

Ethel shook her head, amazed at her beloved's ability to forgive. He really was the world's kindest man. Was it any wonder she loved him so? He could forgive anything, he had said. Ethel counted on that.

'Where are you going?' she asked as he made for the door.

'There's something I have to do,' he said, looking at his face in the mirror to make sure that his eyes weren't too tear-stained; they weren't, but his cheeks had turned pink from the sunburn.

'But I thought you wanted to stay here?' she asked.

'We will, we will. But I have just one last thing to do. I'll be back in an hour or so. I'll see you then.'

Ethel nodded and watched as he left the cabin. Her heart was filled with a mixture of love and fear, but now she knew that there was one task left that she had to perform too. This was the moment that she had been putting off since they had first stepped on to the *Montrose*, and it had finally come. Now they were nearly in Canada and, by the sound of things, they were planning on spending most of the rest of this voyage in their cabin together, which would leave no time for this. She stood up and walked across to the wardrobe, pulling a chair with her, and then stood on top of it, reaching above for the hatbox she had put there a week before. She held it gingerly but without any sense of horror. This was simply the last act which needed to be completed before safety and happiness could accompany them for ever.

Ethel made sure that the box was properly sealed and then she put the wig of Edmund Robinson back on her head, opened the door, checking that the corridor was empty, and stepped outside, holding the box tightly against her body.

*   *   *

'Mr Robinson,' Matthieu Zéla said, opening the door to his visitor. 'I've been expecting you.'

He stepped inside without waiting for an invitation and was immediately taken by the splendour of the Presidential Suite. The first-class cabin that he occupied with Edmund was extremely pleasant, but Matthieu Zéla's suite of rooms was something else: a long couch, several armchairs and plenty of space to walk around. He could hear the shower running in the bathroom which stood in the corner of the living room; at the opposite end were two doors leading to the small bedrooms, one for each of them.

'Mr Zéla,' he said politely, trying not to sound envious of these lavish surroundings. 'I hope you don't mind my visit.'

'Matthieu, please,' he said. 'And no, not at all. Sooner or later the entire ship seems to turn up here. I think they want to see what they're missing. Please. Sit down.'

'Is your nephew around?' Mr Robinson asked, and Matthieu nodded in the direction of the bathroom.

'He's taking a shower,' he said. 'A rare enough thing in itself, so let's not spoil it for him. He slept late this morning and I thought it best not to wake him. After all, when he's unconscious he can't be causing any trouble, can he?'

Mr Robinson allowed himself a brief smile as they sat down, before rubbing his face in exhaustion. 'Actually it's him I wanted to talk to you about,' he admitted.

'I guessed as much. None of us remember last night with any pleasure. For what it's worth, John, I don't blame you for trying to push him over the side. If he had attempted to assault my . . .' He searched for the right word but decided to stick with convention for the moment. '. . . my son, I probably would have done the same thing. Only I wouldn't have let anyone stop me.'

'I didn't want to injure him,' Mr Robinson explained.

'I'm not a violent man by nature, although we do all have our breaking points. But I need to make something clear: there can be no repeat of last night's misadventure.'

'Of course.'

'You see, Mrs Drake just visited me—'

'You have my sympathies.'

'And she knows nothing of Tom's involvement in the events of last night, and I decided it was best to keep it that way. She thinks there was a minor disagreement between Victoria and Edmund and has told me to keep him away from her, which he has agreed to do. However, I think it's important to share this information with you because if she knew what had really happened last night, doubtless she would have gone to the captain about it.'

Matthieu Zéla nodded and thought about it. 'And you, Mr Robinson,' he asked after a moment's thought, 'why didn't you let her?'

'I'm sorry?'

'Well, obviously Edmund is innocent of any wrongdoing last night. My nephew clearly attacked him. He might have killed him. And he might have seriously assaulted Victoria Drake, had he got the chance. So why haven't you informed the captain yourself? You could well be seen as something of a hero.'

'I thought it was best to leave the matter with you,' he said weakly. 'After all, you are the boy's guardian. I didn't think any unpleasantness was called for.'

'That was good of you,' Matthieu replied, although he didn't believe for a moment that this was the real reason for his silence.

The door from the bathroom opened and Tom DuMarqué slowly entered the room, a towel wrapped around his waist, and wiping his wet hair with another. Shirtless, he had more of a muscular physique than Mr Robinson had thought, and he now realized just how

422

much danger Edmund had been in. Tom stopped in the middle of the floor in surprise when he saw their visitor and stared across at Mr Robinson with contempt in his eyes, before turning to his uncle.

'What's *he* doing here?' he asked, rooted to the spot.

'He's come to speak to me, you young ruffian,' Matthieu said chirpily. 'And I believe you owe him an apology. What a perfect time to give it.'

Tom snorted and stared down at his bare feet, mumbling something under his breath.

'Tom, we've already discussed this,' Matthieu said in a stern voice. 'I've told you what the consequences will be if you don't apologize.'

'I'm *sorry*,' he shouted with the voice of a petulant teenager, which was what he was. 'But *he* tried to kill me.'

'And perhaps next time he'll succeed.'

'Have you asked him about—'

'Tom, go and get dressed.'

'But I want to know why Edmund—'

'Go and get dressed,' he repeated sharply. 'Right now. I will handle this from here. And besides, you're dripping all over the carpet.'

Tom frowned, disappointed that he was not going to be allowed to ask his question; he continued to mumble under his breath for a few moments, but he soon disappeared into his bedroom.

Matthieu looked after him for a moment before turning back to his companion and smiling gently. 'I have to try to smooth out his rough edges,' he said apologetically, 'of which he has many. Assuming I don't tire of him in the meantime. He also has a weakness for women and a tendency towards violence, a combination which worries me. Particularly since he's still so young. The DuMarqués never seem to learn from their mistakes.'

'Well, he needs to learn,' said Mr Robinson. 'He may

be still a teenager, but fellows like him have a tendency to grow up and become villains or murderers. But if you're sure you can keep him away from Victoria, then that's all I really needed to know. Thank you for your time.'

'Just a moment,' Matthieu said, urging him to remain seated. 'You still haven't answered my question.'

'Which question was that?'

'Why you didn't tell the captain yourself. Or why you didn't tell Mrs Drake. The truth about Tom, I mean.'

Mr Robinson shrugged. 'I did answer,' he said. 'I told you that I thought it best to tell you and let you deal with it, as the boy's—'

'Yes, but I don't believe a word of it,' said Matthieu. 'I believe you have your own reasons for not wanting to get involved. Perhaps it's something to do with the fact that you can't risk putting yourself in a vulnerable position.'

'Matthieu, I don't know what you're implying, but—'

'Can I ask you a question, John?' he asked in a thoughtful voice. The other man nodded. 'Why would a man travel from Antwerp to Canada with a young woman as his companion and then disguise her as a boy in an attempt to pass her off as his son? What would such a man's motivation be?'

Mr Robinson felt the blood drain from his freshly burnt cheeks and stared at Matthieu Zéla in horror. 'You know?' he asked.

'I am an observant creature, I confess. I knew from the moment I first saw you together.'

'But you haven't told anyone?'

Matthieu shook his head. 'No,' he said. 'It's not really any of my business. But I remain confused, and that is a condition I dislike. Where's the sense in it? What are you gaining by this deception?'

Mr Robinson thought for a moment and decided to come clean. From the first time he had met Matthieu

Zéla he had considered him a respectable man with no interest in involving himself unnecessarily in the private lives of others. If there was anyone he could confide in, then surely it was him. And with Canada so close, why not finally tell the truth?

'You must promise me that this will remain between ourselves,' he began.

'I am not a gossip, John.'

'Then I will tell you the truth. And judge me as you will. You are correct in what you suppose. Edmund is not my son at all, nor is he a boy. He is in fact a young woman whom I intend to marry as soon as I possibly can.'

'Indeed.' Matthieu was intrigued by the romance of it. 'Go on.'

'I was married in London,' he went on, 'to a woman who was deeply unpleasant. We lived together for many years and she made my life, frankly, a living torment. She was unfaithful to me many times, sometimes with fellows only just out of short trousers, so great was her perversion. Added to this, she was abusive, disrespectful and had a foul temper. Sometimes I truly believed that our relationship would end with her killing me. I'm not exaggerating or being overly dramatic. I actually think it was a possibility.'

'I don't doubt you for a moment. I have been married several times myself, John,' Matthieu admitted. 'And I am aware how these affairs can go wrong. Once I married a woman and was nearly killed for my troubles when another man appeared, claiming to be her husband still. She had forgotten to divorce him before marrying me, the little minx, and it was his intention to murder me because of it.'

'That's not something I intend to do. You see, my wife left me recently, for another man, and at the same time I had fallen in love with the young woman you now know as Edmund Robinson. And to my amazement she had fallen for me, too. She told me once that she would do anything at all for me, that she would sacrifice her very life to make me happy. Well, I confess I have never known such devotion. It fills me with hope for the future. I believe that for the first time in my life I can actually achieve happiness. And so, once my wife left, we decided to consummate our relationship and are travelling to Canada to begin a new life. Naturally, I will have to file for divorce from my wife, which might take some months, but in the meantime we simply do not wish to be parted.'

'But why disguise her? Why pretend she's a boy?'

'Mr Zéla, I don't know how familiar you are with the society from which I come, but an unmarried man and woman would never be allowed to share a cabin together on board ship. We would be shunned by all, which would in my opinion make a terrible beginning for our new lives. With the exception of last night's business, we've enjoyed the trip enormously and it has been a wonderful start for us. I know it's an elaborate lie, but it's been almost exciting for us too. And it's nearly over now. When we get to Canada, we will no longer need to pretend. We can be who we truly are.'

Matthieu Zéla considered this and nodded slowly. 'I suppose you know what you're doing,' he said doubtfully. 'Seems like an awful lot of trouble just to avoid a few wagging tongues; but if it's how you feel you needed to act, then I will not criticize you for it. Believe me, I have done some strange things for love in my time too. And paid the price for them.'

'So you won't tell anyone?' the other asked hopefully.

Matthieu shook his head. 'Your secret is safe with me,' he said. 'You have my word on it.'

Mr Robinson smiled and stood up, shaking his host's hand gratefully. 'In the light of recent events, we've decided to remain in our cabin for the last couple of days on board,' he said. 'So I probably won't be seeing you very much again. Also, I think it best if you keep your nephew away from my dear fiancée, or more trouble may ensue.'

'Of course,' Matthieu said. 'I quite agree.' He opened the door and the two men shook hands again. 'I wish you well, Mr Robinson,' he said. 'I really do. But remember, society's opinion of you is as nothing compared to your own self-respect. When you do get to Canada, I urge you to be yourselves. And enjoy life as yourselves. Otherwise, what's the point in living at all?'

'I assure you, Matthieu,' he replied with a broad smile, 'we intend to do just that. Our life is only about to begin. We have wonderful times ahead.'

Ethel LeNeve stepped over a coil of loose rope and walked around a lifeboat to a secluded area that she had discovered a few days before; in her mind, she was neither herself nor Edmund now, but Dr James Middleton, the persona she had adopted in order to buy the poison in the first place. Looking around nervously, she made sure that no one was watching; from where she was standing she could neither see any other passenger nor could she be observed.

She held the hatbox out in front of her and shook it cautiously. Cora Crippen's head, carefully wrapped in layers of newspaper, moved only slightly within. Her hands trembled slightly as she held it over the water. It had been a last-minute decision on her part not to chop up the head and bury it with the rest of the hideous body, but she had believed that if Cora was ever discovered, then the fact that her head was missing might prevent them from identifying her with any certainty. Of course, there was no way she could hide it in London, and she didn't trust the Thames not to wash it back to shore; and so it had come to Antwerp with her. She decided that it was best buried at sea, in the dark waters of the Atlantic Ocean where it would sink to the bottom and never come to light again.

She forced her hands apart and with a muffled cry she let the box fall, gasping as it hit the waves below and rested there for a moment, bobbing along, before slowly sinking under the surface and disappearing from sight.

'May God forgive me,' Ethel whispered, averting her eyes from the ocean beneath her and looking up at the sky, as if pleading with the heavens themselves. 'But love makes us do the most unforgivable things.'

Inspector Walter Dew stood at the bow of the *Laurentic* and stared at the scene before him in amazement. His mouth hung open as he shook his head; he could feel his heart beat faster inside his chest as he wondered what it was he had started. In front of him, appearing in the distance in the port of Quebec were crowds of people, all cheering loudly, their voices rising together and drifting across the water towards him. They were gathered together in their thousands, as far away as he could see, the brightness of their clothing making a rainbow of colour across the harbour.

'This is too much,' he said, looking at Captain Taylor in dismay. 'How can there be so many people here?'

'Well, you're a celebrity now, Inspector,' the captain replied, grinning at him. 'So am I, perhaps,' he added hopefully.

'But I haven't *done* anything yet.'

'It doesn't matter. It's what you're *going* to do that counts. You're going to capture the most evil criminal mastermind who has ever walked the face of the earth.'

Dew raised an eyebrow. 'I hardly think he warrants that description, Captain,' he said.

'As good as. Wife-killer. Cannibal.'

'Oh, for heaven's sake,' Dew said, frustrated. 'Who starts these rumours, anyway? Dr Crippen is *not* a cannibal. The idea is preposterous.'

'Oh no? Then what did he do with the head?'

'The head is missing, so everyone assumes he ate it,' Dew said in a flat tone. 'That's wonderful logic. I admire your detective work there, Captain.'

'I'm only saying what I've heard,' he replied, ignoring the sarcasm. 'Pretending it isn't so doesn't make it not so.'

Dew sighed. He found his emotions torn asunder as the ship pulled in to the harbour and he was forced to wave to the crowds, who were cheering him relentlessly. One part of him was enjoying the attention very much; he worked hard as a Scotland Yard inspector – he'd worked hard all his life – and had solved some interesting and worthwhile cases, but as yet he had to receive any public recognition for his efforts. Now, here was something special: a once-in-a-lifetime crime, in which the killer had so caught the public imagination that the man who captured him would be hailed a hero and would suddenly become the most famous policeman in the world.

'I'm not the true hero,' he admitted to Captain Taylor as they made their way down the gangplank to the waiting police vehicle, the crowds held apart on both sides by a file of Canadian police officers. 'That honour should really go to Captain Kendall.'

'Of the *Montrose*?' Taylor asked, surprised, smiling widely as he waved to the throng, despite his irritation that Dew should say such a thing. 'Why, for heaven's sake? What has he got to do with anything?' He was forced to shout in order to be heard.

'Well, Captain Kendall was the one who realized that Crippen and Ethel LeNeve were present, in disguise, on board his ship. It isn't everyone who would have made the connection. If he hadn't contacted us, there's no way I would have tracked him down this far away. He would have arrived in Canada safely and disappeared for ever. We never would have caught him. All I've done is get on a boat and wait for another to arrive. Not so heroic really, when you think about it.'

'Nonsense,' said Taylor, unwilling to allow the captain of another vessel to claim any of the credit. 'We are the ones who gave chase. We are the ones who risked life and limb in our pursuit of the madman. You and I, Inspector. And if I hadn't pushed the Laurentic to her full capacity, why, they might have got here first and he would have escaped. I wouldn't like to suggest that I should be considered a hero, but there are those who will.'

'With all these crowds here?' Dew asked sceptically, ignoring the other man's bravado. 'I don't think he could have escaped somehow. He would have been arrested immediately.'

After disembarking and allowing his picture to be taken by the hordes of newspaper photographers gathered at the port, Inspector Dew was escorted to the headquarters of the Québécois police force, where he was introduced to Inspector Alphonse Caroux, his opposite number, who had been tracking both ships ever since the chase began.

'You made good time, Inspector,' Caroux said, looking him up and down with interest. He had spent the past week waiting to see what the famous Walter Dew looked like. Very English, he decided. Overweight and pasty. 'We weren't sure at first whether you would manage to get here in time or not. Of course, we would have arrested this Crippen fellow ourselves if you hadn't.'

'No need now,' said Dew, becoming suddenly aware how everyone else wanted to take the credit for this capture. 'Although I do need to get in touch with Captain Kendall as soon as possible. How far away is he now?'

Caroux consulted a file on his desk and ran a finger along a line of numbers. 'Less than twenty-four hours,' he said. 'It's four o'clock in the afternoon now. The *Montrose* will arrive by three tomorrow.'

'Right,' said Dew. 'Well then, I need to send a telegraph to Captain Kendall immediately.'

'Of course.'

'Tell him to come to a full stop at noon tomorrow, three hours before he reaches Quebec.'

'A full stop?' Caroux asked suspiciously.

'I'm going to sail out to the vessel myself and arrest Crippen before he arrives in Canada. I'll need a boat and sailor to take me there.'

Inspector Caroux frowned. 'That's not a good idea,' he said. 'I've already alerted some of our newspapers. The photographers will be returning here tomorrow afternoon. They will want to capture the moment. It's best you arrest him on Canadian soil.'

'This is not a free-for-all, Inspector,' Dew said irritably. 'And the poor man does not need to be involved in some sort of media circus, no matter what he's done. No, I will sail out to the *Montrose* and arrest him, and then the ship can continue on for Canada. After that, he will be immediately transferred to your prison here until the 3rd of August when, I believe, the next crossing to England will take place.'

Disappointed, but in no position to get his own way, Caroux nodded and wrote out Dew's instructions on a piece of paper, before handing it to one of his officers to transmit.

'Don't worry, Inspector,' Dew said, aware of the other man's disappointment. 'The photographers will get their pictures. Just tell them to be ready when we lead Dr Crippen in handcuffs off the boat tomorrow afternoon. That's their front-page story.'

'You've met him before, haven't you?' Caroux asked. 'This *Dr* Crippen.' He emphasized the title, as if he did not believe it for a moment.

'Twice,' Dew admitted.

'But you didn't arrest him then?'

'No, I didn't believe he'd committed any crime.'

'Really. But it was you who discovered the body of his wife, was it not?'

Dew sighed. 'I went back to tie up a few loose ends at his home and discovered that Dr Crippen and Miss LeNeve had fled. So I searched it. That's when I found her. In truth, he would have got away with his crime if he hadn't run off. He must have thought that I knew something.'

'But you didn't.'

'No,' he admitted without embarrassment. 'I didn't suspect a thing.'

'Well, don't forget to tell him that,' Caroux said, laughing. 'He'll die laughing, the poor fool. How did you find him anyway?'

'Find him?'

'His character. What did you think of him when you met him?'

Inspector Dew thought about this. Despite all the questions he had answered about Dr Crippen since discovering the messy remains of Cora Crippen, no one had ever asked him for his own personal opinion concerning the man's character. Not his superiors at Scotland Yard, not the news reporters, and not the inquisitive passengers on board the *Laurentic*. All any of them wanted was the gruesome details, the stuff of nightmares. 'I found him a very pleasant, mild-mannered man,' he said. 'Educated, friendly and polite. In all honesty, I would have said that he couldn't hurt a fly.'

18

Life After Cora

London – Paris – Antwerp: 1 February – 20 July 1910

Hawley slept late the morning after the disastrous card evening with Mr and Mrs Smythson, but he did not wake up in his own bed.

After Cora's attack of hysterics when she had thrown him out of the house, he had wandered the streets for an hour, not knowing what to do or where to go, afraid to go home in case there was more violence to follow. A light drizzle was falling in the streets but he did not seem to notice it, despite the fact that she had evicted him from their home without a coat, hat or an umbrella to keep him dry. He walked the streets and lanes of west London, ignoring the tramps, the prostitutes and the flower girls packing up their wares for the night. He avoided the public houses as he did not trust himself with alcohol. Eventually, without planning it as such, his feet brought him to the home of Ethel LeNeve and he found himself ringing her doorbell at one o'clock in the morning. It took a few minutes before a light came on in the hallway, but finally she opened the door a little way, wearing her dressing gown and clutching it

433

tightly to her neck as she peered out to see who could be calling this late at night.

'Hawley,' she said, astonished to see him there and opening the door a little wider. 'What on earth are you doing here?'

'I'm sorry,' he replied in a low voice, only now realizing what the time was and considering what he was doing. 'I shouldn't have come at this hour. I've woken you up.'

'It's fine, I wasn't asleep yet. But what's happened? You're soaked through. Come in, come in.' She opened the door fully now and stepped out of the way as he trooped in slowly, his head bowed, his entire body weakened by embarrassment and humiliation. 'Look at you,' she muttered, shaking her head. 'Come upstairs. Quickly, before we wake up any of the neighbours.'

He followed her up the stairs to the top floor of the house, which she had inherited upon the deaths of her parents, barely noticing anything there, but collapsing into an armchair and covering his face with his hand. He could feel tears of self-pity getting ready to pour from his eyes and did not want her to see them.

Her home consisted of four small rooms and a hall-way, each one neatly arranged with not an object out of place, a bedroom, a kitchen, a bathroom and a cosy living room in which they sat now.

'I'm very sorry,' he repeated. 'Waking you up at this hour. It's unforgivable. But I couldn't think of anywhere else to go. You're about the only friend I have left in the world.'

'Hawley, I told you that you could come here at any time. And I meant it. We *are* friends, so stop apologizing and tell me what's happened. But let me get you a towel first and put some water on for tea. You'll catch your death, walking around the city at this time of night without any coat on.'

He nodded, happy to let her mother him, and she disappeared into the bedroom for a few moments while he began to take a little more notice of his surroundings. She must have had a fire lit earlier in the evening, for the coals were still glowing and giving off some heat and she had placed the fireguard in front of it before retiring. Above the mantelpiece was a picture of a bearded man with dark eyes standing beside a terrified woman with piled-up hair; they looked as if each was preparing to kill the other. He assumed these were Ethel's late parents, of whom she had few good things to say. Indeed, the only compliment he had ever heard her pay them was her suggestion that they had both had the decency to die while she was still young enough to enjoy a life of her own. On the shelves some porcelain teapots and decorative plates were scattered, family heirlooms that had been passed down to her following their deaths. Feeling the chill now, shivering in his chair, he rubbed his hands together and held them in front of the smouldering fire. When Ethel returned, she brought with her a tray with a teapot and two cups, as well as a towel which he used to dry his hair.

'It's ridiculous, really,' he began, sipping his tea. 'I don't know why I put up with it. The woman must be demented to behave the way she does.'

'What did she do this time?'

He sighed. 'She invited some of her friends around for the evening. Two people whom I don't very much care for myself and who I know care little for me either. The woman is part of Cora's Music Hall Ladies' Guild.'

'Her what?'

'A society she attends which she believes offers her an extra social standing. A group of ladies who gather together and attend concerts and afterwards organize evenings where they sit and discuss the music, drinking tea together.'

'Sounds frightfully boring,' Ethel commented.

'I'm sure it is,' he said. 'But she's always believed that she was meant for better things than I can offer her, and

435

somehow these people make her feel important. They're rich, for one thing. And some of them are titled, which she assumes means they're better than her. Anyway, things haven't been going well there recently. I think there might have been some sort of scene when she had too much to drink, and the implication tonight was that she might not be a member for very much longer.'

'Oh dear,' said Ethel, delighted to hear that. 'That must have annoyed her.'

'If she had any dignity,' said Hawley, clenching his fist in anger, 'she would simply have turned the other cheek and let the matter drop. She shouldn't let these people know they can get to her. I mean, who are they anyway? Just a bunch of ill-educated harpies who've managed to snare idiot husbands with an inheritance and a house in the country. But she doesn't see them like that, of course. Instead, she just grew angrier and angrier, and then a full-scale altercation took place. Before any of us knew what was happening, she was insulting Louise Smythson and her husband, and they were storming out of the house. A few minutes later, she threw me out too.'

'And what had you done?' she asked.

'Nothing in particular,' he explained, almost laughing at the absurdity of it. 'I'm just the easy target for whenever she flies into one of her tempers. She grabbed me by the ear, opened the door and flung me out.'

'As if you were a child.'

'My back feels quite sore, actually,' he said. 'I fell down the steps. There's a twinge.'

Ethel shook her head and felt the anger building inside her. She had never met a more gentle, thoughtful human being than Hawley Harvey Crippen. Or a more hideous hound from hell than his wife Cora. She could not understand how anyone could treat their spouse with such inhumanity.

'I'm sorry, Hawley,' she said, unable to contain her

feelings any longer. 'I hate to say it, but that woman is a demon. You have no business staying with her.'

'I know, I know,' he sighed, close to tears. 'But . . .' He struggled to find the words, knowing what he wanted to say but ashamed to admit it. 'The truth is, Ethel, that she scares me.'

'She *what*?' she asked incredulously

'She scares me. I know it sounds ridiculous but it's the truth. Her tempers, her anger, everything about her. I don't believe I am naturally a weak human being, but there is something about Cora Crippen that reduces me to nothing. I simply do not have any strength around her. And I can't help but feel that one day her violence will get entirely out of control.'

Ethel nodded. It was too bad. What he predicted she had often foreseen herself. She had witnessed her friend arriving at work, bruised and battered, one time too many; on the rare occasions when he arrived late, she always feared the worst. Tears were streaming down Hawley's face now and she reached out and put an arm around him. 'Hawley,' she whispered, kissing his cheek, 'you don't have to stay with her, you know.'

'I can't leave her though. She would never allow it,' he said with a hollow laugh. 'If only *she'd* leave,' he added, between sobs.

Ethel reached out and dried his cheeks with her hand. He turned to face her and they kissed.

'I can't go back to her,' he muttered. 'And yet I have to. I have no choice.'

'But not tonight,' she said quietly, kissing him again. 'You don't have to go back tonight.'

'I'd be risking my life if I went back tonight,' he admitted, smiling wanly at the absurdity of the situation.

'Then you must stay here,' she said determinedly. He pulled away from her and looked at her nervously. 'You must stay with me.'

'I can't,' he said. 'It's wrong to impose upon you.'

'Hawley,' she said, holding his hand tightly and making her meaning clear, 'I want you to stay. *With me.*'

He swallowed nervously and nodded. 'Are you sure?' he asked.

'More sure than I've ever been about anything,' she said truthfully. 'You should never go back to her. You deserve better than her. I would never treat you the way she does. You know that. I would value you. Take care of you.'

Hawley grimaced. 'Why couldn't I have met you years ago?' he asked bitterly. 'Why did I ever have to get involved with Cora in the first place?'

Ethel reached across and took the cup from his hand and placed it on the table. Standing up, she held out her hand for him and he took it, following her into the bedroom, where slowly and quietly, they made love for the first time. Hawley was surprised by her body, which was quite the opposite of Cora's. Ethel was small and slim-hipped, with tiny breasts and an almost boyish figure; Cora, on the other hand, had developed into an overweight, heavy-set woman whose physical allure had all but died for him long ago. Big-breasted and tartily attractive, she could still turn heads in the street, but not his. Lying in bed beside Ethel, he was moved to reach across and run his hand along her smooth body time and time again. Finally, exhausted by the fighting with his wife, his wandering around the streets of London and his romantic evening with Ethel, he rolled over and fell into a deep sleep, breathing heavily, his dreams filled with images of what life would be like if Cora Crippen was no longer a part of it.

Ethel had never made love to a man before that night, nor had she ever slept beside one, and she was intrigued by the sounds of breathing he made as he slept. She was wide awake now and with only one thing on her mind. From the moment he had arrived at her home in tears, she had decided that it was time to see her plan through and she was simply waiting for this moment to arrive, when he was asleep and she could escape without his noticing.

She crept out of bed and dressed quickly, opening the wardrobe to retrieve the man's overcoat and hat she had purchased before visiting Lewis & Burrow's Pharmacy in Oxford Street to buy the bottle of hydro bromide of hyoscine, a prescription she had written for herself on a pad which was kept locked in a drawer at the pharmacy. No one should be allowed to treat another human being like this, she thought to herself as justification for her actions. That woman stands between Hawley and my happiness; it's as simple as that.

She closed the door of the bedroom gently and went to the bathroom, where she had been storing the bottle in a medicine chest. Placing it in her pocket, she retrieved the fake moustache and attached it to her upper lip, covering up the scar she had received when her mother had beaten her when she was only a child, her ring splitting the lip open, a wound which had never properly healed. She looked at her reflection in the mirror and couldn't help but smile; she really did make quite a convincing man.

It didn't take her long to reach Hilldrop Crescent and she tried to remove herself mentally from the proceedings as she climbed the steps to Cora's room, worried that if she thought about it at all she would lose confidence and change her mind. Her only moment of panic occurred when her victim sat up in bed, waking slowly, and squinted at her, calling out Hawley's name. That had been the moment of no return, but fortunately the woman had immediately drunk the poisoned water and death had come quickly. After that, Ethel had carried her downstairs and begun her dismemberment in the cellar. She wrapped the head in sheets of newspaper and put it in a box which she found in Cora's bedroom.

Before leaving, she reached into the inner pocket of her coat and took out the letter she had written a week before for just such an occasion as this, propping it up against a salt cellar in the middle of the living-room table. Checking that she had not forgotten anything, she left the house and returned home, hiding her disguise in a hallway cupboard and placing the hatbox on top of her wardrobe before removing her clothes and climbing back into bed with Hawley as the sun rose. To her surprise, the sheets were far from warm and, when she reached out to touch Hawley's shoulder, it was cold too.

When he awoke, it was past nine o'clock in the morning, and for a moment he didn't know where he was. Slowly, the memories of the previous night came flooding back to him and he closed his eyes again, wondering what the future held for him now. He dressed quickly and stepped into the living room, where Ethel was finishing preparing breakfast.

'Good morning,' she said in a light, breezy voice, coming over and kissing him on the cheek, delighted that their new life together was about to begin. 'Sleep well?'

'Like the dead.'

'I love you,' she said suddenly, unexpectedly, and he felt his heart skip within his chest. He could not remember when he had last heard an expression of such sentiment that he had truly believed.

'I love you too,' he replied.

They parted an hour later and Ethel agreed to open Munyon's while he went home to change. Walking towards 39 Hilldrop Crescent, there was a skip in his step. He felt like a new man, a re-energized one. The closer he got to home, however, the more his heart began to sink again. He had no idea what was awaiting him there.

He turned the key in the lock with a heavy heart but, stepping inside, he had the sudden feeling that she was not at home. Somehow, the air in the house seemed lighter to him without her presence. 'Cora?' he called out to make sure, but there was no reply. This pleased him and he stepped into the living room to check that she was not simply asleep on the couch; but she was not there either, and he decided to go upstairs for a bath. Once inside, however, his attention was drawn to the letter addressed to him on the living-room table, and he stared at it blankly for a moment before picking it up and opening it.

My dear Hawley (it began),
I have decided to leave you. I do not believe that you and I can live together any longer. I have met another man. I am sorry to tell you this way, but we are in love and he has asked me to go to America with him. We leave today. Please do not try to contact me, it would be best if we said goodbye like this. We will never speak again. I am sorry for all I have put you through. You are a kind and decent man and deserve more happiness than I could ever provide you with. Do not hesitate to seize it if it presents itself.
Yours,
Cora.

Hawley gasped and sat down, dropping the letter to the floor. 'I don't believe it,' he said out loud, staring at it in surprise and reading it again as he tried to piece together the many thoughts running through his head. At the forefront of them, however, was a feeling of utter happiness.

'Nicholas!' Mrs Louise Smythson cried, calling up the stairs to her husband, who was getting dressed in preparation for a busy morning's idleness. 'Come down here quickly! The most amusing thing has happened!'

She returned to the sofa where she had been sitting, enjoying her morning tea, and re-read the letter from start to finish in a state of increasing delight and surprise. Ever since the terrible evening at the Crippens' a few nights before, she had been torn between her desire to visit her one-time friend and tear out every hair in her head for the things she had said, and her need to remain ladylike in the face of great provocation, for if the other Smythsons ever heard about her disgracing them in public there would doubtless be trouble. However, she no longer needed to make this decision, since Cora had taken matters into her own hands.

Nicholas appeared, fumbling with his cravat, and sat down opposite his wife. 'What is it?' he asked. 'Bloody thing,' he added in a mutter, referring to the cravat. 'I don't see why I need to wear one anyway.'

'A letter,' she said, ignoring her husband's present difficulties. 'A letter from Cora Crippen.'

'An apology, I hope. I've never witnessed such rude behaviour in all my life. And I've sat in the public gallery at parliament.'

'Of sorts,' she replied. 'Listen. Let me read it to you.

'*Dear Louise* (she says),
Firstly let me apologize for my abominable behaviour on the evening you and your husband came to visit us at Hilldrop Crescent. I am clearly a sick woman and unable to control myself in public. There are those who suggest I am mad, a deranged harridan, but I reject this as too strong. Perhaps I am simply a bad human

being who finds it impossible to maintain any semblance of pleasantry towards anyone, even the most worthy. Regardless of this, I do apologize to you both. I would also like to make it clear that my husband Hawley is an innocent in this affair as the poor man has suffered under my whims and moods for longer than anyone should ever have to. It's disgraceful the way I've treated him. Really, I should be taken out and horsewhipped. But anyway, this is all going to change. My main reason for writing to you is to offer my resignation from the Music Hall Ladies' Guild, effective immediately. I have heard from a relative of mine in America, a dear old uncle who has fallen ill and has not long to live. Terribly sad. He has asked me to visit him in California and tend him in his last days. I see this as a way to make up for my terrible behaviour of recent times and I intend to go. By the time you receive this letter I will have already left for America and so will not see you again. However, rest assured that when I return to London I will make things right with you and Nicholas and behave towards my kind, thoughtful and beautifully sensitive husband Hawley in the way that I always should have. With respect and love. I hope you remain well and look forward to seeing you and Nicholas again soon.

Yours sincerely,

Cora Crippen (Mrs).'

While his wife had been reading the letter to him, Nicholas had stopped fumbling with his cravat and had taken to staring at her in amazement. He had never heard such a piece of prose before and was genuinely shocked. Looking up from the pages, Louise turned to face him with equal astonishment before they both burst into spontaneous laughter which left them both incapacitated with mirth for the best part of three minutes.

'Oh, I'll wet myself,' Louise cried eventually, reverting

to the gutter in which she had been reared as she tried to call a halt to her laughter.

'Has the woman lost all her reason?' Nicholas asked. 'Or has she been reading romance novels with the most purple prose? That has to rank as the strangest apology of all time.'

'And not just that, but her sudden conversion to the rank of dutiful wife beggars belief. What was it she called him? "Kind, thoughtful and beautifully sensitive Hawley." Do you suppose she was drunk when she wrote this?'

Nicholas shook his head and shrugged. 'Hard to tell,' he said. 'She never struck me as being the full shilling anyway. Perhaps she's finally gone over the edge. Anyway, it saves you a job.'

'Me?'

'Well, you won't have to go round there and officially expel her from your club, now will you?'

'No, I suppose not,' Louise said, growing serious now. 'It's rather odd though, isn't it? I didn't even know she had relatives in America. To go so quickly, too. She's never struck me as the Florence Nightingale sort. And all this self-condemning business. It's so unlike her.'

'Well, if you ask me, it's for the best,' he said, standing up and checking his cravat in the mirror. 'Right,' he added, pleased that the difficult act of dressing was finally behind him. 'That's me ready for the day. Now, if you want me, I'll be in the study reading the newspaper.'

'All right, my dear,' she said distractedly as he left the room. She sat down and read the letter through one more time, on this occasion with less hilarity than before. Despite her newly realized contempt for Cora Crippen, she could not help but think that this was an odd situation. Very few people in her experience ever behaved entirely out of character, and every line of this note appeared to be exactly that. While it was her custom to dispose of correspondence after she had dealt with it, she resolved on this occasion to keep the letter in her possession for the time being.

20 FEBRUARY

Mrs Margaret Nash never had and never would understand Shakespeare, while her husband Andrew found the theatre a terrific bore. But Señor Eduardo Del Poco, the head of the Mexican firm that was providing much of the labour for his company's work in that country, considered himself something of a literary man and had specifically asked to be taken to see a Shakespeare production while on holiday in London. To this end, Andrew had acquired four tickets to see *A Midsummer Night's Dream* for his wife and himself, along with Señor Del Poco and his travelling companion, an eighteen-year-old muscle-bound youth with a pencil-thin moustache who was known only as Ramon. The play was being performed at the Garrick Theatre and the Nashes had sat through the first three acts with increasing levels of boredom, Margaret at one point amusing herself by trying to recall place names in England beginning with each of the letters of the alphabet. She had got as far as Newcastle before getting stuck on 'O'. When the curtain finally fell for the interval, Andrew Nash breathed a sigh of relief and looked forward to visiting the bar.

'Wonderful stuff, eh?' he said, clapping Señor Del Poco on the back heartily and pushing him out to the aisle. 'Margaret and I don't get to the theatre often enough. About time we started, though. I enjoyed that very much. Always been a big Shakespeare fan, of course. *The Merchant of Verona*, *Richard IV*, *The Tragedy of Terrors*, wonderful plays, every one. But you know, if we hurry, we could just make it to the Savoy in time for dinner.'

'But it is only an intermission,' said Señor Del Poco,

narrowing his eyes and reading him for the illiterate fool he was. 'There are another two acts to come yet.'

'Of course there are,' Andrew replied after a moment, his heart sinking. 'I was just testing you. No need for food with such wonderful entertainment taking place before us. Long, are they, these other two acts?'

'Perhaps we should get a drink during the interval, Andrew,' Margaret Nash suggested, ignoring her husband's *faux pas*. 'There's a bar upstairs. Ramon looks as if he's about to die of thirst.'

'Ignore him,' said Señor Del Poco, looking the boy up and down with a mixture of lust and contempt. 'He is worth less than the dust which clings to the under soles of the lizards which feed on the flies of the Sierra Madre mountains.'

'Right,' said Andrew cheerfully. 'Nothing for him, then. But you'll take a whisky with me, surely?'

'Of course. My mouth feels like a leaf which has been blown from sand dune to sand dune across the Sahara Desert for thousands of years, always in sight of an oasis but never allowed to land on one, due to the cruelty of the Sirocco winds.'

'Bit thirsty myself, old man,' Andrew replied.

The four companions made their way to the bar, all chatting amiably enough except young Ramon, who possessed only two words in English. (Señor Del Poco had not brought him to London for his conversational skills.)

'Two whiskies and a sherry, barman,' said Andrew, propping up the bar and looking around the room distractedly. He didn't have an awful lot of time for the kind of people who visited the theatre. They seemed a terribly effete lot to him, and there was nothing he could stand less than an effeminate man. He himself had made his money in construction, which he considered to be a real man's occupation, good, honest work that built muscles and bank accounts. The building work which his firm was undertaking in Mexico had been going on for eighteen months now and he had almost doubled his fortune in that time. A sixth of his earned income from that investment as a matter of course went to Señor Del Poco, who had secured the services of the Mexican peasants at a fraction of their true worth while he himself spent his money on foreign holidays and paid companions such as the two-worded Ramon.

'Andrew, look!' said Margaret Nash, tapping his arm as her eye was caught by something across the room. 'Look over there.'

'What?' he asked as the three of them turned to look in the direction she was indicating. 'What is it?'

'That's Dr Crippen, isn't it?' she said.

'Dr who?'

'Crippen. Oh, you remember him. We spent that awful evening at his house, some time ago. With Nicholas and Louise. His wife kept arguing with him in public.'

'A wife who argues with her husband should be taken out and strung up at the top of the city while the people throw the stones at her and make her curse the day her father climbed on top of her horse of a mother,' Eduardo suggested. 'She should be made an example of.'

'Oh yes. Crippen,' Andrew said, recalling him only slightly. 'Well, what of it? Why are you staring at him?' he asked irritably, not happy that his discourse on the problems of modern Britain had been interrupted by his wife.

'It's not him I'm staring at,' she replied defensively, turning to them and stepping forward at the same time to make their group seem more conspiratorial. 'It's who he's with. His wife left him, you see. Apparently she went to tend a sick relative in America, but Louise Smythson and I think there's more to it than that. Now, here he is at the theatre with another woman.'

'In my country, a man can have the many women,'

said Señor Del Poco with an air of triumph. 'They are as plenteous as the stars in the sky.' In truth, it had been many years since he had laid a finger on a woman, but he was not about to admit that. 'There is only one thing more important to a Mexican man than women. Money. Because with money you can buy anything.'

'It's a disgrace,' said Margaret, sneaking another look. 'He's escorting that woman who was at the dinner that night. I can't remember her name but it was something common. She's an ugly little thing, too. With that hideous scar on her lip. Look at her, all dressed up as if she's somebody. And his wife doing such a wonderfully charitable act. It's disgraceful. Do you think I should go over and say something?'

'No, leave him alone,' said Andrew. 'He's a frightful bore anyway if I remember correctly.'

She waited for as long as she could, but eventually her anger got the better of her and, despite Andrew's urging her to leave well alone, she excused herself from the three men and walked quickly over to the corner of the room where Hawley and Ethel were chatting and standing close together, his hand affectionately holding her elbow.

'Dr Crippen?' she said, standing beside them and poking her neck forward like a turkey. 'It is you, isn't it?'

He looked at her, a little dazed, and his smile faded. 'Yes,' he said.

'It's Margaret Nash,' she said. 'My husband and I spent a lovely evening in your home some time ago.'

Hawley nodded and waited a few moments, before realizing that he had no choice but to respond. 'I remember,' he said. 'How are you?'

'Very well,' she said. 'Andrew and I do love the theatre so. We come as often as we can. Are you a regular theatregoer?'

'Not really,' he replied, looking towards the auditorium. 'Anyway, we must get back to our seats.'

'Oh, do wait a moment,' she said, blocking his way and turning to look at Ethel. 'Hello,' she said, adopting a false smile. 'We've met before, haven't we?'

'I don't think so,' said Ethel.

'Oh yes, of course we have. I remember your face. I remember that scar very well. It's very distinctive.'

'Miss LeNeve is a colleague of mine,' said Hawley brusquely. 'Now we really must get back to our seats.'

'And such a beautiful necklace,' Margaret said, reaching out and taking a tight hold of the blue sapphire pendant which hung around Ethel's neck. Holding it any tighter would have choked her. 'But I've seen it before, haven't I?'

'I doubt it,' said Hawley, desperately trying to get away from her.

'Of course I have. It's Cora's. As are those beautiful ear-rings you're wearing. How kind of her to let you wear them while she's away. So typical of her good nature.'

She stared at Ethel with a frozen smile, her upper teeth jutting out slightly above her lower lip, while Ethel stared back, refusing to admit anything. 'It was kind, wasn't it?' she said. 'She's a very charitable woman.'

'Indeed,' said Margaret, flicking open her fan.

'Goodbye then,' Hawley said abruptly, pushing past her and taking Ethel by the hand to lead her back to their seats.

Margaret Nash watched them for a few moments, before returning to her party, seething with rage.

'It's infamous,' she announced, interrupting their conversation. The three men turned to look at her. 'The nerve of the woman.'

'What's she done?' Andrew asked, surprised to see his wife's face growing so red. It had been a long time since her passions had been raised to such a pitch.

'That little trollop is parading around on Hawley Crippen's arm, wearing his wife's jewellery – which, if you ask me, is more than a little strange, because I don't know any woman who would go away for any period of time and leave her finest jewellery behind.'

'I wouldn't get involved if I was you,' said Andrew, not particularly interested in the comings and goings of people who did not affect him directly. 'It's none of our business.'

'But I'm already involved, Andrew. Cora Crippen's my friend. No, first thing tomorrow morning, I'll get to the bottom of the matter, I promise you that.'

The bell rang to announce the imminent start of the next act of the play and they trooped back inside, only one of the four with any sense of excitement. Before the lights went down, however, Margaret Nash looked around, trying to see where Dr Crippen and Miss LeNeve were seated, but she could not spot them anywhere. She did, however, notice two empty seats, some rows ahead of her, which she was sure had been occupied before the interval.

30 MARCH

They decided to take a brief holiday together and they spent four days in Paris, their first opportunity to put their old lives behind them and to look forward to a happier future. They stayed in a hotel near the Arc de Triomphe and the receptionist did not bat an eyelid when Ethel announced themselves with different surnames.

'That's the French,' Ethel said happily. 'They don't care about such things. Only the English couch their hypocrisy with such indignation.'

Hawley wasn't so sure; he had tried to persuade her to call herself Ethel Crippen for the duration of their trip, as he still held fast to the idea that they would be shunned by anyone who discovered the truth; but she refused, stating that she would never call herself by that name until it was legally true.

'But it could be a long time before Cora gives me a divorce,' he pointed out. 'For one thing, I have to track her down first.'

'Then I will be Ethel LeNeve until then,' she said. 'It has been a good enough name for me for the last twenty-five years, it will suffice until we can eventually marry.' She had not yet worked out how she would surmount this obstacle; after all, there was little chance of a dead woman being able to sign any divorce papers, but naturally there was no way she could tell Hawley the truth about what she had done.

They spent the next few days in sightseeing. Their first trip was to the Eiffel Tower, which had been constructed only a few years before and which they had read about in the newspapers. Standing underneath it and staring upwards, Hawley was struck by a moment of dizziness and had to sit on the ground with his head between his knees, a position of weakness which embarrassed him. They visited the churches of Notre Dame and Sacré Coeur, lying on the grass in front of the latter in the spring sunshine for hours. Children ran up and down the lawn while old people struggled with the steps leading up to the church. Ethel had brought a picnic lunch with her and they sat eating it, feeling far removed from the violence they had both known in London. Some distance away from them, an old man sat on a bench with a large bag of breadcrumbs. He sat as still as a statue, sprinkling breadcrumbs on his shoulders, head and knees and allowing the pigeons to congregate around him, dining off his body. He never blinked and seemed oblivious to the amused glances of the other visitors.

'Hawley,' Ethel said as they sat there, after she had considered this for some time and had formulated her argument in her head so that it would not seem too suspicious, 'I've had an idea.'

'Oh yes.'

'It's about Cora.'

He groaned. 'We're having such a lovely afternoon,' he said. 'Do we have to talk about her?'

'It's important,' she said. 'It has to do with what you were saying the other day about divorcing her.'

Hawley sighed and put his sandwich back in the bag. 'Go on,' he said.

'It occurred to me that it will be very difficult to find Cora in America. After all, she didn't tell you the name of the man she ran off with, did she?'

'No.'

'And you have no idea who he was?'

He shook his head. 'I was aware of some of her infidelities over the years,' he admitted, 'and some of the men she associated with. But this one came as a bit of a surprise. I didn't know she was seeing anyone. In fact, I thought that a lot of her bad temper at that time was because she was *not* involved in any infidelity.'

'Which makes it all the more difficult,' she said. 'She may not even be in California any more, if that was where she was really going.'

'What are you trying to say, Ethel?'

'Only that if we want to have any hope of eventually marrying, it might not be with Cora's consent. After all, you know what she's like. Do you really think, if you were able to contact her and tell her that you had found happiness, that she would simply be prepared to let you go? The chances are that she would put every possible obstacle in your way.'

He nodded. 'That's true,' he said. 'But I don't see how—'

'I think we should simply carry on as if Cora did not exist any more.'

'How so?'

452

'We could say that she died.'

'Ethel!'

'I mean it, Hawley. Who, after all, do we really need to tell? Not many people. She has no family anywhere. No one will be looking for her. Her friends are few and far between. But we don't want any more incidents like the one we had with that dreadful Nash woman at the theatre last week. Any time we are seen out together, we will subject ourselves to similar rudeness. And it's not as if we can spend our entire lives hidden behind the door of 39 Hilldrop Crescent. We wouldn't want to anyway. We want to enjoy ourselves. We have lives to live.'

Hawley considered this. 'It's true that it would be easier,' he said. 'But how would we get away with it?'

'It's simple,' she said, having considered every possibility. 'We send a telegram to one of her friends, informing them that you have had word from America that Cora has died tragically, and you have decided to take a few days away in order to come to terms with the news. Obviously you're very upset about what has happened. Then, when we return, we simply avoid all of her friends anyway. We can find new ones. Trust me, I have little ambition towards joining the Music Hall Ladies' Guild.'

'But saying it is so won't make it so,' he said. 'We still couldn't marry.'

'No, but you could try to track her down in your own time and, if you can't, well, we can cross that bridge when we come to it. Either way, no one can object to our keeping company if we are both supposedly unmarried.'

He was sceptical but Ethel was insistent. She leaned across and took him by the hand.

'Do you love me, Hawley?' she asked.

'You know I do.'

'Then trust me on this. I'm sure this is the right thing to do. You will earn sympathy as the grieving widower, and in time we will be able to show ourselves in public together. Society won't care because we won't be part of it. We will simply live our own lives, you and I. Without condemnation from anyone.'

They discussed it for some time before Ethel was finally able to persuade him, and that evening they visited the Gare du Nord, where they composed a telegram to be sent to Mrs Louise Smythson in London.

Tragic news STOP, it said. Cora died in America STOP Buried with sick relative STOP Have taken time to myself in Paris to recover STOP A loss to us all STOP Hawley Crippen (Dr).

'Perfect,' Ethel said, paying the few francs from her own purse that it cost to send.

'I hope so.'

'Trust me, Hawley. I know what's for the best. Those friends of hers can't stand her anyway. They'll pretend to feel devastated by their loss, then they'll forget about her, and us, and move on with their lives.'

Unfortunately for Ethel, Louise Smythson was a woman possessed of a particularly suspicious mind. She was shocked to receive the telegram, even though she had no intention of further contact with Cora following her disgraceful behaviour a couple of months earlier. Immediately, however, she discussed the matter with her friend Mrs Margaret Nash, who informed her about her chance meeting with Hawley and Ethel at the interval of *A Midsummer Night's Dream* and the incident with the jewellery. Being the kind of woman who thinks badly of everyone until she is proven otherwise, she decided she did not believe Hawley's telegram for a moment, and her vivid imagination told her that some harm had come to her one-time friend.

Instantly, she set aside her enmity and decided that (for the time being) they were still fast friends and she planned a visit to Scotland Yard the next day, where she first met Walter Dew and announced her concerns to the disbelieving inspector.

In the meantime, Hawley and Ethel ended their Paris sojourn and returned to London, unaware of the conspiracy theories which were being formulated in their absence.

28 MAY

She didn't have much, but what she had she brought with her to 39 Hilldrop Crescent. This included two suitcases, her collection of souvenir teapots, and a tightly secured hatbox which, she informed Hawley, contained her most private possession and was not for his eyes.

Hawley had waited several weeks before agreeing to her suggestion that she give up the rooms in the house where she had grown up and move in with him. He was concerned about what the neighbours would say and what the effect would be on Munyon's Homoeopathic Medicines if a scandal broke out.

'But she's in America, Hawley,' Ethel protested. 'With her new lover. I'm sorry to put it in such blunt terms, but there we are. She said so herself in the letter: "Do not try to contact me and we will never meet each other again." You have to take her at her word. And if she can do that, well, why can't you?'

'The old Queen may have been dead these ten years,' he said, 'but we still live in a society with Victorian values. There would be a scandal.'

'Hawley, I spend practically every night here as it is. It's not as if much would change. All I would be doing would be bringing my things to your home so I don't have to go to mine every few days to collect clean clothes.'

He sighed, but he knew that she had a point. Ever since he had received Cora's letter and had told Ethel its contents, he felt at far greater ease about their new relationship, but nevertheless it still worried him. Despite the fact that it was no secret that his marriage had been an unhappy one, he had insisted on informing her friends that she had gone to America to tend a sick relative before announcing her death; only that way, he believed, could he maintain some dignity. He had allowed her many infidelities during their marriage, but for her to leave him for another was more than he could stand.

'We can be happy now, darling,' Ethel said, coaxing him towards her point of view. 'Without her. Soon you can divorce her and we could marry.'

'I want that more than anything,' he said. 'You know that. And if you truly want to move in here and you find you have the misfortune to be trapped with an ageing curmudgeon, then who am I to stop you?'

Delighted, she moved in the next day.

For several weeks they enjoyed a harmonious time together. They maintained their positions at Munyon's, but then Ethel started leaving work several hours before Hawley in order to return home to prepare a meal. She liked the idea of playing the dutiful housewife and revelled in her new role.

He had given up his practice as a dentist a few months earlier when his patients had finally dried up, but while Cora was still living at Hilldrop Crescent he had been loath to return home to her in the early evening. Instead, he had sought out the comforts of public houses and would drink for several hours before coming back to Cora's abuse and screaming matches.

Not any more. Now he left Munyon's at six o'clock on the dot and practically ran down the streets to return home. Everything about the house seemed to have changed. Ethel opened the windows in the evening to let the air in. She kept lights blazing everywhere at all hours, even in the rooms they were not using. While working in the kitchen, she listened to music on the small gramophone he had bought her and she sang along to the records in a sweet voice (much sweeter than Cora's, who liked to think of herself as a professional singer). The centrepiece on the living-room table always contained a bunch of flowers whose fragrance hit him the moment he walked through the door. For the first time, he believed he had found true happiness.

The first sign of discord, however, came when the landlord, Mr Micklefield, called around one evening to collect the rent. Typically, he entered the house after only the quietest of knocks, surprising Hawley and Ethel, who were engaged in washing the dinner dishes and kissing at the same time.

'Dr Crippen!' he cried out in an exaggerated tone. 'Well, I never did!'

'Mr Micklefield,' Hawley said, turning around in surprise and cursing his luck. He had remembered earlier in the week that the rent would be due in a few days' time and had decided to send Ethel out on an errand at the appropriate time. However, it had completely escaped his memory in the mean time, and he was now confronted by a very angry landlord who was looking at Ethel with barely disguised indignation.

'Might I ask what is going on here?' the man asked in mock outrage, his voice becoming a little more posh as he spoke, as if this made him all the more offended. 'This woman is not Mrs Crippen.'

'Mrs Crippen is away at present,' Hawley said, glancing nervously at Ethel, who had gone quite pale.

'Is she, indeed? And while she's away, this is how you carry on, is it? For shame, Doctor. I thought better of you, I really did.'

'And might I ask who you are?' Ethel asked, recovering herself and stepping towards him, wondering how a complete stranger came to be suddenly standing in their living room, condemning them.

'You certainly might, miss,' he replied. 'My name is Joseph Micklefield, the owner of this 'ere house. And as I recall it, I rent these premises to Dr and *Mrs* Crippen, no one else.'

'Mrs Crippen is in America,' said Hawley.

'So you say.'

'Mr Micklefield, I must apologize,' he continued. 'The truth is that my wife has gone to California to tend a sick relative and I don't believe she will be back for some time.'

'And that justifies this, does it?' the other man asked. 'I'm sorry, Doctor, but I can't condone this kind of thing going on in my own house. I have a string of houses in this street, as you know, sir, and if word of this got out, well, I can't say for sure that I'd have a single tenant left at the end of it. They'd think I approve of these shenanigans.'

'Oh, come now,' Ethel said, irritated by his puritanism. 'As if anyone would care.'

'I care, thank you very much,' he said loudly, not enjoying the tone she was taking with him.

'As do I,' said Hawley, hoping to appease him. 'Miss LeNeve is simply a friend of mine, who very kindly—'

'She seems like a *very* good friend, if you ask me,' said Mr Micklefield. 'And it wasn't an act of friendship I caught you engaged in when I came in here.'

'If you would just let me explain—'

'There is no need for explanations, sir,' the landlord said, raising his hand to silence him. 'I have a list of names as long as my arm of people who want to rent my houses. I'm sorry, sir, but I'm afraid I'll have to give you your notice.'

'Surely not,' said Ethel, blanching at the idea. After all, what if the new tenants wanted to use the cellar? It was true that Hawley had not set foot down there in years, but there was no guarantee that their successors would feel the same way. They might want to use it as storage space. They would certainly be upset to find a dismembered corpse under the flags.

'I am a Christian man,' he replied, 'and my brother-in-law happens to be the Bishop of Wakefield. If news of this got to him, well, I wouldn't like to say what would happen.'

'Mr Micklefield, my wife and I have lived here for years. We've never given you any problems. Surely you can see your way clear to overlooking this little indiscretion.'

'No, sir, I'm sorry. If you check your lease, you'll see that I have the right to give you notice at any time. And so I'm doing it. Two months is the amount of time you have to find somewhere new, which gives you until, let me see . . .' He made some rapid calculations in his head. 'The end of July. And even at that I'm being very generous as this is only May. That's time enough for you to find somewhere else to live. You and your fancy piece.'

'I am no man's fancy piece,' Ethel said through gritted teeth. 'Hawley and I are in love. We intend to marry.'

'That's your concern, and you can explain it to Mrs Crippen when she returns home. It's that poor woman I feel sorry for. Acting as a nurse to a sick relative and you take advantage of it when her back's turned, and get up to all sorts. It's a disgrace is what it is.'

'Please, Mr Micklefield,' Hawley pleaded. 'We're really very—'

'I don't want to hear it,' he said, heading for the door. 'The end of July, and not a day later. And you can thank your lucky stars I'm not getting in touch with Mrs Crippen myself. Good day to you, sir.'

And with that he stormed out, leaving the two lovers staring at each other sadly. 'Well that was a bit of a to-do and no mistake,' said Hawley, considering it a little hypocritical of the landlord to take such a high moral stand when he had made several advances to Cora himself in the past.

'Why did you say she was in America?' Ethel asked, appalled. 'We're after telling her friends that she's dead.'

'I know, I know,' he said, shaking his head. 'I forgot. I can't keep up with the lies, you see. I become confused. Still, maybe it's for the best. After all, if we are to start afresh, why do it in this house?'

'Because I like this house,' said Ethel, a sick feeling beginning in the pit of her stomach as she considered the trouble which could very well lie ahead.

'And so do I, for the most part. But it also contains many unpleasant memories for me. And the truth is, Ethel, that, no matter how hard you try, it will always be more Cora's home than yours. No, I realize that was not a pleasant scene for you and I apologize for it, but we will be better off in a new home. Trust me about this. At last we will be able to put the memory of Cora Crippen behind us for ever.'

She nodded, but she was scarcely listening to him as her mind was fully focused on the problem in the cellar. She heard him say something else and she snapped out of her reverie. 'What's that?' she asked. 'What did you say?'

'I said, there was one good thing about all this,' he repeated, smiling at her. 'He forgot to collect the rent.'

8 JULY

'This,' he muttered to himself as he turned around and made for home, 'is all far from over.' Hawley Crippen made his way back from his lunch with Inspector Walter Dew, worried about the future. Initially he had been surprised when the inspector had arrived on his doorstep to enquire after Cora's whereabouts. Although

Dew had not admitted it, it was obvious to Hawley that it had been Mrs Louise Smythson who had been to see him with her ridiculous theories. Who knew what she might have suggested? However, Hawley thought he had found a kindred spirit in Inspector Dew, who was not looking for anything other than a reasonable explanation, which was why Hawley had eventually confided the truth to him: that Cora had not visited America to attend a sick relative, but had in fact left him for another man. It was humiliating, but it was what had happened. Fortunately, the inspector had appeared to overlook the original white lie and accepted his explanation and his reason for having lied.

For some reason unknown to him, however, he had told the inspector that he knew the name of the man with whom Cora had eloped. Dew had made it clear that he needed this in order to close the file on the case, which left Hawley in something of a dilemma as he neither had the man's name nor had he kept Cora's letter in which she had told him about her plans. He wondered what to do for the best and consulted Ethel on the matter that evening.

'From Scotland Yard?' she asked, swallowing nervously. 'And what did he want?'

'It seems that Louise Smythson told him that she did not believe the story of Cora dying in America. I think it had something to do with Margaret Nash seeing us at the theatre and the fact that you were wearing Cora's jewellery at the time.'

'That was a mistake,' Ethel admitted. 'I shouldn't have done that.'

'Well, what's done is done. Either way, the two women must have consulted each other and thought there was more to this story than met the eye because one of them – Louise, I suspect – went to Scotland Yard and reported it.'

Ethel thought about it and regretted the fact that she

had not been present at the interview herself. 'And how did he seem?' she asked. 'Did he believe you?'

'Up to a point. But then he needed details of who the relative was, and where he lived. It all became too complicated, so I was forced to tell him the truth in the end.'

'You did *what*?' she asked, appalled.

'It's all right. He understood perfectly. I told him that my wife had left me for another man and that I had been too embarrassed to tell our friends. And so I concocted this ridiculous story about a sick relative. It was just a white lie, to save face, but I did express regret.'

'And what did he think of that?' she asked. 'Surely that must have raised his suspicions even further.'

'On the contrary, I think it provided some sort of connection between us. Before I knew what was happening, he was taking me out to lunch. We had a most entertaining conversation, as things turned out. He struck me as quite a lonely man. I think he took rather a shine to me.'

'Oh, Hawley, you're so naïve. He's probably trying to trap you into making some sort of confession.'

'Confession?' he asked, raising one eyebrow. 'But a confession of what? I haven't done anything wrong. Neither of us have.'

'Well, you're the one who's always worried about what people will think of us. Living in sin as we do.'

'Yes, but that's not a criminal matter. It's hardly something Scotland Yard would involve themselves in. The inspector simply wanted to be reassured that there was nothing suspicious about Cora's departure. I really do think it was for the best that I was honest with him. Once you start lying, you can never escape it.'

Ethel wasn't convinced. She didn't like the way things were developing. First, there was the fact that they had to vacate 39 Hilldrop Crescent within the next month, something that was keeping her awake at nights when she considered the gruesome evidence which might be discovered in the cellar. And now there was a Scotland Yard inspector involved. This could only lead to trouble.

'Don't look so worried, my dear,' he said, surprised to be the one offering solace for once. 'We haven't done anything wrong, and I don't believe Inspector Dew thinks we have. In fact, I think we might have struck up something of a friendship.'

'Oh really, Hawley,' she said, exasperated. 'You can't be serious. You've only just met him.'

'I know, but one can tell a kindred spirit when one meets one.'

'And this is what you think he is?'

'Perhaps. Anyway, you might have a chance to meet him yourself. He's coming back in a few days.'

'What for?'

'He wants the name and address of the fellow Cora ran off with.'

Ethel blinked and looked at him as if he was mad. 'But Hawley,' she said in a steady voice as if she was dealing with a child, 'correct me if I'm wrong, but you don't actually have that.'

'Yes, I know, but—'

'Did you tell him you had it?'

'Yes.'

'Well, why did you do that, for heaven's sake?'

'I don't know,' he said, his voice rising as he grew more and more confused. 'It seemed like the right thing to do at the time. He was so casual about needing it that I just said it wouldn't be a problem and he could call around and collect it.'

Ethel sighed. 'And when you don't have it,' she said, 'what's he going to think then?'

'That I've lost it.'

'No, Hawley. He will think you lied in the first place. He will think that you lied when you said that Cora had gone to America, you lied when you said she had died there, and you lied when you said she'd run off with another man. He will start to believe that everything you've told him is a lie and that anything that awful Smythson woman tells him about us is the truth. Before you know it, he'll be poking around in our business until he traps us.'

'Traps us?' he asked. 'Traps us in what?'

She hesitated; she could not tell him the truth. 'I just don't like it,' she said. 'I've come around to your way of thinking, in fact. About our living situation. The only reason those stupid women are all talking about us is because we clearly attended that play as a couple. They're outraged by it, the hypocritical old tarts.'

'Ethel!'

'Well, it's true. And if we allow them to, they will make our lives even more miserable in London than Cora ever did. They may well have despised her towards the end, but she was still one of them. They'll do whatever they have to in order to destroy our happiness. And presumably this inspector will have to report back to them on his findings here.'

'Ethel, I really think you're exaggerating.'

She reached across and took him by the arm. 'Will you do something for me, my love?' she asked.

'Anything.'

'You must try not to see Inspector Dew again. It's perfectly possible that he won't bother to return and collect that name. Particularly if you both got on as well as you claim. He may just let the matter drop. However, if he does show up here, you must let me deal with him.'

'You?' he asked, surprised. 'Why ever would you want to do that?'

'Because I can handle people like him. Interfering people. You must let me speak to him and stay out of it yourself.'

He stared at her, surprised by her ardour and yet moved by her insistence.

'Trust me on this, Hawley, please. I know what I'm doing.'

'Well, if it means that much to you, my dear,' he said doubtfully.

'It does. More than you know.'

He waited a few moments before shrugging and nodding his head.

Several nights later, he had the opportunity to see his promise through as, walking back towards Hilldrop Crescent from work, he caught sight of Inspector Dew standing in his living room speaking to Ethel. His first thought was to go inside and welcome his new friend back to his home, perhaps invite him to stay for dinner and a leisurely drink afterwards; but then he recalled what Ethel had said and he held back, standing under a tree in the rain while he watched them talking. He stayed there for some time before leaving, looking a little disappointed with himself. When the inspector turned the corner and left the street, Hawley ran across the road and entered his house, shivering.

'Did you see him?' Ethel asked when he was inside. Hawley nodded. 'He did *seem* like a pleasant enough fellow,' she admitted, 'but it's hard to know for sure. He could be trying to catch us out.'

'And what if he is?' Hawley said. 'Let's just tell him the truth. We have nothing to hide. We'll be out of here soon anyway. It won't be much longer before we have to leave Hilldrop Crescent. Let's just move away and put this whole business behind us.'

'I was thinking the very same thing,' said Ethel.

'Really?'

'Yes.'

'Perhaps we could move to Chiswick or to Kent. Or further south if you prefer.'

Ethel smiled. 'I was thinking of somewhere a little more exotic,' she said.

'Such as?'

'Canada.'

Hawley stared at her in surprise. 'Canada?' he asked. 'Are you serious?'

'Perfectly.'

'But why? Why on earth would you want to go there?'

'Because I've lived in London all my life, Hawley, and I'm tired of it. We *both* have bad memories of this city, you know. It's not just you. We're starting a new life together. Why not go somewhere far away, where no one knows us? And if it comes to it, we can simply pretend to be married over there. Remember, there is no guarantee that you will find Cora, and if you don't then you can forget about a divorce.'

'Well, that's true, but to travel to the other side of the world—'

'Will be an adventure. Listen, I've done some investigating and we could go to Antwerp first. There's a fleet of ships that travel to Canada from there, the Canadian Pacific Line. We could take one of those and leave all our troubles behind.'

He considered it; it was not such a terrible idea. In fact the idea of leaving England, although one he had not thought of himself, rather appealed to him. 'But why Antwerp?' he asked. 'Why not just travel from Liverpool?'

'Because it will be more of an adventure,' she lied, not wanting to be on a British ship in case the inspector tracked them down. 'And we can holiday there first. We had such a wonderful time in Paris and I've always wanted to see a little more of Europe. We could sail to Paris again and this time travel slowly from there up to Belgium, before leaving for Canada. A new world. A new life for us. Oh, please say we can, Hawley. We have to leave Hilldrop Crescent anyway.'

He thought about it. She was holding on to both his hands and staring up at him pleadingly. He knew now that he could never refuse her anything; he was far too much in love for that.

'All right,' he said. 'Let's do it.'

19 JULY

They travelled through Europe for three weeks, before finally reaching Antwerp. They spent a week on a converted ship, called a 'botel', on the River Vltava in Prague and it was in that city that they first felt truly alone, without interference from others. The air was crisp and they took long walks across the Charles Bridge, over towards the Old Town, arms linked, cheeks red and noses pink from the summer sun. In the afternoons, they would sit in a café window, looking out at the Old Town Square. Ethel gazed at the Astronomical Clock with its dramatic changing of the hours; Death consults his hourglass and slowly pulls on the bell cord as Christ appears from behind; the cock crows, the hour changes, the crowds disperse into the Hall and the streets behind.

After that they moved on to Antwerp, where they spent another week waiting for the *Montrose* to set sail. On the afternoon of the 17th Ethel was walking through the streets on her own and she stopped at a small café for a cup of tea and a sandwich. She had purchased a copy of the London *Times* before entering and it lay on the table beside her while she ate her food. Like Hawley, she was not a person who typically kept up with the news, but she had found that a single woman in Europe was easily harassed if she did not make it clear that she was not interested in being seduced. A book or a newspaper was a convenient way to achieve this.

Finally she poured herself another cup of tea and opened the paper, glancing through the headlines briefly before turning to page three, where her breath was almost taken away in surprise. Across the top of the page was a picture of Hawley and another of Inspector Walter Dew. She could feel the blood drain from her face, and she set her cup down carefully, almost dropping it on the ground in shock. The headline under the photograph stated 'Body Found In London Cellar'; it was over, she realized. She had been found out. Dreading what would come next, she read the article from start to finish.

Murder most foul has been discovered in the home of a respected London doctor. On the afternoon of July 13th, Inspector Walter Dew of Scotland Yard entered 39 Hilldrop Crescent, Camden, the home of one Dr Hawley Harvey Crippen, intending to question said fellow regarding the disappearance of his wife, Cora, known to some as the popular stage entertainer Bella Elmore. Mrs Crippen had been missing for some months but it was believed she was in America, tending to a sick relative. However, suspicious of her continued absence, Mrs Louise Smythson, a close friend of Mrs Crippen, alerted Scotland Yard, who immediately launched an investigation.

Upon entering the home of Dr Crippen, Inspector Dew quickly deduced that neither he, nor his living companion, one Ethel LeNeve, were present. A brief search of the premises led him to the cellar, where the most gruesome discovery awaited him. Buried beneath the stone panels of the floor were the carved-up remains of a body, believed to be that of Mrs Crippen. The *Times* has learned that the only body part missing was her head.

'Neither Dr Crippen nor Miss LeNeve have returned to Camden and it is believed they have gone on the run,'

Inspector Dew told our reporter today. 'At present we have no confirmed details as to their whereabouts but we ask all people to be on the lookout for them both. Dr Crippen is a middle-aged man of average height, with a moustache and a forlorn expression. Miss LeNeve is in her mid-twenties and is five feet and five inches in height, with a scar above her lip.'

She read on to the end of the story, but it contained only a sensational description regarding the manner of Cora Crippen's death. The only bright spot was that no one knew where she and Hawley were and it was unlikely that they would ever be looked for in Antwerp. For the moment, she thought to herself, we're safe. All we have to do is get to Canada.

She persuaded Hawley to shave off his moustache and grow a beard in its place.

'It's the latest look,' she told him. 'Surely you've seen the European gentlemen wearing them like that.'

'No,' he admitted, 'I haven't.'

'Well, you should keep your eyes open then. Because they do.'

He relented and took out his razor.

It was Hawley's idea, however, that they behave as father and son once aboard the *Montrose*, and again this came about thanks to his puritan beliefs. She protested at first, thinking this was something of a perversion on his part, but she finally relented, realizing that it would be a useful ruse if anyone on board the ship had been reading the papers recently. He bought new outfits for them, and a wig for Ethel, and on the morning of 20 July they left their hotel for the last time and walked the short distance to the port.

'Well, there she is,' he said, staring up at the ship and reaching into his pocket for the two first-class tickets he had bought. 'Last chance to change your mind.'

'I don't want to change it,' said Ethel. 'This is the start of our future. We will be happy, won't we?'

'Of course we will,' he replied with a wide smile. 'What could possibly prevent it? We have our whole lives to look forward to now. New lives. Two people together who love each other. What more could either of us want?'

Ethel looked at him and she felt safe and happy. Her old life was behind her. They had escaped. Their suitcases were in their cabin already, one of which contained the hatbox, the contents of which Ethel was keeping for disposal later in the trip. 'I love you,' she whispered, wanting to reach up and kiss him but aware that in their current disguises that was impossible.

Hawley opened his mouth to reply, but he was prevented by a car horn sounding suddenly behind him, that of Bernard Leejik, the Dutch taxi driver who had brought Mrs Antoinette Drake and her daughter Victoria to the ship. 'These new motor cars will be the death of everyone,' he said, recovering his balance and directing his attention towards his youthful companion. 'I think someone should do something about them before we all get knocked over and killed. Don't you agree?'

'I've never driven in one. *Father*,' Edmund replied.

19

The Capture

Inspector Walter Dew awoke early on Sunday morning in the small guest house where Inspector Caroux had arranged for him to stay. He had been kept up late the night before while the landlady had put clean sheets on his bed, something of a ruse, he felt, since she had known all day that he would be staying there. During the interminable length of time it took for her to finish, he was forced to sit in the living room with the other guests, each of whom stared at him with a mixture of awe and terror, peppering him with questions about Dr Crippen. Unlike the passengers on the *Laurentic*, however, most of whom had seemed to be concerned with the method he had used to do away with his wife and the gruesome discovery in the cellar, the Canadians appeared to be obsessed with what would happen to Crippen upon his return to London.

'He'll be hanged, of course,' suggested one.

'Almost immediately,' said another.

'No need for a trial, I shouldn't think.'

'There is *always* need for a trial, madam,' said Dew, who did not much like the idea of Hawley Crippen swinging from the end of a rope, regardless of what he might have done. 'We live in a country where one is innocent until proven guilty. As, I believe, do you.'

'But Inspector, surely, when someone has committed such a hideous crime, there's no point waiting around? When you think about it, taking someone's life in such a—'

'All the more reason for us to be slow to judgement,' he replied. 'After all, murder is a capital offence which holds with it the mandatory punishment of death. If we are not sure that what we are doing is correct, then we merely reduce ourselves to the murderer's level.'

They seemed disappointed with his answer, hoping for something a little more graphic. 'Will he be shot or hanged?' asked an ancient hag with the most wrinkled skin Dew had ever observed on a human being.

'Hanged, I expect. *If* he's found guilty. But I cannot stress too much how—'

'Have you witnessed a hanging before, Inspector?'

'Several.'

'Are they very exciting?'

He shook his head. 'No,' he said. 'Not at all. They are tragic. They take place because someone has already lost his or her life, and they end with another death. They are nothing to take either pleasure or satisfaction in.' He was becoming convinced that his fellow guests had clubbed together and paid the landlady to take a long time preparing his room in order for them to quiz him some more.

'What time will you be going down to the harbour in the morning?' asked the human wrinkle again. 'No one has seen such excitement in Quebec in the longest time. We can't wait to see what happens.'

'I will not be arresting Dr Crippen on Canadian soil,' he stated firmly. 'I'm sorry to disappoint you. So the time of my departure is of little or no relevance.'

'Not arresting him here? Well, where then?'

He considered it, realizing there was nothing to be

lost by telling them; after all, the *Montrose* had received her instructions and was effectively cut off from the rest of the world until she docked. 'I will be taking a boat out to Dr Crippen's ship and arresting him on board,' he said.

'Oh no! Surely not,' they cried together, disappointed.

'I'm afraid so.'

'But you're ruining it for everyone.'

'Madam, this is not a theatrical production to be played out for the amusement of all. This is the arrest of a man on a charge of murder. I apologize if I cannot make it more entertaining, but there we are.'

'Well, it's a shame for us,' said the landlady, bustling in now, having obviously been listening from the hall-way. 'Your room's ready,' she added irritably, as if the whole thing had been too much trouble for her.

'Thank you,' he said. 'Then I will wish you all a good night.'

Despite the earliness of the hour when he arose, the same group of people was gathered in the parlour when he made his way through, the following morning. He stared at them in surprise; they appeared not to have moved since the night before, but on this occasion they did not question him but merely followed him with their eyes while he left for the police station, staring after him as if he was no better than Dr Crippen him-self.

Inspector Caroux had also risen early and was dressed in his finest uniform, aware that later in the day photographs would be taken. He had used a little wax on his moustache and tonic on his hair. The scent he gave off was overpowering and made Walter Dew take a step back in dismay, the aftershave catching in his throat and making him cough.

'Such a day we have ahead of us, Inspector,' he said. 'Can I call you Walter?'

'If you like.'

'I have arranged for a boat to take us out there at ten o'clock. The *Montrose* has already been in touch to confirm that they will be coming to a full stop.'

'To take *us* out there?' asked Dew. 'Us who?'

'Why, you and I, Walter. As the senior representatives of Scotland Yard and of the Canadian police force in Quebec, I naturally assumed that you would want—'

'No,' he said firmly, shaking his head. 'That won't be necessary. I'll go alone. Just give me a man to sail the boat and that's all I'll need.'

'But Walter!' he cried, disappointed. 'The man is a crazed killer. You don't know what you're walking into.'

'He is not a crazed killer,' Dew said sternly. 'And he's not a cannibal either before you suggest it.'

'*Mon Dieu!* I never knew that he was one.'

'Well, he isn't.'

'So why did you suggest he was?'

'He's a perfectly reasonable fellow who has perhaps made one mistake in life, that's all. I assure you, I am in no danger whatsoever over there. After all, Captain Kendall will be present together with any number of his officers that I may require. But from what little I know of Dr Crippen, I do not believe he will be any trouble.'

'I hope you're right,' said Caroux in a petulant voice, like a child who has not been given his treat. 'But if he chops you up and eats you too, you will have no one to blame but yourself.'

'I'll bear it in mind.'

Crowds saw him off as he stepped into a small twin-engined boat and was driven away from Quebec by an old sailor who seemed to be the only person with no interest whatsoever in what was taking place. If anything, he seemed irritated by the vast number of people shouting and cheering as they left the harbour, and he barely spoke to Inspector Dew as they made their way out to sea. For his part, Dew was perfectly happy to maintain a silence. He sat against the side of the boat, his arms stretched out on either side of him, enjoying the sensation of the wind blowing in his face and the smell of the sea air. A little over an hour later, the *Montrose* appeared in the distance and he sat bolt upright, his stomach starting to betray his nerves a little as the final chapter in his pursuit of Dr Hawley Harvey Crippen approached.

'Yonder,' said the sailor, pointing towards the ship, before lapsing back into silence. Finally they slowed down and pulled up alongside her. One of the officers had been assigned to watch out for their appearance, and he directed them towards the ladder which ran down one side of the ship, out of sight of any of the passengers. Thanking his guide, Inspector Dew set foot on the steps and climbed aboard.

'Inspector Dew?' said the officer, as if he could be anyone else.

'Yes, hello. I'm here to see Captain Kendall.'

'Of course, sir. Step this way, please.'

First Officer Billy Carter had informed the officers the previous night about their mysterious passengers and they had been sworn to secrecy until the arrest was made. Aware of the punishments Captain Kendall could hand out if the mood took him, they maintained their silence.

Dew was brought immediately to the captain's cabin, where he and Billy Carter were sitting, enjoying a cup of tea. This morning they were all smiles and Kendall could hardly contain his joy.

'I'll be sorry to lose you, Carter,' he said, not really meaning it but willing to be magnanimous. 'You've been a good first officer on this voyage. Kept our little secret well. I'll be mentioning it to your superiors.'

'Thank you, sir,' said Carter. 'But I expect you'll be

glad to have Mr Sorenson back. Delighted to hear the news, by the way, sir.'

'Yes, it's excellent, isn't it?' the captain said, beaming, his cheeks pink with pleasure. A wire had come through on the Marconi earlier that morning from Mr Sorenson himself, recovered and released from hospital and ready to resume his duties on the *Montrose* once she returned to Antwerp. The news had been everything that Captain Kendall had been waiting for, and he had hardly stopped marching around the ship since in order to burn off the excess energy with which his excitement was providing him.

'You are close friends, aren't you?' Carter said suspiciously, trying to learn a little more about the relationship.

'Well, he's an excellent first officer, you see,' said Kendall in a distant voice, as if he had given the matter almost no thought at all, as if the state of Mr Sorenson's health had not obsessed him since the morning they had set sail. 'Not that you weren't, of course, but we've travelled together a long time. We're like an old husband and wife. We know each other's ways so well that we're lost without the other.'

'Indeed,' said Carter, trying to suppress a smile. He was thinking how their relationship was nothing like that of a husband and wife, as he recalled his own marriage, but he stopped himself from saying anything when he considered that perhaps Kendall had a point. 'Do you have anniversaries?' he asked mischievously. 'Give each other presents? Paper for the first, silver for the tenth and so on?'

Captain Kendall raised an eyebrow suspiciously, wondering whether he was being mocked, but he was prevented from saying anything by a tap on the door. 'Come in,' he roared, and the door opened to reveal his visitor. 'And you must be Inspector Dew,' he said, standing up and shaking his hand. 'We meet at last.'

'I am,' the newcomer replied. 'Delighted to meet you, Captain.'

'This is my first officer, Mr Carter.'

'Mr Carter,' he said, nodding and shaking his hand too.

'Well, the moment of truth, eh?' said Kendall. 'Imagine if I'd been wrong all along.'

Dew laughed quickly. 'Let's hope not,' he said. 'Have you any idea how the world is waiting for this? We're all celebrities. I assure you, Captain Kendall, you'll be a hero for discovering him.'

He puffed out his chest and beamed. 'Kind of you to say so, Inspector, but I was only doing my job. Now, what's the best way to do this? They're staying in one of the first-class cabins. Calling themselves Mr John Robinson and his son Edmund. Shall we go down there?'

Inspector Dew shook his head. 'I'd rather not involve them both,' he said. 'Would it be all right to send someone to the cabin and ask Dr Crippen – Mr Robinson, I mean – to join you here in your cabin? Then, when he arrives, I can make the arrest without Miss LeNeve being present or any of the other passengers being put in danger.'

Kendall shrugged. 'As you like, Inspector,' he said. 'Now?'

'Now.'

'Mr Carter, be so kind as to ask Mr Robinson to join me here.'

'On what pretext, sir?'

'I don't know,' he said irritably. 'Make something up. Use your imagination. Just don't tell him the truth, whatever you do. And get back here with him as quickly as possible. Also, tell a few officers to keep an eye out and, after you both come in here, they can stand outside the cabin in case there's any trouble.'

'Yes, sir.' Carter stepped outside and, a bundle of

excited nerves, made his way to the first-class cabins.

'Nervous, Inspector?' Kendall asked.

'Not particularly,' he replied. 'Hopeful would be a better word.'

And despite himself he couldn't decide where that hope lay: in the idea that Mr Robinson really was Dr Crippen, or that he was actually an innocent man anyway and the truth of Cora's death had still eluded him? They waited, side by side, for Billy Carter to return.

Hawley and Ethel were busy packing their belongings when the knock came on their cabin door. They had brought only three suitcases with them on to the *Montrose* and this constituted all the worldly belongings they had decided to keep. Most of the furniture at 39 Hilldrop Crescent had been rented from the landlord, Mr Micklefield, and Hawley Crippen had never been a man much interested in possessions. Ethel had decided to leave most of her things behind; when she considered it, she realized that almost everything she owned had once belonged to her parents and she had continued to hold on to them out of mere sentimental attachment. All they needed were some clothes and their money and, fortunately, they had plenty of the latter. Hawley had been a scrupulous saver over the years and had kept much of his wealth from the eyes of Cora, while Ethel had held on to her savings as well as her inheritance. There was no question that they would be able to purchase a nice home in Canada and begin their new lives together in comfort.

'I can't believe we're almost there,' Ethel said, checking her watch as she sealed one of the suitcases. 'This voyage seems to have gone on for ever.'

'Well, thankfully we will never have to see any of these people again after today,' Hawley replied. To Ethel, he had seemed a little distant all morning, as if his mind was concentrating on something else.

'And I can become a woman again,' she said. 'Really, it was quite entertaining pretending to be Edmund Robinson, but I have had absolutely enough of him. I think I will celebrate my liberation by buying some new dresses in Quebec.'

'We will be happy there, won't we?' he asked. 'I can trust you?'

'Of course you can, Hawley. Why ever would you ask such a thing?'

He looked at her, and he realized that the moment had finally come. All this time he had waited and prayed for her to tell him the truth but his hopes had come to nothing; he loved her desperately and needed to clear the air before they reached Canada. For a long time he had considered whether it was worthwhile opening this can of worms; after all, there was always the possibility that, some time in the future, it could come between them. Was it better to feign ignorance of the truth?

'We have to be honest with each other, Ethel,' he said. 'You do understand that, don't you? From the moment we set foot on dry land we can never tell each other a lie. That's the only way our relationship can survive. And anything that's happened in the past, well, it's in the past. We don't need to refer to it again after today. But if there's anything you want to tell me, now is the time to do so.'

She stared at him in surprise, wrinkling her nose at the strange nature of his comments. She could not tell what he was getting at. 'I don't know what you're talking about, Hawley,' she said. 'I don't have any secrets from you.'

'Nor do I from you, Ethel. And I believe I know all your secrets. But somehow I would like to hear them from your own lips.'

She shivered. 'You're scaring me, Hawley,' she said, unable to catch his eye. 'What's wrong with you? Are you ill?'

'No, I'm fine,' he said, smiling and putting his arms around her. 'Just be aware that I know you love me and that I love you, and nothing can break that apart. You have done so much for me and, if it came to it, I would lay down my life for you.'

'But we are unbreakable, Hawley,' she said, confused.

He wrapped his arms tighter around her and pressed her close to his body, leaning his head down and clutching her with such force that she could scarcely breathe in his grip. Pressing his lips to her ear he whispered in a sharp, quick voice: *'I know what you did, Ethel. I know what you did to Cora.'*

It took a moment for the words to settle into her mind, and when they did her eyes opened wide and she struggled against him, trying to wrestle free from his grasp, but he held her too tightly. She could not believe what he had just said and she felt almost afraid of him, as if he, not she, was the murderer of Cora Crippen and he was now preparing to claim a second victim.

'Hawley,' she said, her voice muffled against his chest. 'Hawley, let me go.'

She kicked loose and stumbled backwards across the cabin, her face pale, her real hair slipping down from under Edmund's wig. She could hardly bear to look at his face in case he hated her, but finally her eyes moved there; he was watching her with a gentle smile. With understanding. With appreciation.

'It's all right,' he said. 'I've known all along.'

'How?' she asked, gasping. 'How did you know?'

He shrugged. 'Cora and I were married for a long time,' he said. 'And you and I worked in the pharmacy together for many years. Do you think I can't tell the difference between your handwritings?'

'I don't understand,' she said, her legs feeling weak beneath her.

'The letter, Ethel,' he said. 'The letter you wrote, supposedly from Cora, telling me that she was leaving me. I knew you'd written it. I always knew.'

'But you never said anything.'

'Because I hoped you would tell me yourself. I hoped you'd trust me enough. And now I'm telling you that you can.'

Ethel gasped. He had known all along and never said? It was incredible. 'How long?' she asked finally, sitting down on the bed to prevent herself from collapsing. 'How long have you known?'

'That first night when I stayed in your home,' he said. 'The night you killed her. I woke up while you were leaving. I could see you dressing and putting on the overcoat and hat. When you passed by the bedroom door, I saw you were wearing a false moustache. The first appearance of Master Edmund Robinson, I believe. Although a somewhat older version.'

'Hawley, don't . . .'

'I couldn't understand what you were doing, so, the moment you left, I dressed quickly and followed you, leaving the door on the latch so that I could get back in. I followed you all the way to Hilldrop Crescent and waited outside. I saw you pulling a bottle out while you were still in the street – I assume that was the poison – and I could tell that you thought there was no one around. Instantly I knew what you were planning; it was as if I could already read your mind.' He bowed his head regretfully and sat down beside her on the bed. 'I wanted to stop you,' he said, 'but at the same time I wanted you to see it through. I knew it was the only way we could be together. And I knew I could never do it myself.'

Tears were streaming down Ethel's face. 'I did it for you,' she said. 'For us.'

'I know. And I let you. I am as guilty as you are.'

'But you never said.'

481

'I hoped you'd tell me yourself. I kept up the illusion with you that Cora had left me because I was waiting for you to tell me the truth. I lied to Inspector Dew. I did everything as if I was an innocent party, but I am not. I may not have been the one who killed her, Ethel, but by God I was the happiest one to see her dead.'

'Don't you hate me?'

'How could I?'

'Because of what I've done. It's monstrous.'

Hawley laughed. '*She* was the monster,' he said, between gritted teeth. 'She deserved to die. I thought you might have guessed that I knew.'

'Never.'

'Really, Ethel,' he said, teasing her gently. 'That business with the hatbox. It was a little macabre, wasn't it? At one point I thought you were going to keep her head with us for the rest of our lives.'

Ethel stared at him and felt a chill run through her body. Although she had of course been the one to poison, dissect and bury Cora Crippen, there was a certain sinister aspect to him now that unsettled her. She had done what she had done as a crime of passion, in order to be with the man she loved. She had protected him from the truth and he had deceived her entirely, proving to be an even better liar than she was. And he had followed her own deceptions with something approaching amusement, as if the whole thing was little more than a game. She looked around, convinced that the porthole was open because the room felt as if it had been filled with ice.

'I'm not sure I understand you,' she said nervously. 'Why would you keep so quiet about it?'

'Because I love you, Ethel,' he said simply. 'And because I believe that we can be happy together. As I know you do. We are each other's only chance of happiness. And I would gladly lay down my life for you if I had to.

But I hoped that you would trust me enough to tell me what you had done. I gave you the entire duration of the voyage to be honest with me, but I knew this morning that you would keep it a secret. And I wanted no more secrets between us.'

'The day Inspector Dew came to see me,' she said. 'When you were outside under the tree. You knew then?'

'I came back inside, shivering from the rain, and had to pretend that I understood why you wanted to see him alone. In my mind, I kept thinking we only had a few days to get out of London. If you hadn't suggested going anyway, I would have. We were of the same mind all along, Ethel, only you didn't know it. We're the same, you and I. It proves how much we are supposed to be together.'

She swallowed. For the first time she felt a degree of guilt over what she had done. Taking another person's life. Her stomach churned and she felt sick at the way she had committed the act, her callousness, her cruelty, the macabre way she had disposed of the body. This is who I've become? she thought. This is what I can do for love? The walls of the cabin seemed to be closing in around her and she thought that if she stayed there for another moment in Hawley's presence she would faint away. She stood up quickly, ready to climb to the ship's deck and the fresh air, but she was stopped in her tracks by a knock on the door. Hawley looked around irritably.

'Oh, who can that be?' he muttered. 'Hello?' he called out.

'Mr Robinson, it's First Officer Carter,' came the voice from outside. 'Can I have a word, please, sir?'

'It's a little inconvenient at the moment,' he shouted. 'Can't it wait?' Looking towards Ethel, he was suddenly aware how much her face had changed. She no longer looked excited at the prospect of Canada; she looked as if she had been cheated of something. 'What's wrong?' he asked her.

'I'm afraid not, sir,' Carter called back. 'If you could just open the door.'

He sighed. 'I'd better get this,' he said to Ethel. 'Are you all right?'

She shrugged and adjusted her wig. 'I'm fine,' she said in a dead voice. 'Let's just get to Canada and work everything out there.'

He looked at her and his face filled with worry. 'I did the right thing, didn't I?' he said. 'Telling you, I mean?'

'I suppose so,' she said, not sure of anything any more.

'Mr Robinson!'

'Just coming,' he called. 'Let me see what he wants,' he said. 'We'll finish talking afterwards.'

He walked over to the door and opened it irritably. 'Yes?' he asked. 'What can I do for you?'

'Sorry to disturb you, sir. Captain Kendall needs a word.'

'Well, can't he speak to me later? My son and I are in the middle of an important conversation.'

Billy Carter looked into the cabin, where he saw Edmund Robinson standing forlornly, his cheeks growing damp with tears, looking almost unaware of his surroundings. Carter could not help but think how much he suddenly looked like a woman after all. It was obvious. The clues had been scattered everywhere, if he thought back on it. He had just never fully realized it until now because of the presentation. Everyone assumed that Edmund Robinson was a young man, therefore it must be the case.

'I'm afraid not, sir,' he said. 'If you could just come with me, please.'

Mr Robinson hesitated, staring at him impatiently for a moment, before relenting. 'I'll get my coat,' he

484

said, reaching behind the door for it. 'I won't be long, Edmund,' he said. 'We'll continue this later, yes?'

Ethel nodded and watched as he left the cabin. For the first time since she had met Hawley, she didn't know who or what to trust any more, and she wished she was a thousand miles away. 'What have I done?' she asked herself aloud. 'What have I done?'

They were stopped in the hallway by Mrs Antoinette Drake and her daughter Victoria, who looked at Mr Robinson distastefully even as they stopped to speak to the First Officer.

'Oh, good afternoon, Mr Carter,' said Mrs Drake. 'So nice to see you.'

'Mrs Drake,' he said with a quick nod, hoping to move on quickly past her.

'We must be getting pretty close to Canada by now, surely,' she said.

'A couple of hours and we'll be there. Best to get on with your packing, I'd say.'

'But we've stopped,' said Victoria with a snarl.

'What's that?' Mr Robinson asked.

'We've stopped,' she repeated. 'The boat's come to a full stop.'

'She's right,' said Mrs Drake, addressing all her comments to Billy Carter; she had still not forgiven Mr Robinson for his behaviour of a few days before, and it irritated her that he had kept out of her way since then, not even bothering to offer an apology.

'We've just slowed down,' said Carter, thinking on his feet. 'Standard practice when you're getting near the harbour.'

'We haven't slowed down,' Victoria insisted. 'We've come to a full stop. What's the sense in that?'

They stood and stared at each other for a few moments while he tried to think of a reason; fortunately this was not necessary, for at that moment the engines started up again and the boat shivered into action, cleared to continue now that Inspector Dew was safely on board. 'See?' he said, smiling. 'Just a brief stop, that's all. On our way again.'

He started to walk on, but Mrs Drake grabbed his arm. 'And where are you taking Mr Robinson?' she asked, worried that he might be about to be included in something that she was not.

'To see the captain.'

'Why?'

'I'm afraid it's a private matter, Mrs Drake,' he said. 'Nothing for you to worry about, though.'

Mr Robinson frowned; his mind had been concentrating on the conversation he had just had with Edmund; now he started to wonder why Captain Kendall wanted to see him at all. If he was true to form, the captain probably just wanted him to be near by when they approached Quebec. He had insisted on spending an increasing amount of time with Hawley during the voyage, and it had begun to grate on him as he found the captain a dull companion, obsessed with only two things: the sea and the health of some former officer about whom he couldn't stop talking.

'Well, I dare say I shall see you on deck later, Mr Carter,' she replied doubtfully, wondering what was going on that she was not being allowed to participate in.

They walked on, and Mr Robinson was aware that both Mrs Drake and Victoria were watching him suspiciously. Climbing the steps towards the deck, he noticed Martha Hayes sitting with Matthieu Zéla and he looked away quickly, not wishing to have to speak to them either. No such luck. The two men passed directly by them, and Martha turned around to speak to them.

'Isn't it exciting?' she said. 'We're only a couple of hours away from our new lives. I can't wait to step ashore in Canada.'

'Yes,' said Mr Robinson. 'We're all looking forward to it, I think.'

'Is there a problem, Mr Carter?' Matthieu asked, looking at him suspiciously. The officer seemed keen to move on and was hopping from one foot to the other as if his bladder was full.

'No problem,' he said irritably. 'Just need to get to the captain's cabin, that's all.'

'Mr Robinson, the most wonderful thing,' said Martha, taking his hand. 'Mr Zéla and I – Matthieu, I mean – well, he's invited me to stay with him and Tom for a couple of weeks in Quebec. He needs an assistant with a business venture and has given me a job. Just until I find my feet, you understand.'

'Congratulations,' said Mr Robinson. 'It seems that you've found good fortune on this voyage then, after all.'

'As have I,' said Matthieu. 'It will be pleasant having another adult around as I suspect Tom is only going to grow more and more troublesome as time goes on. I dread to think what the next year or two of his life will bring.'

'Well, that won't be anything to do with me, Matthieu,' Martha said, laughing. 'I don't intend to start acting as anyone's mother.'

'Mr Robinson, we really should get on,' Billy Carter said.

'Yes, of course. I'll see you both later.'

'Goodbye, Mr Robinson,' said Martha, turning back to watch the horizon and wait for the harbour to come into sight.

'If you ask me,' Matthieu said quietly as they walked away, 'he's been caught out at last.'

'Caught out?' she asked. 'Caught out at what?'

'Ah,' he replied. 'Perhaps now that we're almost in Quebec, it will do no harm to tell you.' She leaned forward as he began to reveal what he knew.

'Are we not going to the wheelhouse?' Mr Robinson asked, surprised when Billy Carter did not lead them in the direction of the captain's usual station.

'Not today, sir, no,' he replied. 'The captain is in his cabin.'

'He wants me to go there?' he asked, surprised. 'Look here, Mr Carter, can't you tell me what this is all about?'

'I really couldn't say, sir. But we're almost there now. If we just make our way down this flight of stairs.'

They stepped down towards the crew's quarters, but not before Mr Robinson caught sight of Tom DuMarqué skulking in a corner, watching him carefully like a vulture waiting for a body to expire before soaring down and chewing on the still warm flesh. His dark eyes met Mr Robinson's and the boy's mouth twisted into a snarl. He could see how much the boy despised him, but it was nothing compared to the anger he had felt when he saw him attacking Edmund. He ignored him and moved on.

Mr Robinson was surprised to see two strong crewmen standing outside the captain's cabin, but he did not comment on it. They parted as Billy Carter knocked at the door; there was only a brief pause before a voice from inside instructed them to enter. He opened the door and stepped inside, followed by Mr Robinson, who looked around him pleasantly.

'Captain,' he said. 'You wanted to see me.'

Captain Kendall nodded and the door closed behind him. He nodded towards a figure behind Mr Robinson's shoulder, and he turned around to see who was standing there. For a moment, the face didn't register. He knew it, of course, but it seemed so unexpected and so out of place that it took him a few seconds to remember who exactly he was looking at. When he did, he felt a sudden mixture of horror and calm, as if the worst had happened and he could finally be at peace.

'Dr Hawley Crippen,' said Inspector Dew, stepping forward and extending his hand politely, as if they were old friends. His face wore a look of utter relief that he had found his man. 'I hope you remember me. I'm Inspector Walter Dew of Scotland Yard.'

'I remember you,' he replied calmly. 'In a way, I'm glad it's all over.'

Epilogue

They were kept in separate cabins on the ship taking them back to England. Among the passengers on board was Billy Carter, released from his duties on the *Montrose* and returning home for the birth of his son, who would be born prematurely, six days after he arrived home. (The doctors and nurses thought the young man deranged, but he insisted on being present while his wife gave birth.) Although he had hoped to see Mr Robinson again – or Dr Crippen, as he was gradually learning to call him – Inspector Dew saw to it that his prisoner was not allowed on deck except for exercise periods late at night when the other passengers were asleep. Several of them had raised their concern about his presence at all, pointing out that they did not want to be eaten by London's most infamous cannibal, but he had to return for trial and there was no way of getting him there other than by sea, so they had little choice but to accept it.

The day before they arrived in Liverpool, Inspector Dew entered Dr Crippen's cabin and unlocked his handcuffs. He had brought the accused's lunch with him and had decided to join him today, for there were several things he needed to explain to him about the ordeal that lay ahead.

'Ah, Inspector,' Hawley said, pleased to see him, for he had spent most of his time alone in the cabin and was desperately in need of company. 'How nice to see you. We're dining together today, I see,' he added, noticing the two plates on the tray.

'For the second time,' Dew said, recalling the afternoon they had lunched together in London.

'Yes,' said Hawley, staring at the meagre contents of his plate with some disappointment and sensing the note of reproach in the other man's voice. 'I must confess that I was not entirely honest with you on that occasion, was I? I should apologize for that.'

'Well, you never mentioned that you'd chopped your wife up and buried her in the cellar, if that's what you mean,' Dew replied. 'Although I have to admit, you had me fooled entirely.'

'Did I? I seem to be rather good at that.'

'What astonishes me – and disappoints me about myself – is the fact that I caught you in a lie – when you said that your wife had gone to tend a sick relative in America – but that I actually believed your follow-on lie as well. It makes me feel rather foolish.'

'I wouldn't worry about it, Inspector,' he said. 'After all, from what I'm told, I seem to be something of a criminal mastermind. How could anyone have seen through me?' Despite being secluded in his cabin for the past week, the gossip of the other passengers and the reports of his activities in the newspapers had been relayed to him via a number of members of the crew, and he had developed a rather bleak sense of humour about it.

'Really?' said Dew. 'Is that how you see yourself?'

Hawley smiled; he wasn't prepared to incriminate himself any further than he already had.

They ate their food in silence for a while, before the

inspector remembered his reason for visiting.

'When we reach Liverpool,' he said, 'I expect there will be something of a crowd gathered. I don't want you to be nervous of them. I've ordered reinforcements to keep the people back and to protect you.'

'Am I really in that much danger?' he asked, almost amused by the idea.

'Not if we protect you. But feelings are running high, you must understand that. What you did seems to have captured the imagination of the public.'

'And I am a despised man.'

'Feared. Despised. Misunderstood.'

Hawley nodded; he could tell that the inspector had some sympathy for him; his use of the word 'misunderstood' gave that away.

'Then we'll take you immediately on a train back to London, where you will be housed at his Majesty's pleasure, awaiting trial.'

'And when will that be?'

'Quite soon, I expect. As early as October.'

'Good,' said Hawley. 'The sooner this business is over, the better.'

Dew stared at him, confused. 'But Dr Crippen,' he said. 'You realize that the outcome is obvious; the evidence against you is overwhelming. Not to mention the fact that you have admitted your guilt. You stand virtually no chance of being acquitted.'

'Of course I realize that.'

'And that the hangman's rope awaits you then?'

'It will be sweet relief.'

From the moment Inspector Dew had confronted him in Captain Kendall's cabin, Hawley had grown resigned to the fact of his imminent death. Although innocent of murder, he had to an extent colluded in it. His main priorities now, however, were accepting full responsibility for Cora's death, maintaining the innocence of Ethel LeNeve and keeping her alive.

'And what about Ethel?' he asked, trying not to reveal his concern on this topic. 'She will be released, of course?'

'Certainly not,' Dew snapped irritably. 'She will stand trial too. Separately, of course.'

'She will?' he asked, putting his fork down. 'But why? She is entirely innocent of any wrongdoing, I've told you that several times. She knew nothing about it.'

'So you both maintain. But that's for the court to decide.'

'But, my dear inspector. I have confessed. I admit my guilt. And I assure you that Ethel LeNeve knew nothing of what I did. Her only crime has been falling in love with me.'

Dew shrugged. 'As I have said, I am not the one who can determine her innocence or guilt. That will be up to a judge and a jury. You may maintain whatever you like, but I am not the one you have to convince.'

For his part, Walter Dew was not quite sure that what he was being told was the simple truth anyway. He had interviewed Ethel LeNeve several times in her own cabin, and he found himself confused by her. She appeared to be telling the truth when she swore how much she loved Hawley – that seemed to be her over-riding motivation – but she refused to admit any guilt when it came to the murder of Cora Crippen. Naturally, she was unaware that Hawley himself had taken full responsibility.

'Miss LeNeve backs up your story,' said Dew. 'She says that she is innocent.'

'Well, there you are,' he said, relieved.

'But if that was not the case, well then, there might be a chance for you yet. This could be seen as a crime of passion. If you were goaded into it by another, then—'

'Inspector, you are wasting your time. There is no way that I will allow Ethel to be led to her death, if that is what you are trying to get me to do. She is the only woman who ever truly loved me, you see. She is the one who saved me, who would have sacrificed all for me. How could I assist in her own death?'

'Sacrificed what, though, Dr Crippen?' Dew asked, leaning forward. 'What sacrifices did she make exactly?'

'Her home, her life, England. She was willing to leave it all behind and run away with me, bearing the badge of a scarlet woman since she did not know that Cora was actually dead. If you think I will turn against her now, you are quite wrong.'

Dew sighed; he did not know what to believe and he was glad that his responsibilities, with the exception of any evidence he had to offer, would end when he delivered his prisoner into the hands of the crown court. 'What was she like, anyway?' he asked finally, standing up. 'Your late wife, I mean. What kind of woman was she?'

'She was a demon,' Hawley replied, after giving it some thought. 'Regardless of what happens to me now, the world is a better place for her absence from it.'

'No regrets then?'

'None.'

That, Walter Dew considered, might all change soon.

Mrs Louise Smythson and Mrs Margaret Nash, along with their husbands Nicholas and Andrew, were seated in the front row of the public gallery on the afternoon of 25 October 1910, when the verdict was announced. The court was filled to capacity with lawyers and barristers, newspaper men, and as many members of the public as could be fitted inside. Outside, the streets were lined with people, all awaiting the news with great excitement. The Smythsons and the Nashes, however, had been given front-row seats because of the roles they had played in capturing the murderers in the first place. Mrs Louise Smythson herself had achieved a certain notoriety and had been interviewed by several newspapers, her photograph appearing prominently on their front pages. There was talk of a commendation by the police commissioner, the first such honour to be given to a member of the public, let alone to a woman.

'Nicholas, did I read about your brother in the newspaper this week?' Margaret Nash asked, looking across at Louise's husband. 'I'm sure I did.'

Nicholas nodded and broke into a smile. 'You did indeed, Margaret,' he replied. 'And what a headline: "Lord Smythson Scales The Matterhorn!" Never thought I'd see such a thing in print.'

'Nor did I,' said Louise bitterly. The health of her brother-in-law Martin had changed from being a cause of constant hope for her to one of disappointment. Martin's wife Elizabeth had given birth to a son a few days before and, from the moment she had informed him that he was to be a father, the once sickly Lord Smythson had begun an almost miraculous course of recovery which had amazed his physicians. Not only did he appear to have conquered his chest problems but he had begun a new health regime which had seen him try ever more adventurous tasks. His most recent escapade – climbing the famous mountain – would surely have killed him a few years earlier. Now it made him a hero.

'It's amazing how his health recovered, isn't it?' said Andrew.

'It was the idea of fatherhood, I believe,' said Nicholas. 'He simply refused to be sick any more. Strength of character, if you ask me.'

'And after all the years when he's been ill.'

'Elizabeth says she plans on having a dozen more,' Nicholas said with a laugh. 'Just to keep Martin healthy.'

With each new birth, the chance of her becoming Lady Smythson would become ever more remote for Louise; indeed, she had all but given it up now and had transferred her desires from the death of her brother-in-law to the death of her own husband. After all, if Nicholas was to succumb to some unexpected disease, she reasoned, she would be a wealthy society widow and could surely find an unmarried or widowed lord of her own to marry. She watched him constantly for any signs of ill-health but, to her disappointment, he displayed ruddy form. For a time she had taken to sleeping with the bedroom windows open, hoping that he would catch pneumonia, but instead he had declared that it made him sleep all the better, while she herself had come down with a bout of influenza.

'It's so thrilling to see justice served, isn't it?' said Louise, aware that many of the eyes in the courtroom were fixed on her and enjoying her new-found celebrity. 'And to have been such an important part of it.'

'But what a shame that it needs to happen at all,' Margaret agreed. 'Our poor, dear Cora. Such a tragic end.'

'Indeed. Our lives will never be the same without her. Our Music Hall Ladies' Guild has lost a valued member,' Louise agreed, repeating the words she had used to a *Times* reporter on the steps of the courthouse a few days earlier. 'Nevertheless, we shall always remember her.'

'A fine friend,' said Margaret Nash.

'A wonderful woman,' said Louise Smythson.

'Nonsense, none of you could stand her,' Andrew Nash blustered. 'Less of the hypocrisy now, ladies.'

'Andrew, that's an outrageous lie,' said his wife. 'You know perfectly well how close we all were to Cora.'

'If you insist, my dear,' he replied with a sigh. 'Anyway, this whole matter will be over and done with soon, and then we can finally move on with our lives. Although I have to admit, it's been very good for business. Ever since our names started appearing in the newspapers, there's been a rush of interest in my mining projects in Mexico. I have hopes that a lot of new investors are going to come on board. Stand to make quite a tidy profit if all goes well. I heard from Alec Heath yesterday, and he's become something of a local celebrity too.'

'Oh, hush, Andrew, the jury is returning.'

Three thousand miles away in Canada, Matthieu Zéla and Martha Hayes were at the offices of the *Quebec Gazette*, where news of the verdict was expected to be reported as soon as it was announced. They had followed the case eagerly since the morning when Dr Crippen had been arrested on board the *Montrose*, and they had been shocked by it.

'He seemed like such a pleasant fellow,' said Martha, controlling her tears but seeking comfort on the shoulder of her new employer and friend. 'To do such a hideous thing. It just defies humanity.'

'He may well *be* a pleasant fellow,' Matthieu pointed out. 'After all, just because he committed a brutal crime does not mean that he doesn't have a good heart.'

'Oh, Matthieu! How can you say such a thing?'

'I just mean that circumstances can lead us into actions sometimes, and we cannot necessarily be held accountable for them. Who knows what this Cora woman was like?'

'She could have been the most awful human being who ever lived, but that does not justify such a cruel end.'

'Of course not. I simply mean that one malevolent action does not a monster make. We liked Dr Crippen – or Mr Robinson, however you care to describe him – while we were on board the *Montrose*, and we should not automatically assume that we were wrong, simply because of this.'

'You are a very forgiving man, Matthieu,' said Martha, smiling at him warmly.

'Well, he hasn't done *me* any harm,' he replied with a shrug, 'so I can't condemn him.'

'I can,' said Tom DuMarqué, listening to their conversation from a distance and recalling the late-night events on board the ship. 'I'll be happy when he hangs. After all, I could have been his next victim.'

'Yes, well, you probably would have deserved it,' said Matthieu.

'He tried to push me overboard! He tried to drown me!'

'Only because you attacked his . . . his . . .' He searched for the right words. '. . . Edmund. Ethel. His friend,' he said finally, lost for words.

'His fiancée,' said Martha.

'It's sick and twisted,' said Tom, who could not quite get over the fact that he had never managed even to kiss Victoria Drake, while Ethel LeNeve, a *woman*, had. It did nothing for his self-confidence. 'I hope they publish pictures of the hanging. I'd stick them on my wall.'

'Oh really, Tom,' said Martha. 'How can you be so callous?'

'He comes from a callous line,' said Matthieu, staring at his nephew with barely disguised contempt. 'I believe I got the honourable genes in our family,' he said.

'Oh yes,' said Tom. 'You're wonderful. You would have let me drown. That's very honourable.'

'But I didn't, did I?'

'You would have,' he repeated petulantly.

Matthieu shrugged. 'Well, that's my point,' he said. 'We don't know what we're capable of. Come the moment, come the man. Or the woman, pretending to be a man. We can do the strangest things in the name of love.'

In New York, two other people were looking forward to hearing the verdict. Mrs Antoinette Drake and her daughter Victoria were finishing their four-month trip to North America with a two-week sojourn in Manhattan, where Mrs Drake was regaling all who would listen with stories about her intimate knowledge of the evil Dr Crippen.

'The man was positively obsessed with me,' she told friends at a dinner party. 'He followed me around everywhere. I believe he was lining me up to be his next victim. And as for Victoria, well, that evil creature Edmund chased her too. Or Ethel, as she wishes to be called now. It's infamous, the entire thing.'

Victoria was scarcely listening. Her eye had been taken by one of the guests at the dinner party, and she could hardly stop staring. Naturally, the news that Edmund was in fact a girl had shocked her initially. She was embarrassed by how intently she had been pursuing him on board ship, and when she recalled some of their conversations she could only blush with mortification. And yet, the more she thought about it, the more she had to admit to herself that there was no one she had ever been more attracted to than him/her. The memory of the kiss they had shared behind the lifeboats on that dreadful night of violence remained in her head; no one had ever kissed her quite like that, either before or since. Nothing made her shiver when her skin was touched quite like the fingers of Ethel LeNeve.

'Really, Victoria,' said Mrs Drake later that evening when they were returning to their hotel room. 'You were quite distracted tonight. What was wrong with you?'

'Nothing,' she replied in a dreamy voice, her mind elsewhere.

'And the way you kept staring across at young Miss Hartford. I realize she's a pretty girl, but why on earth were you looking at her in that way?'

'I wasn't staring,' she protested, 'I was simply interested in her conversation, that's all. She seems like a fascinating girl.'

'I dare say she is,' said her mother, not caring much one way or the other. 'But did you see her brother, Luke

Hartford? I believe he took quite a shine to you. *And* he's very wealthy and handsome, don't you agree?'

Victoria frowned and considered the prospect. 'I don't recall,' she said. 'I don't remember noticing him at all. However, I have arranged to lunch with Miss Hartford tomorrow.'

'Oh, Victoria!' said Mrs Drake, frustrated by her daughter's lack of matrimonial intentions.

'Here they come,' said Louise Smythson at the same moment, leaning forward in her seat, anticipating the verdict with great excitement.

The courtroom went silent as the prisoner stood in the dock.

'Foreman of the jury,' intoned the aged judge, whose wig seemed to overshadow his entire face. 'Have you reached a verdict upon which you are all agreed?'

'We have, your Honour.'

'And on the charge of murder, do you find the defendant guilty or not guilty?'

The foreman swallowed and cleared his throat quickly, aware that he had the attention of the entire world. He felt an overwhelming urge to burst into song – which, to his credit, he resisted. The atmosphere was electric and no one breathed while they waited for him to speak.

'Not guilty,' he said, to the surprise of all.

Some weeks later, on the morning of 23 November 1910, Ethel LeNeve walked along the corridor of Pentonville prison to the cell where Dr Hawley Harvey Crippen was being held, her hands clasped together inside a muffler, and wearing a black dress and a veil. She had wept all night long and could hardly imagine what the rest of the day would be like. To her surprise, the cells were cleaner than she had expected them to be. When the door to Hawley's cell was opened, she found him sitting, quite relaxed, in a corner, reading a book. He rose when he saw her, smiling warmly, and enveloped her in his arms, kissing her gently. He had grown thinner, she could tell, but he did not seem afraid of what was to come.

'My dearest one,' she said, sitting down beside him and bursting into tears. 'They've said I can only have a few minutes with you.'

'Ethel,' he said, embracing her again. 'Don't cry. You'll make *me* start. This is a good day.'

'How can it be?' she asked desperately. 'What have I done to you?'

'You have done nothing,' he said, and she marvelled at how relaxed he seemed. 'The happiest moment of my life came when I heard you had been found not guilty.'

'But I *am* the guilty one,' she protested. 'Not you.'

'I am just as guilty,' he replied, shaking his head. 'I was pleased that Cora had died. I even took pleasure in how she died.'

'Yes, but you didn't kill her, did you? I could still admit my guilt, you know. I could tell them—'

'You cannot,' he stated firmly. 'You must promise me that you will not. I will die anyway. For you to admit anything will simply lead to your joining me, and I couldn't bear that.'

'But I *want* to join you.'

'You're still a young woman, Ethel. You can live a life yet. And you can remember me. I am happy because I know I die loved. And I don't remember *living* loved until I knew you.'

Ethel shook her head, distraught. 'It just seems so unfair,' she said. 'That you should die for my crime.'

'I'm not afraid of death,' he said. 'But if I knew you were meeting the same fate, I would die miserable. As things stand, my conscience is clear. And I am prepared.'

The guard reappeared and indicated to Ethel that her two minutes were up. She could hardly cry any more, and they held each other for a few moments before she was led away, with protestations of love.

When she had gone, Hawley turned around and stared up at the barred window above his head through which the light streamed. Since he had been held here, he had discovered that if he stood on his bed and raised himself on his toes he could see through it, and he did so now and watched as Ethel left the building and walked slowly down the street. She stopped for a moment and turned around, unable to see him watching her, before hailing a hansom cab. Unaware that he could watch her every move, she blew a kiss in his direction and, stepping inside the cab, was driven away.

Later that evening, standing alone at the bow of the *Mercurial* as she left Liverpool behind and set sail for America, Ethel gripped the railing firmly in her hands and closed her eyes, thinking of her dear, dead love. She planned on avoiding the passengers entirely during the trip and speaking to no one – although she knew this might be difficult since her steerage compartment also housed three other young ladies. It was only a matter of time before they discovered who she was, and she dreaded the commotion that would take place then, but for the moment this was far from her thoughts.

Instead, she remembered the day they had arrived at Antwerp harbour, preparing to board the *Montrose*. How excited they had been, how filled with love. And how they had nearly got away with it, too. But Hawley had been right: she was young, she could survive. She had a future ahead of her and she owed it to him to make the most of it. After all, he had sacrificed his life so that she might have one. She had loved him dearly, there was no question about that, but then he had been the first man she had ever known. Perhaps, she thought, reflecting on it, it had merely been an obsession, a romance that she could enjoy and get carried away by. And if she had felt like that about Hawley Crippen, then surely she could feel it again towards another?

She smiled and looked out to sea. Ahead lay America.

Author's Note

When mentioning the name of Dr Crippen to people during the writing of this book, I found myself time and again excusing his actions with the rather odd comment that he 'only' killed one person, his wife Cora. Common perception seemed to have placed him as a vicious serial killer, with his eternal tenancy of the Chamber of Horrors assured. Obviously the Hawley Crippen presented in the novel is a different one from that whom we have been encouraged to accept over the years. But then my Crippen is a fiction, and the events of the night on which Cora Crippen met her bloody end are entirely a supposition on my part.

While many of the characters and situations in the book are taken from the facts of the case – Inspector Dew really did chase 'Mr Robinson' and 'Edmund' across the ocean; Louise Smythson really was the first person to suspect foul play; Captain Kendall really did discover the truth about the 'father' and 'son' by chance and use the newly installed Marconi Telegraph to alert Scotland Yard – many others were created to serve the plot.

However, readers may be interested to know that when Ethel LeNeve was acquitted of Cora's murder, she left England for a new life and finally settled in Toronto.

She changed her name, found work as a secretary, married, became a mother and never again referred to the events which led her to Munyon's Homoeopathy Store, the *Montrose*, or Dr Hawley Harvey Crippen. She died in 1967, at the age of 84.

Dr Crippen's last request of his executioners was that a photograph of his lover be buried with him; in her will, Ethel left instructions that a picture of Crippen also be placed in her hands before her coffin was sealed. Both requests were granted.

The Absolutist
John Boyne

SEPTEMBER 1919: Twenty-year-old Tristan Sadler takes a train from London to Norwich to deliver some letters to Marian Bancroft. Tristan fought alongside Marian's brother Will during the Great War, but in 1917, Will laid down his guns on the battlefield, declared himself a conscientious objector and was shot as a traitor, an act which has brought shame and dishonour on the Bancroft family.

But the letters are not the real reason for Tristan's visit. He holds a secret deep in his soul. One that he is desperate to unburden himself of to Marian, if he can only find the courage.

As he recalls his friendship with Will, from the training ground at Aldershot to the trenches of Northern France, he speaks of how the intensity of their friendship brought him both happiness and self-discovery as well as despair and pain.

The Absolutist is a novel that examines the events of the Great War from the perspective of two young soldiers, both struggling with the complexity of their emotions and the confusion of their friendship.

The House of Special Purpose
John Boyne

'An exciting, fast-paced story . . . absorbing and richly satisfying'
THE TIMES

RUSSIA, 1915: Sixteen-year-old farmer's son Georgy Jachmenev steps in front of an assassin's bullet intended for a senior member of the Russian Imperial Family and is instantly proclaimed a hero. Rewarded with the position of bodyguard to Alexei Romanov, the only son of Tsar Nicholas II, the course of his life is changed for ever.

Privy to the secrets of Nicholas and Alexandra, the machinations of Rasputin and the events which will lead to the final collapse of the autocracy, Georgy is both a witness and participant in a drama that will echo down the century.

Sixty-five years later, visiting his wife Zoya in a London hospital, memories of the life they have lived together flood his mind. And with them, the consequences of the brutal fate of the Romanovs which has hung like a shroud over their marriage . . .

'John Boyne brings a completely fresh eye to the most important stories. He is prepared to look at the dark, yet somehow manages to find whatever light was there in the first place. He guides us through the realm of history and makes the journey substantial, poignant, real. He is one of the great craftsmen in contemporary literature'
Colum McCann

'Boyne writes with consummate ease, and is particularly good at drawing the indecently rich world of the pre-revolutionary Romanovs'
INDEPENDENT

Mutiny on the Bounty
John Boyne

Portsmouth 1787

PICKPOCKET JOHN JACOB TURNSTILE is on his way to be detained at
His Majesty's Pleasure when he is offered a lifeline, what seems
like a freedom of sorts – the job of personal valet to a departing
naval captain. Little does he realize that it is anything but – and by
accepting the devil's bargain he will put his life in perilous danger.
For the ship is HMS Bounty, his new captain William Bligh and
their destination Tahiti.

From the moment the ship leaves port, Turnstile's life is turned
upside down, for not only must he put his own demons to rest, but
he must also confront the many adversaries he will encounter on
the Bounty's extraordinary last voyage. Walking a dangerous line
between an unhappy crew and a captain he comes to admire, he
finds himself in a no-man's land where the distinction between
friend and foe is increasingly difficult to determine . . .

*'An excellent story . . . written with a total command of naval expertise,
without ever spilling into pedantry,* Mutiny on the Bounty *is
storytelling at its most accomplished'*
INDEPENDENT

*'A memsmerising tour-de-force . . . this is a remarkable
and compelling piece of storytelling'*
IRISH TIMES

The Congress of Rough Riders
John Boyne

WILLIAM CODY GROWS up surrounded by his father's tales of Buffalo Bill, to whom he is distantly related, and his fantasies of the Wild West.

Though he escapes his heritage by fleeing abroad and starting a new life for himself, he finds that he is always drawn back to England and to his ancestry.

When his father proposes that together they should recreate Buffalo Bill's stage show, 'The Congress of Rough Riders of the World' for a contemporary audience, William refuses to have any part of it. When tragedy strikes, however, it is to his father that he must eventually return.

'A rollicking ride . . . Compelling'
THE SCOTSMAN

'The charm of history in this book lies in imagining how exciting it would have been to live there'
OBSERVER

'Boyne is an engaging writer who succeeds in making his readers care'
DAILY TELEGRAPH

The Thief of Time
John Boyne

MATTHIEU ZELA HAS lived his life well. In fact, he's lived several lives well. Because Matthieu Zela's life is characterised by one amazing fact: his body stopped ageing before the end of the eighteenth century.

Starting in 1758, a young Matthieu flees Paris after witnessing his mother's brutal murder. His only companions are his younger brother Tomas and one true love, Dominique Sauvet. The story of his life takes us from the French Revolution to 1920s Hollywood, from the Great Exhibition to the Wall Street Crash, and by the end of the twentieth century, Matthieu has been an engineer, a rogue, a movie mogul, a soldier, a financier, a lover to many, a cable TV executive and much more besides.

Brilliantly weaving history and personal experiences, this is a dazzling story of love, murder, missed chances, treachery – and redemption.

'An extraordinary debut'
SUNDAY EXPRESS

'A minor masterpiece'
TIME OUT

'Boyne should be congratulated for his spirited take on an old theme'
GUARDIAN

'Boyne is a skilful storyteller, expertly weaving differing stories together'
SUNDAY TRIBUNE

The Boy in the Striped Pyjamas
John Boyne

What happens when innocence is confronted by monstrous evil?

NINE YEAR OLD Bruno knows nothing of the Final Solution and the
Holocaust. He is oblivious to the appalling cruelties being inflicted
on the people of Europe by his country. All he knows is that he
has been moved from a comfortable home in Berlin to a house in
a desolate area where there is nothing to do and no-one to play
with. Until he meets Shmuel, a boy who lives a strange parallel
existence on the other side of the adjoining wire fence and who,
like the other people there, wears a uniform of striped pyjamas.

Bruno's friendship with Shmuel will take him from innocence to
revelation. And in exploring what he is unwittingly a part of, he
will inevitably become subsumed by the terrible process.

NOW A MAJOR FILM

The Heart's Invisible Furies
John Boyne

Cast out from her West Cork village, sixteen years old and pregnant, Catherine Goggin makes her way to Dublin to start afresh. She has no choice but to believe that the nun to whom she entrusts her child will find him a better life.

The baby is named Cyril by his adoptive parents, Charles and Maude Avery, a well-to-do but deeply eccentric couple who treat him more like a curiosity than a son. You're not a proper Avery, they tell him. And perhaps he isn't. But through them he meets Julian Woodbead who, even from childhood, seems destined for an infinitely more glamorous and dangerous life.

And so begins one man's funny and moving search to find his place in a world that seems to delight in gently tormenting him at every turn. Buffeted by circumstance and, at times, the consequences of his own questionable judgement, Cyril must navigate his emotions and desires in a search for that most elemental human need . . . happiness.

'A substantial achievement'
GUARDIAN

'A bold, funny epic'
OBSERVER

'Written with verve, humour and heart . . . at its core,
The Heart's Invisible Furies aspires to be not just the tale
of Cyril Avery, a man buffeted by coincidence and circumstance,
but the story of Ireland itself'
IRISH TIMES

A Ladder to the Sky
John Boyne

You've heard the old proverb about ambition, that it's like setting a ladder to the sky. It can lead to a long and painful fall.

If you look hard enough, you will find stories pretty much anywhere. They don't even have to be your own. Or so would-be-novelist Maurice Swift decides very early on in his career.

A chance encounter in a Berlin hotel with celebrated author Erich Ackerman gives Maurice an opportunity. For Erich is lonely, and he has a story to tell; whether or not he should is another matter.

Once Maurice has made his name, he finds himself in need of a fresh idea. He doesn't care where he finds it, as long as it helps him rise to the top. Stories will make him famous, but they will also make him beg, borrow and steal. They may even make him do worse.

'A deliciously dark tale of ambition, seduction and literary theft . . . compelling and terrifying, powerful and intensely unsettling. In Maurice Swift, Boyne has given us an unforgettable protagonist, dangerous and irresistible in equal measure. The result is an ingeniously conceived novel that confirms Boyne as one of the most assured writers of his generation'
OBSERVER

'Maurice Swift, the novelist protagonist of John Boyne's A Ladder to the Sky, *is a bookish version of Patricia Highsmith's psychopathic antihero Tom Ripley'*
THE TIMES